AWAY
FROM THE
DARK

OTHER TITLES
BY ALEATHA ROMIG

The Light Series
Into the Light

The Infidelity Series
Betrayal

Cunning

Deception

Entrapment

Fidelity

The Consequences Series
Consequences

Truth

Convicted

Revealed

Beyond the Consequences

and companions

Behind His Eyes: Consequences

Behind His Eyes: Truth

Tales from the Dark Side
Insidious

AWAY FROM THE DARK

Book Two of The Light Series

ALEATHA ROMIG

THOMAS & MERCER

Published by Thomas & Mercer, Seattle

www.apub.com

Amazon, the Amazon logo, and Thomas & Mercer are trademarks of Amazon.com, Inc., or its affiliates.

ISBN-13: 9781503938724
ISBN-10: 1503938727

Cover design by Shasti O'Leary-Soudant

Printed in the United States of America

To Mr. Jeff. Without your love and support, my dreams wouldn't be complete. I love you.

Forever is composed of Nows.

—*Emily Dickinson*

AS WE LEFT THE END OF
INTO THE LIGHT . . .
Jacob

Taking a deep breath, I recalled the number I'd memorized and stored away. I steadied my hand as I fired up the other burner phone and dialed. Running my fingers through my hair, I listened to the rings.

Special Agent Adler, my handler, answered on the fifth one. "Agent McAlister?"

"Yes, sir," I answered through gritted teeth.

"Fuck! We haven't heard from you in over two years. Tell me you're calling because you've got the evidence. Tell me to get the bureau ready, that you're ready for the raid. Tell me you've got what we need to bring Gabriel Clark down."

"Special Agent, we have a problem."

CHAPTER 1
Sara

More than a week earlier

The granulation was off. From what I was seeing, that had to be the answer. I wasn't sure why it had caught my attention or whether I should mention it to Brother Raphael or Brother Benjamin; however, the more I scrolled and clicked, the more apparent the problem became. From what little I'd picked up over the months I recalled working in the chemical lab, I understood the medications we created allowed Father Gabriel's vision to be shared with the world.

Due to the energy constraints at the Northern Light, most of our electricity coming from the hydropower, we were forced to use dry granulation in the manufacturing of the pharmaceuticals. If the granulation of this new medication was off, slightly larger than that of its model medication, it could affect the absorption rate. I'd overheard many of Brothers Raphael and Benjamin's formulation discussions.

The difference in the weights of the finished products was what caused me to question.

"Sara?"

Why am I questioning?

"Sara!"

Small beads of perspiration dotted my brow as my research all but drowned out the sound of Dinah's voice. I reasoned that with most patients this minor difference might not be a significant issue, but I also worried that in others it could be life-threatening.

"Sara, what are you doing?"

Dazed, I looked away from the computer screen into Dinah's concerned expression. My coworker, friend, and Assembly wife sister had an expression of sheer terror as she scanned the screen of my computer.

"I'm . . ." My words faded away as I looked from the report beside the keyboard to the screen. My mouth dried. I wasn't in the program I was supposed to be in. I wasn't adding the data and quantities I was supposed to be adding.

My pulse suddenly quickened. "Oh, Dinah, I don't know what I was doing."

She looked toward the wall and my eyes followed hers to the clock. It hung near the ceiling and was simple, plain, with a round silver frame. It reminded me of the clocks in my elementary school when I was a child.

When I was a child!

I recalled a clock in my past. It was the first thing I could recall in nearly a year.

Shutting my eyes, I tried to see beyond the twelve numbers and the hands in my memory. As if it were right in front of me, I saw it. I even saw the skinny red second hand running circles around the black minute and hour hands. I blinked twice, wishing for more of the scene to materialize and at the same time fearing that it would. Below the clock from my childhood was a large green blackboard.

Wait, that didn't make sense. Blackboards weren't green. Besides, my elementary school would've been in the dark, a place that was gone to me forever. How then could I remember that clock?

Dinah was speaking, and finally her words broke through my thoughts. ". . . Brother Benjamin will be back from Assembly. What will he say when he sees you've not completed your assignment, but taken the liberty—"

I moved my head back and forth as I exited screen after screen that I didn't recall opening. "You're right. I don't know what I was doing. It was because something in the numbers seemed wrong, like it didn't fit. I was curious. I started looking . . ." I pulled my lip between my teeth. "I'll confess." My head hung in shame. "To Brothers Benjamin and Jacob."

Dinah's arm moved protectively around my shoulders. "We still have a few minutes. I'm not saying you shouldn't tell Brother Jacob. You should. But if I help you, maybe we can get the data entered before Brother Benjamin gets back from Assembly. Besides, Brother Raphael won't be here for another hour. He still has the Commission meeting. Depending what Brother Benjamin wants us to do, I'm sure we can get this entered before then."

I let out a long breath. "Thank you, Dinah. I'm not even sure how I knew what I was doing. I don't know. It was just—" I knew the answer. It was the same problem I continued to battle. It was my curiosity. "I didn't want anything to be wrong. Father Gabriel's mission is too important."

Its importance was real. We all believed in his mission.

Dinah pulled a high-backed stool from her workstation up next to mine. The wheels easily glided across the smooth cement floor. "Do you want to read or enter?"

I pulled the correct screen back up on the computer. "I'll enter. You read. Start with yesterday's production . . ."

It was only a few minutes past ten when Dinah stopped reading and asked, "Sara, how did you know how to get out of our program? I mean, we don't know any of the passwords."

As I tried to recall, the memory was a blur, as if someone else had taken control of my movements. My lip disappeared between my teeth. I wasn't trying to be deceitful or cunning. What I'd wanted to do was to help, to figure out why the weights weren't matching. Finally I replied, "I don't know. I don't remember."

It wasn't like me to be secretive, but as I answered, I willingly shadowed the truth in ambiguity. Brother Benjamin had created this program. I recalled entering Raquel's name and *05*. Raquel had told me once that she and Benjamin had been together here at the Northern Light for five years. It was a guess, but I'd been correct on the first attempt. From that moment on, I hadn't thought, I'd just clicked and scrolled as if propelled by a sense of inquisitiveness that felt familiar yet foreign.

I replied to Dinah the way I did because if I confessed to Brother Benjamin that I'd been outside my program and he changed the password, I'd never be able to go outside it again. And though my conscience weighed heavily upon me, the yearning to keep access and learn more was too strong to ignore. Therefore, as we worked to complete my early-morning duty, I simultaneously contrived a way to confess without disclosing everything.

As the last number was entered, the door to the lab opened and Brother Benjamin came inside. The summer months at the Northern Light required less outerwear than the cold, dark months. Brother Benjamin hung his light jacket on the row of hooks near the door and ran his hand through his hair.

"Good morning, Sisters."

"Good morning, Brother Benjamin," we answered in unison.

His brow was furrowed as if he were deep in thought. I knew that things had been stressful with the Assembly lately, and Jacob had been spending more and more time away at other campuses. I didn't know the particulars, only that it had something to do with Xavier, The Light's other pilot, being ill, and a new pilot helping.

Swallowing my shame at my unusual bout of disobedience as well as an unusual, overwhelming desire to hide my behavior, I nodded to Dinah, who squeezed my hand. "Brother Benjamin," I said, "may I speak to you about something?"

The creases in his forehead deepened. "Is this a private matter? Would you like me to call Jacob?"

My natural reaction was to shake my head, yet my training was too strong. I lowered my eyes. "If it's your will. In the meantime I'd like to tell you about something that happened this morning."

With my head down, I couldn't see his expression.

"Sister Dinah, would you go to the coffee shop and get three coffees?"

My chest heaved at his calm tone. This was my chance. If I confessed outside of Dinah's hearing, I could do it without admitting to everything.

"Yes, Brother," she said, giving my hand another squeeze.

Once the door closed, Brother Benjamin asked me to continue.

I lifted my gaze. "This morning, I was entering the data like I always do. Well, the products, batch 3F789, the weight seemed wrong."

His lips formed a straight line.

"I know it isn't my place to question. I'm not questioning." Silently I said a prayer to Father Gabriel that Brother Benjamin wouldn't tell Jacob I had been questioning. "It was an observation. I went back to previous orders. The weight isn't off by much, but it's not the same. If the quantity is equal, the weight should be too."

Though I waited for his reprimand, it never came. Instead he said, "Show me."

I nodded, swallowing what little saliva I could muster, and walked back to my workstation. The report with the data we'd successfully entered was on my screen as I moved the mouse and brought my computer to life. I pointed to the numbers. Brother Benjamin stepped closer and stared at the screen. Without asking he took my mouse and began clicking and accessing past reports. The entire time I stood motion-less, afraid that he would look at the search history and learn that I'd accessed information outside my scope.

It was bad enough that I'd done it, but to not confess and be caught would be worse.

"Sara, copy and send me the last three weeks of reports on 3F789. I know you have other work to do, and I don't want to take your computer."

"Brother, I'm sorry if . . ."

"Don't be sorry." He sounded genuine. "This is Father Gabriel's vision. We don't want there to be a problem."

My exhalation of relief filled the lab.

"Sara, we won't say another word about this."

I wanted to ask whether that meant he wasn't going to tell Jacob, but I stopped myself, suddenly aggravated by the whirlwind of unruly questions and thoughts infiltrating my mind.

The mental image of the clock had me confused. The simple, insignificant timepiece was burrowing into my consciousness. How did I know it was a memory? Maybe it was something I'd seen at the Northern Light. After all, there was a school here. Children went to day care at five weeks and began school at four years.

That didn't answer why the image had expanded—why I now envisioned myself sitting behind a small wooden desk with my name scrawled on colorful paper taped to the upper edge.

This line of thinking was wrong. I'd been taught that. I needed to confess to my husband and study Father Gabriel's word more diligently.

CHAPTER 2
Sara

Two days later

Each Wednesday night, everyone on the Northern Light campus attended service, but before it began I needed to meet with a follower at the day care. She and her husband had arrived at the Northern Light at about the time of my accident, and she'd requested help with her transition. Her husband was under Jacob's supervision, which left her walk in The Light to me.

As I walked from the lab to the day care, I told myself to focus on Sister Priscilla and forget the fog of uncertainty that seemed to have settled around me. Strange visions plagued my thoughts. I planned to talk to Jacob. He could help, except he was still gone, and I hadn't had the opportunity to confess my actions at the lab or my thoughts to him.

Whatever was happening with The Light had him gone more often and for longer periods of time. I didn't even think he'd return tonight, as services on the other campus would have already started. All I could hope was that he'd be back to the Northern Light sometime tomorrow.

The reality was that Jacob's schedule—like everything else—was up to Father Gabriel.

My thoughts went back to Priscilla, the female follower I was about to meet. We'd been meeting once or twice a week for a few months. I tried to do for her what Sister Lilith had done for me after my accident, recommending lessons for her to study and talking about Father Gabriel's teachings. Part of my duty as an Assemblyman's wife was to remind her of her place and role as helpmate to her husband.

Though Dinah's and my workday was done at the lab, the non-chosen followers' workdays lasted longer. As I made my way inside the large metal structure situated near the school, the voices of young children filled my ears. As soon as the children could speak they were taught to recite Father Gabriel's word. I smiled at the sound of repeated verses and edicts. No doubt these children would grow to be strong soldiers and workers for The Light.

My boots clicked on the concrete floor as I passed partition after partition, making my way toward the youngest followers. Some classrooms were allowing free time, which I knew from my visits was precious to the young children. As little faces turned my way, "Sister Sara" echoed around me.

Even the children knew the chosen. Though perhaps it was prideful, my heart grew a fraction at each recognition. I'd spent many hours getting to know the wives and children assigned to Jacob as an Assemblyman. In my heart I hoped they saw me as a friend and confidante as well as an Assemblyman's wife.

Once I entered the infant room, Priscilla looked up and her eyes smiled. It wasn't her entire expression, but I saw a sense of relief as I approached.

"Sister Priscilla, can I help you for a little while?"

"Oh, Sister Sara, thank you. Thank Father Gabriel. I know not to complain, but today has been"—her words trailed off—"it has been a challenge, but one I'm happy to conquer."

The baby room wasn't nearly large enough for the number of occupants. Apparently the followers were taking "Be fruitful and multiply" quite literally. There were two and three babies in each crib; some had bottles propped while others cried, waiting for their afternoon meal. Thankfully, not all were anxious. Some were sleeping, somehow immune to the wails reverberating off the walls.

Taking it all in, I shook my head. How had I never before noticed how many babies there were, or how short-staffed the day care was?

I went directly to a chubby little boy I'd held many times before. His cheeks were red and his nose runny as his little chest heaved with cries. As I lifted him, the weight of his diaper caught my attention. "Priscilla, I believe he's wet."

She nodded. "Father Gabriel set a limit on the number of diaper changes per day. It's designed to teach the children control. Unfortunately, little Tobias must have had an upset stomach. He's already used his daily allotment. And while maybe I shouldn't have used them so early, he was very messy."

I shook my head in disbelief. "Tobias is an infant. He's what? Three months?"

"Four."

"When was his last diaper change?"

Tears teetered on Priscilla's lids. I wasn't sure whether they came from my questioning or her own frustration.

"About four hours ago. I-I can't . . ."

"How many changes per day are the children allowed?" My question came louder than I intended and more selfishly than Priscilla could possibly understand. I wanted a baby—for Jacob and me to have a family. I understood Father Gabriel's reasoning for the day care, but *control*? These were babies. They needed comfort, not control.

"I-I don't . . ."

My shoulders straightened. "I'm a member of the chosen. Answer me."

"Three. If more are needed, the family's credits are reduced and the parents must put in extra hours at the plant to make up the difference. If they don't, other credits are cut." Her explanation came quickly and quietly. "Sister, Tobias has two other siblings. His mother asked that I not exceed his limit. It's my fault; I shouldn't have changed him so many times this morning."

My lips formed a straight line and an internal battle raged. Had I never heard this before? Why did it suddenly upset me? It must be my desire for a baby. My maternal instinct was rearing its ugly head.

The stacks of cloth diapers filling the bins below the only changing table in the room caught my attention. "There are plenty of diapers." As soon as I spoke I realized my error. Priscilla might be a female, but questioning Father Gabriel's decree was unacceptable. "Perhaps"—I looked down to the calmer child in my arms. Simply the act of holding him and swaying my body back and forth had settled his cries. I lifted my cheeks in a weary smile—"perhaps Tobias will be fine until his mother arrives."

Priscilla took a deep breath and pushed strands of hair away from her face. "Thank you, Sister. Sometimes I wonder . . ."

This time tears fell from her eyes.

I reached for another baby and tucked one in the crook of each arm. Sitting on one of the two rocking chairs, I smiled as the babies' eyes closed. "You can talk to me, Priscilla. It isn't questioning to ask another woman. What do you wonder?"

For the next thirty minutes I rocked the small humans in my arms as Priscilla fluttered around the room taking care of the other babies. She spoke about her studies and answered my questions. She also confessed her uneasiness with some of the ways in which her life had changed since she and her husband joined The Light as fully committed followers.

Though I couldn't admit it, I envied her perspective. She could compare life in the dark to life in The Light. My accident nearly nine months ago had taken that from me.

Priscilla never voiced disappointment in their choice, only a sense of disillusionment. I asked all the right questions: Did she love The Light? Did she want to follow Father Gabriel? Did she believe in his word? Did she love her husband and trust him with their life decisions?

These conversations had been going on long enough in Priscilla's transition that I knew I should tell not only Jacob but also Elizabeth. As new-follower coordinators, Elizabeth and her husband, Brother Luke, knew what to do. When lingering signs of doubt occurred, there was a prescribed course of action.

The last question I voiced—Did she love her husband and trust him with their life decisions?—caused a faint flicker of shame. I hadn't trusted Jacob with the decision to stop my birth control. I'd done it on my own.

Maybe that was the cause of my new uneasiness. I felt guilty. After all, with each hour it seemed as though I continued to amass new transgressions that I would eventually need to confess to my husband.

By the time I left the day care and made my way to our apartment, my head and heart were heavy. Though I didn't want to experience correction at Jacob's hands, I longed for the peace that came with giving my concerns and infractions over to him. If only he'd come home tonight, but he wouldn't. He was with Father Gabriel at another campus. I think he'd said the Eastern Light.

Priscilla's talk of the dark had me wondering about the image of the clock. I didn't know whether the image was real or whether it was something that had been planted by a benign conversation with one of my sisters. If there were more childhood memories, I couldn't retrieve them. Only the classroom with the clock above a green chalkboard, a vision that had now expanded to include an elegantly swirled cursive alphabet separating the board from the clock. The teacher in this image was a mystery, but on the small desk before me was my name carefully scrolled. It wasn't on the desk, but on a piece of colorful paper. The *S* was tilted to the right and connected to the *a* and the *r* and the *a*.

Even though I wasn't trying to remember . . . the images continued to appear behind my eyes, creating a fog that distorted my reality. Our apartment building appeared different—the same as it had been, yet more run-down. No. More basic. Unpainted siding showed the effects of the Alaskan weather. My shoes scuffed the worn boards of the stairs as I made my way up two flights to our apartment.

I shook my head, trying to clear away the uncertainty.

Sighing, I made my way inside and collapsed upon the sofa. Rubbing my temples, I closed my eyes and wished for Jacob.

"Stop it!" I said aloud to no one.

Our empty apartment mocked me.

"I don't want these thoughts." My head ached with an uncommon pain behind my eyes. If only I could go to bed and forgo service, but that wasn't an option. I had to move forward.

My mind swirled with a whirlwind of thoughts; pieces and fragments unable to create a complete image floated about as service concluded and Father Gabriel's image faded from the screen at the front of the sanctuary.

"Sara, are you not feeling well?" Raquel asked in a whisper.

I forced a smile as I stared at my closest friend. "I think I'm tired, and I miss . . ."

Raquel's forehead came close to my own. "You miss Brother Jacob. Of course you do. I could ask Benjamin if you could come over for a little while. We could have coffee."

The mention of her husband's name reminded me of what I'd done a few days before at the lab, and that I hadn't had the chance to confess my exploration to my husband. "Thank you. I think I'd like to go home. Maybe I just need a good night's sleep. I don't sleep as well when he's gone."

"I can't imagine. From the day Benjamin and I were married, I've never had to sleep alone."

"Were you married in the dark?"

Raquel's eyes grew wide as she peered from side to side. "Sara!" Her voice was a hushed whisper. "We're in the temple, surrounded by the chosen." She lowered her tone even more. "Not the place to discuss such things."

My lips formed a straight line. "I'm sorry," I said with an edge to my voice. "I didn't realize I was speaking to Elizabeth."

The recognition in her dark eyes told me she understood my remark. Elizabeth was our friend; however, she never strayed from the straight and narrow. Besides her job with new followers, she was the poster child for obedience. She would never mention the dark, anywhere, and definitely not in the temple.

"What?" Elizabeth said as she turned toward us, her green eyes shining and her lovely red hair pulled back to the nape of her neck. "Did I hear my name?"

Raquel shot me a *just stay quiet* look and scoffed. "Sara and I were discussing going back to our apartment building. Will you and Luke be walking with us?"

"That's up to Luke," she answered without reservation. Then her eyes narrowed. "But Sara, you can't go alone."

I sighed. "I walk alone during the day. It's July. It's daytime all the time."

She shook her head dismissively as the other Assembly and Commission wives were claimed by their husbands one by one. Beyond our chosen seating I noticed the other followers, mostly couples leaving the benches and heading toward the doors. There were so many people I didn't know. Being chosen was a blessing and a curse. The followers

I saw had the pleasure of sitting with their spouses, yet they all looked exhausted.

When I thought about the hours Priscilla and the others worked, I understood.

Elizabeth was still talking. ". . . if it's light or dark in the sky. Brother Jacob left instructions for either Luke or Brother Benjamin to accompany you. You can't argue."

The pain behind my eyes had intensified, making my response less censored. "I'm not arguing. I'm tired. That's all."

"She misses Brother Jacob," Raquel volunteered.

The judgment present only a millisecond earlier on Elizabeth's face dissolved. "Oh, dear. I'm sorry. Of course you do."

"Ladies." Brother Benjamin's deep voice interrupted our conversation. "It's time to head home."

Beyond Brother Benjamin was Brother Luke. We all nodded in agreement and followed the men from the sanctuary out to the evening sunshine. Though the two men continued to talk, I allowed myself to fall into silence. It was the obedience I'd been taught, but more than that, it was my private way to make sense of the rush of uncertainty I was now feeling. I wanted nothing more than to climb into bed and wake revived.

In the morning I'd feel like my old self.

That was my last thought as I closed my eyes with my head on Jacob's pillow. His signature leather scent surrounded me as I fell asleep.

CHAPTER 3
Sara

Shrill screams echoed throughout our dimly lit bedroom, accelerating my heartbeat and pulling me from the terrible nightmare. I waited for more, until the realization struck. The screams were my own.

"Jacob?" I called, my voice shaking with dread as I reached for my husband. Instead of reassurance, my fingers met cold empty sheets. He was gone—still away at another campus.

What just happened? Was it a dream?

I clung to the covers as I puffed my cheeks and slowly exhaled. While each breath helped to still the chaos, the exercise wasn't enough.

Who am I? Who is he?

Jacob's questions from months ago came back. They were my security. They'd worked before.

I am Sara Adams and my husband is Jacob Adams.

Pushing the images from my dream, or nightmare, away, I imagined Jacob's comforting embrace. Slowly I threw back the down comforter and willed the cool air to soothe my perspiration-drenched skin. From the way my heart galloped in my chest, I might have been running a marathon, not sleeping.

In my sleep I'd been battling to escape a vehicle, and then an explosion of heat.

It had been a dream, I reassured myself—a nightmare. The accident I'd had, nearly nine months before, had been different. I couldn't remember it, but I'd been told that I'd been injured and gone unconscious. In the nightmare I had been out and away from the wreckage.

I shook my head.

It seemed so real.

In my dream I hadn't been able to see past the darkness, yet I'd known I wasn't injured.

My arms surrounded my midsection as the memories replayed like pictures in my mind. Someone was hurting me—purposely harming me, and there was a voice—a deep voice.

Jacob's voice?

No. He wouldn't hurt me.

My entire body shuddered as goose bumps peppered my skin. Sitting upright, I reached for the bedside lamp. With trembling fingers I turned the knob and my eyes adjusted as the soft light combined with the sun's perpetual summer glow.

I closed my eyes and tried to concentrate on Jacob's questions.

Who am I? Who is he?

This time I said the words aloud, praying that if I spoke the truth, the images would disappear. "I am Sara Adams. He is my husband, Jacob Adams." I pulled myself from the bed and walked to the bathroom. Turning on the light and the faucet, I cupped the cool water and splashed my face. As I reached for the cup and began to fill it, a metaphoric dam that had been constructed to hold back my past burst.

My mind was flooded—no longer with simple images, but with scene after scene.

For the first time since I could recall, I *knew* the woman in the mirror. I knew me.

The colorful paper taped to my childhood desk hadn't read *Sara*.

The *S* was still there, but the rest of the name was different.

I knew my own soft blue eyes and blonde hair.

I recalled its length and the way it used to flow over my shoulders.

Though I met my own gaze for only a millisecond, I also saw my own panic—not only that, I felt it. In the pit of my stomach I knew that what I'd just experienced hadn't been a nightmare. It was my reality—my past, the one I'd thought was forever gone.

At the realization, my muscles lost their ability to grip. Water splashed about the vanity and onto the mirror as the cup I'd held fell to the base of the sink. No longer capable of supporting my weight, my knees buckled and I slid to the floor.

"Oh my God! Is this real? It can't be." I spoke to the empty bathroom. "Jacob? The accident. It didn't happen. Did it?" I longed for him to make it right, to take it all away.

Acid bubbled from the depths of my stomach. The dinner I'd eaten long ago refused to stay down. My nightgown clung to my moistened skin and I lunged for the toilet. Like an old film reel, the scenes continued to play behind my tear-dampened eyes: the accident, my awakening, my crash course as an Assemblyman's wife, our temporary banishment, my reminders . . . nearly a year of my life—of Sara's life. Everything within me ached as my body convulsed. Over and over I heaved, purging all I'd known, been told to believe, told to *remember*— all the lies.

When the running water finally registered, I stood, rinsed my mouth, and splashed my face again. This time, as I stared at the woman in the mirror—at myself—the terror I'd seen was gone, replaced by betrayal. Hurt and anguish washed over me, crashing down, drenching my body, soul, and mind.

I tried to fight it, to argue with myself. *If only Jacob were here to help me understand.*

Turning off the water, I slid back down the wall and settled on the cool tile. Hugging my knees to my chest, with tears coating my cheeks, I re-created the timeline that was supposed to remain forever lost.

For the first time in nearly a year, I could answer Jacob's question—I knew.

"I am Stella Montgomery!" My verbal declaration reverberated against the walls as my heart ached.

It had to be real.

Lies! I'd been fed lie after lie. And like the ice chips after my awakening, I'd accepted each and every one.

Sobs replaced my voice as I fought to make sense of what had happened. Nothing made sense. All the people I held dear—my husband, friends, sisters, and brothers—were all a sham.

Lifting my left hand, through blurry vision, I stared at the simple gold band. I wasn't Sara Adams, nor was I married. My chest ached as my heart begged me to be wrong, to believe the life I'd lived was mine, but I couldn't.

I am Stella Montgomery, an investigative journalist for WCJB in Detroit.

I knew that was true.

I had a career and a life, with a real family and friends. I recalled blue eyes—piercing blue eyes. I had a boyfriend named Dylan, Dylan Richards, who was a detective.

My breathing hitched at my internal monologue warning me not to question. It wasn't my place. As a woman, I needed to accept. I should pray to Father Gabriel and confess to Jacob.

The hell with that!

Questioning was what I did—what I had done. It was part of my job. No wonder this had been so difficult.

Holding the walls for support, I walked back to our bedroom.

Our bedroom.

Again I hugged myself as my now-empty stomach twisted. Jacob and I weren't really married. I wasn't against premarital sex; memories of me with Dylan confirmed that. But as I stared at the bed where I'd made love with my husband, a new question surfaced.

Have I been raped?

I shook my head. No. Despite the lies at every turn, my heart confirmed that I hadn't. Never had Jacob forced himself on me, but then again, were the lies he'd fed me any better?

Had he? Did he know the truth?

I couldn't think about that . . .

Shit! The nausea. *What if I'm pregnant with his child?*

I didn't even know his name. Mine wasn't Sara; maybe his wasn't Jacob. I couldn't have the baby of a man whose name I didn't know. Pulling my robe tightly around me, I looked at the clock—nearly four in the morning.

With the whirlwind in my head, I knew I'd never be able to fall back to sleep. Instead I slowly walked through our quiet apartment, taking in everything anew as I passed down the short hallway, through the living room, and into the kitchen. With the drapes opened, even at this early hour, the summer's perpetual sunlight allowed me to see our world. Everything around me was my *past*, the only one I'd thought I'd ever have, the one Jacob and I had created together, the one that only a few hours ago had held the potential for a promising future.

No longer.

Deceit tarnished everything, everywhere I looked.

My hands trembled as I stood and turned slowly, mindlessly, around and around. Everything was wrong. I was surrounded by lies.

How had it happened? Why had it happened? Who had done this to me?

I grasped at a shred of hope.

Perhaps Jacob was disillusioned too. Maybe he believed we were truly married. Could we both be victims?

I wandered to the table and sat, not sure which of my thoughts to believe.

"Dear Father Gabriel," I said between sobs, "please take away these impure thoughts. I confess I remember my life before . . . no, I confess I have allowed evil . . ."

I took a deep breath.

The thoughts weren't evil; The Light was.

I stared at the stove where I'd cooked dinners for my husband. I was a good cook, even though I remembered that as *Stella* I didn't cook. As *Stella* I hadn't been ready to co-own a fish, yet in this life that I'd been forced to live, I'd been ready to have a baby.

Why had I been forced to become someone I wasn't?

Yet I was . . . I'd been Sara. None of it made sense.

Standing, I walked toward the cupboards and reached for a bag of decaffeinated tea. As I began to fill the teakettle with water, I decided I wanted coffee. I needed coffee. I'd gotten the decaffeinated tea in preparation for pregnancy. With the confusion and hurt filling my heart and soul, I refused to consider that pregnancy was possible. After all, I'd been without my birth control for only . . . I did the math . . . almost two weeks. People didn't usually get pregnant the first month.

How had they done it? Why had they done it? What would happen now that I knew?

While the coffeepot began to sputter, I made my way to the kitchen table and collapsed back into a chair. I needed more than coffee. I needed to get away from the Northern Light and back to *my* life. I needed to find a way to be free from The Light.

The Light!

The incomplete slivers of scenes were forming complete movie reels. I, Stella, had been investigating The Light. It was the last thing I could recall doing in Detroit.

Other facets of my life came back: my parents, my sister, Dylan; Bernard, my boss; Tracy, my friend; and Foster, my coworker.

Although the lies that I'd been fed and willingly consumed sickened me, to have a past—when I'd had none—excited me. My head ached as

the gaping holes that I'd accepted would forever remain void were closing with record speed, filling with a real past that had been hidden away.

Or was it more lies? I couldn't be sure.

If I didn't belong here, why was I here?

And then it hit me. I wasn't the only one here.

I thought about Tobias, all the other babies, and the children who
called my name from the depths of the day care. I envisioned the followers, the chosen and the ones I didn't know as well—the women, men,
children. How many of them were living lies? How many were lying?

My friends . . . more heartbreak. Did they know they were lying?

My thoughts were all over as my eyes roamed our small apartment
and I clenched my teeth.

Father Gabriel lives as we do—bullshit!

Bloomfield Hills. The new images clawed at my newly founded
belief system: Father Gabriel had a huge, sprawling, multi-million-
dollar mansion in Bloomfield Hills with a landing strip.

My heart continued to crumble.

For the past nine months I'd been conditioned to turn to Jacob,
to seek not only his approval but also his guidance. Admittedly, there
was still part of me that wanted that. I wanted to close my eyes in his
arms and give this all to him, but the newly awakened part of me knew
I couldn't.

Jacob had told me stories of our past, a past I now believed had
never existed. Our entire relationship was based upon lies that he'd per-
petuated over and over until I believed his every word. Had he invented
those stories, or had he been told to tell them to me? He'd said more
than once that he had rules to follow too.

Despite the evidence, I wanted to believe that my husband had
done what he believed.

My head fell onto my folded arms as I willed my new thoughts to
stop.

He wasn't my husband.

An internal battle raged between desire to know and willingness to accept. My heart told me that Jacob loved me and would always do what was best, but the images, the memories, all painted another picture.

Grudgingly I acknowledged that Jacob had to be part of this deception. After all, not only had he played into the lies about our being married and about our past together but also he flew planes. He flew Father Gabriel. He was with him right now at the Eastern Light.

A new thought surfaced.

Could the Eastern Light be Detroit, more accurately Bloomfield Hills?

If it was, Jacob knew about the mansion. He knew about the landing strip. He knew that Father Gabriel didn't live as he professed.

My recently emptied stomach continued to twist. Not only did I need to get away but also on the off chance I was pregnant, I needed to get my baby away from this madness.

I peered out the window at the bright, clear summer sky. I was in Alaska—Far North, Alaska. There were walls and polar bears. This wasn't only a physical prison but a mental one. I had to think. I had to plan. I had to tell my heart to forget the man who'd been my comforter, disciplinarian, and rock. For my survival, my possible child's, as well as others', I needed to think.

I poured a cup of coffee, and as the cream swirled through the darkened liquid, questions continued to swirl within my consciousness. As flickers of my former self fought through the uncertainty, I realized that I no longer needed Jacob's approval to question. I granted it to myself. My mind went to my parents, my sister, and Dylan, and how they must be suffering with my disappearance. It had to be as it had been with Mindy's disappearance.

Shit! Mindy!

My hand fluttered over my heart. Mindy was here too, with me. I was confident. I remembered the blonde woman who'd spoken to

Elizabeth a few months ago. Now it made sense that she'd looked familiar. She wasn't Mary; she was Mindy Rosemont, my best friend from the dark. However, just as I hadn't recognized her, she hadn't recognized me. More than likely her past had been erased, leaving her without memories of her true identity.

How many of us were there? How many of the women and maybe men had been programmed?

Sitting back at the table, I reached for the warm cup of coffee and timidly moved it toward my mouth. I'd learned to be careful. Since heat no longer registered with my fingertips, I'd burned my mouth before. Heeding the steam's warning, I sucked my lip between my teeth and lowered the too-hot coffee back to the table. With a sickening realization, I rolled my wrists and stared at the ashen flesh on the tips of my fingers.

Oh my God!

I was one of those women—the ones with the burned fingertips, the ones from Dr. Tracy Howell's table at the Wayne County morgue. The women who'd ended up dead.

A new chill ran through me, and I pulled my robe tighter. I wasn't investigating a life-and-death story—I was living it!

CHAPTER 4
Sara

After waking early to my revelations I spent most of the day trudging through the thick fog of confusion. Everything took effort and concentration. Tasks that had become second nature now seemed foreign. Something as simple as making my own breakfast set my mind back. As the slices of bacon fried in the iron skillet, I had flashes of smoke and firemen.

I questioned the validity of each recalled image. Were these memories, or were they thoughts that fleetingly appeared real? Without warning doubt would creep in. What could I believe? Was I recalling my life or was it my imagination? As my bacon crackled in the pan, I reasoned that since we didn't have firemen at the Northern Light, the images of men with heavy coats and helmets were real—a memory from the dark.

Here, in case of fire, there was an understanding that every male follower would do what was needed. I wouldn't know that if I hadn't overheard Jacob speak of it to one of the followers under his supervision. The threat never seemed to be a concern, but given that most of the construction—besides the wall surrounding the community—was wood, fire could be devastating.

Methodically I managed to complete each task: breakfast and work at the lab.

I was keenly aware of everything I did and said, weighing each word of my conversations, no matter with whom. As I entered the data into my computer, waves of urgency flowed through me, an undeniable desire to obtain information. Questions such as I hadn't allowed myself to ask in months bombarded my thoughts. Why had I been placed in the chemistry lab? Did anyone know what I'd done before? What was the truth behind the manufacturing of medications by the followers? Was there more to it, or was it purely philanthropic?

With my fingers hovering above the keys and Brother Benjamin's password repeating in my brain, I wasn't sure what I wanted to find or even what I was looking for. And then a moment later, I'd return to my prescribed task with guilt squelching my inquisitiveness and reminding me of my place as a woman and a member of the chosen.

The entire process—from the elation of memories to the doubt and shame of questioning—was infuriating, unsettling, and tiring.

By lunchtime I was exhausted. Needing a change of scenery, I asked Dinah to accompany me to the coffee shop for a sandwich. The new surroundings didn't help. Something about my revelations had changed everything. No longer did I see a thriving small town, but a compound or camp of sorts. I fought the need to lift my eyes and truly study the world in which I lived.

I'd been taught to keep my eyes cast downward. Yet I longed to stand and stare as I had alone in my apartment. I wanted to take in the buildings along the dirt-packed streets and paths. They now seemed solid, yet basic. While some, like the coffee shop and school, were made of sheet metal, most were made of wood like the pole barn.

The investigator in me who was trying to break free made connections I'd never before stopped to consider. Jacob had told me that near the power plant, just outside the walled community, was a small mill where followers worked to convert hundred-year-old trees into lumber. How else would they have built this place? It was in the middle of nowhere. Flying in all the construction materials would have been

difficult and more expensive. From what I could remember of the planes
Jacob had shown me, neither one was large enough for that.

"Do you ever think about the people Father Gabriel's medicines
help?" I asked, as I nibbled on my cold turkey sandwich.

Dinah shrugged. "I guess not really. I mean it's a wonderful thing
his ministry does. I can't imagine not having all of my needs met."

"Are they?"

"Are they what?"

I leaned closer. "Are all of our needs met?"

Dinah nodded. "Mine are. That's what Father Gabriel teaches. Any
needs not met aren't necessities but desires."

"Yes, that's what he says. What do you think?"

"Sara! I don't know what's gotten into you, but I don't question
Father Gabriel's teaching and neither should you."

"I'm not questioning it. I'm curious."

"Are you without food, a roof, or clean clothes?" she asked.

"No."

"How about your spiritual needs?"

"What about them?" I replied.

"Are they met?"

I swallowed a sip of my water. "Yes, of course."

"It isn't our place to have curiosity."

"I know." I hung my head. "I think I'm just missing Jacob." Thank
God I had that excuse. Otherwise I didn't know how I'd be able to
explain my odd behavior.

As we were about to exit the shop, a group of three female followers
entered, their heads bowed as they scanned the room with their eyes.
All of their heads were covered with scarves, something I'd seen on the
women who worked in the greenhouse that grew fresh fruit and veg-
etables for our daily consumption. It wasn't until the pale-blue eyes of
one of the women looked in my direction that I recognized her. They

were eyes I'd known for years. I had no doubt. I was looking at my friend Mindy Rosemont.

Without thinking I stood and moved in her direction. The pain at her disappearance, the visits to the morgue, all came back. A lump formed in the back of my throat as my arms ached to hug her. She was alive, here, and safe. Before I could process or filter my thoughts, I reached for her hand.

"Mi—" I stopped the name from rolling from my lips as I registered the look of shock on her face.

"Sister, did I . . . is there a problem?" she asked, her voice soft and weak. The other two women stood dumbfounded, staring at me, as did Dinah.

My mind raced. I remembered seeing her before at the temple, speaking with Elizabeth. I had to think of something.

"No," I reassured her, hoping I'd see any recognition in her eyes. I didn't. "I-I—" I struggled for words. My audience listened expectantly. "Sister Mary? Correct?"

"Yes," she replied, her eyes now down to where I held her trembling hand.

"Please look up."

She did.

"Sister Elizabeth asked me to speak to you. May we talk for a moment?" The lie left a disgusting taste on my tongue, but I couldn't think of anything else.

Mary nodded, first to me and then to her friends. I looked over to Dinah, whose eyes were wide with wonder.

Shit! I needed to think of something to tell her too.

"Sister," I said toward Dinah, "I'll be back to the lab in a few minutes."

"I can wait."

"That's all right. This won't take long. Elizabeth asked me to do her a favor." My explanation seemed to satisfy Dinah, because she simply smiled and walked toward the door.

Letting go of Mary's hand, I walked back to the table where Dinah and I had eaten our lunch. "Please, have a seat."

"I-I don't have long," she said as she obediently lowered herself to the chair.

Of course she didn't. She must be on her break from her workday.

"I don't want to interrupt your lunch, and I want you to know that nothing we say will be repeated."

"What?"

"On occasion I help Sister Elizabeth and Brother Luke. You can only imagine how busy they are." With each word and sentence the lying became easier.

"Sister Elizabeth has been very helpful."

She continued to stare toward her hands, which were now on her lap. The sight of her with the two other women had brought back an image of women crossing the street in Highland Heights. I couldn't think about that now.

I lowered my voice. "Mary, please look at me. Do I look familiar?"

Mary peered upward and back down. "Yes."

My heart leaped.

She went on, "I've seen you in the temple, with the other chosen."

And it sank.

My long-ago conversation with Elizabeth about abusive husbands came back to me. I scanned Mindy's face and body. Her long-sleeved blouse covered her arms, while jeans covered her legs. But thankfully I didn't see any signs of abuse on her face. "Are you all right?"

She nodded.

"Are you sure?"

Her pale-blue eyes glistened with moisture. "Are you going to tell Sister Elizabeth something? Will it get back to Adam?"

"No!" I lowered my voice. "No, Mary. There's nothing wrong. I'm not telling Elizabeth anything. I'm sorry. I didn't mean to scare you."

"B-but I thought you were speaking to me for Sister Elizabeth?"

"I am. Just take a minute and think. Have we met before?"

"Before?" she asked. "I'm sorry. I don't remember *before*." She looked up. "You mean in The Light? We aren't allowed to talk about the time before that."

"Do you remember the dark?" I asked in a whisper, hopeful and suddenly curious about whether others had had their memories taken away.

"No. Adam says that we were married before we came here. I don't remember that either."

I tilted my head. "Did something happen to affect your memory?"

Her lower lip disappeared between her teeth in a familiar habit. "I don't remember. Adam said I fell. I woke in the clinic about a year ago. That's all I know."

My heart beat rapidly as I contemplated this happening to all the women of the Northern Light. "Did you hurt yourself when you fell?"

"Yes, I broke my arm and hurt my head." She fidgeted in her seat as she sought out her friends. They were seated at another table, eating. "I-I am sometimes quite clumsy. Was there anything else Sister Elizabeth wanted you to ask me?"

Guilt settled heavily in my stomach.

Lies, questions, and now I was stopping her lunch.

My eyes went to her friends' table. "I'm sorry. I didn't mean to make you miss your lunch. Did they get you food?"

Her head moved back and forth. "We only have rations for our own meal. No one can get more than one."

She and I were sharing the same life, yet it wasn't the same. Mine was chosen. Often Dinah or I would make a run for sandwiches for everyone at the lab. How had I not fully noticed or understood the hierarchy in The Light before?

"Oh. Then please go. I'm sorry, Mary. But the next time you see me, please don't be afraid of me."

"I-I'm not. You seem nice. Sister Elizabeth is nice and so is Sister Esther, our overseer's wife. I don't know any other chosen. I don't even know your name."

I tried to smile. "My name is St-Sara, Sister Sara. Please feel free to speak to me anytime."

She looked back at her hands, waiting for me to dismiss her, as my stomach twisted. "If you hurry, will you have time to eat?"

"Yes," she answered quickly.

"Then please go. Thank you for talking to me."

"Thank you."

I sat silently as she hurried from the chair to the line and then the counter. From the depth of her pocket, she removed a slip of white paper. It was her lunch ration ticket.

More questions came to my mind. Did everyone experience an "accident" upon arrival? Why? How many hours a day did she and her friends work? What did they do in the greenhouse? What did others do in the production plant?

Walking back to the lab, I contemplated the dichotomy of Mary and Mindy. No longer was she the confident woman who'd been my roommate, classmate, and best friend. Somehow The Light had turned all of us into Stepford wives.

When I entered the lab, Dinah looked up at me, silently questioning my unusual behavior. It wasn't until we were alone that she finally asked, "Elizabeth? What did she want you to do?"

I licked my lips and lifted my shoulder in a shrug. "She wanted me to ask that follower about a memory she'd had."

Dinah's nose scrunched. "A memory? Of what? And why you?"

My eyes widened. "I don't know. Elizabeth is our friend. I can't imagine her asking me to do anything that I shouldn't. Can you?"

"No. It seems odd."

"I thought so too. It doesn't matter. The follower didn't remember."

Though Dinah seemed satisfied, I silently said a prayer. *Please, Father Gabriel, don't let Dinah say anything to Elizabeth.*

Before the end of our workday, Brother Benjamin came to my work desk. "Sister, this morning at Assembly, I learned that Jacob will be returning this afternoon. He'll be home by dinner."

A smile spread over my face, before I had the chance to respond differently. "Thank you, Brother Benjamin. That's the best news I've heard in days."

He winked. "Why don't you go home early and get ready for his return. I'm sure he's missed your home cooking."

Although I was suddenly worried about facing him, the man who had worked so hard to make me believe I was his wife, my body and mind were conflicted. Truth be told: I had missed him.

CHAPTER 5
Jacob

I'd called our apartment telephone as I passed the final gate to enter the community. It was nearly five o'clock, and I hoped that Sara would be home from work. On this trip I'd been gone for three nights. I didn't like leaving her for hours, much less days.

This trip had been spent solely at the Eastern Light. While Father Gabriel did whatever he did in his mansion, Micah and I stayed down past the pool and tennis court in the small outbuildings.

When I'd first started this assignment, I'd considered investigating the big house, until I saw the cameras. Every move Micah and I made on the property, or at least inside the outbuildings, was watched. Late at night I'd sit on the steps and watch the big house. In the darkness I was hidden, but the large mansion was visible, its windows often lit, the house looking like a Christmas tree. Even from the distance of the outbuildings, I could see the multitudes of people celebrating with our leader.

Although my job was to infiltrate The Light, my training told me that I could accomplish my goal only by following Father Gabriel's rules. He specifically forbade my or Micah's presence closer to the mansion. I wouldn't have gotten where I was today if I'd broken that simple an order.

Whenever I was at the Eastern Light, I rarely left the grounds. If I did, it was to attend temple. Usually Elijah, an Assemblyman from the Eastern Light, drove us. This past Wednesday, Brother Uriel, the senior commissioner at the Eastern Light, had been with him. During our drive to and from the estate, I'd had the distinct impression I was being interviewed. If I was right, hopefully, my duties would be increasing and so would my knowledge of The Light.

I believed that I was very close to learning more about the pharmaceutical distribution. Each new piece of information was another step closer to getting away from this assignment and resuming my real life.

While that thought of leaving The Light used to motivate me, now it also saddened and worried me. As I walked up the stairs toward our apartment, the most recent piece of my life that demonstrated my obedience and commitment to The Light—my wife—was the one piece I couldn't imagine living without.

I took a deep breath and pushed thoughts of the dark and life beyond The Light away. Reaching for the doorknob, I inserted my key, waited for the sound of the lock, and opened the door.

Standing precisely where she'd been told to stand was the most beautiful woman in the world. Though her head was bowed, with her hair pulled back to a short ponytail, I could see her raised cheeks. I reached for her chin and brought her light-blue eyes to mine.

"Mrs. Adams, I've missed you."

Her head tilted and her eyes closed as she brushed her cheek against the palm of my hand.

"I've missed you."

The stress of the assignment, the tension of the flight, everything disappeared into the melody of Sara's voice. As soon as I entered the apartment, the aroma of something cooking brought to life a different hunger from the one brought on by the sight and touch of my beautiful wife. I pulled her close and kissed her soft lips.

Almost immediately I reached for her shoulders and stepped back. With her at arm's length, my dark eyes narrowed as I searched her face. It had been only a second, but something seemed off—different.

"Sara?" I evened my tone. "Is there something you need to tell me?"

Her eyes widened and then dropped.

"I've missed you," she said. "I don't like you being gone for three nights."

There was more. I sensed it. Taking her hand, I led her to the couch. "Tell me. Do you want me to ask again?"

Her breasts heaved with deep breaths as her shoulders straightened. "Two days ago, at the lab, I found an error. It wasn't my place to find it. I wasn't looking for it, but once I noticed it, I did more research . . ."

I didn't interrupt as her confession came one word on top of the other. While she spoke I prayed to Father Gabriel that whatever she'd done didn't warrant correction. If it did, I would do it. However, after my being away from her, the last thing on my mind was punishment.

". . . Brother Benjamin said he was glad I found it. He said we wouldn't need to mention it again, but I knew you needed to know."

"Was Brother Raphael involved?"

She shook her head. "Not with me. I don't know if Brother Benjamin spoke to him. It was never mentioned again, but Dinah saw me looking into it. She had to help me catch up with my work. Well, she didn't have to—she offered."

"Was this before or after you told Brother Benjamin?"

"Before."

I reached for her hands, neatly folded on her lap, and felt the slight tremble. "Sara, look up at me." Obediently she lifted her eyes. "Tell me again what Brother Benjamin said."

"He said it would never be mentioned again."

I lifted her hands to my lips. With each kiss of her knuckles, the tension melted from her grasp, and I looked back up to her trusting gaze. "It was right of you to tell me. We won't mention it again."

The tips of her lips moved upward.

"Thank you, Jacob."

"Now, what do you have cooking? It smells wonderful."

As if I'd taken the weight of the world from her shoulders, she bounced up from the couch and headed toward the kitchen, the menu she'd prepared spewing forth from her lips. I listened to not only her words but also the sound of her voice.

Over the past nine months I'd fallen for my wife. Part of it was undoubtedly the training and manipulation of The Light. But that wasn't all. I had an overwhelming desire to protect her from the darkness that lurked within The Light.

Father Gabriel's word taught each husband to bear the weight of his family. It was my place. Yet there were times when I wondered what it would be like to be in a more equal relationship, one where I could share my burdens as she'd just done.

It wasn't that Sara didn't do everything she could to help me. She did. It was that I couldn't talk to her. I couldn't talk to anyone. That had never bothered me before. Now, each time she confessed a misdeed and gave it to me, I longed for the relief she obviously felt.

According to Father Gabriel's teachings, men received that sense of relief through confessing to the Assembly or the Commission. My case was different. Confessing my anxiety over the termination of my FBI mission could not happen. It was up to me.

CHAPTER 6
Sara

My heart beat frantically as I rambled on about our dinner, something about wanting Jacob to have a home-cooked meal. I wasn't sure of what I was even saying. I was more aware of what I wasn't saying, what I wasn't admitting. Somehow in this messed-up scenario, this pretend, ridiculous, outrageous life I'd been sentenced to live, the man listening to my ramblings knew me. He knew my thoughts without my so much as saying a word. Only seconds after he arrived, he'd known there was something, something I hadn't said.

That new realization shook me to my core.

Jacob knew me, in many ways perhaps better than I knew myself.

Yet he didn't know the real me. He knew the me he'd created.

It was such an odd thought. As I continued to talk about food, the lab, and anything else I could think of, I wouldn't allow my mind to dwell upon the ramifications of his intimate knowledge.

I fought the urge to confess my memories. As bizarre as that sounded, it was a real battle. The investigator and independent woman I'd once been knew that telling Jacob or anyone in The Light was dangerous, perhaps even a death sentence. Memories of bodies in the Wayne County morgue worked to keep my confession at bay. Yet the conditioning I'd experienced for the last nine months kept the words *I remember the dark* on the tip of my tongue.

As Jacob reached for my hand and blessed our meal, the carefully prepared food lost its appeal. A sheen of perspiration dotted my brow as I worried I wouldn't be able to stop the words.

What if I admitted to memories in my sleep?

What if he asked and I couldn't help myself?

My internal battle raged throughout dinner and as I cleaned the kitchen. I spent more time than usual assuring cleanliness, purposely avoiding what I knew was coming. Jacob had been gone for three nights. The way his warm hand encased mine even after he blessed the food and his soft lips met mine when he entered the apartment alerted me to his future intentions.

I tugged my lower lip between my teeth, contemplating our immediate future. If I confessed my newfound knowledge, or recovered knowledge, as an Assemblyman, Jacob would be bound to take my confession to the Commission.

Would he condemn my memories as lies? Would he punish me for entertaining such thoughts? Each question added fuel to my concerns.

I wanted to believe he'd listen and help. My heart wanted that. Yet my inquisitive mind feared the worst. At best he too was a pawn and wouldn't believe me. At worst he was intimately involved in the lies, and my knowledge would be a threat.

If I were to survive and find a way out of the Northern Light, I needed to continue to maintain the farce that I was Sara Adams, the content Stepford wife of Assemblyman Jacob Adams.

Wringing the excess soapy water from the dishcloth, I decided to take another swipe at the countertop. Just as I was about to turn back toward the counter, the signature leather-and-musk cloud announcing my husband's presence penetrated the scent of my dish soap. I'd been too caught up in my thoughts to hear his approach. I closed my eyes as his strong arms surrounded my waist and his lips neared my neck.

"I've missed you."

His deep voice tugged at my heart, while the warmth of his embrace tore at the flimsy walls I'd constructed in an effort to keep him away. My head fell back against his chest as my pulse raced. I'd always had the option to tell him no, yet I never had.

If I did now, would he suspect something was different?

Butterfly kisses skimmed my skin as the scruff of Jacob's tightly trimmed beard heightened my senses.

My head told me the truths. We weren't really married. He was part of the lie.

The words that hours ago had been loud and convincing grew dim as Jacob's hands began to roam.

The dishcloth dropped back into the soapy water as I ran my hands over his forearms. Jacob not only knew me, he knew my body. With the perfect combination of baritone words and ministrations, my insides began to respond.

Agreeing to him, to this, was what I needed to do to survive.

It was the mantra my consciousness tried to recite.

Convince him nothing is different. Don't hesitate. He will know. I heard the words though they weren't audible.

It was interesting the deals one made with oneself in an effort to excuse what could be perceived as unacceptable behavior. After all, I was about to sleep with a man who wasn't really my husband, a man who'd lied to me, punished me, and yet my body was willing—more than willing. As I slowly spun toward him, my arms encircling his firm torso, I pushed my new revelations out of my mind and concentrated on the man who wanted me.

As he led me down the hall, I didn't think about the deception or the lies. I thought about the excuse I'd given others for my unusual behavior—I'd missed Jacob.

Later in the night, while the heavy curtains kept the ever-shining summer sun from our room, Jacob pulled me against his chest and sighed. His breath moved across my hair as his heart beat against my back.

"Did anything else happen while I was gone?"

In the afterglow of our lovemaking, I battled against my training. In his arms I longed for the openness we'd shared and the relief that came from complete honesty. And then, just as quickly, I reminded myself that it wasn't real openness or honesty—not on his part. If it had been, he wouldn't have lied to me.

"I'm not sure why you keep asking," I replied.

His chin moved over my hair as he shook his head at my slyly worded question. I couldn't help but smile as I turned toward him.

"That wasn't a question," I confirmed.

He kissed my forehead. "No, Mrs. Adams, it wasn't. But I could infer—"

"You could," I said with a hint of laughter, trying to steer him away from his initial question. His use of my surname sounded so familiar, the falseness of it barely registered.

"If I did, after I took matters into my own hands"—he playfully cupped my behind—"I might say that you seemed different somehow when I first got home. When did the incident at the lab occur?"

I took a deep breath as I lowered my chin against my chest. "Monday."

"Hmm."

Though I wondered what that meant, I knew not to ask.

"I see," he said.

I shook my head as I closed my eyes. Maybe if I stayed awake I'd know what he meant. Yet if I stayed awake, I risked saying more than I wanted. Even though I hadn't been completely honest, in his arms my lids grew heavy and Jacob's breathing evened. In no time at all we both drifted to sleep.

~

As a week passed, each day was more difficult than the one before. Each day memories came mixed with emotion. I'd be working at the lab or doing a mundane task such as sorting our laundry, and something from the dark would infiltrate my thoughts. Some memories were benign: my apartment or Dylan's house. That was always the way they began, the prelude to more, my fish (his name was Fred), or Dylan's backyard and the way he grilled steaks or salmon in the warm Detroit air. Some were so intense; they were more than images, also sounds and smells. The authenticity of them made each one difficult to dismiss.

Even in the summer, the outside air at the Northern Light held a chill. I found myself longing for the oppressive Michigan humidity I used to detest.

Somehow I learned to shut off the old me when I was with Jacob. I'm not sure how I did it, but I did. I concentrated on him, on us. Whenever the old me tried to break through, I became hyperalert, fearing a change in Jacob's expression, afraid he could see my internal battle raging. Maybe it was simply paranoia, or perhaps it was real. Either way, I worried constantly that I'd give myself away.

My other battles came around female followers. As time passed I deduced that those women who recalled the dark, like Elizabeth, had come to The Light of their own volition, while others, like Dinah and Mary—Mindy—had come as I had, forced to accept a life they couldn't question.

As we all pressed our fingers into the prayer sponge and I contemplated our lack of fingerprints, the women in the morgue fueled my desire to leave The Light. The world needed to know what was happening.

I was an investigative journalist. Fate had somehow given that job to me. I had the responsibility not only to expose this travesty but also to rescue my sisters and the children of The Light.

While I used to look forward to my visits to the day care, now entering the doors and seeing the small trusting faces broke my heart. The babies and children hadn't chosen this life. They were prisoners behind the campus's walls as much as we all were. I couldn't decide about the men. I wanted to ask whether they'd all come freely, or whether any of them were here as the result of an "accident." Of course I couldn't.

As days passed, the old me found ways to glean information.

I spoke less and listened more. As Jacob spoke to other men, I bowed my head and took in as much as I could. While I sat quietly at the coffee shop, retrieved our groceries, or did laundry, I listened. Since we'd all been trained to leave the dark in the past, I learned little about that, but I did pick up other things.

At one point Raquel mentioned medications. When I first woke, I had been given many of them. I didn't want to ask in front of Elizabeth, but the simple comment that I might not have noticed before now had me wondering. Did The Light possess medication that made us more adaptable—more accepting? Obviously they had something that had taken away my memories while allowing new memories form. Since the only medication I had taken regularly after leaving the hospital had been birth control, I concluded that in those pills was where I'd been receiving the memory suppressant. It wasn't until I stopped taking the birth control and after the medication had time to leave my system that my memories came back. If The Light could do that, then I assumed that anything was possible.

Since the return of my memories, I was constantly on edge. Though I'd been pretty diligent, speaking about my birth control was one of the glaring mistakes I'd made. Thankfully it had occurred with Raquel. I told myself that I could chalk it up to the building stress or perhaps a sense of friendship, but whatever the cause, once the words were out of my mouth, I feared the worst and prayed for the best.

I hadn't meant to say anything.

With each such instance, my fear and paranoia grew.

I had a plan.

I would leave the Northern Light with Jacob.

Over a month ago I'd mentioned that I wanted to travel with him. That was what I'd wanted, then—to spend more time with him. Now I wanted to get away. He'd never told me that he'd petitioned the Commission; however, one day at the lab, Brother Benjamin let it slip.

My plan was to leave with Jacob. I didn't care where he took me. I didn't care whether it was to Fairbanks for supplies—he did that often—or to another campus. I'd already deduced that the Eastern Light was Highland Heights. No matter whether it was the Western or Eastern Light, wherever we went had to be less remote than the circumpolar North.

Once Jacob flew me to another destination, my plan was simple: I'd find a phone and call for help.

As days and nights passed, I contemplated whom I would call. I considered my parents, Bernard, and Dylan. No matter how I looked at it, Dylan was the best possible alternative.

I recalled an Internet thread I'd found while researching The Light. It was about a woman who claimed to have been taken by a cult.

Even today that word sent shivers down my spine.

The woman on the thread claimed that the authorities didn't believe she'd been held against her will. They claimed her story was tainted because she'd abused illegal drugs before her abduction. I hadn't. I reasoned that my story would be more believable. And even if local authorities didn't believe me, Dylan would, and he was a detective. More than that, I couldn't wait to let him know that I was alive.

The last memory I had of my old life was from late October of last year.

As I sat in service and listened to Father Gabriel preach, it took all my control to smile, nod, and bow my head. What I really wanted to do was scowl and ask how he could do this to so many people—people who not only followed but also trusted him.

With each passing minute, the truth became clearer. I needed to get out of here!

CHAPTER 7
Sara/Stella

It was morning, and Jacob had already left for the hangar. He'd told me that he was heading to the Western Light and wouldn't be back until tomorrow. The pressure to gain freedom was mounting. With our breakfast dishes clean and more than an hour before I needed to report to the lab, I decided to take a walk. Each day the weather was warmer. Though I hoped the fresh air would help clear my head, I'd also become addicted to exploring and witnessing the community through my new perspective.

Each glimpse of the world around me showed a new paradigm. No longer did I see a bustling community. Now, as an investigative journalist, I saw things as they were. Our coffee shop and stores were simply warehouses, similar to the pole barn, divided by partitions and filled with only the supplies the Commission deemed necessary. The walls surrounding the community no longer served as our protection; they were our cage, designed to keep us all peacefully within.

I wondered whether they truly were necessary. After all, it wasn't as if, on the edge of the circumpolar North, we followers had many options for leaving. Nevertheless, the walls made any notion of escape impossible.

I recalled from when Jacob and I had been sentenced to our temporary banishment at the pole barn that the only acceptable way to pass beyond the walls and the multiple gates was within a vehicle. No one walked away.

For that reason few people had access to vehicles. Primarily it was the chosen men and those followers who had clearance to work beyond the walls, those who needed to access areas such as the pole barn for supplies, the power plant, or the mill.

The world where I'd been forced to live became clearer with each passing day. Our buildings were mostly accessible by foot. Snowpack paths in the winter and hard dirt paths in the summer connected one to another. The apartments where we lived were closer to the temple and main buildings than those housing the non-chosen followers. While ours were in what looked like three-story barracks, theirs were in what resembled dorms on a run-down college campus. Each building was sufficient to protect people from the elements, not constructed for visual appeal. Since vehicles weren't needed to get from housing to work or community centers, when not in use, they were parked away from the main cluster of buildings.

As I took my morning walk, I made my way past the followers' housing and toward the outskirts, the direction in which Jacob and I often ran. Because it was at the opposite end of the community from the greenhouse and production buildings and more remote, fewer people were in this area. The solitude gave me a sense of freedom, allowing me to lift my eyes and truly see.

It wasn't until I reached the place where many vehicles were parked that I noticed what I believed to be Jacob's truck, parked along a row of vehicles. It caught my attention because Jacob was gone. He would have left it at the pole barn and hangar. Making the only logical deduction, I figured that Thomas, the new pilot, was the one who had driven it into the community.

At nearly the same moment, my heart began to thunder in my chest: Thomas was my ticket to freedom.

I scanned the area. Seeing no prying eyes, I hurried to the truck and hid under a blanket on the floorboard in the backseat. With each passing minute, I contemplated Thomas's return. I'd seen him before within the community. I wasn't sure why he was allowed to enter. Xavier never had. However, I knew he'd done it. One time in the coffee shop with Raquel, I'd noticed him. He was a large man, about Jacob's age, with short hair in a military cut.

Raquel and I had both recognized Thomas as new. There was something about him, the way he behaved: nodding and making eye contact with females before he said hello. The men of The Light didn't do that. In general male followers didn't acknowledge female followers. As Elizabeth had once told me, they didn't owe us their words. If a man and woman crossed paths, the woman looked down and the man moved on.

That was the way it was.

I sucked in a breath as the door opened and slammed shut. From my hiding place, I caught a glimpse and knew I was right. Thomas was in the driver's seat. Slowly he backed up and turned toward the gates. I feared he could hear my racing heart as the truck slowed and he pressed the code on the first, the second, and finally the last gate.

As the truck lunged forward, a sense of freedom bubbled from deep inside. Elation at passing the final barrier fought with the fear of the unknown. I hadn't been out of the community since Jacob's and my banishment. And up until a week ago that hadn't bothered me. Given the way the tires bumped against the floorboard of the truck, the road was as uneven as it had been all that time ago.

I fought the urge to take a deep breath and fill my lungs with the air outside those walls. I couldn't. I wasn't really free, not yet. Once I made my presence known to Thomas, if he decided to take me back, I knew that I'd be punished. What I didn't know was how severely.

Would I end up dead, like the women in Tracy's morgue? Would it be Jacob's decision, the Commission's, or Father Gabriel's?

Although what I'd done was a risk, I couldn't stay at the Northern Light another day. I needed to get back to my life and do whatever I could to help my sisters and the children. I wanted to save Mindy. After all, she'd been part of the reason I'd first learned of The Light.

I silently said a quick prayer to Father Gabriel that I wouldn't fail her or everyone else.

My heartbeat echoed in my ears as the road noise faded and the truck came to a stop. Though it'd been a long time since our banishment, I was relatively certain that we hadn't driven long enough to reach the hangar. I held my breath as the driver's door opened and then the one beside me. When the blanket was ripped off me, I didn't know what I feared more: Thomas, my possible punishment, or the polar bears that could be near.

Thomas smirked as he leaned back on his heels, as if to get a better look, and shook his head. "Look what we have here."

I moved from the floor to the seat. "Please, I'm begging you to help me."

"You're begging me? I like the sound of that."

My stomach rolled. "If you'll take me wherever you're going, I can pay you."

"You can?" He touched my cheek as I resolved to remain still. "Tell me, pretty lady, why are you hiding in the back of this dirty old truck?"

Oh, shit! Maybe I should have waited for Jacob to get approval.

I willed my eyes to look at his and found it interesting how well I'd been trained. Even now, when I knew it was wrong, I had physical difficulty doing what I used to consider natural. Nodding, I swallowed and asked, "You're Thomas, Xavier's replacement, right?"

He nodded. "I didn't think they let you women know what was happening."

"They don't, not really." *Should I tell him that I'm Jacob's wife?* "I'm a good listener."

"And, Miss Good Listener, what do you expect me to do to help you?"

I had to try. "I don't belong here. I don't even know how I got here. I've been here for almost a year, but I have a life off the Northern Light." My words came fast, each one landing on the one before. I hoped he was listening well enough to understand. "I have . . . had a job, a good job. I have money and so does my family. If you can get me off this campus and away, I'll make sure you're compensated."

His golden eyes narrowed as they scanned me from head to toe and back again. The jeans and sweater I wore seemed to evaporate as his expression morphed. It was as if he could see what was underneath. Finally he said, "So you're saying The Light kidnapped you?"

I nodded.

"What would Father Gabriel say if I turned this truck around and took you back?"

Tears threatened my eyes. "P-please, you're my only hope. If you take me back, I don't know what will happen, but it won't be good."

The longer he stood with the door open, the more concerned I became about the bears. "You do know there are polar bears around, don't you?"

He laughed. "Is that what they tell you?"

I sat straighter. *Is everything Jacob told me a lie?*

He opened the door to the front passenger's seat. "Here, pretty lady, sit up here." He patted the seat. "And convince me to help you."

Convince him?

Slowly I moved from the backseat. When both of my boots stood upon the hard ground, I scanned the sparse trees at the side of the road. If there weren't really polar bears, maybe I could make a run for it. Thomas's hand grasped my arm.

"In the truck."

I swallowed and nodded as I moved to the front seat. After he'd shut both doors and as he walked around to the driver's side, I once again considered the idea of running. The opportunity was short-lived as Thomas opened the driver's door and eased himself into the truck.

"Go," he said, his cocky grin back in place. "Convince me."

"I-I'm not sure what you mean. I told you that I don't belong here. I just need someone to take me away, someone to believe me."

One of his cheeks rose as his lips thinned. "I've heard stories. You see, there are rumors. That's why I wanted to go into the community. I wanted to know if they were true."

"I'm not sure what you've heard, but please help me." The truck still wasn't moving. "I won't tell anyone that you're part of this. I promise." My breath caught in my throat as he reached out and again brushed my cheek. "Please, don't touch me," I pleaded as I backed away and my nausea returned.

Pushing my now-longer hair behind my ear, he leaned closer. "See, pretty lady, what I've heard is that you bitches in The Light like to *obey*. If you don't, I heard you get punished." His eyes moved up and down my frame, lingering too long at my breasts. "Is that true?"

Oh, God, what am I doing?

"I-I promise, my family will pay you."

He laughed, the stench of his stale breath filling the noncirculating air in the cab. "If you think your family will pay me better than Father Gabriel, your daddy must be Bill Gates, and I ain't heard nothing about Bill Gates's daughter gone missing. But don't worry, sweetheart, I think we can work this out." He traced a line from my ear and down my neck to my breast.

I slapped his hand. "Forget it. Take me back. I made a mistake."

Thomas started the truck and laughed a deep echoing laugh. "I like a bitch with spunk. She's all the more fun to tame."

Biting my lip, I sat in silence as he drove toward the hangar. My mind searched for possibilities. Brother Micah. If he was at the hangar, maybe I could convince him that Thomas had taken me against my will. As I contemplated my options, I didn't care what Brother Micah or anyone else thought or about my possible punishment. I just wanted to get away from Thomas.

Even though I'd lived at the hangar, in the living quarters of the pole barn, for two weeks, I'd never really seen the outside of the building, the landing strip, or the hangar. When Jacob had first driven me to it, my eyes had been covered, and when I could see, it was winter and everything was cloaked by darkness. Now, as we approached in full light, I scanned the area for vehicles and saw how truly massive the building was. Even though I didn't see any other vehicles, I didn't give up hope. Obviously the building was big enough that Brother Micah could have parked inside.

My pulse increased again when Thomas hit the button on the garage and pulled Jacob's truck into the bay near the living quarters. This was wrong. This was Jacob's truck and Jacob's parking area. It was where he'd brought me, where I'd felt like a newlywed. In reality I had been. I just hadn't known it.

Thomas hadn't said a word since he'd told me he wanted to *tame* me.

I didn't know who was telling the truth about the polar bears. Nevertheless, I waited for the garage door to close before I opened my door. As soon as the door stopped, I opened my door and ran toward the hangar. Opening the door on the opposite side of the garage from the living quarters, I screamed, "Micah, Brother Micah! Are you here? Help! Brother Mic—"

Thomas's hand covered my mouth and stopped my words. I closed my lips, swallowing the disgusting taste of grime and sweat.

"Shhh," he whispered menacingly in my ear as he pulled my back against his front. "You're going to be a *good girl*, or we'll start that punishment right now."

When he spun me around to face him, I nodded, all the while listening for the sounds I'd heard when others were at the hangar. Even though I didn't hear anything, I couldn't let Thomas take me, not if there was a chance I could save myself. His eyes narrowed in warning as he slowly removed his hand from my mouth.

As soon as I was free, I screamed, "Help! Micah! It's Sara! Please . . ."

My world spun as Thomas's hand stung my left cheek.

"Shut the fuck up!"

I swallowed, tasting the telltale copper of my own blood. As I fought the dizziness his slap induced, my feet obeyed as he pulled me toward the living quarters. As soon as Thomas opened the door my chest ached with memories of Jacob's and my past. I needed to leave The Light. I wanted to leave. But no matter the injustices I'd endured, never had Jacob treated me the way Thomas was doing right now.

Thomas shoved me forward. Awkwardly I caught myself and landed in one of the kitchen chairs.

"Sit here. Don't fucking move." He rubbed his obviously hardening erection. "I'd love to get a better look at Father Gabriel's gift, but I don't know who's coming out here." His lips separated into a broad smile, exposing his stained teeth. "And I don't plan on making this quick. I guess it'll have to wait until we get to Fairbanks. Don't you worry, pretty lady, once we're there we'll have all the time and privacy we want."

My stomach knotted. "T-Thomas, I'm going to be sick."

He pulled me up by my arm and pushed me toward the bathroom. Undoubtedly my arm as well as my face would be bruised.

"Go in there. Don't make a fucking mess. I'm not losing this job over you."

I nodded as I rushed to the bathroom and shut the door. There wasn't a lock.

Shit!

My heart sank.

"I'm getting my stuff from upstairs," he called through the door. "When you come out, sit where I put you. If you don't, I'm taking my

belt to that pretty little ass." The sound of his laughter trailed away as
his footsteps climbed the stairs.

Looking at the woman in the mirror, I noticed the way my left
cheek was already beginning to swell. Though the tips of my fingers
lacked feeling, as I pushed on the reddening and slightly purple skin,
I felt the tenderness. Shaking my head, I contemplated my options. I
could take off running. If I did, I'd need to run back to the community.
I'd never survive in the wilderness on my own, with or without polar
bears. Even if I made it back to the community and was allowed to live,
I feared I'd never get away from the Northern Light.

Better sense—or was it delusional thinking?—told me that this
could be my only chance.

My thoughts went to Mindy and the others. If I left with Thomas,
there was a possibility of my saving not only myself but also the others. Taking a deep breath, I surrendered to my decision. I opened the
bathroom door and scanned the living area.

Conceding to my choices didn't mean giving in to the man walking
upstairs. With the sound of Thomas's footsteps echoing from above, I
rushed to the kitchen and opened a drawer. I peered into its depths,
knowing what it contained. Lying side by side were varying knives. I
scanned the possibilities; I needed one big enough to do harm, but
small enough to be concealed.

When the sound of footsteps stopped, I held my breath. Quickly
I turned toward the stairs, but Thomas wasn't there. When the steps
began again above my head, I grabbed a four-inch paring knife and concentrated on Thomas's footsteps as I quietly shut the drawer. Raising the
leg on my jeans, I slipped the knife into my boot, and quickly moved
to the table. Counting his steps on the stairs, I sat and tried to calm my
breathing. Since I'd been unable to see when Jacob and I first moved
to the pole barn, I'd memorized the number of steps. Thomas still had
four more before he reached the bottom.

Only my eyes moved as I watched him enter the lower level. He glared in my direction before walking past me to the bathroom. "Good girl," he called, just before the sound of his urinating echoed through the living quarters.

I scrunched my nose. *Gross!*

Clenching my teeth, I thought about how much I hated the phrase *good girl*. It was such a condescending form of praise.

The toilet flushed and Thomas returned. "I thought you might try to leave something in there, like a message. Either you're a fast learner and don't want your ass beat, or you're not very bright. Either way, I can't wait to get you to my place and find out." He bent down until our noses were mere millimeters apart. His breath reeked of coffee, twisting my stomach into more knots. "No matter how well you *obey*"—he emphasized the word—"I'm sure I'll find some reason to turn that ass red."

Though I bit my lip and told myself to remain still, I couldn't stop my flinch as he reached out to once again tuck my hair behind my ear.

"Don't look so worried, pretty lady. I'm sure I'm not as depraved as what you're used to." He shrugged. "Or maybe I am." With a smirk he added, "You'll have to let me know."

I swallowed my response: Jacob might have lied to me, but he wasn't depraved.

Why did I think this was a good idea?

When Thomas reached for my arm, I pulled away. "I can walk."

He snickered. "For now."

When I stood he told me to walk in front of him. As we made our way through the length of the pole barn, I scanned each area we passed: the garage, the long hallway, and doors to offices and workshops. Each area confirmed my fear: we were indeed alone. In the hangar, the final, largest area, I saw Father Gabriel's stunning plane. Though months ago I'd only felt it, by all the windows, I knew it had to be the one with the soft leather seats. That meant Jacob had the smaller jet, the one that took only one pilot.

That meant Micah could still arrive any minute. I tried to think of a way to stall, but when Thomas cleared his throat and pointed to a door, I made my way in that direction.

As we stepped back outside into the late-morning sunshine, a cool breeze blew through my hair, causing it to swirl around my face. Fearful the change in temperature would be visible, I crossed my arms over my chest.

We'd exited the building all the way at the other end from the living quarters. Squinting against the brightness, I saw our destination. On the tarmac was a small white plane with a red stripe, and large letters and numbers on the tail. Unlike any of the planes Jacob flew, this one had a single propeller.

Thomas opened the plane's back door. I presumed that on his way to the Northern Light the open area of the fuselage had been filled with supplies. Now, with it empty, he unfolded a seat and tilted his head.

Come on, Sara . . . Stella . . . do this. It's your only chance to get away.

Inhaling, I climbed aboard and sat in a seat very similar to one in Jacob's truck. There weren't even any fancy straps, just normal-looking seat belts. Before I could latch mine, Thomas's large hand reached across me, pulled the belt, and buckled it tight. Once I was secure, he allowed his hand to graze my lap and smiled.

"Three and a half hours." He winked. "You might want to get your rest. You're going to need it."

Not if I put this knife in your artery first, asshole!

CHAPTER 8
Sara/Stella

Thomas had told me to sleep, but as we flew over Alaska with the sun streaming down, my nerves were strung so tight there was no way that was possible. Besides that, each time the plane changed altitude, I was certain I'd vomit. I'd even searched for some kind of bag but found none. Fear of what Thomas would do if I threw up all over his plane was the main motivation keeping my breakfast where it belonged.

All I could think about was getting free. It didn't matter that through the windows and below was some of the most majestic scenery I'd ever seen. I'd always imagined Alaska covered in snow; however, at the Northern Light we never got much snow. It wasn't because it didn't get cold enough. It was that the latitude was so far north there was rarely enough moisture. Mindlessly I noticed that the farther south we flew, toward Fairbanks, the more the landscape below was covered with deep greens, rolling browns, and crystal-clear lakes. I debated my options as the beautiful blue sky I was used to seeing filled ominously with clouds.

The engine and propeller's loud roar made it impossible for Thomas and me to speak. Before we'd taken off, he'd placed earphones over my ears, but unlike his, mine didn't have a microphone. I wasn't sure whether he could speak to me. If he could, he hadn't. Maybe he thought I really would sleep.

As I peered up toward the front of the plane, I saw Thomas's short hair and shoulders from around the seat. I sadly remembered the first time I'd asked Jacob to take me with him on his flights. At that time I'd wanted to be with him. However, now that I was away from the Northern Light and my perspective was different, I reasoned that I neither wanted to see Jacob again nor would allow myself to think about what he would do if he ever found me. Fear turned to indignation at the thought of his possible correction.

With each mile I concentrated not on the man I'd left behind or the one flying the plane, but on the one who would help me. I thought about Dylan.

I recalled everything about him, from his vibrant blue eyes to his toned muscles—everything except his phone number. It had been programmed into my phone. I tried to envision the screen. I recalled the sound of his distinctive ring, yet I couldn't visualize the number. My only choice would be to call the Detroit Police Department. After all, I should be able to find their number with a quick online search.

All I needed to do was slip away for a few minutes and borrow someone's phone. I didn't imagine that it would be easy, since I was being flown by a madman who'd already struck me, causing my cheek to swell. But if I succeeded, the payoff would be worth it.

I would hear Dylan's voice.

He would know I was alive.

A small smile crept across my face with the knowledge that the man I'd imagined while I was without sight *was* real. At the same time, the realization hurt. If only I'd listened to his warnings about Highland Heights. One of the first things I'd do once we were together again would be to apologize for the heartache I'd undoubtedly put him through.

As urban sprawl began to appear below us, I assumed we were nearing our destination. In the distance were more mountains, but beneath us a flat city began to materialize. Slowly the buildings began getting closer together. Though Fairbanks was the biggest interior city in Alaska, I didn't suspect that Thomas would land his small plane at the Fairbanks International Airport. Since he was Xavier's replacement, I wondered whether he flew extensively for Father Gabriel. If he did, he probably flew out of a private airstrip. I prayed it wouldn't be like the one in Bloomfield Hills, that instead it would be more public. To have a chance to get away, I needed people around.

Thoughts of what my future held caused my hands to ball into fists and my nails to bite into my moistening palms. My investigator's mind filled with the possibilities Thomas had in store. Each scenario was worse than the last, and none of them included my ability to place that call to DPD.

Believe in yourself.

The words came back to me. I couldn't project too far ahead; instead I needed to look at my situation in steps. Getting away from Thomas had to be my first priority.

As our altitude began to decrease, I crossed my legs and slowly lifted the hem of my jeans. With my seat directly behind Thomas's, I hoped he couldn't see what I was doing. I also hoped that since he was speaking on his headset, his attention was elsewhere. Lifting the cuff, I slid my hand down inside my boot. The handle of the knife was against my ankle and the sheathed blade was near my foot, but without unzipping my boot, I couldn't quite reach the knife.

"Sara."

I jumped at the sound of Thomas's voice through the earphones and quickly lowered my boot. I lifted my eyes to the front of the plane, and our gaze met in a rearview-type mirror.

"Don't try to talk. I can't hear you, so listen."

I pressed my lips together and nodded. In front of him were windows and gadgets. Casually I lowered the leg of my jeans, thankful he hadn't seemed to notice.

"This airport is small," he said, "but I don't want you making a scene. If you do, I'll be glad to return you to Father Gabriel, but that's not happening until I'm thoroughly done with you."

Fighting the urge to vomit, I pressed my lips together and shook my head.

He turned his head toward the side window as he flipped a switch and began talking to someone else. Just like that, he'd spun my world, warning me about a future I'd already imagined.

Clenching my fists, I concentrated on my second objective. It was to get in contact with Dylan. I knew that if I could reach him, my story wouldn't end like that of MistiLace from my Internet search. Besides, it wasn't as if I could get to the Fairbanks International Airport and fly home to Detroit, even if I wanted to. I didn't have any identification. The TSA wouldn't allow me to travel. I needed the help of the police. Dylan could help me with that.

As the plane touched down, I willed my fist to open and looked at my fingers. Hell, forget about identification, I didn't even have fingerprints.

The small plane bounced as Thomas brought us to a stop near the hangar, and I glanced around. This hangar didn't even seem as big as the one at the Northern Light. This one had only two runways going in opposite directions, a large paved area, and the hangar. An old chain-link fence surrounded the entire compound. I sucked my lower lip between my teeth, waited, and contemplated my knife. It would have to wait. I feared that I couldn't reach it without bringing my movements to his attention. If there was any chance of being successful with it, it had to be a surprise.

Taking off his headphones, Thomas leaned to his side and craned his neck. With a disgusting toothy grin, he said, "Welcome to your new home."

Removing my headphones, I replied, "I know what you think about women in The Light, but you're wrong. Father Gabriel won't let this go unpunished. You stole me from the Northern Light."

I was playing with fire, but I had to try. Through the last few days I'd gotten better at lying, something Sara or any other woman of The Light would never do. Now it was time to go for broke.

"It was a test," I went on, "a test designed by Father Gabriel, and you failed. He *does* care about me. I'm the wife of an Assemblyman. I didn't want to leave. I said what he told me to say. It was for The Light. You're new. Father Gabriel was testing your response. You failed."

With each of my phrases, Thomas's confident grin dimmed as the color faded from his ruddy cheeks. "You're lying. You're lying to save your ass."

I crossed my arms over my chest and turned toward the window. "You can either take me back and suck up to Father Gabriel or you can let me go and I'll contact my husband."

He'd unbuckled his seat belt and was fully turned toward me in his seat. "How the fuck are you supposed to do that? You people don't have phones."

I lifted my chin confidently. "The chosen men do. I've been told how to reach my husband." This was it. It was all or nothing. "Besides, he's a pilot. He'll come get me."

Thomas's shoulders relaxed and he shook his head. "Bitch, you had me going for a minute. I'm going to enjoy tanning your—"

"What?" I asked incredulously. "My husband *is* a pilot."

"No way, I heard how you yelled for Micah."

I shook my head. "Not Brother Micah. I'm Jacob's wife." I fumbled for my necklace, pulling it from beneath my sweater. "See this necklace? It's only worn by the chosen. Jacob's on the Assembly *and* Father Gabriel's pilot!"

"Fuck!"

When he opened his door, I quickly unbuckled my seat belt and scooted toward the other side of the plane. My heart beat in double time as I fumbled with the handle. My efforts were in vain, though; it was locked. My blue eyes grew as big as saucers when Thomas peered through the window, undoubtedly knowing I'd wanted to escape. My mind was a blur. I prayed to God and Father Gabriel for a miracle I didn't deserve.

Just as Thomas began to open my door, out of nowhere two men in dark jackets with badges came running forward. The front door of the plane was still open, and through the wind I could hear raised voices. The men were yelling at Thomas, and one had a gun drawn.

I stared in disbelief as Thomas forgot about me and spun in their direction. There was a split second when his body twitched in indecision. He might have considered running, but just as fast, he lifted his hands in the air. Between the wind and my blood rushing in my ears, it was as if the rest of the world were on mute. I couldn't make out their words. Instead, it was as if I were watching a silent film and praying the good guys would win.

I sat statuesque as one of the men secured Thomas's hands behind his back and led him away. Maybe if I remained still, they wouldn't know I was here. And then the other man in a dark jacket looked through my window. When he nodded, I knew my wish wouldn't come true.

Opening the door, he asked, "Ma'am, are you all right?"

I let out the breath I'd been holding and replied, "A-are you the police?"

"No, ma'am, US Marshals." He offered me his hand.

I stepped from the plane, contemplating which story I should lead with: I was taken against my will almost a year ago, or I was taken earlier today. "Thank you," I said softly, forcing myself to look into the older gentleman's eyes.

"Ma'am, what happened to your cheek?"

I lowered my eyes. "It was him."

The marshal's jaw clenched as he reached for his phone. "Excuse me, I need to make this call."

I stared momentarily at his phone, then nodded and wrapped my arms around my body as the wind blew my hair around my face. While the marshal spoke quietly, I turned completely around and took in the small private tarmac. It wasn't the way I'd planned it, but I didn't care.

I was finally free.

Relief flooded my system and a renegade tear slid down my cheek. It was over. It was really over.

I was no longer trapped in someone else's life in the circumpolar North. I was alive, with a US Marshal, in the city of Fairbanks.

When he finished his call, the marshal turned back my way and offered me his hand to shake. "Ma'am, my name is Deputy Hill."

Willing the inner voice, the one I'd worked hard to suppress, the one I now knew was the real me—Stella—to emerge, I trepidatiously accepted his hand. "Thank you, Deputy Hill, may I please use your phone?"

I supposed I should have introduced myself, but I wasn't thinking straight. With my first objective accomplished, I needed to call Dylan.

Deputy Hill's dark aviators reflected the afternoon sun as he glanced from his phone to my face. "Let's get you to the safety of the station first. You've had a traumatic experience." If he only knew. "We have a female marshal who can assure your well-being and then we can progress."

The cloak of freedom that I'd lost nearly a year ago weighed heavily on my shoulders. At the same time relief overwhelmed me. My tense muscles gave way, causing me to stumble.

Deputy Hill reached for my elbow. "Are you all right? Can you walk?"

Sucking my lower lip between my teeth, I nodded. "I'm just so relieved. I was frightened of what he was going to do."

"Yes, ma'am, we received a tip and have been waiting for his arrival."

"A tip?" I asked, more than slightly concerned. "From whom?"

Had it been The Light? Had they known I would be with him?

"Ma'am, the important thing is that you're safe." Deputy Hill continued to speak as he led me to a dark, unmarked SUV and helped me into the backseat.

Once he was in the driver's seat and we began to pull away, I asked, "What happened to Thomas?"

"My partner took him. We thought by that shiner you're sporting you'd prefer not to ride in the same vehicle."

My fingers fluttered near my eye as I leaned back against the seat. "Thank you. Once we get to the station, I need to make a call."

"Did Mr. Hutchinson take you against your will?"

"Mr. Hutchinson?" I asked.

The deputy's eyes met mine in the rearview mirror. "The man who was with you, Thomas Hutchinson."

"Yes, but . . ."

"But?" he repeated.

I shook my head again. "Please, once I make a call I can explain everything."

"Yes, ma'am. After we get to the station and get your statement."

I settled back and watched the city streets. There were more people out and about in the community at the Northern Light than I saw on these urban streets. As we drove I marveled at the world I used to take for granted. Stores and fast-food restaurants clustered at each intersection. I'd forgotten how normal the dark was. It wasn't scary and unknown like The Light had told me. Instead, it was comfortingly familiar.

The US Marshals' station was small, reminding me more of a house than a police station. Deputy Hill pulled onto the gravel lot, mostly filled with SUVs. As soon as he parked, he opened my door and helped me out. It wasn't until we began walking that the rubbing against the outside of my foot reminded me of my knife. I thought about confessing that I had it, until he asked whether I'd like anything to eat or drink.

Suddenly the thought of food monopolized my thoughts. I hadn't eaten since I'd cooked breakfast for Jacob. "What time is it?"

As we entered the building Deputy Hill looked up at a clock hanging above the empty front desk. "It's nearly four."

The clock was large, round and plain, like my first memory of the dark. Despite my feeling weak from hunger, it made me grin. "Thank you, I'd love something to eat."

Below the clock was a large circular sign that read **DEPARTMENT OF JUSTICE, UNITED STATES MARSHAL**. The US Marshals must not be very busy in Fairbanks. I remembered a Detroit police station, from the few times I'd gone there for work or to visit Dylan. It was always bustling with activity. This office seemed abandoned in comparison.

Deputy Hill walked me down a hall, opened a door, and ushered me over the threshold. "Please have a seat. I'll get you something to eat. There's a restroom across the hall, and in a few minutes Deputy Stevens, the female officer I told you about, will be in to talk with you."

"Thank you," I replied as I sat. Before the door closed, I asked, "Will Deputy Stevens be taking my statement? I'd like to make that call."

"It will be just a few minutes."

The door closed, and I sighed. I glanced around the stereotypical interrogation room, seeing the pale walls, tile floor, and metal table with four chairs. There weren't any windows to the outside, but one wall contained a large mirror I was relatively certain was actually a one-way window. From my side of the glass, I saw only my own muted reflection. Though the colors didn't seem right, I could tell that my eye was getting worse.

After a few minutes, I took Deputy Hill's offer of a restroom. When I slowly opened the door, I peered in both directions. Though I'd expected to see someone, instead there were only empty hallways. Entering the bathroom and turning on the light, I cringed at the woman in the mirror.

Damn, Thomas had done one hell of a job on my cheek. The bruising was much more visible under the incandescent lighting.

Not wanting to miss Deputy Stevens, I hurried and returned to the room.

Eating the turkey sandwich and stale chips Deputy Hill delivered, I debated my statement and decided I'd first tell the marshal that Thomas had taken me. Then, once I was granted my telephone call, I'd call Dylan and tell him I was alive and about The Light. If I told the marshals that story first and they didn't believe me, I might not get the chance to call Dylan.

I suddenly thought about the time difference between Fairbanks and Detroit. I didn't know what it was. I knew Pacific time was three hours behind Detroit. I believed that made Alaska four hours. My heart sank. Dylan wouldn't be at the station this late.

Undeterred, I decided I could persuade them to give me his number. I would do whatever I could to avoid staying in this hell, even if it were nighttime in Detroit.

Drinking from the water bottle, I continued to wait for Deputy Stevens. Maybe it was the nourishment or perhaps the rush of freedom, but with each passing minute, I started to become more anxious. Silently I watched the door.

As I waited, for the first time since the night my memories came back, I mentally returned to the accident—the *supposed* truck wreck that had not only taken my memory and resulted in banishment but also marked the end of my life as Stella Montgomery and the beginning of my life as Sara Adams. Even now I couldn't recall what had preceded the accident. My last memory from before that was of a parking lot in Detroit. I remembered waking in the mangled truck without sight, crawling from the wreckage, and scrambling in the darkness. My teeth clenched as I recalled the intense pain in my leg and ribs. My hand fluttered to my now-swollen cheek, the same cheek that had been swollen then.

Pacing the small room, I recounted the hard, vicious blows that had assaulted me as I lay trapped upon the cold, hard ground. Tears formed as I came to the same conclusion I'd come to the night my memories returned. I'd been kicked and purposely abused as, throughout the entire assault, the wind whipped around me, whistled in my ears, and filled my mind with white noise until . . . the voice.

In my mind I heard the deep, demanding voice ordering me to stop, even though I didn't know what I'd done. And then I was lifted into someone's arms.

My turkey sandwich rolled in my stomach as the scent of musk and leather came back. I opened my eyes and peered around the small room. The memory was so intense that it was as if I could actually smell it, but no. It wasn't real.

It was familiar—Jacob's signature scent. I knew in the depth of my soul that Jacob was the one who had lifted me. He had been at my accident. Was he the one who'd yelled, the one who'd hurt me?

I tried to devise another plausible scenario, something other than naming him as my assailant. Nothing came to my mind, no other possibilities.

Eventually Deputy Hill returned, apologized for Deputy Stevens's delay, and promised she'd be there soon.

"If I could please make a call? I just need to use your computer—"

"Ma'am, soon. I promise," Deputy Hill said, as he disappeared again behind the door.

The relief I'd experienced at the airport was beginning to fade. This didn't seem right. Someone should have taken my statement.

With each ticking minute, I remembered who I was. I was no longer compliant Sara. I was Stella, and I was alive. I had parents, a sister, and a boyfriend who deserved to know that I was no longer missing. I had friends who needed to be informed. There were people I needed to help and an organization I needed to expose.

With a huff I stood, scooting the metal chair across the hard tile, and headed for the door. Just as I did, the door opened. Deputy Hill met me and I gasped.

Deputy Hill wasn't alone.

His next sentence took everything away. My newfound freedom disappeared as he spoke. "Ma'am . . . your husband is here to take you home."

CHAPTER 9
Jacob

A few hours earlier

It was a gamble, but it was also our only chance. If Raquel was right and Sara had not only remembered her past but also found a way to leave the Northern Light, Thomas would have been her only option. On the off chance she was with him, his plane had to be intercepted. If Raquel was wrong, then we were without options and time. As I flew toward Fairbanks, all I could think about was getting to her, Sara or Stella, I didn't know. When I left Montana, her whereabouts had still been unconfirmed.

My Citation X flew considerably faster than Thomas's Cessna 206. He might have left the Northern Light with Sara before I left Whitefish, but despite the impending weather, I was able to gain on them.

The entire flight, unsure whether I'd find Sara in Fairbanks, I contemplated Special Agent Adler's plan. It was brilliant and totally contingent upon Sara. If I found her, I would then need to convince her to help. If I accomplished both goals, then we'd be going back to the Northern Light. Going back would give the FBI more time to sync the raids at all campuses. It was the only way to reduce loss of life if, indeed, there was an extermination plan that one raid at one campus would set into motion. If I couldn't find Sara or convince her, then the operation was over.

Everything.

Three years of deep-cover operative work, embedding myself in The Light, learning the ways, proving my loyalty . . . it was all done. I had until tomorrow morning to pass Sara's answer on to Special Agent Adler.

Agent Jacoby McAlister wasn't ready to be done. I'd learned too much and was too close.

As I got closer to Fairbanks, I continued my fervent prayers that she was there. Being certain of her safety became paramount. With that in mind, if she was there *Jacob Adams* decided he wanted Sara to say no. That wasn't completely true. As her husband I wanted to make the choice for her. Ever since I'd taken her as my wife, I'd been worried about how to protect her when the raids finally went down—not if, but when: they were inevitable. I'd been terrified that someone would execute a possible contingency plan while I was away. That was why I'd taken her plea to travel with me to the Commission. She'd always been intelligent and inquisitive, and with her request, I'd hoped she'd provided a way for me to save her.

No matter what decision was made or whether she was found, her life as Stella Montgomery was over. If she found a way back to Detroit on her own, I knew what would happen. The Light would eliminate her as a threat. Under no circumstances could she return to her hometown. It was too dangerous.

Assuming she was found and she chose not to help, the federal agencies were ready to take her into the witness protection program and the raids would happen—tomorrow. If Sara and I didn't return to the Northern Light, the FBI feared it would raise suspicions and put more lives at stake.

On the off chance that Father Gabriel would see Sara's and my desertion as the beginning link in a chain that would bring him down, the sting operation had to be over, and the FBI had to move. The bureau wasn't willing to jeopardize the intelligence I'd discovered. Though there were still unknowns, such as the location of the money, I'd unraveled enough to stop The Light and put Father Gabriel behind bars for a very long time.

Without question, with each mile while I prayed she was in Fairbanks, I was conflicted over whether to take her back to the Northern Light and continue my mission, or to hand her over to witness protection and assure her safety.

When Hill called my burner to tell me they had Sara and what Thomas had done, I was still in the air and unable to receive calls. It wasn't until I landed that I heard the voice mail. Learning that she was safe almost took me to my knees with relief; however, as his message continued and I heard that Thomas had struck Sara, blackening her eye, my death grip on the burner phone almost crushed it.

I reminded myself that the most important thing was that we'd found Sara.

I'd devised a story to help with the cover-up of her escape. I contacted Brother Daniel and told him that Whitefish hadn't been ready for me. I hadn't been able to get the supplies I needed, so I'd flown to Fairbanks.

For that story to be believable, I had to purchase supplies. Since I wasn't leaving Sara alone once I had her, I needed to leave her at the marshals' office where I knew she was safe. Per Special Agent Adler, she'd come into contact only with two marshals, and Deputy Hill was the only one who'd spoken with her.

It hadn't taken Adler long to learn Thomas's flight plans and discover that he had been headed to Fairbanks. Unfortunately, there wasn't an FBI field office in Fairbanks. The only one in Alaska was in Anchorage. That gave the FBI the choice of the US Marshals or local police. Adler chose to contact Deputy Hill and involved the US Marshals in our operation. Without divulging too much, he explained the urgency of finding, securing, and isolating Sara, as well as taking care of Thomas.

After the message about Thomas's hitting Sara, I would've liked to have been the one who *took care* of him; however, undoubtedly my method wouldn't be approved and there wasn't enough time.

With a motel room set, a call in to Brother Daniel about my change in plans, and supplies purchased, I finally arrived at the marshals' office and sat behind a window watching the woman who'd been my wife for nearly a year. Though I'd wanted to go straight to her, Hill insisted that I see her first, see her injury. Even though I saw it only through the glass, my teeth and fists clenched.

"Tell me Thomas is no longer a threat," I said, though my jaw wouldn't move.

"Agent, he'll be lost in the system for more years than you'll need to complete your assignment," Deputy Hill said, shrugging confidently, as only a man with years of experience could do. "With his cocky attitude and affinity for hurting women, he might find more than he bargained for behind bars. Who knows? He may not make it long enough in general population for his messed-up papers to ever be straightened out."

I nodded, the muscles in my neck and shoulders screaming from the tension and strain. "What did she say in her statement?"

"I haven't taken a statement."

I turned toward the older man's blank expression. "What do you mean? You've had her here for hours."

"And if I'd taken a statement, I'd have had to record it. If I forgot to take a statement or record her detention, then maybe it didn't happen."

I inhaled. Puffing out my cheeks, I slowly released the air. "Did she say . . ."

"She hasn't said anything. She's tried, but I just kept telling her we'd be ready soon." He nodded toward the window. "Mostly she keeps asking to make a call."

"If she decides . . . they'll let her call her family." I couldn't say *if she decides to go into witness protection*. As much as I'd convinced myself, as I flew to Fairbanks, that having her safe was the best option, having her in the next room, I couldn't imagine letting her go.

Not that my intentions would convince her. I was probably the last person she wanted to see. Well, looking at her eye, maybe I trumped Thomas, but that wasn't saying much. I had to think of something. Everything and everyone was riding on this.

First I needed to get her away from the marshals' office. I ran my hands through my hair as Sara stood and walked.

"We'd better . . . ," Hill said as he exited the room.

My steps stuttered as I watched Sara move toward the door. Immediately my temperature rose. Something was off with her stride. Hill had said that Thomas hadn't done more than strike her—as if that were OK—but by the way she was walking . . . biting my cheek, I suddenly wondered whether he had done more.

So help me God, if he had touched her sexually . . . once this was over, I'd unravel the fucking paperwork and make him pay.

I made it to the door of the interrogation room, just as Deputy Hill opened it and said, "Ma'am . . . your husband is here to take you home."

As I stepped around Hill, my gaze met Sara's. Though her eyes remained fixed, her feet backed away. In that second I didn't see the horrible purple bruise. All I saw were the most beautiful light-blue eyes staring back at me. In that gorgeous stare was a kaleidoscope of emotion: shock, fear, disbelief, and resentment. They all swirled together with hurt and disappointment. I searched for the love I swore I'd seen that morning. Fear was winning her emotional battle.

Needing to refocus her thoughts, I evened my voice. "Sara."

Her neck straightened. Despite her eye, she had strength. She was fighting not only me but also the months of training, submission, and conditioning. Stella and Sara were battling before my eyes. If only she'd listen to my true intentions. I wasn't Jacob, not completely.

Her protests started softly, and then her eyes widened, and Stella grew stronger. "No," she whispered. Then, after clearing her throat, she repeated, "No. This isn't happening." I closed the gap. "No," she said louder. Turning toward Deputy Hill, she spoke louder: "I'm not his wife. No!" Her face was suddenly tight with terror as she realized he wasn't going to help. "Deputy Hill, please! You haven't even taken my statement."

"Sara," I repeated calmly. "It's time to go home. We need to talk."

As I closed the gap, she slid against the wall, working her way toward the door, as if I'd allow her to escape. Instead of looking at me, her gaze searched for Hill, as she pleaded, "No! Don't listen to him. My name is—"

"Stop!" I yelled, my voice echoing against the walls of the small room. We hadn't told anyone from the marshals her true identity. It wasn't safe. Special Agent Adler had confidence in Hill, but we suspected The Light's power could be far-reaching. We couldn't take that chance.

I didn't mean to scare her, but when she looked back to me I swear I saw raw horror. Her expression was like none I'd ever seen on her before, even when I deserved it. This time I didn't. This time I wasn't going to correct her or punish her. I was trying my damnedest to save her.

She fell to the ground, pulling my heart out of my chest and throwing it to the floor below. Her cries and pleas replaced the reverberating sound of my one-word command. "Please . . . I'm not his wife . . . please believe me . . . I'm not Sara . . . I'm . . ."

I lowered myself before her, needing to stop her words, and keeping my tone even. I lifted her chin, forcing our eyes to meet. The purple bruise taunted me, telling me I'd already failed to keep her safe. Not wanting to hurt her, I brushed the puffiness softly with my thumb and said, "Sara, we need to go. *Now*," I emphasized. "Don't make me repeat myself."

My words came too easily. I'd lived the role for so long.

Sara's head moved from side to side with her chin still in my grasp, her eyes closed in submission. Her despair ripped at my chest, shredding the remaining pieces of my heart.

I reached for her hand. "Sara, it's all right. We'll get this taken care of. I promise."

With her lip between her teeth, she grudgingly stood. Defeat and apprehension rippled from her every pore. After a few steps, she stopped, and with her head still down, she looked at me with only her eyes and asked, "Will you . . . ?"

I placed my hand at the small of her back and directed her toward the door. "Shhh, not here, Sara. We'll discuss it in private."

I guided her to the truck I'd borrowed from the private hangar. Her continued battle raged: Sara versus Stella. She'd straighten her neck and purse her lips, and then just as quickly she'd bow her head. By the time we'd made it to the motel in silence, I'd had enough. No doubt the death grip on the steering wheel was evidence of my own discontent.

What the fuck did I think I was doing, trying to convince her to return? Hell, there was an excellent possibility this plan would blow up in our faces. There were too many variables.

What if Benjamin and Raquel talked to Brother Raphael? After all, Brother Raphael was Benjamin's overseer and one of the original Commissioners. He might be nice and kind, but he knew what really happened in The Light. He was the one who continued to formulate the pharmaceuticals.

I understood why Father Gabriel did what he did. I'd seen his mansion and heard the celebrations from the depth of the property.

But what was in it for Raphael, Uriel, and Michael?

They were intricate pieces of the puzzle. They worked diligently, yet to me they seemed sorely undercompensated.

During our drive Stella continually looked in my direction with a thousand questions, ready to bombard me, and just as quickly Sara would quell every one of them.

Sara knew the repercussion of questioning. She'd experienced it more times than I cared to remember.

Right now I wanted her questions. I needed them. I was a fucking chicken and needed her to begin this conversation, though I had no idea how it would go.

As I parked the truck outside the old motel, I took a deep breath and looked in her direction. When our eyes met, I wanted nothing more than to take her in my arms and make her forget the hours she'd spent with Thomas. I wanted to make her feel safe enough to tell me the truth about what he'd done. I wanted to see the love I thought I had seen nearly twenty hours earlier.

But I was a damn fool, because what I saw in those blue eyes was a whirlwind of contempt and suspicion. Despite what I'd been taught to believe, it wasn't up to me to make anything happen. It was up to her.

I exhaled. "This is where we're spending the night."

"W-we're not going back to the Northern Light tonight?"

My brow rose at her question. I was conditioned as well as her. Lesson after lesson had been recited, learned, and eventually regurgitated to other men followers. Beginning at the Eastern Light, I'd been made to believe that men were the stronger, smarter sex. We made decisions. Women didn't question. They couldn't.

"I-I'm sorry." Her chin fell and her lip quivered.

I reached for that chin and pulled the blue gaze toward me. "No, Stella, it's over. Never be sorry for your questions. I owe you a lifetime of answers, and it's going to start tonight."

CHAPTER 10
Sara/Stella

What did he just say?

Releasing my chin, Jacob said, "Let's go into the motel?" It sounded more like a question than a command.

For the first time since Deputy Hill had handed me off to Jacob—the moment I realized my nightmare was not ending—my chest filled with air and my neck straightened. Incredulously, with my mouth agape, I turned in his direction. It was my turn to narrow my eyes.

Sighing, Jacob reached for my hands.

I pulled them away. "What the fu—? What did you just call me?" I asked, with more anger in my tone than I'd ever used with him.

Nevertheless, the expression that stared back at me didn't frighten me. I didn't understand it and didn't know what had happened, but something was different. No longer was Jacob my disciplinarian: he was my equal. Something in his dark eyes told me that he felt it too.

With only the lights from the outside of the motel, I scanned the man who claimed to be my husband. His face looked older and more tired than I'd ever recalled. Slowly he ran his hand through his dark hair as defeat filled his voice. "We've both had a long day. Let's get out of this truck and go inside where we can talk. You deserve answers."

"Answers? Answers?" My volume rose exponentially with each word. "I fucking deserve a lot more than that!"

"Sara."

"No! No! I'm not Sara!" Blood rushed to my ears and face. My body trembled as nine months of submission boiled out of me. I was losing control, and I knew it. "I'm Stella! And you knew it! You knew! Fuck you! You've *known* it from the very beginning!"

Unable to stay seated, I reached for the door handle and shoved the door open. Though Jacob spoke, his words didn't register. As soon as my feet hit the parking lot, I ran, the sheathed blade of the paring knife rubbing against the side of my foot. With each stride the world lost more focus. I rushed forward, each step becoming more important than the last. I didn't know where I was going, but I had to get there.

Being farther north, the Northern Light had very few hours of darkness this time of year, but thankfully, Fairbanks had some. Since I'd spent so long at the marshals' office, the sky was now black. As I ran I imagined the darkness was my cover, my invisibility cloak, allowing me an escape from my ongoing nightmare. But alas, it wasn't. Before I made it through the next parking lot, Jacob seized my shoulders.

Burrowing his lips into the nape of my neck, in a hushed whisper he said, "You can hate me for the rest of your life. Just, please, trust me for a few more hours. If you don't, I'm afraid the rest of your life won't be long."

I spun toward him. Under the lights of the street, in the eyes of the man I wanted to hate, I saw what I suspected was the most honest expression I'd ever seen. Still I asked, "Are you threatening me?"

He shook his head. "I'm trying to save you."

"I-I don't understand."

Releasing my shoulders, he reached for my hand. I didn't fight as he laced our fingers together. "I'll explain. I'll tell you everything." He lifted our joined hands and kissed my knuckles. "Then it will be your decision." Looking at my hand, he smiled. "You're still wearing your wedding band."

I looked down at our joined fingers and shrugged. He was right. I wasn't sure why I hadn't taken it off, but I hadn't.

"Please," he pleaded, "come to the room and let me try to explain."

With the warmth of his hand and the cloud of leather and musk, I nodded. I didn't understand what had happened, but somewhere between the marshals' station and the motel, *my husband* had changed. Maybe we'd both changed. As we silently walked, hand in hand, I didn't know.

Once we were inside the room, Jacob locked the door and turned in my direction. My heart ached as I watched the handsome man before me. From his dark wavy hair to his brown eyes, defined jaw, and broad shoulders, I saw a storm of emotions I'd never before seen. His normally confident demeanor had been replaced by one of sorrow and fear.

Holding a fistful of his dark hair, he said, "Before I start, I need to know . . ." His chest expanded and contracted. "Tell me the truth. What did Thomas do to you?"

Though his tone wasn't demanding, I had no reason to lie. Sitting on the edge of the bed, I sighed. "He scared me and slapped me, but that was all."

"He didn't . . . ?"

I couldn't help but smile at his genuine concern. I shook my head. "No. He told me he would, once we got to Fairbanks, but as soon as we landed, the marshals were there." Remembering the scene, I stood. "Were they really US Marshals or were they part of The Light? How did they know I was there? What really happened to Thomas?"

Though my questions came fast and furious, the shaking of his head was lethargic and slow. "Sara, there's so much I need to explain."

My back straightened. "Do *not* call me that. You know my real name. Use it!"

"Stella," he said.

My name sounded painful on his lips, as if it ripped him apart, exposing him in an unfamiliar way. The angst resonating from the one word made me want to tell him to forget it and just call me Sara, but I bit my lip, stopping the words. I was the one who'd been living a lie for the past nine months, the one who'd been ripped from her real life; he deserved to feel a fraction of the pain I felt. My eyes dropped to his hips.

Pain.

All I had to do was look at his damn belt to remind myself that this was the man who'd hurt me—controlled me—brainwashed me, not only mentally but also physically. With each second of silence, my contempt grew. Crossing my arms over my chest, I exhaled and turned away.

"Don't," he said, his warm hand reaching for my shoulder and his fingers directing my movement.

Spinning toward him, I yelled. "No! *You* don't. Don't you touch me. I'm not your wife. You know that. You've *known* that and still you . . ." My words began to fail. "You . . . made me . . ." Shaking my head within the confines of the small motel room, I walked as far away as I could, refusing to cry. "Jacob . . . I . . ."

When I turned back toward him, he was sitting on the end of the bed, his elbows on his knees and his hands holding his head. His normally proud broad shoulders slumped forward. Unable to see his face, I stared, feeling the palpable defeat wafting off him.

Finally, still looking down, he said, "My name's not Jacob, not really, but you probably figured that out."

When his dark eyes peered upward, I nodded. "I assumed. I mean what are the chances that *everyone* has a biblical name? I think I've figured out that most of us were given a name that starts with the same letter as our real name."

He shrugged. "You're right. It has something to do with recall. It's supposed to make accepting the new name easier. My real name is

Jacoby McAlister, and what I'm about to say will be the reason Stella Montgomery will never be able to go back to her life in Detroit."

The compassion that continually licked at my heart for this man evaporated.

"Then don't say it," I said with alarm. "Whatever *it* is, Jacob, please don't say it. I want to go back. I need to go back."

Though he sadly shook his head, one side of his lips turned upward. "See, Stella, it isn't that easy. You just called me Jacob. Sara is who you are to me."

I nodded. I hadn't even realized I'd said his name. "Jacoby," I said, the name sounding foreign. "Please don't say whatever it is. Just let me go. I need to. I have connections. I can save Mindy. I can save others."

"Mindy?" he asked.

"She's my friend. She's part of the reason I started investigating The Light."

He sat taller. "What? You were investigating The Light? Are you with the police?"

"I'm not police. I was, or am—hell, I don't know anymore—an investigative journalist. I'd been following some leads that led me to The Light."

He stood, again fisting his hair. "Shit! I didn't know that. They didn't tell me. All they said was that you were chosen."

"What? What do you mean . . . I was part of *the* chosen, or I was chosen?"

"Most men don't get to see their wives until they arrive, but I was different. I'm a pilot." He grinned a real grin. "See, not everything is a lie."

"Army?" I asked.

He nodded. "That's true too, and so was Iraq. Anyway, because I travel to the different campuses, about a week before you were taken, Brother Uriel, from—"

"Eastern Light," I interrupted. "Uriel Harris or Harrison."

Jacoby's eyes grew wide, staring at me as if we'd never met. "Shit!" he exclaimed. "Yes. Well, *he* took me to this festival in Dearborn, Michigan."

It was my turn to collapse onto the bed. "You saw me there? You saw me with Dylan?"

"Yes, I saw you." He sat beside me. "Do you remember me telling you how the first time I ever saw you I knew you were mine?"

I nodded, trying to forget the emotion I'd felt that night, the night he'd started painting me a mental picture of our past.

"Well, it was true. I saw you with Richards . . ."

Gasping, I covered my lips with the burned tips of my fingers. "You know his name?"

He nodded. "But like I said, I *did* know you were mine. I wasn't being figurative. Brother Uriel told me that you were. I remember listening to you laugh, how fucking carefree you were. At the same time, I knew. I knew it was all about to end."

I didn't understand. "Why? Why? Why did you do it?"

Jacob seized my shoulders. "*I* didn't do it. Don't you get it? It wasn't up to me. Father Gabriel said I was to have a wife. I didn't choose you. You were chosen for me."

"So you didn't want me?"

He gently reached for my face and, so as not to hurt my eye, tenderly cupped my cheeks. "I didn't want *a wife*. I'd tried to avoid taking one, but from the first time I saw you, I wanted you."

He released my face and stood. As he paced the length of the room and back, the silence grew. Each step upon the carpet was a beat of a mystical drum, each one increasing the pressure until he exploded. "I know it makes me as fucking wrong as all of them! But I did! Damn it, I wanted you. And once you were there, at the Northern Light . . . once you were there and you were mine, I did everything I could to save you."

Indignation rose as I stood. "Really? Really? Lying to me, correcting . . . fuck that . . . beating me, was to save me?"

"Yes, Sara, it was."

"Stella! Use my goddamn name!"

In two strides he was before me, his large hands holding my shoulders, our noses nearly touching. The heat of our breath grew as his chest touched mine. "Stella." He'd calmed his tone, yet his words were separated, punctuated for emphasis. "Every. Goddamn. Thing. I. Did. *To.* You. Was. *For.* You." With only a whisper of distance between us, his lips crashed over mine. Their warmth was the fire that ignited my body in a way I no longer wanted to admit.

I reached for his shoulders and pushed him away. "No!"

Hurt swirled in the depths of his eyes.

"No!" I continued, "You want me to believe that you didn't get off hitting me with your belt. Well, I don't believe you."

"Think about it, Sara. Just think about the bigger damn picture."

I was too upset to correct my name again. "Bigger picture. Fuck you, Jacob, or Jacoby, or whoever the hell you are! I didn't see a bigger picture. I *don't* see it. Remember me? I'm the one who had the reminders on my ass!"

"We were being watched, continually. Every encounter was a test. If I failed, you failed. If you failed, I failed. The only time I corrected you was when your transgressions were witnessed. It was when it was expected of me. Only once did I do anything without someone to witness it." Remorse filled his words. "It was at the clinic when I slapped you, but even that, like the other times, was for your success."

My mind spun. I thought about all the times he'd corrected me. I tried to recall what had preceded or followed each instance. He was right. There were so many times I'd expected him to do it, and he hadn't. Yet there were other times when I'd thought my transgression was minor, but he had. I sank back to the bed. Every instance had had witnesses.

"Why?" I asked. "Why not just let me fail?"

Jacob's eyes grew as he dropped to his knees near my feet. "You said you researched The Light?" He turned my hand over and touched the tips of my fingers. "Do you know what happens when someone fails?"

I swallowed and nodded.

"From the first time I saw you at that festival, I knew failure wasn't an option. I didn't know for sure why you were chosen. Now I suspect it was because you were getting too close to them, but no matter why, I knew you needed to live. I wouldn't let them banish you."

I shook my head. "But we *were* banished."

"That wasn't real banishment. In all the time I'd been with The Light, I'd never heard of *temporary* banishment, not until us." He ran his hand through his hair. "The night after service when Father Gabriel said that we were to be banished, my heart stopped beating. I was so fucking scared."

I reached for his face and palmed his scruffy cheeks, seeing his pain. "That was the first night I went to service, wasn't it?"

He nodded, his face still in my grasp.

"It was the night you were so quiet. I was afraid that I . . ."

Jacob stroked my cheek. "It was the night I almost claimed you as my wife, your body. Despite all that they'd done to you and all you'd been through, you were still so beautiful, so strong, and yet so scared. I wasn't supposed to, but I wanted to make it better." He shook his head. "But I couldn't. I didn't want to hurt you."

My eyes narrowed. "They? *They* did to me? *You* did it. I remember being hurt. I remember your voice. *You* were the one who hurt me! There wasn't an *accident*. Father Gabriel banished us for something that never happened!"

"Oh, God, no! Yes, I was there, but I wasn't the one who hurt you. They made me watch. I was supposed to be quiet and let God's plan . . ." He stood again and paced. "Fuck that! It wasn't *God's* plan. It was Father Gabriel's. I was supposed to stay quiet, but I couldn't. I yelled at him. I told him to stop.

"If I hadn't been on the Assembly, fuck, if I'd been a mere follower, I never would've gotten away with what I did. But I couldn't watch him hurt you. When he wouldn't stop, I finally stopped him. I was the one who carried you away." He fell back to my feet and reached for my hands. "Of all the things I've done, please know, that wasn't one of them."

"Father Gabriel? He's the one who hit me and kicked me?"

Jacob's head moved back and forth. "No, hell no. He doesn't do any of his own dirty work. He's always a few steps removed."

"Then who?"

Jacob closed his eyes. When he opened them, sadness and regret flowed through the swirling brown. "You know how you said you didn't like Brother Abraham, that he made you feel uncomfortable?"

"Oh, God." My stomach twisted.

"There's a good reason for that."

"Does Father Gabriel know?"

Jacob nodded.

My eyes narrowed. "You're not defending him? I . . . I don't understand."

He leaned back on his toes, kneeling, as he'd told me not to do. With sadness in his eyes, he confessed, "Stella Montgomery, my name is Jacoby McAlister. I've been an agent with the Federal Bureau of Investigation for over seven years. The last three have been spent embedded in a deep undercover investigation of The Light."

I couldn't move or speak. The pieces of the puzzle that I'd tried to arrange over the last year all slid into place. From the first time I'd seen the white building that housed The Light in Highland Heights, I'd tried unsuccessfully to make the pieces fit. Even the pieces I'd managed to maneuver as Sara now combined, fitting into place like a key in a lock . . . a lock that I slowly realized meant the loss of my past.

"That's what you couldn't say? That's what you said would never allow me to go back to Detroit. Isn't it?"

He nodded.

"Then take it back. I don't want to know!"

Jacob reached again for my hands. "I can't take it back. Do you understand now? Do you understand how crucial your success was—is?"

"Because if I failed, you failed?"

His lips formed a straight line. "Yes."

"Jacob." I shook my head. "Jacoby, what do you mean *is*? How did you find me so fast? Did The Light tell you or the FBI?"

He exhaled. "There's much more to The Light than what you know. I've spent the past three years trying to get at its secrets, trying to learn what's really happening. You were my ultimate test. Although I prided myself on how fast and well I learned the ways of The Light and Father Gabriel's teachings, I think they suspected that I wasn't like them. Not until you. You convinced them that I was. I didn't want a wife"—he stood and resumed his trek—"for many reasons. The obvious one was that this was all a sham. It's my job. The other was because I don't agree with all their ways. I could preach it and teach it to new followers." He shrugged. "I thought of it like the military. I justified it as taking and giving orders, but taking a wife made it different. Taking a wife meant I had to live it. I didn't want to do that.

"Though Brother Daniel was always supportive, Brother Timothy was equally as negative. I suspect he was involved in forcing a wife on me. He wanted me to fail."

I hated that man, even the sound of his name. "Why? What is his problem with us?"

Jacob shrugged. "I suspect he doesn't like you because you're my wife. I really don't know why he doesn't like me. To be honest, I never let it bother me, until . . ."

I reached for my hair, which now fell past my shoulders. "Me?"

His cheeks rose and his brown eyes shone. "God, I hated them for what they did to you, but Sara, I loved you so much more. You were so strong. That was the night I fully believed in you. In us. If what they did to you didn't break you, I knew you'd survive, and I knew I'd stop at nothing to not only complete my assignment but get you out too."

I remembered that night. "That really was our first time?"

His Adam's apple bobbed. "I'd promised you—it was when you were still unconscious. I promised I'd give you time. I needed to make you believe you were Sara Adams to keep you alive, but what we did in private was different. I swore I'd never force myself on you." His smile disappeared. "That's not the way it is with all the men in The Light. I'm on the Assembly. I hear stories."

My skin crawled as I thought of Brother Abraham's wife. "Deborah?"

Jacob's jaw clenched. "Abraham is an ass." His eyes pleaded. "I never forced you, nor did I ever lie about my feelings." He ran his hand over his face. "You can hate me forever, and tomorrow we can part ways and never see each other again, but if that happens, I pray you'll give me the gift of letting me know that you understand why I did everything. And that you know I never meant you harm."

It was so much, *too* much. He'd taken too much. I wasn't ready to give him what he asked, not yet. "What do you mean that tomorrow we could part ways? What's happening tomorrow?"

"Tomorrow is up to you."

When has anything been up to me?

CHAPTER 11
Dylan

I ran my fingers through my hair and sighed as my phone continued to ring. Each week the same call. Each week the same conversation. As I stared at my screen and read Beverly Montgomery's name I contemplated hitting ignore.

Ring four.

Ring five.

She'll just keep calling.

"Hello, Mrs. Montgomery," I said, trying for my calmest tone. If I'd let it ring one more time it would've gone to voice mail. Either she'd have called back or left a message. If she'd left a message, I'd be forced to call her back. It was easier to just talk—like ripping off a Band-Aid.

"Bev," she corrected. "How many times do I need to ask you to please call me Bev? I'm not interrupting you, am I?"

"No, Bev. I'm clocked out and on my way home."

"It's been another week since Stella . . ." Her voice momentarily trailed away. "I just can't believe it. My baby's been gone for nearly nine months. Please tell me you've learned something new, something that can help."

I shook my head as I eased my unmarked Charger into early-evening Detroit traffic. "I wish I could. As you know, I'm not on the case."

"We know that, but you're on the force. You're her boyfriend—were."

I considered correcting her, telling her I wished I were still her boyfriend, but it would only take this conversation the way of many others, down an emotional path I wasn't up to navigating this evening.

She went on. "Surely they'd let you know . . ." Beverly Montgomery's words began to crack.

So much for avoiding emotion.

"The truth is that they wouldn't," I explained. "I'm not on the missing-persons task force. They can't tell me every time they learn anything new. Besides, because of Stella's and my relationship, they're less likely to tell me anything until they know for sure. They wouldn't want to get my hopes up."

"But . . . if they found something, that wouldn't get your hopes up. If they found her"—this time she couldn't disguise the audible cry before she whispered—"body."

"Nothing like that has happened. I promise you, if anything like that is found, you'll be contacted."

"It's strange how grown children live their own lives and as parents we're OK with that. Days and weeks can go by without speaking, and it's all right, because it means your children are doing what you raised them to do, to be independent, to be adults, and then in an instant it can all change . . ."

I clenched my teeth as I listened. Stella's mother had told me once that her therapist said talking to me would be helpful, therapeutic even for her loss. Sometimes the conversations were more upbeat, about Stella's sister, the one who'd been divorced. She'd recently remarried. Apparently losing a sister—well, having a sister go missing—had made her reevaluate her choices. The man she'd married had been her friend and now they had a child on the way. Beverly was elated at the prospect of being a grandparent. And then she'd think again about Stella and how much she'd enjoy being an aunt. Some conversations were too difficult to continue.

". . . thank you."

I'd been listening, but also watching the moving traffic. I didn't hear why she was thanking me, but didn't want to ask.

"You're welcome. I look forward to your calls."

"I wish . . . well, a lot of things. I remember how excited Stella was that she'd asked you to our house for Christmas. I'm never giving up hope, but I want you to know, we'll always think of you as part of this family, even if you"—she took a deep breath—"find someone else."

"I'm not dating, but maybe someday. I'm not ready to give up either."

"I meant to tell you." Beverly's voice filled with a new sense of excitement.

"What?"

"Bernard Cooper called me the other day."

I felt my grip tighten around the steering wheel. "He did?"

"Yes. It wasn't much, but since both Stella and Mindy went missing, apparently there's been an internal investigation at WCJB. They hired some computer forensic guy. You know they never found either one of the girls' personal laptops, but they've been able to uncover deleted files from the television station's server."

"They have? What have they learned?"

"Nothing yet. But he was very excited about the possibility of discovering more. I am too. Anything is better than nothing."

"Please keep me up to date on Bernard's progress."

She sighed. "I will. I was afraid he hadn't told you."

"We spoke quite a bit when she first . . . but we don't exactly see eye to eye on everything."

"I get the feeling that Mr. Cooper feels responsible, like a father who didn't do all he should have for his children. Both girls' disappearances have been very difficult on him."

I was sure they were. He should feel responsible. Sending Stella to Highland Heights. I told her over and over to stay away. She wouldn't listen. It was when she went to Gabriel Clark's mansion in Bloomfield Hills that my hands were tied.

Her fate was better than it could have been.

That's what I told myself as I disconnected the call, made my way into my house in Brush Park, and checked on Fred. He was blissfully unaware of all that had occurred as he swam circles in his little bowl.

"It's OK, little guy," I said as I sprinkled betta pellets on top of the water. "The clock's reset. We won't need to have that conversation again for another week."

CHAPTER 12
Jacob/Jacoby

I took Stella's hand in mine, and at least this time, she didn't pull away. I couldn't ask her to go back to the Northern Light. It wasn't fair. Sitting beside her, I tried to smile. If it was our last time together, maybe, just maybe, she'd have some fond memories of me. "Before we get into tomorrow, would you please tell me about your memory?"

"My memories? Of what?"

"No, *your memory*. When did it come back?"

She sighed and lay back on the bed. Though her feet were still on the floor, with her head back, her yellow hair fanned around her face, reminding me of a halo. On her neck was the silver cross necklace that I'd put around her neck the night of her first service. Like the wedding ring, she'd worn it consistently since that day. I didn't deserve her, and she didn't deserve this. Scooting up on the bed, she arranged the pillows and leaned against the headboard. As she did she scanned the room.

"What?" I asked.

She shrugged. "I just realized there's only one bed."

I stood and walked to the small table near the window and sat in a chair. "You can have it. I can sleep in a chair. I did that for over two weeks."

She nodded and smiled at me. "Now that makes sense."

"I promised."

She patted the bed beside her. "I'm not having sex with you, but you can sleep here."

"Are you . . . ?"

"Jacob, I'm not sure how much sleep we'll get. We have a lot to talk about."

I moved back to the bed. "Your memory?"

"Over a week ago, when you were gone for a few nights. You went to the Eastern . . . Detroit."

I nodded. "I can't believe I didn't know."

Crossing her arms over her chest, she shook her head. "I was afraid you did. The moment I saw you again, I knew I couldn't hide it from you. So I didn't try. When I was with you, I turned Stella off. I had to."

"What do you mean, you turned her off?"

She turned to face me. "How have you done it? I mean for three years. That's a long time."

I stared up at the ceiling. It was one of those bumpy ones, painted, but the white paint had discolored to a faint yellow with time. "You know what?" I said. "I get it. When I first went to the Eastern Light, I had to think about what I said and how I acted, but then, with time, I became *Jacob*."

I recalled the earlier training. Women weren't the only ones to be indoctrinated. It wasn't called that with men. It was called training—making it sound military or strategic. The first few weeks at the Eastern Light were a boot camp of sorts. It was where the men deemed unfit were weeded out. It was where Father Gabriel's word became second nature, where The Light's way of thinking was either embraced or rejected.

Those who rejected it didn't succeed. They didn't go on to become Assemblymen. I studied. I listened, and I performed. I couldn't fail.

I sighed at the memories and went on with my answer. "In the back of my mind I kept my objective, but I didn't have to think anymore. I was."

"So with me . . . ?" She left the question open.

There were so many ways I could go. "With you I had time. You were unconscious for a week."

"Did you really stay with me, or did I imagine that?"

"I stayed with you." I didn't want to tell her that Dr. Newton had injured her more between the attack and when I got to her. She didn't need to know how depraved he was too. When she only nodded, I went on. "So I had time to work through my issues. I talked to you. I confessed the truth about our relationship."

"That we didn't have one?"

"No. I said it was new, but I also told you that I'd seen you, and I'd do my damnedest to make you laugh like you had."

Staring straight ahead, she wiped a tear.

"I'm so sorry."

Sara shook her head. "The thing is, you did. In that whole fucked-up world, I wasn't really unhappy. I was at first, but then it felt . . . I don't know . . . right." She turned toward me. Her cheeks were dotted with blotchy red patches, the way they were when she cried. "I want to hate you. When my memories first came back, I hoped you were a victim too. That's what I tried to convince myself. But now, knowing that you knew, that you were part of it . . . I want to hate you.

"The thing is, as Sara I'm so different than I am as Stella. Different, not better or worse. Stella had a career and a fish." She laughed. "I hope Dylan took care of Fred."

I doubted that asshole had done anything, but I wouldn't say that either. "Fred? Was that your fish?"

Her eyes sparkled with unshed tears. "Yes. I feel like I'm two different people. Stella had a fish. Sara wanted a baby."

"Do you understand why I said no?"

She nodded. "Now I do, but I . . ." She looked down.

"I know what you did. It's why your memory came back."

Her gaze snapped back to mine. "You know? How do you know?"

"The drug that kept your memory away was in your birth control medicine. And, well, Raquel told me."

She nodded with the confirmation of her theory and then huffed. "So much for friendship confidentiality."

"In all fairness, she didn't tell me until today."

"Today?"

"Well, it seems like longer ago than that. After the incident with Brother Timothy, Sister Lilith, and your hair, I worried about leaving you alone, especially since I had to be gone overnight. So one of the times I left, early on after we returned to the community, I bought a burner phone. You know, a disposable one, untraceable?"

She nodded, her eyes wide.

"I took a chance. Elizabeth is too conditioned. I knew I couldn't ask her to break rules."

"So you asked Raquel?"

I nodded. "Benjamin knew too. We all prayed that the phone would never need to be used."

Sara reached for my hand. I rolled my wrist so our palms would touch and our fingers intertwine. "See," she said, "I'm so mixed up. I hate that it was all a lie, but things like that make it seem real."

I lifted her hand and kissed her knuckles. "I told you that I didn't lie about my feelings."

Though she sighed, she didn't pull her hand away.

"So," I said, "your memories have been back for over a week, and when you were with me, you were Sara?" She nodded. "This morning, before I left, you told me you loved me." She nodded again. "And that was a lie?"

"Sara loves Jacob." She squeezed my hand. "That's all I can give you."

It was my turn to nod. "What happened with Thomas?"

She quickly turned toward me. "I told you, *nothing.*"

"No, I believe that. I'm asking how you ended up with him. Deputy Hill said that you said he took you against your will, but . . . what did the *but* mean?"

She sighed. "I went for a walk before work, and I saw your truck."

"My truck?"

"I knew you hadn't driven it into the community. You were gone. I'd seen Thomas in the community before. I didn't understand how he did it. Xavier never did, but I took a chance."

My pulse quickened. "You spoke to him in the community where others may have seen you?"

She shook her head. "No, I made sure that no one was around, and I got in the truck. I hid in the backseat, on the floor under a blanket."

Though she'd totally fucked up both of our lives, my cheeks rose as I shook my head with newfound admiration. "Damn, you're brave."

"It was stupid. I took a chance and it almost cost me more than I was willing to pay."

I didn't know how to respond. It *had* cost both of us, it wasn't *almost.*

"I thought I was good until he drove through the gates and then a few minutes later stopped the truck. He knew I was there." Her eyes opened wide again. "Jacob? I mean Jacoby?"

I lifted her hand and kissed her knuckles again. "I'd be OK if we stick with Jacob and Sara. I recently heard something about Sara, and I'm confident Jacob feels the same way."

"I can't . . ."

"I'm not asking you to," I reassured her. "What did you want to ask?"

Her baby-blue eyes held the innocent Sara gaze I'd come to adore. "Are there really polar bears?"

"Yes!" Of all the questions she could have asked, this one made me smile. "I've seen them myself, especially out by the landing strip."

"Then I hope he gets mauled."

"You don't need to worry about him."

"Will you tell me why?"

"I'll tell you anything. You never need to ask that way again."

She nodded.

"I don't know the details, but the US Marshals took care of him." When her expression blanked, I realized what that sounded like. "Not as in dead. Your confirmation that he took you against your will gave them probable cause. Deputy Hill guaranteed that Thomas would be lost in the federal system longer than I needed."

"Longer than you needed? What does that mean?"

"My assignment isn't over. The FBI needs more time to coordinate all the raids, and there's more I want to learn. Today was only the second time in nearly three years that I've spoken with my handler. Thomas is a weak link. He could have easily talked to Father Gabriel. He had to be silenced."

"Are you going back? Did I mess everything up?" She sighed, adjusted her pillow, and lay back.

"It's like I said, it depends on you." When I looked toward Sara, she was on her side with her knees drawn up. "What is it?"

In a short time, her complexion had paled. With her eyes closed, she shook her head. "I think I'm hungry."

"Damn, I'm sorry. I wasn't thinking." I stood. "When did you last eat?"

"Sometime at the marshals' office. It's probably the stress too."

Her forehead glistened with a sheen of perspiration.

"Let me go get you something to eat. It's kind of late. I can get fast food."

She nodded. "Thank you. I think that would help."

"If I leave you alone?" I looked at the phone on the stand near the bed. "I can't. I can't leave you alone."

"I'm not sure I can go with you. I'm suddenly not feeling very well."

Even if I pulled the phone cord out of the wall, she could always walk next door and borrow someone's phone. I couldn't say it, but in reality she too was a weak link.

Looking around, I found plastic cups wrapped in cellophane. Opening one, I filled it with water and brought it back to her. "Here, try drinking some water." Her beautiful eyes opened as she sat back up.

"Thank you," she said, taking the cup. Though the water sloshed in her shaky grasp, she smiled. "This reminds me of the clinic."

I watched the color return to her cheeks. Once she was done, I took the cup and brushed my thumb over her right cheek. "See, we do have a past."

I rolled the handle of the paring knife in my fingers as I paced the room and Sara slept. I should have been sleeping too, but I couldn't. My mind couldn't settle from the whirlwind of thoughts. Though I hated what Thomas had done to her, the knife made me smile. I hadn't been able to believe it when she removed it from her boot. It was obviously the reason I'd thought she was walking oddly, why I was worried that he'd hurt her sexually. She was so much braver than I knew.

I'd finally gotten the nerve to ask her the question that had eaten at me since my call with Raquel. I'd asked whether she was pregnant. Her answer made me feel neither better nor worse. She said she didn't know. It had been only three weeks since her last period, which she said was too early to know. I wasn't sure whether that was totally accurate. Though it'd been three years since I'd watched television—yes, even while in motels, I didn't; I wanted to stay in Jacob mode—I seemed to remember commercials that talked about home pregnancy tests that could determine results earlier than that. With her sound asleep, I considered driving to a store to buy one, but I wasn't sure I was ready to know.

We'd talked about so much, but I'd never posed the question that the morning would require. Once she ate the fast food we'd gone together to get and began yawning, I'd decided it could wait. Obviously the future was something neither one of us was ready to tackle. However, we'd done a bang-up job on our past. Maybe it was because it was relatively short, but we'd covered nearly everything, and I'd done my best to explain the whys behind each decision. The time of forbidding her questioning was over. For there to be a chance at a future, she needed to understand everything. The change in dynamic was refreshing yet unsettling. The conditioned man from The Light wanted to take control and tell her what to do. The man I had once been, and hoped to be again, appreciated a partner, not a submissive.

Sara wasn't the only one who felt like two different people. My two perspectives had me torn.

I didn't want to ask her to come back to The Light. It was too dangerous. Then again, the idea of never seeing her again created a void I couldn't imagine navigating. There was a reason agents stayed unattached. Lying in the bed, in nothing more than her bra and panties, was that reason. No, it wasn't that I'd waited for *Sara*. It was that I fucking hated having an Achilles' heel.

She made me more vulnerable. For that reason alone I should forgo asking and just tell Special Agent Adler that she'd said no. Then I should kiss her good-bye and let her walk away into witness protection. She'd be blissfully unaware of the repercussions, but I'd be confident of her safety.

Sitting at the table, I laid my head on my arms. With my eyes closed, I tried reassuring myself that the entire three years weren't a bust. My testimony alone could put Father Gabriel, the three Commissions, and the three Assemblies away for a long time. They all knew something.

It wasn't as if each individual knew the extent of the wrongdoings. Hell, I hadn't even known about the entire pharmaceutical scheme until recently. But once this was over, deciphering the details and determining the extent of each person's involvement wouldn't be up to me. It would be up to others in the FBI and then the judicial system.

The idea of putting all those men behind bars made me think about the wives and other followers. As the fast food churned in my gut, I feared that if the timing was off—at all—if all the raids didn't happen at the exact same time, Father Gabriel had an escape plan and would use it. The only part of his plan I knew for sure was that it involved flying to an unknown destination. What concerned me was the fate of those he would leave behind. Every day, as I became closer and closer to people like Raquel and Benjamin, I feared more for their safety. I'd never been told of a mass suicide plan, but I was terrified one might be in place.

Sara's hand landed on my shoulder. I hadn't even heard her get up.

"Why aren't you asleep?" she asked.

I covered her hand with mine. "Investigative journalist, huh?"

She walked in front of me, wrapping herself in a blanket she'd found in the top of the closet. Though the lights were off, with the soft glow of a night-light from the bathroom, I watched as she covered her bra and panties. "Yes," she replied, sheepishly adding, "I'm good at asking questions."

"Too good."

"So why aren't you sleeping? You were the one who said we had a long day."

I took a deep breath. "I'm thinking about tomorrow."

"Tell me."

"I can't."

Her volume rose. "I thought you said no more secrets."

"I can't tell you, because it's not up to me, and if it were, I can't decide what I'd choose."

She sat on the edge of the bed. "You're saying that tomorrow is my decision? Then give me my options."

I sat back and ran my hands over my face. My normal scruff had grown longer and softer. "Number one, we say good-bye to each other and you're taken to someplace safe. I'm leaning toward that option, by the way." I didn't know how far I was leaning that way, but her being safe outweighed the alternative.

She nodded. "You want to say good-bye?"

"No, Sara, I want *you* safe."

"And option number two?" she asked.

"Number two, we go back to the Northern Light and resume our lives."

"Option two means that you get to continue your assignment and keep working to bring down Father Gabriel?"

I nodded.

"What happens to Father Gabriel if I choose option one?"

"Well, right now he's at the Eastern Light."

"In that huge-ass mansion in Bloomfield Hills?"

"Jesus, you know about that too? Don't tell me Richards took you there."

"No! He didn't even know that I knew about it." She shrugged. "I guess he did know I knew about the house. I remember him being with me when I looked it up on Google Earth, but the way I figured it out had to do with a trail of ownership. I deduced that Father Gabriel was really Gabriel Clark, son of Marcel Clarkson."

I stared in amazement as she recounted the accurate information. No doubt The Light had taken her before she could expose them. More accurately, Richards had handed her over before she could expose The Light. As she finished speaking, she asked, "So what happens to Father Gabriel?"

"If you choose option one, the FBI will move as soon as it can. They want their raids coordinated. If neither of us returns to the Northern

Light, those in control will undoubtedly get suspicious. I don't know the particulars. There's a lot I'm still learning, but I suspect the Commission on each campus has a plan in case of discovery."

"What kind of plan?"

"Like I said, I don't know."

Sara stood and paced, the blanket falling from her shoulder, revealing the satin strap of her white bra. "A plan, like Jones's Kool-Aid?"

"It's not your concern. You didn't ask for any of this."

"What about all the followers? What about our friends, the women who didn't ask to be there? What about the children?"

I shook my head. "That's not how this works. I can't pick and choose. I can hope the raids happen before the Commissions figure it out. I mean, they all have to be timed perfectly."

"But you said you don't know it all. Why can't you go back without me?"

"Because I can't explain your disappearance. If I show up without you, they'll go after you. That's why you can't go back to your life. You have to go into witness protection."

"What? Wait! That's what you mean by me *being safe*? No way. No fucking way."

I pinched the bridge of my nose as I fought the urge to bring attention to her insolent tone and vulgar language. "Excuse me?"

"I said *no*."

Standing, I towered over her petite frame. "I'm not risking your safety. Besides, what if you're . . ." I motioned toward her midsection.

"Then you're going to send me away to have a new identity, like two aren't enough? And you're never going to see me or our baby again?"

"What the hell? Ten hours ago you were trying to call Richards. Would you have let him raise my kid?"

She crossed her arms over her breasts. "Ten hours ago I thought you were some whacked-out Light fanatic who'd kidnapped and assaulted me. And with that profile, hell yes, I wanted to get away from you."

"Light fanatic?" I asked with a hint of amusement.

She snickered. "Besides, I'm not pregnant."

"What? I thought you said it was too early?"

"It is, officially. I mean I don't know. So we shouldn't base anything off the unknown. Talk to me about what we do know." Before I could answer, she continued, "Let me start. If I don't go back with you, the FBI will raid all three campuses . . . today? Father Gabriel is in the big-ass mansion, which is probably one of the worst places to catch him, and if the raids aren't perfectly timed, there's the chance of Kool-Aid?"

I shrugged. "No confirmation on Kool-Aid."

"If I go back, we continue to live as we did. We continue to gather evidence to bring down Father Gabriel, otherwise known as Garrison Clarkson, and The Light. And we give the FBI more time to coordinate the raids."

"No."

"No?"

"There's no *we*. There's *me*. The FBI can't ask a civilian to enter into an investigation."

She smiled.

At that moment, I wasn't looking at Sara but at Stella. Though her cheek was battered, the beautiful woman before me exuded confidence. With a sexy smile, she dropped the blanket and moved closer. Pushing me back to the chair, she spread my knees apart, walked directly in front of me, and bent closer, until our noses nearly touched. With the mounds of her breasts peeking from her bra and a sultry tone, she whispered, "I don't think it's the FBI who's asking me." Her finger traced my jawline, burning my skin with her touch. "I think it's me saying I want to do this." Continuing her assault, she gently teased the collar of my shirt. "It's me, volunteering to keep your mission going." Placing her petite hands on my shoulders, she moved her lips closer to mine. "Tell me, Jacoby, do you really want to send me away?"

I am so fucking screwed!

CHAPTER 13
Stella/Sara

Jacoby didn't answer my question, but by the expression on his face, I knew I was winning this battle of wills. It was the power I'd learned I possessed months ago. Despite his dominance, there had been times when I had control. Now I wanted to use that power to help him and his mission. I'd told him things I knew about The Light; now I wanted to know all he knew—there were still so many questions. Nevertheless, I was confident that together we could do this. We could bring Gabriel Clarkson's world crashing down, and I prayed we could do it without Kool-Aid or any other plan that would have catastrophic results.

I knew that Jacob and I could help each other. But there was something I needed to do first. "I want to call my parents and let them know I'm alive."

Jacob sighed. "If you choose witness protection, they'll help you with that."

I stood and pulled the blanket tighter. "I don't want witness protection. But I can't not tell them or"—I didn't know how Jacob would respond—"Dylan."

His stare darkened. "It's not up to me. You can't."

"It's not up to you? You're right. It's up to me. I need to call. My parents probably think I'm dead. My mom could call Dina Rosemont, my friend Mindy's mom, and then they'd have hope."

Jacob shook his head. "I don't know who you're talking about, but this is why witness protection is best."

"How long would we need to be back? Days? Weeks? Months?"

"As short as possible. Just long enough for the FBI to get organized on the raids. The best possible scenario is for all three campuses to be raided at the exact same time."

I pressed my lips together. "I don't like it—not calling—but I understand."

I did. Though Jacob had lied in the past, as we'd talked, I'd understood both his motivation and the reason I couldn't call. I even believed that he'd protected me and that our collective success had been contingent upon the success of each of us.

When I brushed my lips against his, his dark eyes widened suspiciously.

I tried for my most innocent Sara expression. "What?" I sat back on the bed and faced him. "Will you tell me a few things, a few things about The Light?"

"I told you, I'd tell you anything you want to know."

"How many of the women, wives, came to The Light like I did?"

He shrugged. "I've only been there for three years, but as a pilot I see more than most. After all, the women have to get to the Northern Light or Western Light somehow."

My stomach rolled as I scrunched my nose and lowered my chin. "Oh, God." My words sounded more like a cry. "*Y-you* transported them—us?"

"Micah and I." He reached for my hands. "Sara, remember why. Remember my goal. I had to gain Father Gabriel's trust. No follower has ever obtained the Assembly in as short of a time as I did. It was because, well"—he sighed—"I convinced them I had PTSD. I convinced them *all* that I reveled in the structure of The Light, and I thrived following and giving orders."

My eyes narrowed. "But you knew what you were doing." Suddenly cold, I released his hands and tightened the blanket around myself. "It's human trafficking."

He nodded.

No denial or even regret.

Shaking my head, I stood. "I've been struggling with what are real memories and what aren't, but one thing I remember vividly, not only from what I've lived but also from what I believe I recall from my research of The Light, was"—I walked to the bed, turned on a lamp, and returned to Jacob. Then I deliberately held out my hand, fingertips up—"this. I was looking for something to tie everything together." I rubbed the tips of my fingers against my thumb. "Women were showing up in the Wayne County Morgue, and their only connection was the burned fingertips. Actually, there were even a few men who had them."

Jacob rolled his hands. I knew his were the same as mine. It was why when my eyes were covered I'd thought his hands were callused. They weren't, not really. It was the roughness of his acid-burned fingertips. "What are you asking?"

"Were those people, those dead people, ones who were banished?"

He nodded. "Some of them. The Eastern Light is the entry point, the place for visitors' assembly. There are also informational hubs that are set up around the country. The Assembly at the Eastern Light is proficient at follower acquisition. They decide who can and can't join. Believe it or not, people are turned down."

I shook my head. "Are there really that many willing to join?"

Jacob nodded. "That was why, when I approached The Light, I had to stand out as a good recruit. The FBI chose me for this assignment not only based on my success in other undercover missions but also based on my history and my lack of family commitment."

I sank back to the bed.

Oh my God! I'd never considered that he might be married to someone else. Obviously my expression gave away my thoughts.

"You didn't ask," he said, "but I wanted you to know. I'm not married, as Jacoby McAlister. I never have been."

I nodded, unable to do more.

"I was also chosen for the assignment," he went on, "because of my real-life military experience. I handled my transition from military to law enforcement well, but I know of others, I have friends, or had them, that didn't. I studied what they went through and like I said, I was able to become a veteran with PTSD. As Father Gabriel's pilot, I had more access to him than others. I didn't take advantage of that—on the surface. I never questioned—"

My brows rose.

He smiled. "Yes, in case you didn't know, questioning is frowned upon in The Light."

"Really?" I said in my best sarcastic voice.

This time his brows rose. "And so is being a smart-ass to your husband."

"So I've been told."

He went on, "I did what I was told to do by Father Gabriel, my overseer, members of the Commission, everyone. Eventually, Father Gabriel began asking me questions about my past. Slowly I wove the story I'd given at the Eastern Light, and it worked. With time I was given more and more responsibilities. Each step in the hierarchy of The Light was a test. At first I only flew with Micah, and then together we flew Father Gabriel from campus to campus. Then I was trusted alone to gather supplies, often coming here to Fairbanks. The first time I was told to transport acquired members, I expected it to be like when I was taken to the Northern Light. I was among seven individuals who'd all come willingly into The Light. Initially there were more in our group; however, only seven went to the Northern Light. We were told that some didn't perform to The Light's requirements and were banished. That term has always implied the ultimate punishment.

"We were also told some went to a different campus. Followers don't know how many campuses exist, other than that the Eastern Light is the point of entry, and, of course, they learn about the campus where they're assigned. Most people who come willingly are men or couples. Rarely do women join of their own accord. Yet some do."

"Elizabeth," I said.

Jacob nodded. "Luke told me that, but she joined before me, so I don't know anything about that."

I looked down.

"What?" he asked.

"I believe I know more about that, about her twin sister, but I'd rather hear what you have to say first. Please keep going."

He took a deep breath. "The operations at the other campuses are different. Men are needed for physical labor. Women are needed for other tasks, but primarily to keep men content."

I clenched my teeth.

Jacob shook his head. "I'm not saying I agree with the philosophy. I'm telling you, honestly, that it's the mind-set of the Commission. The Light needs men. At the Northern Light they're needed to work the production of the pharmaceuticals, to load the merchandise, to work the power plant, I could go on and on—to build buildings, the exterior walls, and fences." His eyes opened wide. "It's a huge operation. Women do some of that work too, as well as female jobs like day care, laundry, cooking. Mostly they're there to provide men with what they need."

"It's so fucking sexist."

He lifted one of his eyebrows. "You're an investigative journalist, and you just now realized that?"

I pursed my lips. "No, I figured it out as Sara. What I don't understand is how I was OK with it." I shook my head. "Because as much as I hate it at this moment, two weeks ago I didn't."

"That's because we all worked to condition you. Assuming we're going back, if we were to end up there longer than a few days or weeks, the time will come when you're expected to help condition others. It's required. Refusing isn't an option, not without punishment and possible banishment. The community as a whole works to welcome new members, no matter how they're obtained. Working together is essential to keeping it all running. In some ways you've already done it. The women you meet with, you're conditioning them to accept the way of The Light and Father Gabriel's word."

I didn't want to think about that—about how I'd helped. "Tell me about the women in the morgue."

Jacob's shoulder rose and fell. "I wasn't at the Eastern Light for very long. I progressed fast and the Northern Light happened to have an opening for a pilot."

"Happened?"

"I don't know. I really don't," he reassured me. "I assume the one before me was banished, but I've never been told. The only people who know are the Commission, and I can't question them."

"Have you asked anyone on the Assembly? It seems like you're close with Brothers Benjamin and Luke."

"We are, but no. I can't let my assignment affect Jacob's behavior. If I did . . . if I became too inquisitive, it would make people leery."

"Dead women?" I asked again.

"Like I said, The Light needs women, not just for sex, but for jobs that men are too busy to do. It's the Eastern Light's responsibility to determine if the women that are chosen or who volunteer will be able to handle it. Once they're brought into The Light, if it's determined they aren't fit to be a follower, they're removed."

"Does that only happen at the Eastern Light?"

"No, but that's where most of it happens. However, every new believer has a probationary period."

"Do you dispose of bodies at the Northern Light?"

"Me personally? No."

"But it happens?"

He nodded.

"That first time you were asked to transport followers, they weren't willing participants, were they?"

"No."

"Women?"

"Yes, all five of them."

I seriously thought I might be ill. "What happened once they got to the Northern Light?"

"You know what happened. You lived through it."

"I've been asking questions, since I started having memories. It seems like many women have similar stories."

"Similar, but they vary," he admitted. "The similarities are injuries. For many they occur at the Eastern Light. It's part of the process to see how well they adapt. The main component is lack of sight. It's been determined that loss of vision is an essential psychological factor in making the new follower dependent upon her husband."

A tear slid down my cheek as I stood. "Well," I said, walking to the end of the bed. "I guess I should congratulate whoever put the plan together. It works."

Jacob came up behind me and wrapped his arms around my waist. Leather and musk fell over us as I laid my head back against his chest. "I'll tell you I'm sorry forever, but I know it'll never be enough."

I turned into his warm embrace. The steady beat of his heart comforted me, as it had over the last nine months. Keeping my cheek against his soft shirt, I asked, "Is it still my decision, if I go back?"

"Yes."

"I was all ready to say yes. I mean, I want to help. I want Father Gabriel to be brought down . . ."

"But now?" His chest vibrated with his words.

I shook my head as tears began to freely flow. "It's so wrong, so perverse. I'm not sure I can watch other women suffer, like I did, or help condition them. The fact I already have sickens me."

"People like Raquel and Deborah, at the clinic, are very good at it."

I nodded, the feeling of betrayal slicing deep inside me. "I thought Raquel was my friend."

Jacob grasped my shoulders and held me at arm's length. Looking deep into my puffy eyes, he said, "She is. Don't doubt that. She's the reason I found you. She risked punishment to save you."

"To bring me back. I'm not sure it's saving me."

His eyes narrowed. "Listen to me." His even tone held an edge of harshness. "Raquel didn't know what kind of man Thomas was, but by getting you away from him, she saved you. What she does know, what she's the most concerned about, is what would've happened if The Light found you. She risked her own well-being to save your life. Her lies were no more malicious than mine. She isn't undercover, but she *believes*. Like many of the others, she sincerely believes that what she's doing is for the greater good. She only wanted your success."

My chin fell to my chest. "It's just so hard to wrap my mind around." I looked back up. When his grip loosened and his arms again surrounded me, I fell back against his chest. "I have so many more questions."

He led me to the bed. "We need to leave this room in a couple of hours. One way or the other. Either we're both going with the FBI or we're both going back to The Light. No matter your decision, we should try to get some rest."

I lay back down, the blanket still wrapped around me, and Jacob covered me with the bed's cover. As I settled against the pillow, I asked, "What if I'd been given to someone like Abraham?"

Jacob's neck straightened and the vein along the side pulsated. He didn't speak, only shook his head.

"How can you watch that and transport women knowing that they could end up like that?"

He kissed my forehead. "I'll need *your* answer when I wake you."

I swallowed my tears. "Will you please lie here with me?"

"Sara?"

"Please, I know it isn't fair. I meant what I said about sex, but I have no idea what I'm going to do." I sniffled. "All I know is I want you near me right now."

Jacob sighed and climbed onto the other side of the bed. Scooting closer, he wrapped his arm around my shoulder, and I nuzzled against his chest.

"I had images of the two of us saving them all," I said, "but that's not what's going to happen, is it?"

His chest moved with his answer. "No. There will most likely be casualties."

"But I can't go back to my life . . . either. Can I? I mean to my life as Stella?"

"No, I'm sorry . . ."

I closed my eyes and refused to listen to the rest of his apology. He was right. He could say it a million times and it wouldn't be sufficient. Though he'd done his best for me, there were others, so many others, and he'd had a hand in their fate. For three years he'd transported unconscious women across the country to enslave them in a life they never wanted or imagined in their wildest dreams. It wasn't as if The Light were a horrific orgy. There were specific rules about the sanctity of marriage, yet it was all a farce. The marriages weren't real. Unless . . .

My head popped up. "Wait. Is Father Gabriel really a minister, like ordained?"

"Yes. He has to be, for tax purposes. He's the head of a church."

"Then . . . does he marry the women—" I jumped to my real question: "Are we really married?"

His embrace loosened as he sighed. "He does. I mean he did. There wasn't a ceremony as such, but he married Jacob Adams to Sara, making you Sara Adams. I'm not Jacob Adams and you're not Sara."

Using my thumb, I turned my wedding band. "I'm so confused. I wish I still hated you."

"You should."

I agreed, I should, but I didn't. "Will I ever know what's real and what's been conditioned into me?"

"Take option one. There are people who help with deprogramming. They'll work with you; they'll help you."

"Will they help the others?"

"All that they can."

The motel room fell into an eerie silence; only the hum of the heating unit near the window made noise. It was our reminder that time was passing, the *tick-tock* telling us that our clock was running. Someone else had wound it up, and neither of us could make it stop.

As I lay in his embrace, sleep stayed out of reach. Despite his even breaths, I was certain that Jacob couldn't sleep either. My mind was in a constant battle. I didn't know if it was Sara versus Stella, or the desire to help Jacob and our friends while bringing down a tyrant versus walking away. All I knew was that I was walking a figurative fence, each thought pulling me from one side to the other. No matter where I landed, Stella was gone, and the pain of that loss was paralyzing.

There was also the man with his arm around me.

Did I love him, or was I only conditioned to love him? Did I dare think about Dylan?

Dylan and I hadn't been that serious, yet it had been more serious than I'd ever been—than Stella had ever been. A tear fell onto Jacob's chest as I remembered Dylan's warnings about Highland Heights. He'd lost his parents and now he'd lost me. The ripples continued to move further and further away.

After everything that Jacob had done, I decided I couldn't leave him without giving him the one thing he'd asked for. Wiping my tears, I sat up and said, "Are you awake?"

"Yes."

"You asked me for something earlier. You asked me to tell you that I understood why you did what you did." I lifted his hand, intertwined our fingers, and kissed his knuckles, as he'd done to me over and over. "It's totally fucked up, but I do. I don't think I could've asked for a better husband. I mean if this was my fate, predetermined for whatever reason, I'm not sorry I was assigned to you, Jacoby. I believe that you made it as good as it could be."

Jacob sighed. "Jacoby?"

"Yes, thank you. I know it could've been a lot worse." Did he understand what I wasn't saying?

His chin fell. "God, I'm going to miss you."

I swallowed the emotion forming a lump in my throat. Witness protection was best. I needed to face that. "Will the FBI . . . will I be able to contact you if I'm . . . ?"

I was so stupid. Why the hell had I risked getting pregnant?

"Not me. They won't allow it. But since it happened as part of a sting operation, I believe there's some kind of financial—"

I sat straighter. "Stop!"

His eyes opened wide. "What?"

"I'm not asking you for money! Is that what you think this is about?"

"No . . . no . . . that's not what I meant. I just mean, you'll need to be able to provide . . ."

I threw back the covers and stood. I was a fucking wreck. One minute I was sad, the next I was mad. I wanted to go back. I didn't want to go back. I loved Jacob and I'd miss him. I hated him and I never wanted to see him again.

Holding my head, I paced along the side of the bed.

"Sara, come lie down."

"No! I feel like I'm going to jump out of my skin. I don't know who the hell I am, or even what I feel." In the darkened room, Jacob sat up against the headboard, but he didn't try to speak, to tell me who I was or what I should feel.

Part of me wanted him to do that.

The Sara part.

That was the part of me that was conditioned to do exactly what my husband said, what he wanted, even before he said it.

"Damn you!" I screamed.

His shadow didn't flinch.

"Did you hear me? I hate this! It might not be your doing, and I may have forgiven you your role, but it was still you!"

"I wasn't . . ."

"I know," I interrupted, "you didn't *choose* me. You didn't even want a wife, but it was you who made it all right. If you were Abraham, I could easily walk away."

His head moved from side to side. "You're right," he said sadly, "I'm so fucking sorry I tried to make it the best I could for you." His tone evened as he stood from the bed. "Maybe that's all you need to push you over the edge into making the right decision." Each word came forth with less and less emotion. Walking toward me, he reached for his belt. "You've always been smart. It scared the shit out of me, but this time, I thank you. You just gave me the goddamn answer."

My breathing quickened as I backed away and he unlatched the buckle. "What the hell do you think you're doing?"

"What I fucking promised I'd never do."

"No way! Don't do this. It's not you."

He pulled his belt from the loops, one at a time, the sound echoing through the room. "Don't worry, Sara, I think you'll have your decision soon."

I swallowed and stepped backward away from the bed until my back bumped into the vanity at the end of the room. His dark form moved closer. By the light of the night-light, I watched as he ran the length of his belt through his hands.

"Jacob, don't do this."

In the semidarkness, the belt dangling from his left hand reminded me of a whip. It didn't take a stretch of my imagination to see it that way. To my left was the door to the bathroom containing the shower and toilet. I lunged for it, making it inside as Jacob's foot entered the jamb. Though I pushed with all my might, I couldn't shut the door.

"Come out here. It's time to prepare."

CHAPTER 14
Jacob/Jacoby

"You can't do this," Sara yelled from the small bathroom. Her volume decreased as she surrendered the door and sank down onto the closed toilet seat.

She was wrong, I could do it. I couldn't do it out of anger. That was Father Gabriel's teaching, but I could do it, as her husband it was my right. Besides, her bravery was nothing more than stupidity. Three fucking years of work down the damn drain because she wanted a baby. She didn't have the right to make that kind of decision, not in The Light. That was up to me. Punishment for that alone was justified.

Opening the door, I narrowed my gaze, and worked to speak calmly. "Don't make me repeat myself."

The blue that stared up at me, veiled by the bowed head and long lashes, would haunt me forever, but I knew what I was doing. Sara couldn't go back and neither could I. The operation was over. It was up to me to make her feel right about leaving me and about telling me to go to hell.

She didn't need to tell me, because without her and our possible child, I'd be in hell—figuratively as well as literally. As I fought my own fight against my three years of personal conditioning, I was standing at the entrance to fire and brimstone. The twisting in my stomach told me it was a one-way door.

I stood silently watching the conflict between the two women inside her as it continued to rage. With each ticking second it was as if I could see both individuals. Slowly Stella was relinquishing control to Sara. This was, after all, Sara's world; nevertheless, Stella wouldn't go away quietly. Even as Sara's shoulders rolled forward, Stella spoke.

"Fuck you," she muttered.

I shook my head. "Vulgarity was never a real problem at the Northern Light, but I've had quite enough for tonight."

"Too fucking bad!" Stella's eyes sent daggers through my heart. "I was wrong to accept your apology. You're an asshole!"

I reached for her arm. "Sara, stand." As I pulled her to her feet, she looked back down at the ground. "Tell me, how many lashes per transgression?"

Her jaw clenched as she fought with herself to answer. Finally she whispered, "Five."

"Now tell me how many times you've used vulgarities tonight."

Her body trembled in my grasp, yet when her eyes fluttered back to mine, her neck straightened with defiance. Raising her chin, she spoke clearly and resolutely. "If you fucking do this, I will press charges. I'll tell the FBI what a whack-job they have for an agent."

Undeterred by her threat, I smirked. "Remove your underwear."

"Fuck you," she whispered, lowering her chin again to her chest.

I straightened my neck and spoke as I'd been trained to do, as I'd trained others to do. "Vulgarity and disobedience are only two transgressions. I've heard you use two vulgarities in the last thirty seconds. As always, the severity of your correction is at my discretion." I grabbed the waist of her panties and pushed them down. Spinning her around, I unlatched her bra and pulled the straps from her arms. "I recommend you stop saying any more before I decide to give you the accurate number of lashes."

"Jacob, please don't do this." She spun back, her firm breasts pressing against my chest, as she appealed with her gorgeous blue eyes. The left one was a stark contrast, the color of her iris so light compared to the purpled skin surrounding it. Her cheeks were sprouting red blotches as we stood. When I narrowed my gaze, she obediently turned back around. However, her stare never left mine, now glaring at me through the reflection of the mirror. She gripped the edge of the vanity and asked, "Please . . . why?"

I ran the length of the leather through my hands, not allowing myself to sense the despair seeping from her every pore. "Enough questioning."

Her lips came together, forming a straight line. She didn't need her mouth to tell me her thoughts. I saw both the pleas and the insults shooting from her eyes.

"You know what to do."

"I hate you," she whispered.

I stood unmoved and maintained my stance. As I made Sara wait, her words gave me the strength to continue. With each second her proclamation darkened the remaining shreds of my heart. If making her hate me would save her, then I'd do it. Everything she'd said was right; though I hadn't wanted a wife, I'd taken one. I was the one who had done this to her. I was the one who had held her hand while she lived in that hell. I couldn't take her back there, not again.

As I slapped my belt against my hand, the sound echoed throughout the room. Gasping, Sara spread her legs and leaned forward. Just as her cheek contacted the cool vanity, she whispered, "I really do."

Blonde hair fell over her battered cheek as her body shuddered with tears.

In nine long months she'd awakened something inside me that had been dead for over a decade. I'd suspected what she was capable of doing to me the first time I saw her, when Brother Uriel showed her to me. Now it was time to shut it off. This was different from being in

The Light. Taking her back wasn't saving her. She'd been given to me to protect. It wasn't up to her. It was my decision. Now that she had the real chance to be free and safe, I wouldn't take that away from her.

Sara's lip disappeared between her teeth as she finally shut her eyes. The way the muscles in her legs and behind tensed, I knew she was ready for the correction to commence solely for it to end. The wait was nothing more than part of the game, psychological warfare, and Father Gabriel made sure that every male follower knew how to play.

The reason she was in this position, bent over the vanity, was my fault and Father Gabriel's teachings. She'd been conditioned too well. If she hadn't been, Stella would have fought more. The FBI would help her—help Stella—deprogram her. This was for the best, no matter whether she was or wasn't carrying my child. Nothing about going back to The Light was right.

I bit my cheek, not allowing myself to smile at her latest declaration. She'd said she hated me. It was what I wanted. Lifting my belt, I said, "Good, I'm glad to hear that. Now I'll give you a reason not to forget it." I twisted the proverbial knife. "Tell me, Sara." I leaned above her beautiful body. "Tell me what helps you not forget."

She pressed her lips together defiantly.

I slowly ran the rough underside of the belt over her bottom, watching her muscles flinch, as if the leather were fire. Even so, she maintained her tight hold on the counter's edge. "I'm waiting," I whispered.

"Go to hell."

I stepped back and lifted the belt, its weight multiplying exponentially with each millisecond. "Sara."

Her eyes opened at the sound of her name. Seeing my stance in the mirror, she replied, her words drenched in tears as well as defeat, "Reminders."

"What do they do?"

"They help me to not forget."

I stepped closer and rubbed the leather over her round behind one more time. "Don't forget it's your job to count."

With her lip still between her teeth, she nodded. I stepped back. The belt cut through the still air, creating a whistling sound; however, the *crack* never came. I'd stepped just out of reach. The *clank* of the buckle as it hit the linoleum floor bounced off the walls.

Sara's eyes opened, questioning what had happened, yet she remained as statuesque as I'd taught her.

Reaching to the ground, I picked up her bra and panties. All the while her frightened eyes in the mirror watched my every move. Placing them next to her on the vanity, I said, "Get dressed, Stella. I'm calling my handler. This is over. The FBI will help you."

Her back collapsed as she exhaled in relief, her small breasts flattening against the fake marble.

I expected an expletive, something. Instead she slowly straightened herself and stood. Staring at me incredulously, still through the mirror, I found the acidic contempt I'd sought. After gathering her underwear as well as her jeans and sweater, she walked into the small bathroom containing the lavatory and shower. The *click* of the lock eroded any lingering pieces of my heart.

Sinking to the bed, I rubbed my hands over my face.

Fuck!

That wasn't what I'd wanted to do.

Holding her and explaining everything felt right. Risking her life didn't.

I'd told her it was her decision, and it was. Her conflict was clear. And then, the way she'd used my real name when she accepted my apology, I'd known she was leaning toward the best decision, toward taking the offer of deprogramming and witness protection. I also knew that if I was the reason she returned to The Light and anything went wrong, I'd never forgive myself. Though she might not have said her decision in words, she had in her tone and actions. I knew her well enough to hear it loud and clear.

I heard the shower through the thin walls. Reaching for my jacket, I pulled two phones from my pocket. The one that I always used, my The Light phone, blinked. I looked at the screen and my heart sank. Though it was only nearing four in the morning in Fairbanks, in Detroit it was nearing eight. That meant the Assembly and Commission would be meeting soon.

I had a voice mail from Father Gabriel.

Apprehensively I pushed the sequence of buttons that allowed the voice mail to play.

"Brother Jacob . . ."

I replayed the message again, hoping I'd imagined it. After all, I hadn't slept much in the last twenty-four hours. Maybe it was nothing more than a mirage.

Can mirages be auditory as well as visual?

Running my fingers through my hair, I turned on the burner phone. Special Agent Adler answered right away. I turned away from the bathroom and lowered my voice. "She knows a lot, not everything, but she's not going back."

"Then that's it. Stay where you are, we'll send a plane. We'll bring you both back to the Anchorage field office."

I swallowed the bile. "Yes, sir. We'll be waiting for the call."

"McAlister, you've done your best. Going back without her wouldn't work. Hell, going back with her would've been risky."

"Yes, sir. I know it's not up to me, but I need to tell you, move fast."

"You know we can't possibly get enough people to the Northern Light for at least three hours. Even then it would take most of our Alaskan agents. One or two more days would allow us to get more agents there and be prepared."

I fisted my hair, pulling it from the roots. "Sir, I woke to a message from Father Gabriel."

"And?"

"As I told you, he's in Detroit right now, at the Eastern Light."

"Yes, and . . ." My handler was beginning to sound impatient.

"He instructed me to take my supplies back to the Northern Light and leave tonight for the Eastern Light."

"Tonight?"

"Yes, sir. It's approximately a four-and-a-half-hour flight, but with the time difference if I leave Northern Light at nine tonight, I'd arrive at Eastern Light by six in the morning, Detroit time."

"Is this an unusual request?"

"Part of it was," I said, having trouble coming up with the words to explain it.

"Agent, I'm waiting."

"A few weeks ago, I petitioned the Commission to allow me to take Sara with me when I flew. They hadn't made a decision. That's why if I tell them I took her, it'll be a punishable transgression."

"Yes, you mentioned that yesterday during our short debriefing."

"Sir," I said, "Father Gabriel said in his message that my petition was granted. I was told to bring Sara."

"Oh my God! What does that mean?"

I spun at the sound of Sara's voice. Her hair was wet, and her complexion matched the tips of our fingers.

"Agent, it's time to stop this," Special Agent Adler said.

I nodded, relief flooding my synapses.

"What?" Sara came to the bed and sat beside me. "What does that mean? Does Father Gabriel know what I did, that I left?"

"Yes, sir," I said into the phone, while turning toward Sara and shrugging.

"You can't just shrug. If I go back, will it give you more time?"

"Agent," Special Agent Adler said in my ear, "I'm assuming that's Miss Montgomery that I hear?"

No, it's Sara Adams.

That was what I wanted to say, but unlike Stella, I had the ability to bite my tongue. "Yes, sir, it is. I didn't know she was listening." My eyes narrowed her way, but instead of Sara's demure response, Stella gave me a close-lipped *fuck you* smile as she cocked her head to the side.

"Give her the phone."

"Sir?"

"I know you've been living in the dark ages when it comes to men and women, but give her the damn phone. I want to hear her response, from her."

My teeth clenched as I covered the mouthpiece and turned toward Sara. "This is my handler. You may call him Special Agent. The less you know the better. I already told him your answer. It's over. You're going into witness protection."

She reached for the phone.

"Sara," I said, in my customary warning.

Her brows rose.

"Don't—"

Taking the phone from my grasp, in a stage whisper she quipped, "Embarrass you? Oh, I wouldn't fucking dream of it." Placing the phone to her ear, Sara said, "Hello, Special Agent, this is Sara . . . I'm sorry, Stella Montgomery."

A smile crept over her lips as she stood and walked farther away. "Thank you . . . I'm all right." She looked my way. "I'd like to say it's the first time I've ever been struck, but I can't."

Holy fuck!

"Yes, he told me . . ." She went on, "Yes, I do understand . . . Sir, may I ask, if I change my mind . . ." Again she looked toward me. "If *I* change my mind, would that give the bureau more time to arrange the raids in a way that may eliminate the loss of life? . . . That's what Jacob/Jacoby said, sir . . . I do . . . I am . . . One more request, if I may . . . If something were to happen to me before we get out of The Light, would the FBI please contact my parents and those of Mindy

Rosemont? . . . Yes, sir, she is . . . Yes, I've seen her . . . And a Detroit detective, Dylan Richards."

She shrugged as she wrapped one arm around her midsection. "We were dating. He used to say I should join the DPD. Maybe he'd understand what happened if he knew I was working with the FBI . . . I understand." She nodded. "Nothing until . . . Yes, sir. I hope you don't either . . . Yes, I'll give the phone back to him. Thank you, I believe it's an honor . . . Good-bye."

She handed the phone back to me. "Here, he needs to work out the details with you. We're heading back immediately."

What the fuck just happened?

"Sir?" I asked.

"If this weren't so damn serious and dangerous, I'd like to hear how you managed to keep that woman oppressed in The Light. She seems very strong-willed."

"You have no idea."

CHAPTER 15
Stella/Sara

Scenes of normal life passed by the windows of Jacob's borrowed truck. Though it was still early, not even five in the morning, this far north the sun was shining, illuminating the empty streets and giving me a glimpse of what life could be. Sighing, I took another bite of the breakfast bar Jacob had gotten for me from a convenience mart. If it weren't for the bottle of water, I wasn't sure I'd be able to swallow. I remembered Bernard saying that I ate cardboard for breakfast. I'd never thought I did, until now.

From my peripheral vision, I watched as Jacob took the last few bites of his breakfast sandwich and thought how strange it was that even my tastes were different now than they'd been as Stella. He'd offered to buy me something from the fast-food restaurant for breakfast, but after what we'd eaten late last night, I hadn't thought I could stomach more grease.

"How's your sandwich?" I asked, needing to hear his voice.

Swallowing a drink of his coffee, he replied, "Not as good as your cooking."

"Good."

"How's your"—he nodded toward my remaining bar—"whatever that is?"

I shrugged. "I'd rather have my cooking too. Which is hilarious, if you knew how I, or Stella, used to cook."

"Sara, no more Stella. It's too big of a risk."

I nodded, heeding his warning—more than resenting it.

"Coffee?" he asked, holding his cup for me.

I shook my head. "No, thank you." He'd offered earlier to get me my own cup, but the idea of drinking the caffeine still ate at my conscience.

But the idea of putting yourself in greater danger doesn't?

I ignored my inner monologue and turned back to the window. With each passing mile I became lost in the promise of Fairbanks. It wasn't until Jacob's voice registered that I came back to the present.

"Sara, are you listening?"

"No, sorry."

"I've decided that our story is that you never left the Northern Light."

I turned toward him. "You've decided?" Though I asked my question with a bit of resentment, the relief that came with his control surprised me.

"Yes," he simply replied.

"How? I didn't go to work yesterday. You said you spoke to Raquel, and she and Brother Benjamin looked for me."

He nodded, his profile revealing the concern his words refused to utter.

"I'm sorry, Jacob. I'm sorry that I've messed up all your hard work and that now we're in this situation."

Dark eyes overflowing with remorse settled briefly on me before turning back to the road. "Don't be."

Apparently our time for heart-to-heart talks was over. Since we'd spoken to his handler, I had been lucky to get more than a couple of words strung together. Though I wanted more, I knew the man beside me. I knew that when he was thinking and worrying, he was quiet. He was the one currently devising a plan for our future, not necessarily one where we were together, but one where we were both alive.

"Something you must remember," he began, "is that since you didn't leave the Northern Light, you can't be on the plane. All of our planes have what is essentially a black box. It records everything. Once you're on the plane you can't speak, and I can't speak to you."

"All right. Hopefully I won't snore," I said, trying to break the tension.

A corner of his lips moved upward. "If you do, I'll throw something in your direction."

"Hey, are you saying I snore?"

His shoulders moved up and down.

"If we can't talk on the plane, please, fill me in on our cover story."

"I've spoken to Benjamin and promised I'd be at Assembly this morning. Thankfully, since it's Saturday, you don't have work at the lab today. I told Benjamin that you spoke to Thomas, which you shouldn't have done, and he took you against your will. I told him that after Raquel's call, I flew to Thomas's hangar and found you before anything happened, other than your blackened eye. I also asked him to keep the truth a secret. We both know what happens to people who leave The Light."

His words sent a chill down my spine.

"He won't even tell Raquel. The fewer people who know the better. But since Raquel was so worried, I said she could come check on you later today. And you'd be back to work after our trip to the Eastern Light."

"That scares me."

He simply nodded.

Was he scared too, or simply acknowledging my concern? I didn't want to think about Jacob being scared. Instead my hand fluttered to my darkened eye. "And this?"

He shook his head. "Isn't it obvious? I did it."

"You?"

"I corrected you, probably for questioning too much." He added the last part with a smirk.

I shook my head. "I thought you said that I could now—"

"When we're alone, but the point is, correction is my right. No one will question it. I've also decided it's the reason you didn't go to work yesterday."

Yesterday? Has it only been twenty hours since I left the Northern Light?

"Sara, we can't utter one word, or even think in terms of Stella and Jacoby. No one, and I mean no one, not Benjamin, not Raquel, no one can know what we've discussed. Brother Benjamin believes what I told him. I also told him that you hadn't remembered your past. When I found you, you were mostly scared and afraid I'd be upset."

Well, *some* of that was accurate. "Other people have their memories," I protested. "Why can't I?"

"Because other people weren't investigating The Light when their memories were suppressed."

I turned in his direction. "Do you really believe that's why I was taken?"

"You said you Google Earthed the mansion in Bloomfield Hills?"

"Yes, but no one knew that. The thing is, I went there too."

His head snapped in my direction. "You did what?"

"I went there. I went to the front gate and pushed the button and asked for Uriel Harris."

"Jesus, Sara!"

"The voice from the box said I had the wrong address and asked me to leave."

"So you did, right?"

"No."

Jacob struck the steering wheel with the palm of his hand. "Of course fucking not. What did you do?"

I sat taller. "I'm an investigative journalist. It's what I do, did, whatever. I walked around the front fence and tried to take pictures." I shrugged and looked back out the window. "When I left I saw a surveillance camera. Unfortunately, it probably recorded everything I did." Thinking about the timeline, I added, "That was a few days before we went to that festival in Dearborn." The realization made my stomach turn. That was the day Jacob had seen me for the first time. "Oh, God, my future was already set by then. Wasn't it?"

With his jaw clenched, Jacob nodded. "Yes, do you see why *you* cannot get your memory back?"

"What about my medicine? Raquel and Benjamin know I'm off it."

"Medicines work differently on different people. Just because you quit taking it, doesn't guarantee that your memories will return. Beginning at the Eastern Light, acquired wives are given high doses of the medication intravenously. Brother Raphael has hypothesized that in some individuals that initial regimen is all that's needed. The idea being that the receptors become permanently blocked. He's said that the daily boosters in many women are merely an insurance policy. Not everyone's brain responds exactly the same way. As soon as you have your period, you're going back on the medicine."

"What? No, I'm not!"

"Sara."

Panic filled my chest as I tried to suck in air. Closing my eyes, I reminded myself that this was the world where husbands made the decisions, but we were still alone, and I had a chance. "No, Jacob," I implored. By the way he turned, my response obviously surprised him. I kept going. "I can't help you if I don't have memories. Think about it. What if the medicine blocks everything I learned at The Light?" I sucked my lip between my teeth and put my hands between my legs to hide their trembling. "I can't go back to that. Besides, how would we explain it if I suddenly forgot all Father Gabriel's teachings or my job or how to cook, or what if I forgot you?"

"Fuck," he said, pulling the truck into the small airport. "I guess I hadn't thought about all of that." Once Jacob had the truck inside a hangar, he turned toward me. "Give me those hands."

Though I looked down, I obeyed.

As he took my hands, it wasn't his words but his tone that pulled my gaze to his. "If we have any chance at all of getting through this alive, you and I both have to put on the best performances of our fucking lives. That's why I wanted you to resume your medicine. I thought it would make it easier for you, but"—he kissed my knuckles—"you've always been so smart, and you're right. I don't want you forgetting what you've learned in The Light. You worked too hard. Just please remember, no one is trustworthy, no one. Everyone is programmed, not just the acquired wives. Most of the men aren't on medication; their programming is more environmental, tribal mentality really. It keeps everyone content to work toward Father Gabriel's goals. If they weren't programmed, they wouldn't accept everything Father Gabriel says as gospel and they even may try to question his authority. That can't happen.

"It's literally you and me against The Light. We have to convince everyone that nothing has changed. The next eighteen hours are crucial."

I nodded, knowing I needed to put my full and unyielding trust in the man who held my hands, the one who'd kept me alive so far.

"Leaving The Light," he went on, "is a transgression punishable by banishment. *No one* leaves The Light and lives to talk about it. *No one.* You, Sara Adams, are an Assemblyman's wife. We love each other, and you're usually well behaved. Thursday night after the prayer meeting, once we were home, you weren't. I corrected you. You were embarrassed that it resulted in a blackened eye. Since I left early Friday morning, you went running on the campus, like we do. It's summer and you chose to stay out in the north acres. Being upset with me, you forgot about the lab. That's why you weren't in our apartment when Raquel came to find you."

I sighed. What he'd just done was the comfort that came with being Sara. The story, my choices, everything was up to my husband. Jacob told me who I was and what I thought. It was a realization that bothered the Stella side of me, but I knew that to survive what we were about to do, I needed to keep Stella quiet. I could use her keen thinking and survival skills, but in everything visible, I needed to be Sara.

Thankfully, last night I'd been granted something that I hadn't previously had. Last night I had been given permission to question. "I'm scared. Why can't we tell everyone that Thomas took me? I hate people thinking you did this to me."

"Because this"—he looked out through the hangar's open garage door and over the airstrip. I followed his gaze and suddenly realized we weren't at the same airport where Thomas had brought me yesterday—"is where I fly in and out of for The Light. I'm not sure how I'd be able to explain to Xavier or Father Gabriel how I knew Thomas's destination."

I swallowed. "H-how did you know?"

"My handler searched flight plans. Flight plans are supposed to be filed in advance. VFR, visual flight rules, don't require it, but for safety, especially with such large areas of unpopulated wilderness, most pilots do it. Thank Father Gabriel, Thomas had. He'd filed his plans before leaving for the Northern Light. They included his estimated time of return to Fairbanks and listed the airport. Technically, there's no way I could've made it from the Western Light to Fairbanks in time to save you, which was the story I gave Benjamin and the reason the US Marshals were there instead of me. But Benjamin has no way of knowing that. He hasn't left the Northern Light in years. Father Gabriel would know and so would Micah, if he were questioned."

I shook my head. "This is such a mess."

"Well," he said coldly, "I'm sorry you're still involved."

My neck straightened. "Now, as in because we're going back, or you're sorry I was ever assigned to you?"

Jacob's narrow gaze silenced me—Sara—the way only he could. "No more. We've been through this. Now we're going back as Sara and Jacob. Later today I'll take you to Brother Raphael and you'll need to explain and apologize for your absence. He's a Commissioner. Correction will be at his discretion."

"No, Jacob. No more, ever."

He lifted a brow. "You had that option. You chose otherwise."

I felt suddenly nauseous.

"We need to hurry," Jacob said, "so I can make it to Assembly."

"What about Thomas?"

"I told you, he's no longer a threat."

"But won't The Light question his disappearance?"

"Minimally, that's not our concern. It's his. Like I said, no one enters The Light and leaves. Theoretically he shouldn't have been in the community. Once Xavier is informed of what Thomas did—entering the community on more than one occasion—even Xavier won't question Thomas's sudden disappearance. Benjamin knows what Thomas did to you, so he won't question his disappearance. Once Father Gabriel learns Thomas entered the community, he won't question it either. He'll assume there was a problem, and it was handled."

I shrugged. "Maybe there are advantages to not questioning."

Jacob reached for my hand, and with a grin said, "It's taken you long enough to figure that out."

My cheeks flushed as I glanced toward our intertwined hands.

"This hangar doesn't have cameras or surveillance inside," Jacob explained. "That's why I didn't park outside. I'm going to help you onto the plane, and then I have some last-minute things that need to be done. Remember, do not talk."

As he helped me from the truck, I replied, "Yes, Jacob."

His lips curled upward as his gaze devoured me. "Life would be so much easier if you could remember that is always the correct response."

I was exhausted, had a battered cheek, had been gone nearly a day from a place *no one leaves*, and had my hand in the hand of a man whom twenty-four hours ago I'd never wanted to see again. I was out of fight.

With a shy smile, I lowered my chin, looked up through my lashes, and repeated what my husband wanted to hear. "Yes, Jacob."

Just before entering the plane, he stilled our steps. With his free hand he surrounded my waist and pulled me close. "I pray that one day I'm able to call you by another name, but in the meantime, you're my wife, my Sara Adams, and while I do and will respect the boundary you placed on sex, right now I want to kiss my wife, and I plan on doing it. Do you want to stop me?"

Before I could answer, he pulled my hips tighter against his, causing our chests to collide. Needing to see his face, I lifted my chin and looked into his dark gaze. As leather and musk enveloped us, he rephrased, "More importantly, do you think you *can* stop me?"

I shook my head. "No, I don't want to stop you. After all, you're my husband."

He smiled, an exhausted smile, just before our lips reunited. For a few moments, in the drafty hangar, our world was right. After all we'd said and done, the danger I'd put us in and how he'd tried to push me away . . . after *all* of it . . . our bodies knew their rightful place. Drawn like magnets with an irresistible pull, they carnally remembered what my mind believed it wanted to forget. As his kiss deepened, heat radiated from my head to my toes, melting everything in its wake. Simultaneously his touch made me liquid, molding me against his solid warmth.

I didn't fight as fingers twined in my hair and tugged my head backward. When Jacob's tongue slid across the seam of my lips, I willingly granted him entrance, accepting the invasion that gave our tongues license to dance. He swallowed my moans as the friction from his broad chest pebbled my nipples, and my arms wrapped around his firm torso.

When our lips finally parted, I settled my cheek against his chest and held tight, listening to the steady beat of his heart.

We both knew that there was a possibility we'd never make it out of The Light, and still, when he lifted my chin and stared deeply into my eyes, I couldn't say the words my heart longed to say; instead I did the next best thing. With a soft kiss to his cheek, I whispered, "Sara loves Jacob."

He kissed my forehead. "And Jacob loves Sara. Please never forget that."

I shook my head. "Neither Sara nor Stella will."

"I never thought of myself as a bigamist," he said with a grin.

When Jacob opened the Northern Light's smaller plane, I quietly climbed aboard.

Though the fuselage was filled with boxes, Jacob pointed to one of the jump seats, and I sat. Next he strapped me in. Its seat belt was much more elaborate than the one in Thomas's plane. Briefly I wondered whether this was how the unconscious women were transported—how I'd been transported. Instead of allowing myself to dwell on that thought, I surveyed the boxes, assuming they were filled with supplies; however, as in my first few days in The Light, I couldn't ask. My speech was once again restricted.

The difference was that this time I understood why. I knew that Jacob's rules weren't to dominate me, but to save me. As we flew away from the dark and back into The Light, the weight of our mission settled over me. It was up to us. If we failed there were others who would never be saved.

CHAPTER 16
Sara

My heart was ready to beat out of my chest as the full impact of Jacob's words, "The next eighteen hours are the most crucial," settled over me and he left our apartment for Assembly. All it took was one person who saw the truth or knew what had really happened.

I should have been tired, but I was mostly scared—scared to be separated from Jacob, and of what could happen at Assembly. More than once I'd prayed that Brother Benjamin had kept our secret. After all, Jacob said that Brother Benjamin and Raquel were believers, and that what they were doing by helping us was against Father Gabriel's teachings. Just as all of my thoughts and behaviors belonged to Jacob, all of our husbands' thoughts belonged to the Commission and Father Gabriel.

What if Brother Benjamin confessed to the Commission?

I bit my lip and continued to pace.

We'd gotten into the community without anyone's seeing that I was in Jacob's truck. Riding in his truck wasn't forbidden. I did it from time to time. It was leaving the community that was forbidden. No one could know I'd been out to the pole barn, much less into the dark.

To corroborate our story, as soon as we entered the community, I stayed hidden inside the truck while Jacob drove as close as he could to our apartment, went in, and returned to the truck. As we drove to the parking area, I came out of my hiding place in the backseat. Then together we walked to the coffee shop.

Since the story was that I was upset with him about leaving the reminder on my cheek, taking me into public was his punishment for my missing work yesterday. The thing that I continued to mull over was that he hadn't explained any of this to me—any of the reasoning. Nevertheless, I understood it.

No matter how I fought it, I was conditioned. Sitting at a table at the coffee shop with my eyes down, I obediently waited for him to return with our drinks. Of course he didn't ask what I wanted, and I wouldn't have refused whatever he'd ordered; however, when I peered into the cup and found tea instead of coffee, I smiled. Though he briefly returned the smile and whispered, "It's decaffeinated," his gaze immediately narrowed, reminding me that I was supposed to be upset with him.

Jacob was right about my blackened eye. No one seemed to notice it. If I allowed myself to think like Stella, the unspoken acceptance of my husband's correction was more evidence of the perverse nature of The Light. I hoped that the unique position of having both perspectives would be an advantage as we continued *the best performances of our fucking lives.*

A knock on the apartment door startled me as it brought me back to the present. I took a deep breath and steadied myself to open the door. I'd known Raquel would be coming ever since Jacob told me he'd given Brother Benjamin permission for her visit. I reached for the doorknob as I prepared to see the best friend I'd had while in The Light.

In the coffee shop I'd needed only to look the part, now it was time for speaking. There was more riding on this performance than before I'd left the Northern Light. Now my success wasn't just for me, but also for Jacob and his mission. It was for everyone.

I opened the door to Raquel's questioning blue eyes.

"Come in," I said, "Jacob told me you'd be coming."

She shook her head and waited for me to close the door. Once I did she wrapped me in an embrace, her slender arms squeezing with all her might. "Oh, praise Father Gabriel. I was so worried about you." Backing away, she playfully hit my shoulder. "I should be mad at you . . ." Her words trailed away as she noticed my eye.

I wasn't sure how she hadn't seen it first thing, but then again, she'd been too busy hugging me. I reached for the puffiness and a tear fell. "I know. I'm sorry I worried you."

Raquel wrapped her arm around my shoulders and led me to the sofa. "Sara, it's all right. I'm sorry. I shouldn't have responded like that. It just surprises me." As we sat she asked, "Have you thanked Father Gabriel and God for your husband?"

I nodded as more tears flowed. I didn't know where they were coming from, exhaustion probably. I'd slept a little on the plane, but the flight was much faster in Jacob's plane than it was in Thomas's. We had been in the air for under an hour.

Raquel hugged me again. "Benjamin and I were so worried when you didn't go to work."

"I'm sorry. I was selfish." I lowered my chin. "I honestly didn't think about anyone but myself. I was embarrassed. I mean, it's the first time I ever remember this"—I tilted my head to the left—"happening, and I didn't want anyone to see it."

"We're sisters. We understand. It happens. No one will think less of either you or Brother Jacob." Raquel smiled her biggest, shiniest smile.

Gratitude for all she'd done for me from the beginning of my journey in The Light came bubbling out. "Thank you, for always being so great. I'm so glad we're friends, and sisters," I added.

"I had so many thoughts running through my head. I was afraid you were . . . were taken, that you were lost in the dark."

"Taken? Why would you think I'd been taken? By whom?"

"This is going to sound crazy, but by that pilot guy, Thomas. I don't like that he comes here into the community. I told Benjamin that I was afraid that's what had happened, and he said he'd bring up that Thomas comes into the community to the Assembly. I mean, it just isn't right."

If she only knew! "He does give me the creeps. I'm sorry I worried you. Jacob said you went looking for me."

Raquel nodded. "When I couldn't find you here, Benjamin drove me to the pole barn. Brother Micah was there. He's the one who said Thomas had recently left. I guess Brother Micah arrived just after Thomas took off. I was the one who jumped to conclusions." She squeezed my hand. "I'm sorry. I should have known you'd never willingly go back to the dark, not after the last time."

"I don't remember doing it then either."

"Sometimes," she said, seeming to weigh her words, "when people stop taking their birth control medicine, it does something to their chemical balance and they remember things. Have you had any memories?"

I shook my head. "No, not really. It's still as if the day I woke from my accident was the day my life began."

She nodded and laid her head back against the sofa. "The other day you said something in the temple about the dark. I remember the dark. I didn't at first either, but now I do. If you do, talk to Brother Jacob. Benjamin helped me more than I can say." A tear slid down her cheek. "I'd never go back. I'd never leave The Light."

"Raquel, what is it?"

She pressed her lips together and swallowed. "Nothing, I was just so scared that you were out there, and I wouldn't wish that on anyone."

"I know we're not allowed to talk about the dark, but if it would help you, I promise not to tell."

Shaking her head, she whispered, "No, I can't. I know you wouldn't tell, but I don't want to be the cause of any secrets between you and Brother Jacob." Taking a deep breath, she forced a smile. "The most important thing is that we're here now. We're in The Light and you're safe. Benjamin said that when I came looking for you, you were out running?"

"Yes, I was in the north acres, but that won't happen again, not without Jacob."

"So this"—Raquel tilted her head toward my eye—"happened before Brother Jacob left?"

"Yes, Thursday night after prayer meeting." I looked down. "He's really patient—usually. It's my fault. I need to stop questioning. I think that's why I'm so embarrassed. I don't want anyone to think of him like Brother Abraham."

Just speaking his name gave me chills.

"Oh, don't worry. That could never happen." Raquel paused. "Why won't you be running without Jacob? You like running."

I nodded. "I'm no longer allowed. Jacob wasn't happy when he arrived this morning. He knew why I didn't go to work." I sighed. "It's like he always knows everything. Instead of staying here and discussing it, he made me go out into the community with him, to the coffee shop."

Raquel's eyes widened. "Were there many people?"

I shrugged. "I kept my eyes down, but even though it was early, yes. I didn't see any chosen, but there were many followers."

"I guess that was his way of easing you out of your embarrassment."

Really?

"It was mortifying, and this afternoon after the Commission meeting concludes, he's taking me to Brother Raphael and Sister Rebecca's apartment." I lowered my voice. "I have to apologize for missing work."

She squeezed my hand. "It could be worse. You seem to be sitting fine."

"Now," I interjected. "He said my correction will be up to Brother Raphael."

Raquel shrugged. "I guess I'll know how that went tomorrow morning at service."

I sat straighter and opened my eyes wide. "Tomorrow! Oh, do you remember me telling you that Jacob petitioned the Commission for me to travel?"

"Yes."

"Apparently it was approved. Father Gabriel told Jacob to bring me with him when he comes to pick him up from the Eastern Light."

Raquel's expression clouded. "The Eastern Light? He's supposed to take you there?"

"What's the matter? Do you know where that is?"

"Do you?"

I feigned a smile. "I'm assuming east of here."

She nodded. "I guess, since it's not the dark, I can say. I remember the Eastern Light. I was there for a little while before I was brought here."

Oh. My stomach sank. *What happened to her?*

I couldn't stop my inquisitive mind. "You say that like it's a bad thing."

"It was just different, harder. If you're allowed to see other campuses, Father Gabriel must really trust you."

"I don't understand. Isn't the Eastern Light like here?" Though I was doing my best to keep her suppressed, the Stella part of me was dying to ask more probing questions.

"Not really. You can tell me what you think when you get back."

I couldn't push too much, or she might become suspicious. As I sat there with Raquel, I understood what Jacob had meant last night when he'd said he couldn't allow his assignment to affect his behavior. Though it was tempting, I wouldn't either.

"Thank you for coming to see me. Again, I'm sorry I scared you." I admired her clear, bruise-free olive complexion as her round cheeks rose.

"Hey, now that you're all right, let's talk about something more exciting."

I genuinely smiled. I was doing it, being Sara, and if my best friend since I'd awoken in The Light wasn't suspicious, I must be doing a good job. Settling against the sofa, I stifled a yawn and listened as she chatted away.

My sleep-deprived nerves were stretched to the point of breaking as we walked silently to Brother Raphael and Sister Rebecca's apartment building near the temple. Though Jacob hadn't told me, I assumed he'd spoken to Brother Raphael at Assembly, because when we arrived, they seemed to be expecting us. The only other Commissioner's apartment I'd visited was that of our overseer, Brother Daniel, and his wife Sister Ruth. The Commissioners' apartments were bigger than the Assemblymen's, but not by much. Since all of the Assemblymen's apartments were similar, I wasn't surprised that Brother Raphael and Sister Rebecca's was similar to Brother Daniel and Sister Ruth's. What made theirs bigger than ours was that it contained an office, which was where Sister Rebecca led us as soon as we arrived.

Brother Raphael greeted us as he stayed seated behind his desk. Sister Rebecca moved a chair next to her husband and sat, leaving Jacob and me standing. It was probably their way of making our visit about the matter at hand and not a friendly visit.

Though Brother Raphael had always been nice to me in the lab, as we stood before him and Sister Rebecca, I remembered his position. Not only was he a Commissioner, he was second in command at the Northern Light, second only to Father Gabriel. With Father Gabriel gone, he was in charge. Nothing, not even banishment, was outside the scope of his power. That knowledge, plus Jacob's warning about the next eighteen hours, weighed heavily on my mind as I waited to speak. If our story was to be disputed, it would probably be here and now.

"Sister Sara, I'm glad you're not ill. Go ahead. Brother Jacob said you wanted to say something to me."

Though I didn't remember having said I wanted to do this, I nodded and began, "Brother Raphael and Sister Rebecca, I'm here today . . ."

I attributed my emotional outbursts to my lack of sleep. Just as had happened when I talked with Raquel, as I apologized to Brother Raphael, tears coated my cheeks. It wasn't an ugly cry, but it was enough that Sister Rebecca stood, even as I spoke, handed me a tissue, and gave me a hug.

I didn't tell them why I didn't go to work, only that I was upset and selfish, thinking only of myself. When I was done, Brother Raphael asked me whether I enjoyed my job at the Northern Light. I assured him—I did. Then he asked me a similar question about my husband, did I love him and accept his decisions? When I turned toward Jacob and saw the pride in his eyes, more tears flowed. "I do. I really do," I answered.

I didn't think about Stella or how wrong this was. I didn't think about how I was essentially telling the person in charge that I was all right with my husband blackening my eye, which he hadn't. In that moment all I thought about was what Jacob had told me to remember when I had the nightmares: I was Sara and he was Jacob.

Sara loves Jacob, and Jacob loves Sara.

Brother Raphael didn't respond; instead he looked at his wife. "Rebecca, please take Sister Sara into the kitchen. I need to speak with Brother Jacob privately for a few minutes."

As far as Commissioners' wives went, Sister Rebecca was more like Sister Ruth than like Sister Lilith. Though she was thin and always well dressed like Sister Lilith, she was also sweet, with the maternal quality of Sister Ruth. Whenever I'd spoken with her, she'd been kind, and her lessons during Tuesday and Thursday prayer meetings were thought provoking and often emotional. We Assembly wives didn't know which Commission wife would lead the meetings until we arrived. Whenever I learned it was Sister Rebecca, I knew I wouldn't be disappointed.

Once we were in the kitchen, Sister Rebecca gave me a new tissue and smiled. "My dear, I'm glad you're all right. When you weren't at work, Brother Raphael was concerned that you may've been ill. I heard Brother Benjamin was concerned too." She patted my hand. "It'll be all right. My husband's a fair man."

My head began to ache as I hiccupped and nodded. After the way Jacob had scared me the night before, I knew I didn't want correction or reminders. I also knew that it wasn't up to me.

Setting the teakettle on the stove, Sister Rebecca said, "Let me make you some decaffeinated tea. That always helped me relax. Though I did miss coffee while I was pregnant."

My eyes opened wide. "W-what did you just say?"

Her soft hazel eyes sparkled. "Come now, you heard me."

"I-I'm not . . ." I shook my head. "I don't know if I am."

"But you want to be, don't you, Sister?"

"I'm really not sure anymore."

"Is that why Brother Jacob corrected you? Did you not tell him?"

Oh, shit! Where is this going?

I swallowed. "Sister, I have a problem with questioning. I try, I really do, but sometimes I think all I do is try his patience."

"Brother Jacob seems to be a patient man."

"He is. That's why I'm so embarrassed. I don't want people to think less of him."

"You do love him," she asked, "don't you?"

I smiled a closed-lipped smile. "I do. I know that God had a reason for bringing us here. I'm so thankful I've had Jacob to help me, and"—I lowered my eyes—"to correct me." Though the words once again hurt my pride, they flowed easily from my lips.

Again she patted my hand. "Let me get you that tea." Once she set the cup in front of me, she whispered, "I doubt Brother Raphael picked up your signals. You know how men are."

"My signals?"

"Your hand protectively covered your stomach the entire time you were apologizing, you're emotional, and the way you looked at your husband . . . goodness, if you're not sure yet if you're expecting a child, you certainly think it's a possibility."

I shrugged as my cheeks blushed. "I mean, I know how it works. There's a chance."

"When I was pregnant, I had all sorts of strange cravings." Her eyes lit up. "Oh, and odd memories. I'm not even sure they were real. They seemed real. Have you had any of that?"

I bit the inside of my cheek. She was good, and she was sneaky. I shook my head. "No, I haven't. Do you think that means that I'm not pregnant?"

"No. Everyone is different. Besides, this is early, if you aren't sure."

I nodded. "Very early, I haven't even missed a period."

"Well, when you know something, do tell. I just love babies. Sometimes I go to the day care just to be around them."

"Sister?" I asked, "Your child, or children, are they here, in The Light?"

"One, our son. He was raised under Father Gabriel's teachings, even before The Light. He's not at this campus, but he's an Assemblyman."

I smiled. "I'm sure you're proud. You only have one child?" As soon as the question left my lips, I regretted it. A shadow of sadness fell over her expression, returning the tears to my eyes. "I'm sorry. Please don't answer."

Her neck straightened. "Not all stories have happy endings. I'll always remember my beautiful daughter; however, Father Gabriel knows best. I trust in him and Raphael in all things."

The opening of a door and footsteps alerted us that our husbands were coming down the hallway. When Sister Rebecca pressed her lips together and patted my hand again, I knew she was silently telling me not to say anything about their daughter. I nodded my understanding as the men entered.

As we were about to leave, Brother Raphael said with his still-thick Boston accent, "Sister Sara, we'll welcome you back to the lab as soon as Father Gabriel sees fit to return from the Eastern Light. I trust your husband to do what is best."

It took all my willpower not to look toward Jacob; instead I lowered my eyes. "Thank you, Brother Raphael."

A few minutes later, as Jacob and I walked along the sidewalk with my hand in his, I whispered, "What does that mean? What Brother Raphael said."

Though Jacob didn't turn, his grip tightened, and he simply replied, "Sara."

"You said I could—"

"When we're alone. Does this look like we're alone?"

No. We weren't alone. We were walking among followers who were going from here to there. However, in my opinion, they all seemed preoccupied, all heading to their own destinations. No one was paying attention to us, except the occasional male follower who'd address Jacob with a nod and a "Brother Jacob." I assumed that most of those were the followers he counseled. I should know their names and for a few I did, but mostly I didn't. I probably knew their wives' names. I rarely saw couples together. Whenever I counseled the wives they were alone.

"No. I'm sorry," I said softly, pressing my lips together.

CHAPTER 17
Sara

Ascending the stairs into Father Gabriel's private plane, I was in awe of the splendor. Taking a deep breath, I immediately remembered the rich aroma of leather. Of course my husband wore it like cologne, but it was different as I stepped across the cabin's threshold. It was the new-car smell that everyone loved, only amplified. The only other time I'd been inside this jet had been when I was without sight, during Jacob's and my temporary banishment, when he'd given me a tour of the planes. Now my vision was overloaded and my eyes darted about. From the shiny wooden facade of the cabinets that greeted me as I stepped inside, to the beautiful cream-colored leather chairs up and down the aisle, everything was over-the-top luxury.

It was definitely nothing like the plane I'd flown in this morning or Thomas's plane. The cabinet near the door held a sink, refrigerator, and coffeemaker. Wineglasses hung upside down from a rack. For only a moment, I wondered whether there could be wine. No one in The Light drank alcohol, but the Stella part of me questioned whether Father Gabriel did when he was flying or in Bloomfield Hills.

"Sara," Jacob instructed, "go sit near the back. You won't have to listen to Brother Micah and me in the cockpit."

I nodded and obediently walked toward the rear of the plane. With each step down the aisle, the backs of my fingers brushed the soft leather. Closing my eyes, I remembered the first time Jacob had brought me onto this plane—I remembered our past.

There were eight seats. Consecutive rows faced in opposite directions, creating clusters. I chose a seat all the way in the back. From it I could see up to the cockpit, but I was far enough away that their talking wouldn't bother me. Scanning the seat belts, I smiled. They were normal, not the jump seat kind like in the other plane.

Having difficulty suppressing my curiosity at Father Gabriel's extravagance, I opened the bathroom door and peered inside. With my mouth agape, I covered my lips, physically stopping myself from making an audible gasp. Even the bathroom was over the top. The cabinetry matched the stunning, shiny cabinets in the cabin, and the fixtures glistened. Lowering my hand and closing the door, I was glad I'd remembered to stay quiet. During the drive out to the hangar, I had been reminded more than once that everything within the plane was recorded.

Since we weren't sure when we'd have privacy, and couldn't be assured that we weren't being recorded, Jacob had spent most of the truck ride preparing me for what I might see. While he did, he admitted he was nervous about this trip. When he'd asked permission for me to go with him, he'd assumed that meant going to Fairbanks for supplies. He'd never expected permission to take me to another campus, especially back to the Eastern Light. The fact that he'd been specifically told to bring me only added to his concern.

When I asked about the mansion, he said he'd never been invited up to the house. There were small buildings closer to the landing strip. I remembered seeing those on Google Earth. Apparently they were similar to the living quarters in the pole barn. When he was required to spend the night at the Eastern Light, that was where he and Micah stayed. When Father Gabriel came to the airplane, he was driven through a side gate. He didn't walk through the yards to the back of the property. The only people from the mansion who ventured close to the outbuildings were those who played on the tennis courts or swam in the pool. Jacob said it wasn't uncommon for there to be many people around and it often sounded as if parties were being thrown. Father Gabriel referred to them as *celebrations*.

Jacob also told me that sometimes, if he was at the Eastern Light for any length of time, he could leave the property, as he had when he was taken to see me in Dearborn or when he went to service at the Eastern Light's temple. Since we'd be arriving early Sunday morning, more than likely we wouldn't just pick up Father Gabriel and return to the Northern Light. Father Gabriel always broadcast his Sunday and Wednesday sermons live. That meant he actually did each sermon three times, one for each time zone. The first in Detroit—in Highland Heights—was at nine Eastern time. Since we had been told to be there before then, there was a good probability that we'd be told to attend.

All I could do as he spoke was stare. There'd been a time when I'd longed to see inside the white building in Highland Heights. I reminded myself that now was my opportunity to do as Sara what I hadn't been able to do as Stella.

The Western Light was on Mountain time, which meant the next sermon would be two hours after the first, and the final sermon would be four hours from the first and broadcast to the Northern Light. With that schedule, we couldn't possibly be ready to fly back to the Northern Light until three or four in the afternoon at the earliest. Since everything was contingent upon Father Gabriel, Jacob wanted me to be prepared to spend the night in Bloomfield Hills.

He'd reminded me several times that Sara had never seen the mansion before. She'd never Google Earthed it nor stood outside its gate. I needed to act as if everything was new, while at the same time turning a blind eye. Jacob credited his quick rise to the Assembly to his ability to ignore the wealth and exuberance that occurred behind the scenes.

That begs the question, Why is Father Gabriel willing to expose his secrets to me?

We'd both napped after our visit with Brother Raphael. Nevertheless, I was still worried about Jacob's lack of sleep over the last twenty-four hours. He'd promised it would be all right, that the Cessna Citation X used instruments for navigation and Brother Micah was there. They were both confident in each other's abilities as a pilot and alternated as copilot. Jacob had volunteered to be the copilot on the way to Eastern Light, claiming that he wanted to be able to check on me. Personally I wanted to sleep. Making it through our return to the Northern Light undetected had left me more exhausted than relieved.

If I was supposed to be corrected after I apologized to Brother Raphael, Jacob had never done it. Though I'd tried to ask about it while we walked home, I hadn't tried since. Even though he'd given me permission to ask questions, my correction was a subject I preferred to avoid, mostly because it made me mad.

Why hadn't I restricted corporal correction before I agreed to return?

Instead I'd restricted sex. I liked sex, being struck with a belt—not so much.

As I settled into the soft leather seat, I looked around and realized that even seeing what was before me was a privilege. I doubted any of the regular followers, or even most of the chosen, knew how extravagantly Father Gabriel traveled.

Once we were in the air at the right altitude, Jacob came back and showed me how to swivel and recline my chair. It didn't just recline, it lay flat, creating an incredibly comfortable bed. The last thing I remembered was being covered with a blanket and Jacob's kissing my forehead, before he kissed me again, letting me know we were almost to the Eastern Light.

Maybe it was all the flying and lack of sleep, or maybe it was the idea of being back at the campus where I had originally been taken

after my abduction and where they'd begun suppressing my memories, I wasn't sure of the reason, but as I moved my seat from reclined
to upright, my stomach violently twisted. Shaking my head, I shoved
Jacob out of the way and ran toward the bathroom. Once I'd successfully emptied all the contents of my stomach, I turned and saw Jacob's
stare.

Be careful what you say. We're being recorded.

The warning was loud and clear in his dark eyes. Shaking my head,
I moved to the sink and rinsed my mouth. Under the cabinet I found
mouthwash and swooshed away the terrible taste. Though I'd have liked
a toothbrush, I was probably already overstepping my bounds by using
the mouthwash. When I looked up, in the mirror I noticed how the
bruise around my eye was less swollen but darker than it had been. As I
splashed water on my face, Jacob entered the small bathroom and shut
the door. While the bathroom was lavish, it was also small. His presence backed me up against the wall. In a hushed whisper, he demanded,
"Tell me."

My eyes opened wide. "Tell you what?"

"You know, don't you? You're pregnant."

"I don't know, but seriously, there's a lot happening right now, a lot
to make me nauseous. I'm scared."

He wrapped his arms around me, and kissed the top of my head.
"So am I, but no matter what, you're my first priority."

I shook my head. Still whispering, I replied, "No, you have a first
priority, and I'm here to help you with that, not mess it up any more
than I already have."

"We're about ready to land. Once we're at the Eastern Light, stay
close to me at all times and keep your eyes down."

"I know you don't want me to, but I can help. I'll have access to
women followers, unlike you. I can learn things too, things to help your
case. This is what I do—what I did. I want to help gather evidence."

Jacob's expression hardened as a tendon in his neck pulsated. "No." He laced our fingers together. "I'm not letting this go on much longer. It's not worth the risk."

"Don't worry about me. I'm in a much better place than I was. At least now I know what's happening."

He closed his eyes and exhaled. The hardness from before morphed to a look of pain. "It's not better. You were perfect at Brother Raphael's. You have to keep that up. Sara must always be in control."

I nodded. "I promise, I understand. But think about it. I'll act the part of Sara and help you at the same time."

He took a deep breath as the plane began to descend, and continued our whispered conversation. "I said no."

The words were definitive, as though any argument I made would be wasted breath.

He continued, "I'll do my best not to leave you alone. If I'm not with you, Brother Micah will try to be. Remember what I said about each move being a test?"

I nodded.

"I don't know why or what it's about, but I know that somehow bringing you here is a test. I just don't know which one of us is being tested. I honestly believe it's me. Somehow you're involved."

A chill ran through me. Jacob must have felt me begin to tremble, because he released my hand and hugged me again. His signature leather and musk filled my senses.

In the middle of our storm, I relished the peace. "I trust you," I whispered with my cheek against his shirt.

With his chin on the top of my head, his words skirted warm breaths across my hair. "Thank you, I didn't know if you'd ever be able to say that again, after everything."

"*Everything* is why I do." I craned my neck upward, searching for the honesty in his stare. "I can see now that everything you did was done for a reason. Besides, I wouldn't be back here if I didn't trust you."

As the urgency of what we were about to do threatened, our lips collided and a new fire replaced my earlier chill. Though I wasn't ready to forget the restriction I'd placed on our relationship, the hunger in Jacob's kiss drew me closer, filling me with desire. Without a word he claimed my body, allowing my tense muscles to relax in his embrace. Our lips remained firm, giving and taking with an unquenchable need to be nearer. Without provocation, I willingly surrendered to his craving. As I did I realized what I'd probably already known—I'd already trusted Jacob with *everything*: my mind, body, and life. Even now, with Stella awake inside me, I knew—*both parts of me* knew—the trust wasn't misplaced. We also knew we'd never trusted anyone else so completely, ever—not even Dylan.

After all, I'd only shared the key to my apartment with Dylan the day . . . the last day . . .

My entire body shivered. I couldn't let my mind go there, not now.

When our fervent kiss ended, Jacob smoothed my hair and reached for my hand. "Let's get you seated before we land."

I nodded and smiled at his choice of words. For once it wasn't an order.

As I flipped off the light switch, I caught a glimpse of my reflection. I didn't notice only the blackened eye, but from our kiss, my lips were red and slightly swollen. Grinning as I buckled my seat belt, I realized how our brief passionate kiss had provided us with an alibi. Obviously we'd been together in the bathroom to make out.

"Keep your eyes down," Jacob reminded me after we'd landed, as he opened the door and lowered the steps.

With my hand in his, we took the steps down. A light breeze blew, sending strands of blonde fluttering about my face as my long skirt billowed. As I inhaled the familiar scent of Michigan summer, humidity and heat filled my lungs. Even in the still of the morning, the promise of the sun's rays taunted, creating an ache that I could satisfy only by raising my chin and exposing my cheeks to the radiating light. It'd been too long since I'd truly felt the sun's warmth. As I fought the building desire and maintained Jacob's demanded pose, my heartbeat echoed in my ears.

Keeping my eyes veiled, I took in the open area of the landing strip, seeing only the edge of the surrounding trees. This was the wooded area where Dina Rosemont's witness had said her children saw the abduction. It was where they'd seen Mindy carried to a plane . . . a plane possibly piloted by the man beside me—my husband. I couldn't think about that, not when I needed to trust him.

Placing his hand on the small of my back, Jacob directed me to turn. Lifting only my eyes, I saw that beyond the outbuildings, upon a hill, was the mansion. I sucked in my breath as Jacob frantically whispered, "Eyes down! Don't look up there."

It was too late. I couldn't unsee.

I reached for Jacob's arm, my knees no longer able to support me. "How? Why?"

"Sara, not now." His words were harsh, coming from between clenched teeth.

From the distance the man on the balcony couldn't hear us or maybe even recognize me, but I knew. I knew in the depth of my heart that the man standing and watching the plane land and the passengers disembark was the man I'd imagined while I was without sight. Perhaps if I hadn't known every inch of him intimately, I wouldn't have been able to identify him from so far away, but I did.

By the time Jacob got me into the first building, my cheeks were covered with tears, and words were difficult to form. It was all right. From Jacob's expression I could tell he didn't want me to speak. Instead he casually walked the perimeter of the room before disappearing behind a door and, moments later, returning. Taking my hand, he silently led me to another bathroom.

Closing the door, he grabbed a towel and rolled it before placing it near the bottom of the door. Then, once again speaking in a whisper, he said, "I saw two cameras out there. There's nothing visual or audible in here."

I nodded, hearing but not comprehending. My mind swirled with too many thoughts and memories.

Uncharacteristically, Jacob violently seized my shoulders. Instead of his normal calm, anger exuded from his touch. Through clenched jaws, he said, "Hold it together. Don't you see? That's it. That's the fucking test. You had to know, in your heart. Think about it. How did Brother Uriel know you were at that festival?"

My head moved from side to side.

No. There is some mistake. I didn't. I never even suspected the blue-eyed man I'd trusted.

"I don't know what Father Gabriel knows," Jacob said, "or why he'd even suspect that you remembered your past, but what bigger test could he present than to make you face Dylan Richards?"

CHAPTER 18
Jacob

"Maybe not. Maybe he's been kidnapped too?" Sara questioned, her blue eyes begging me to make this right, but I couldn't.

I should've told her about Dylan Richards when we were at the motel; however, at the time, I was afraid she wouldn't believe me. There was too much she was trying to comprehend. It wasn't that she wasn't intelligent enough to do it. It was me. I'd seen the distrust in her eyes at the marshals' station. I was afraid that if I told her about Richards, she'd think I was lying, and I'd promised no more lies.

Taking a deep breath, I loosened my grip on her shoulders. "Sara." My tone was low and hushed. "I need you to trust me. Look at me. Do you trust me?"

Her dampened cheeks, combined with the pain in her expression, made me hate that bastard more than I already did.

"Do you?" I asked again.

Her shoulders drooped. "I told you I wouldn't be here if I didn't."

"Then believe me, Richards knew your fate. I remember being shocked when Brother Uriel took me to Dearborn, and while we were watching the two of you, Brother Uriel let it slip that Richards was a cop. I didn't know then what his connection was with The Light. Now, I've come to the possible conclusion that as a cop, he helps with acquiring women. I don't know, but Sara, not only did he know your fate, he delivered you on a platter."

"Why?" she cried more than spoke, as her chin fell to her chest.

Gently lifting her chin, I bent down until our noses touched. "So that I could meet the most intelligent, beautiful, amazing woman, and she could royally fuck up my life."

She didn't speak as her eyes searched mine. Just before I released her chin, I gently kissed her lips, and she melted against my chest. I wrapped her in my arms as her body shuddered with silent sobs. Time stood still as I rubbed her back. Finally I looked at my watch. It was after three in the morning at the Northern Light, but that meant it was after seven here. We'd been here for nearly an hour and I'd done nothing to help Micah.

"I don't know what's going to be expected of us. Why don't you lie down and rest while I help Micah?"

She nodded against my chest. "I'm sorry."

"Why?" I asked, once again pulling her eyes up to mine.

"For messing up your life."

"Don't be. It wasn't your doing." I kissed her. "I'm sorry I didn't tell you or warn you. I didn't think they'd be that cruel."

"I wouldn't have believed you." Her red-blotched neck straightened as she took a deep breath. "I've been thinking about it as we stood here. I think there were clues, but I missed every one. So much for being a kick-ass investigative journalist."

"Shhh. Don't even talk about it. I'd suspect the exact opposite. Not only do I believe you were very good at your job, but I believe that's the main reason you're here."

"It just doesn't make sense."

I wanted to fix it, to make everything make sense for her. After all, that had always been my role. She was to give her sadness to me and I was to take it. That was Father Gabriel's teaching. But I couldn't make this better. Stella needed to deal with it. I just wanted her to do it without bringing attention to her or us. Instead of telling her it was done, as The Light proclaimed, I changed the subject. "I'll show you where the bed is, and I want you to rest." When she looked as if she were about to argue, I stood straighter. "Sara?"

Lowering her eyes, she said, "Yes, Jacob."

"Look at me." When she did, I continued, "We didn't talk about your friend Rose?"

Sara's forehead furrowed as she shook her head. "Rose? No, not Rose. Her name is Mindy, Mindy Rosemont. She goes by Mary at the Northern Light, and all I know is she's married to a man named Adam."

"Do you remember when you saw her?"

She nodded.

"What did you do or say?"

"The first time, I don't remember . . . oh, yes, I told Raquel she looked familiar, but I didn't know why until—"

Though she was whispering, I touched her lips with my finger. "That's what you need to do, exactly like that. Please tell me you can do it."

"I'll try."

Holding her hands, I found my even, demanding tone. "No, Sara, you must not try. Tell me you *will*."

Through her lashes, she obediently replied, "Yes, Jacob. I will."

It wasn't unusual for Micah and me not to hear from anyone up at the mansion when we arrived. Since this was only a landing strip and not a functional hangar, our job had always been to call for the refueling truck and wait. It'd never bothered me before, nor had the cameras I knew were in the outbuildings, but today everything bothered me. My nerves were frayed.

With Micah next door and Sara sleeping, I paced the living room and waited for my phone to ring. A little after eight, Detroit time, it did.

"Hello?"

"Brother Jacob?"

"Yes," I replied, not recognizing the number or the voice.

"Father Gabriel expects you and your wife at service in less than an hour. A car will arrive to transport the two of you and Brother Micah. It'll be there in ten minutes. Be ready."

"We will."

The line went dead.

My mind filled with thoughts; most weren't good or even promising. Surely Father Gabriel wouldn't do this little reunion of Richards and Sara in front of the entire church, not that there were that many people at the Eastern Light—but still.

As I went to wake Sara, I thought about breakfast. There was no way we'd have time to eat much of anything. When I entered the bedroom, she was under the covers, curled on her side. Her light-blonde hair covered part of her cheek. The side with Thomas's bruise was against the pillow. She looked more peaceful than I'd seen her in what seemed like forever—since before she left.

Part of me wanted to keep her that way, allow her to sleep, and let her remain in whatever dream world she was visiting. Wherever it was, it had to be better than here.

When I sat on the edge of the bed, she turned toward me with her knees still pulled up and reached out for my leg. For only a second, her sleepy eyes opened and a smile graced her lips. And then it was gone. For only a second, she'd felt safe, knowing I was here, but then just as fast the memories and reality had come back. The sleepy blue of her eyes had clouded with doubt and fear.

I smoothed her hair away from her face, revealing her bruise. "It's time. I just received a call. There's a car coming to take us to service."

She nodded.

"Are you feeling all right? Can you get up?"

Slowly she sat, assessing. "I do feel all right, as good as I can, I guess. I'm a little hungry."

I shook my head. "If you get yourself ready, I'll check the kitchen and see if there's anything to eat."

We'd already determined that even the bedroom had a camera. When I pulled back the covers, she was still fully dressed. Her skirt was some kind of gauzy material that didn't wrinkle, and other than shoes and whatever she needed to do privately, she was ready.

In the kitchen I found bread and hurriedly put it in the toaster. In the refrigerator I found her favorite flavor of Preserve the Light preserves—strawberry. I looked up as she walked toward the small galley kitchen. She looked so pretty. I was glad she'd rested, if only for a little while. Despite the ugly bruise, her coloring had improved, bringing back the pink to her cheeks and lips.

When she reached for the plate with the toast, she gasped, "Oh!"

I narrowed my gaze.

"I just remembered," she said, recovering quickly, "how much I love the strawberry preserves. We've been out of it at the Northern Light for a while."

I suspected that she had remembered something other than that, but I could play along. "I knew it was your favorite. It always has been."

She shrugged as she chewed. Once she swallowed, she said, "Sometimes I forget that you remember further back than I do. All I remember is liking it." She wrinkled her nose. "It's much better than the blueberry."

I exhaled and prayed. Just maybe we could pull this off.

As I handed her a glass of water, we both turned toward the sound of knocking.

Taking a quick drink, she asked, "Is this like our service? I'm nervous."

"It is, only smaller."

I opened the door to Micah. Beyond him, on the driveway that passed the buildings and ran out to the landing strip in one direction and to the road in the other, was a black SUV. Under the warm Michigan sun stood a driver, waiting ominously by the car door. Sunglasses covered his eyes, and a white button-down shirt stretched over his large arms, a stark contrast to his dark skin. I immediately recognized him. Although Brother Elijah was on the Assembly, from my experience at the Eastern Light and the way he resembled a professional football player, I believed he also acted as a bodyguard whenever Father Gabriel was present.

"Hello, Brother Elijah," I said.

He nodded. "Brother Jacob. Brother Micah."

Although Sara followed closely behind, with her eyes down, Elijah didn't acknowledge her. He wasn't expected to, nor was I expected to introduce her. When she glanced up and saw Brother Elijah, her lip disappeared between her teeth and she reached for my hand. Damn, I wanted to know what she was thinking. Instead I searched her expression as I helped her into the backseat. She was true to our plan, and other than the fact that the pink had left her cheeks, her expression revealed nothing.

Though Brother Elijah often accompanied Father Gabriel, thankfully, Father Gabriel wasn't in the SUV. I sat next to Sara in the backseat and tried to silently reassure her as I squeezed her hand. With Micah in the front seat, we rode in silence as Elijah turned the SUV around, headed into the trees, and drove toward the gate. After he entered an access code, the solid, wide gate moved, allowing us to leave the mansion's compound. It wasn't until we entered Highland Heights that Elijah spoke.

"Brother Jacob, as an Assemblyman, you'll sit with the Assemblymen, and Sister Sara, you're expected to sit with the Assembly wives."

Her hand flinched within mine, but her head never moved. "Of course," I replied. "I'll show Sara where that is. When we were here before, I wasn't on the Assembly."

Shit! Now it was me who was rambling.

Elijah's head turned slightly toward the rearview mirror. I nodded, doing my best to keep my tone and facial expression neutral. Fuck, it wasn't going to be Sara who messed this up, it was going to be me, if I didn't calm down.

"My wife," Elijah went on, "is Sister Teresa. I told her to tell the other Assembly wives to expect a guest. They'll be ready."

I hoped that was a good thing, because given the way Sara was clinging to my hand, I didn't want to be separated from her, not even in a church filled with followers, and I was certain that she felt the same. So much for keeping promises. Not only couldn't I be with her but also neither could Micah. The two of them knew each other only from services, but each had heard the other's name often.

Micah was also married. His wife and their young son were back at the Northern Light. He and I both knew this entire situation of taking Sara to the Eastern Light was highly unusual. When we were getting the Cessna ready for the trip, he had reached for my arm and whispered, "I don't understand this. I piloted Father Gabriel for years before you came. I've never transported a woman *back* to the Eastern Light."

I nodded, my concern obviously visible.

"Brother, I'll do all I can to help," he reassured me.

"We just have to bring her back."

Micah nodded. "I hear you. I mean, we don't choose them, but once they're ours . . ." His words trailed away. Micah was a good man, a good pilot, and a good husband. There weren't a lot of men who treated women the way Abraham did, at least not at the Northern Light. I mostly credited Luke with that. He worked hard, monitoring and doing what he could to keep the wives safe. If someone else had his job, the outcome could have been much different. I didn't know how it was at other campuses.

We pulled up to the back of the large white building housing The Light, located on the corner of Second and Glendale Avenues. When I turned, Sara's eyes were closed. She was concealing her fear visually, but damn, from her pulse and grip I felt it. Hell, I even smelled it, if that was possible. It emanated from her, creating a cloud.

The Northern Light had grown to nearly five hundred followers, and yet the Eastern Light had stayed relatively stable, its population hovering around one hundred. With that number, its temple was much smaller than ours, composing only a small part of the total building. Taking Sara's hand, I led her through the doors. Each step was smaller than the one before, the old tile floor became figurative quicksand, sucking my shoes into the muck, slowing our steps as dread glued our hands together. Even the thought of letting go of her seemed impossible.

Perhaps I was paranoid, but as the followers made their way to their seats I sensed a different atmosphere from the one at the Northern Light. Everyone here seemed more tired and reserved. It made sense. The only male followers who remained at the Eastern Light were the ones who worked on either recruitment or logistics. Most of the female followers worked in the building across the street. While they had a small Preserve the Light operation, mostly they made illegal substances. It was Father Gabriel's backup plan, his way to deflect law enforcement from the bigger illegal operations, if operations behind The Light were ever questioned. These followers were more aware of the dangerous side of The Light because they lived it.

Using the seating at the Northern Light as my guide, I took Sara to where I assumed the Assembly wives sat. I must have been right, because a woman stood.

Bowing her head, she said, "I'm Sister Teresa, my husband said to expect a new sister."

New? What? Not new, just visiting.

"Sister Teresa," I said, "this is my wife, Sister Sara. We're visiting from another campus. I'll return for her after service."

She looked to the empty seat beside her and then reached for Sara's hand. "Welcome, Sister."

I made my way to the front, where Elijah too had an empty seat beside him.

"Brother," Elijah said, "before service begins, I believe you're wanted for a few minutes in the offices, on the second floor. Do you remember where you're going?"

I swallowed my concern. I didn't want to leave this room, not with Sara out there alone. "Yes, I remember."

He nodded. "I'd try to be back before Father Gabriel gets here."

My gaze narrowed. "Father Gabriel isn't the one who wants to see me?"

Elijah shrugged.

I took a deep breath and looked out toward the congregation and sighed. I felt a little better seeing Teresa and Sara speaking.

The Eastern Light's temple was on the first floor. This building was quite large and used for many purposes. When I'd first entered The Light, like most voluntary followers I'd spent most of my time in this building. The second floor held offices as well as classrooms for new-follower training. Part of the introductory process was learning and retaining Father Gabriel's teachings. The third floor had testing centers—individual cubicles where daily examinations were performed. There was constant analysis of a follower's dedication to The Light before that follower could be assigned to one of the other campuses. The fourth floor had dormitories for new followers and apartments for permanent residents. The Assemblymen and Commissioners' apartments were in the far end of the building across the street, giving them some privacy.

As I rounded the corner at the top of the stairs for only a brief second, I saw Richards as he stepped in front of me.

What the fuck?

"Let's see how you like it, asshole."

I didn't have time to process his words before his fist contacted my jaw, catching me off guard and sending my face flying to the left. Instinctively I reached to the wall. Before I steadied myself enough to retaliate, my arms were seized from behind.

CHAPTER 19
Sara

I couldn't believe I was in the building I'd watched. Memories of my investigation came back, reviving my curiosity. As I looked around, I contemplated the size of the temple. There had to be more in this building. I wondered what that included. And then I remembered the abandoned school building across the street—the one I'd seen women walk to. For only a moment, I considered asking the other wives what they knew, but then I reminded myself that Sara wouldn't question.

When I first sat, I had a strange sense about the other Assembly wives making me wonder how we at the Northern Light would react if a new wife came to us. Almost immediately my unwelcome feeling faded as Sister Teresa and the woman on my other side, Sister Martha, seemed to relax and greeted me. Soon the other Assembly and Commission wives were shaking my hand and telling me their names.

Since they were all part of the chosen, I could tell them that I was from the Northern Light. While the followers weren't as informed, the chosen knew about the other campuses. It was as Sister Teresa spoke that I realized what had facilitated their acceptance.

"Sister Sara, have you thanked God and Father Gabriel for your husband?"

Aleatha Romig

Lowering my eyes, I nodded. "Yes, Sister, I have. I'm thankful he loves me enough to correct me."

It was a bond—a sick, twisted bond, but somehow, in this fucked-up world, it gave the women of The Light a connection. For only a moment, I thanked Thomas for the bruise that had opened these women's hearts. I didn't want to be here among them, but if I had to be, I was glad we could find a common denominator to keep me from being the outsider.

"How long have you been in The Light?" Sister Martha asked.

"My husband said we've been at Northern Light for over three years."

"Your husband?"

I nodded. "Yes, about a year ago I had an accident. I don't like to talk about it, but I must have hit my head. I don't remember anything before that."

"Oh," Sister Teresa said, "that must be terrible."

I sighed. "It was, but everyone's been so helpful." I shrugged. "I think I've just accepted that my earlier memories weren't important. If they were, and if remembering them was God and Father Gabriel's will, I'd get them back."

"It's good to have you with us, Sister," Sister Martha said.

From time to time, I'd try to look about. I searched for the piercing blue eyes in my memory. However, Dylan's being at service didn't make sense. He'd never left on Sunday mornings or Wednesday nights when we dated. Not that I'd spent every Sunday and Wednesday with him, but I had spent some.

I watched the room as men and women of all ethnicities continued to enter. The sanctuary wasn't only smaller than ours, it was much older. The walls were painted cinder block, and everything was clean, but obviously worn. The threadbare carpet was in need of replacement. From what little I'd seen and learned, I believed The Light's money went other places.

Polished wooden beams peaked at the center of the ceiling, and long cylindrical lights hung from cables. Toward the front was a raised stage. Where some churches might have had a choir was the seating area for Commissioners and Assemblymen. I held back my panic as I realized that Jacob wasn't there. I'd watched him walk in that direction, but as I took in the surroundings, I realized something must have happened. The chair next to Brother Elijah was empty.

I turned, searching for Brother Micah. He wasn't too far behind me. When our eyes met, he opened his wide and slightly shook his head.

What does this mean? Where is he? Where did he go?

Biting my lip, I debated my options. I knew that Jacob wouldn't leave me. Besides, Micah was still here. If I had been the one to go missing, he would have searched for me. I owed him the same.

"Sister Teresa," I asked, "is there a restroom that I could use before service?"

"It's about to start."

I wrinkled my nose. "I haven't told anyone," I whispered, "but I think I could be pregnant."

"Oh, I understand. Yes, let me show you . . ."

Just as we were about ready to stand, the room quieted, and Father Gabriel entered the stage from a door on the right, and walking behind him was Jacob. Sister Teresa shook her head as I nodded my understanding. We wouldn't be leaving our seats until the service was done.

I narrowed my eyes, trying to see my husband more clearly. Though he appeared fine to all the followers as he took his seat by Brother Elijah, I could tell something was off. Continuing to stare, I waited until his dark eyes met mine. When they did, his jaw clenched, and even from far away, I saw the anger in his eyes and the tension in his shoulders just before his expression changed.

Something had happened, and he was trying to shield me. I just didn't know what.

Throughout the entire service I waited for something, for anything from Jacob or Father Gabriel. I didn't know whether he would make a big deal about our visitor status or whether he'd make some kind of announcement. Instead the service progressed as it would have at the Northern Light. I stood and sat at all the right times, recited the responses and verses as well as anyone.

I'd learned my lessons well.

As I began to relax, I noticed Sister Teresa's hands upon her lap. With her dark skin, the burned tips of her fingers were even more pronounced. Rolling my wrist and seeing my own fingertips fueled my need to help end this travesty. And then everything changed.

CHAPTER 20
Jacob

Minutes earlier

"What the hell?" I said, as my arms were pinned behind me. I couldn't see the person holding me back, but I sure as hell could see the asshole in front of me.

"I saw her face," Richards said, his jaw clenched.

Heat boiled in my chest as I worked to relax my arms. Apparently he was done with his little right-hook demonstration.

"What are you talking about?" I asked.

"Stella! That's her fucking name."

"Stella?" I did my best to sound confused. Moving my shoulders, I said, "Let go of my damn arms. I'm not going to hit this asshole."

"No, of course not," Dylan replied. "You only hit women."

Whoever was behind me released my arms, and I took a step toward Richards. "You're talking about *my wife*. And what happens between me and my wife is none of your damn business."

He ran his hand through his hair. "It is my damn business, more than you fucking know."

I took a deep breath and spoke louder than I should. "Father Gabriel gave *Sara* to me." I emphasized her name. "If I choose to correct her, it's my decision. Not yours."

When I turned I saw a large man I didn't recognize. Though he'd taken a step back, I had no doubt that if I went for Richards, he'd go for me.

"She's . . ." Richards turned away before spinning to face me again. "She's walking around like the zombie women around here. What did you do to her?"

"What did I do?" *Fuck you.* "Go to hell! I remember you. You were with her in Dearborn. You had her and you turned her over. She's mine now, and I'm keeping her."

"You're keeping her? Like she's a fucking possession? This is insane."

"No, not a possession, my wife."

"Gentlemen."

A chill went through me, silencing us all, as Father Gabriel emerged from a doorway farther down the hall. The man behind me and I immediately shifted our stances, standing taller and bowing our heads, to reflect the reverence we felt for Father Gabriel. Conversely Richards casually leaned against the wall and shoved his hands in the pockets of his jeans.

Patting Richards's shoulder, Father Gabriel said, "This is The Light, we don't argue, we don't fight, and"—he leaned toward Richards, his voice low and methodical—"We. Don't. Drop. Fucking. F. Bombs. Am I clear?"

"Yes, Uncle," Richards said, though it appeared it pained him to do so.

"Brother Jacob," he said, looking in my direction.

"Yes, Father."

"We have much to discuss." He pulled up the sleeve of his silk suit, revealing a watch, as well as cuff links that I would guess could have been sold to pay off the debt of a few small nations. "However, now is not the time. Service is about to begin." His brow rose. "I assume Sister Sara is seated with the other Assembly wives?"

"Yes, Father."

"Very well." He turned back to Richards. "Won't you join us? It'd be good for you."

Pulling himself away from the wall, Richards again ran his hand through his hair. Although he was answering Father Gabriel, his stare never left me. "No, I need to get the hell out of here."

I'd never in three years heard anyone tell Father Gabriel no, but from the way Richards walked away without waiting for Father Gabriel's response, I got the distinct impression that neither of them found it unusual.

"Children can be so disrespectful," Father Gabriel said, looking at me.

Child? Richards had said *uncle*. They were related?

I wanted to ask what all of this meant, for me, for Sara, but of course I couldn't.

"Brother," he said, laying his hand on my shoulder. "I see you have questions and admire your restraint. I always have admired that about you. The thing is that I have questions too." He patted my shoulder. "The difference is that I can ask mine. Before I return to the Northern Light, we *will* talk."

What the fuck does that mean?

"Yes, Father."

As he walked past me and the other man, he casually asked, "How is Fairbanks this time of year?"

Thoughts bombarded my mind. "Fairbanks? It's fine. Whitefish was out of some of our supplies. I called Brother Daniel—"

He waved his hand. "Never mind that right now. Do you have my envelope from Brother Reuben?"

Envelope. What envelope? I had a faint recollection of Brother Reuben's handing me something at the Western Light. I couldn't recall anything after that.

"I do. It's at the Northern Light." I hoped it was. Was this the test?

He nodded. "I see." Walking away, he said, "Come, it's time for service."

I followed him down the hall and down the stairs. The other man followed closely behind, as if he needed to be sure I wouldn't make a run for it. There was no way I'd do that, not with Sara in the congregation.

As I sat, Brother Elijah nodded.

Had he been doing Father Gabriel's work or Richards's by telling me to go to the offices? Did Richards possess the power to direct Assemblymen? With each minute, the questions multiplied.

Looking out to the congregation, I found Sara and exhaled—she was all right. When her eyes met mine, I tried to relay calm, to let her know that it would be OK. At least I knew Dylan Richards wouldn't be surprising her here during service.

I responded correctly as Father Gabriel preached. I stood and sat, and even recited. However, what I didn't do was listen. My mind was too aghast at the turn of events. I tried to remember what I'd even done with the envelope from Brother Reuben. I'd taken it right before all hell broke loose. At the time I hadn't thought it was important. I also tried to decipher Richards's connection to The Light. Whoever he was, he had the most casual relationship with Father Gabriel that I'd ever seen.

My thoughts continued to swirl from subject to subject with no answer in sight, until Father Gabriel's words cut through my confusion.

"Therefore, do you not agree with our Lord, that we would rather be away from these earthly bodies, for then we will be at home in The Light?"

Away? Was this the Kool-Aid?

"Yes, Father," came the congregation's response.

"Are you certain, my children?"

"Yes, Father."

"Remember the Lord detests lying lips, but he delights in men who are truthful. People in the dark lie, but you are in The Light. You've taken off your old self and become new. Who among you would like to go back to the dark?"

No one replied, and heads shook.

"It is taught that outside are the dogs, those who practice magic arts, the sexually immoral, the murderers, the idolaters, and everyone who loves and practices falsehood. Is that where you want to be?"

"No, Father."

"Where do you want to be?"

"In The Light."

"But can everyone stay in The Light?"

"No, Father."

"What have we been told to do with our eye if it causes us to stumble?" He didn't wait for the response as his voice rose in volume. "We've been taught to gouge it out. For it is better to go through life with one eye than to have two and be thrown into the dark!"

"Yes, Father."

"Brother Abel, you and Sister Salome may come to the front of the congregation. Brother Uriel, please also come forward."

I sat in awe and horror. My gaze searched for Sara's, but she wasn't looking at me. She was looking down, as were many of the women. No doubt they all suspected what was about to happen. I'd heard of services with banishments, but I'd never witnessed one. At the Northern Light the only banishments I'd known about had been done privately. When they were made public, it was more of a production for the other followers than for the ones who were to be banished—their fate was set.

A solemn hush fell over the temple as a young couple, probably in their late teens or early twenties, made their way to the front. She was crying and holding on to his arm. Apparently they'd needed encouragement to come forward, because the man who'd been behind me in the upstairs hallway was walking behind them. Brother Uriel stood from the row of Commissioners and moved to the center of the stage.

"Followers of The Light," Brother Uriel said. "Do you trust your lives and souls to Father Gabriel?"

"Yes, Brother," was said by all. The volume was considerably lower than it had been, the sense of impending correction falling like a damp blanket.

"What have we learned about disobedience?"

"It deserves correction."

"Brother Abel, tell us what happened in production distribution."

The young man bowed his head and began to tremble. "I'm sorry. It won't happen again."

"Brother?" Father Gabriel asked.

"I-I didn't take . . . it wasn't much . . . I just needed . . ."

"Brothers and Sisters, the product you toil to make is for what?" Brother Uriel asked.

"The Light."

"Apparently Brother Abel forgot that as he was working to package product for shipment." The followers inhaled collectively. "Not caring about The Light, he chose to keep some for himself." Brother Uriel turned toward Sister Salome. "Sister, is Brother Abel your husband?"

"Y-yes."

"And as such he's caused you to stumble. Isn't that correct?"

"F-Father, p-please, we won't—"

"Congregation, is it better to gouge out these followers or allow them to drag us all into the dark?"

My empty stomach churned. When I looked for Sara, she was bent forward with her blonde hair falling down. However, as I stared, she momentarily sat up. Though her eyes were closed, I saw the telltale red blotches covering her cheeks and knew she was crying. I balled my fists, willing myself with every bit of self-control I possessed to remain seated.

I couldn't comprehend.

Father Gabriel had invited Richards to this service. Surely Richards knew what was going to happen. Could he really have watched this and turned a blind eye? He was a fucking cop, but then again, I was a federal agent and I was watching.

"Yes, Father." The response to Father Gabriel's last question was the softest yet.

"Children, do you follow me?"

"Yes, Father." It was a little louder.

"Do you believe in me?"

"Yes, Father."

"Do you trust in me?"

"Yes, Father." It was getting louder each time.

"Brother Uriel, the decree."

Brother Uriel pulled two syringes from his jacket and handed them to Brother Abel and Sister Salome. Though they hesitated to take them, they did.

"Father Gabriel's word tells us that all are to follow the rules of The Light. Correction is to be quick and appropriate. Brother Abel, you chose to take merchandise from the production center for your own use. You put yourself above The Light. As your punishment, Father Gabriel's decree is to grant your desire and give you more."

"Roll up your sleeves and show everyone your punishment."

"P-please," Sister Salome cried.

The big guy from the hall held her arm while another follower came forward and injected the contents of the syringe.

"N-no, she didn't do anything," Brother Abel cried, as his wife fell to the floor.

I wondered what the drug was and how much they were being given.

Was the intent to kill them?

"Brother Abel, your turn."

Slowly, he did as he was instructed. Immediately after the contents of the syringe were injected he fell to the ground. Their mouths began to foam and their bodies twitched. Without being asked, the big guy and three others came forward, lifted the bodies, and carried them out.

"Children," Father Gabriel said, bringing everyone's attention back to him. "Correction isn't pleasant. It's not meant to be pleasant. It's meant to keep everyone within The Light safe. When we have malfeasance among us, no one is safe. What do you say for the privilege of knowing that you are now safe?"

"Thank you, Father."

Blood seeped from my cheek as I bit the soft flesh, controlling my protests.

For the next fifteen minutes, Father Gabriel continued to preach his sermon, talking about the beauty of correction and the importance of obedience.

CHAPTER 21
Sara

Oh my God.

I couldn't watch and I couldn't run, but I wasn't alone. The other wives around me were responding the same way. Women I'd met only an hour ago held my hands. The toast Jacob had made me for breakfast threatened to return. Closing my eyes, I concentrated on keeping it down and not vomiting all over the worn carpet or my new sisters. It was a welcome distraction, because I couldn't concentrate on what was happening in front of me. I'd seen dead bodies; however, I'd never watched someone die, or, more accurately, be murdered.

This had to stop. The evidence was mounting and both Jacoby and I were witnesses. With each passing second, I wanted nothing more than for the FBI to come running through the doors and stop this horror show. I wanted to look Father Gabriel in the face and tell him who I was and that I was helping to bring him down.

I took deep breaths, concentrating on my role. Although I recognized Brother Uriel as Uriel Harris, the developer, I couldn't dwell on it. When the scene finally ended, the other wives and I released hands and fell into our own thoughts as Father Gabriel continued to preach.

I wasn't listening to what he said, nor did I care. With my eyes down, I waited. Eventually people began to move around me, but I remained still, paralyzed by the correction I'd witnessed. And then I heard the one voice that could free me. With the one word, *Sara*, in his deep tone, the tone that had praised me as well as corrected me, I was able to move.

Looking up with just my eyes, in the midst of this chaos, I was safe again, because Jacob was beside me, offering me his hand. It was another realization, one that the old me would never have admitted or probably experienced. Even with the mental checklist of laws I'd witnessed broken, I wanted the relief that came with giving my cares over to Jacob.

As I placed my hand in his, his warmth washed through me, alerting me to how cool I'd become. As I stood I wanted to fall into him and be surrounded by his strong arms. I wanted the only sound to be that of his steady heartbeat as my ear lay against his broad chest. I wanted him to protect me and to take me away from all this madness.

When our gazes met, his told me that he knew my every thought. Surrounded by the Eastern Light's followers, without words, we spoke not only words but also an oration to each other. We both wanted out. This had to end. Coming back had been a mistake, but we would survive.

I couldn't process what had happened, how it had happened, or why no one had tried to stop it. Biting my lip, I trapped the protests and declarations of indecency that had surfaced in my thoughts.

How could everyone just sit and watch two young people murdered—people who'd end up on Tracy's tables at the Wayne County Morgue—people whose fingerprints were gone?

I knew the reality. No one would question their deaths. A young couple dying of a drug overdose, their bodies found in Highland Heights, wouldn't even make WCJB's news. No one in the dark would question. Why should they? No one in The Light had.

Silently we walked to the black SUV, my hand tightly encased in Jacob's grip. Across Second Avenue from the parking lot was the old school building I'd watched. The curiosity I'd possessed even at the beginning of service no longer existed. Like my fingerprints, it was gone. I didn't care what they did over there. Maybe I should restart my medicine after my period. Maybe then I could forget what had happened. As the tragedy of what we had witnessed consumed me, my only desire was to know that Jacob and I were safe and away from The Light.

Jacob, Brother Micah, and Brother Elijah spoke during the drive back to the compound, but I didn't listen. Only the final words of the young couple, Sister Salome begging and Brother Abel pleading for her life, replayed in my mind.

Did things like that happen at the Northern Light? I'd never seen it or even heard of it. If leaving The Light wasn't possible, at the very least, I wanted to go back to Alaska.

As we drove north on Highway 1, sitting straight took every muscle I possessed. The urge to melt into Jacob's warmth was stronger than it had ever been. I knew it wasn't an option. We were chosen. Public displays of affection weren't permitted. When we arrived back on the compound, I dutifully followed Jacob into the outbuilding's living quarters. Though the Michigan sun was shining and warm, I was chilled to the bone as I collapsed on the sofa.

Before I could speak, Jacob did. "Sara, cook Brother Micah's and our dinner."

I gazed up at him in disbelief. He wanted to eat after that?

He reached for my hand as his tone softened. "There's food in the refrigerator. It only needs to be warmed." As I stood he continued, "It'll give you something else to think about."

I nodded as I walked to the small kitchen. Jacob was right. I needed a distraction, but it wasn't enough. I could have cooked a five-course meal and it wouldn't have erased the images of what I'd seen. Besides, what I warmed wasn't a five-course meal. Quite honestly, I would've rather cooked, but there weren't ingredients. Pilots usually occupied these quarters, and they wouldn't be expected to do more than warm their food.

After I cleaned up the dishes and the kitchen, Jacob took my hand. "Let's go for a walk."

"All right." I didn't care what we did. We knew Father Gabriel had two more sermons to preach before he'd be ready to fly back to the Northern Light. Besides, I wanted to talk to Jacob, and since the only place that was possible was in the bathroom, we couldn't. Surely if we spent too much time in there together it would be questioned.

As we stepped outside, the sun and breeze warmed my skin. Lifting my face without sunglasses, I squinted. I didn't care that I was supposed to keep my eyes down. Allowing the summer sun to kiss my cheeks reminded me of how much I loved fresh air. "I wish we had running shoes."

Jacob smiled. "We have to walk toward the rear of the property. We aren't allowed up near the mansion." He took my hand and led me toward the landing strip.

As we walked past the Cessna, I said, "I want to leave."

"I should have forced you to," he replied sadly as we made our way farther and farther away from the cameras.

"I don't mean that," I corrected him. "Although yes, I want away from The Light. I meant I want to go back to the Northern Light." I took a deep breath. "Tell me the truth. Does anything like what we saw today happen there?"

"I promised you no more lies. I'll always tell you the truth. You don't have to ask for it. And no, at least not that I've ever seen. There've been a few banishments since I've been on the Assembly, but they've been done privately.

"The Eastern Light is different than any of the other campuses. It's in the middle of the dark. No one can walk away from the Northern or Western Light, not easily. They're too isolated. So dealing with disputes or corrections doesn't need to be as public or as severe. Here, obedience on every level is mandatory."

"Are you defending what happened?" I asked, staring up at him.

"Hell no. There's no defense. I'm justifying it, to you and to me."

"I don't want it justified. I want it stopped. Those kids will be left in some abandoned house in Highland Heights, and no one will question their death, just another drug casualty."

"If you were a follower here, after what you just witnessed, would you steal drugs or even a paper clip?"

I shook my head.

"Would you disobey any directive?"

"No."

"Those kids served as reminders for the entire Eastern Light."

I shook my head. "I've always hated reminders."

Jacob squeezed my hand. "By the way, Brother Raphael left your correction up to me."

"And?" I asked, with my eyes open wide.

"And I took you to the coffeehouse. It's done. As if it never happened."

"Thank you."

Jacob led me past the open space near the landing strip and into the woods at the perimeter. Looking up, I saw the tall trees and the way the leaves rustled in the breeze. Now that we were away, not only from cameras and microphones, but also from eyes that could peer from the mansion's balcony or windows, the tension surrounding us lessened, and I leaned against his arm.

"Jacob, where were you right before service?"

"Oh, shit. With all that happened, I actually forgot."

"What?"

"I received an invitation to go up to the offices on the second floor."

"Father Gabriel?"

"No. Although he was there, eventually," Jacob said, rubbing his chin. "It was from your . . . well, I don't like to think of him as your anything. Ex, maybe?"

I stopped walking. "Dylan? You saw Dylan?"

Jacob nodded. "He punched me."

My eyes opened wide. I couldn't imagine it. I remembered how people had told me that Dylan was a hothead, but Jacob was bigger, much taller than Dylan. "Why?"

"He said he'd seen your face. It must have been on the cameras. I doubt he'd have been able to see it from the balcony, especially with your eyes down."

"That doesn't make sense. He turned me over to The Light, and then punched you because he assumed you're the one who did this to me?"

Jacob shrugged. "I don't get it either. Did you know he's related to Father Gabriel? Probably he's related to Garrison Clarkson."

My brow furrowed. "No, no, he's not. His parents died when he was eighteen. He said his grandparents were dead, and he didn't have any siblings."

"I promised you honesty. I'm telling you what I heard. After he punched me, we exchanged a few words, and Father Gabriel came out of an office. Richards called Father Gabriel *Uncle*."

I stopped walking and sat on the ground with my back against a tree. Pulling my knees up to my chest, I searched my memory. "No, I'm not doubting you," I said quietly. When Jacob sat beside me, I reached for his cheek. Running my fingers along his jaw, I pouted. "I'm sorry he punched you. You didn't do this. You didn't deserve it."

He inclined his face to my touch. "I don't deserve it for that, but I'm sure I deserve it."

"Well . . . that could probably be true," I admitted with a grin. Glancing over his shoulder, I nodded in that direction. "What's that over there?"

Jacob turned. In the distance was a concrete wall. With the trees I couldn't see how high it was, or see the rest of the building. I didn't remember seeing other buildings at the rear of the property when I'd looked on Google Earth.

"It's a wall, like we have at the Northern Light. Although I'd guess polar bears aren't too much of a problem around here. When I first started flying here it wasn't here. I assumed they thought the woods would keep them safe, but a little under a year ago"—he reached for my hand and smiled—"about the time my life became fucked up, I saw the construction as I'd fly in. It took them a few months, but it completely encases the rear of the property."

Even if I hadn't seen Dylan on the balcony, what Jacob had just said confirmed that Dylan was involved, and that he'd lied to me. "You may think I'm crazy, but I think I'm the reason they built the wall."

"You. Why?"

"My friend, Mindy Rosemont—Mary at the Northern Light," I added to help him remember. "Besides researching The Light for a drug story and missing persons and fingertips . . . I was trying to find Mindy."

"So how does that connect you to that wall?"

"I wasn't finding anything. It was like Mindy had disappeared into thin air. Anyway, her parents live in California, and they wanted to do something to help find her. About a month after Mindy went missing, her parents came back here and posted a bunch of fliers all over the city and suburbs. I thought it was a waste of time. I mean, this is the digital age, what good would paper fliers do?

"I was wrong. A while after they were posted, Dina, Mindy's mom, received a call from a woman who said her young kids liked to play in the woods behind their house. She said they played near a landing strip, and one day they said they saw a woman being carried onto a plane. Dina called and asked me to look for the landing strip. She was told it was near Highway 1 and Eastways Road. That was the day I drove up here. I had the address of the mansion, but after I couldn't get in or even get any good pictures, I drove around for over an hour trying to find the landing strip. I couldn't find it. After today, I know why. It was because of all the gates.

"At the time I assumed if there were a landing strip, there'd be an access road. I never imagined it would be gated."

Jacob scooted against the tree. When I looked up, he was staring at me. In his eyes I saw something I didn't recall having seen before.

"Why are you looking at me funny?" I asked.

He lifted my hand and kissed my knuckles. "I'm not looking at you funny. I'm looking at you with utter amazement. You *are* a kick-ass investigative journalist. I can't believe they assigned me—an FBI agent—a wife with so much knowledge on The Light."

I grinned. "I'm pretty sure they don't know about you."

He shook his head. "No. If they did, that would've been me in the front of the temple."

I closed my eyes. "Please don't say that. Don't even joke about that." A tear ran down my cheek, and Jacob gently wiped it away with his thumb.

"I'm not joking. We're getting out. I just need a burner phone so I don't alert The Light by using my phone. It's been more than twenty-four hours. They should have enough manpower in Anchorage very soon."

"What happened to the phone you had in Fairbanks?"

"I had to destroy it. I couldn't risk having it on me when we went back. I wasn't sure we'd get away with what we did, getting you back into the Northern Light." With our hands still united, he laid his head against the tree and sighed.

"What now?" I asked.

"I remembered something else. Before service, Father Gabriel asked me about Fairbanks. Before I went there, I called Brother Daniel and told him that Whitefish was low on supplies so I was going to Fairbanks. There would be record of me being there, and I needed to justify it."

"What did Father Gabriel ask?"

"Just how the weather was in Fairbanks this time of year."

My pulse increased. "That's weird. Don't you think?"

"Yes, but then he asked me for an envelope someone gave me after my delivery. For the life of me, I don't remember what I did with it."

I didn't ask about the envelope. If I did, I knew Jacob would tell me—he'd promised. I also knew there was still so much about The Light I didn't know, but at this moment my curiosity was waning. I knew too much. That's why I was here, with my make-believe husband, sitting on the cool ground in the shadows of tall trees, within the compound of a man I believed to be mad, one who'd authorized the killing of two people in front of more than a hundred witnesses.

When I turned toward my make-believe husband, his eyes were closed, and his breathing steady.

How much sleep had he gotten in the past seventy-two hours?

It was hard to comprehend that I'd only left the Northern Light on Friday morning, and now it was Sunday. So much had happened.

Releasing his hand, I gently traced his jaw with my knuckles and enjoyed the abrasion of the stubble against my skin. My cheeks rose as I remembered how I'd traced his face before the bandages were removed from my eyes. When I'd done that, I'd been trying to *see* him, to envision the man in my bed. He wasn't the man I'd envisioned.

Now I knew he was so much more.

As I began to stand, Jacob reached for my hand and pulled me back.

"No," he said, as I landed on his lap.

"I thought you were asleep. I was going to look around." Not that I could be looking around now, not with the vise grip he had on me.

"You're not allowed out of my sight."

"Allowed?" I asked with more than a bit of rebellion.

"We're still in The Light, so yes, *allowed*."

I shook my head and kissed his cheek. "You were sleeping. I wasn't in your sight."

The light brown staring intently back at me sparkled with the flickers of sunlight raining through the leaves.

"Yes, you were. You're always there." He kissed my nose. "I even see you in my dreams."

Framing his face, I puckered my lips. Our kiss was soft and understanding. Loosening his embrace, Jacob reached for the back of my neck and pulled me closer. As the fervency of our connection grew, our kiss and need deepened. When his tongue teased my lips, I willingly parted them, releasing a moan as our tongues danced.

When Jacob's hand sought the hem of my shirt, I remembered the boundary I'd placed, but instead of reminding him, I pulled my blouse from the confines of my skirt. His touch was warm as he unfastened the clasp of my bra and released my breasts. Sighing, I closed my eyes and enjoyed the sensations as the scarred tips of his fingers heightened my desire, caressing and taunting my beaded nipples. I pushed my chest toward him, wanting more of what he could do to my sensitive skin. Bowing his head, he delivered, sucking and nipping and sending pulsations elsewhere.

"Oh, Jacob," I purred, weaving my fingers through his dark wavy hair.

The ground where we sat was hard and dry, hardly the place to make love. It was also private and isolated. Moving from his lap, I lifted my shirt over my head and laid it on the ground. Discarding my bra, I reached for Jacob's hand and tugged him over me as I lay back with my head on my shirt.

"You said . . . ," he reminded me.

"Please, I want you."

Jacob's eyes never left mine as he bunched my skirt to my waist and removed my panties and shoes. "I," he said between kisses, "will always want you."

Reaching for his belt, I smiled as I rubbed the erection straining against his jeans. His groan rumbled through the trees. Ever since the first time—that I now knew *had* been our first time—when I'd asked to be the one to unbuckle his belt, he'd always left it for me. As I pulled it from its loops, I realized it was one of the ways he'd never forced me. I'd always wanted to make love with him. It'd always felt right.

Leather and musk replaced the scent of dry leaves, and my back arched upon the solid ground as he slid inside me. Humming, I adjusted to the delicious fullness as we moved in sync. Leaving a trail of fire, Jacob peppered my skin with kisses as he teased my neck and breasts and everything in between.

Unbuttoning his shirt, I ran my fingers along his chest and reveled in the way his muscles hardened and flexed beneath my palms. When I opened my eyes, the brown I sought was staring down at me.

"I love you," I said, choking on the emotion in my own voice. It was true. It wasn't Sara or Stella who loved Jacob; it was me, the new combination of each individual I'd once been.

Jacob reached behind my head and removed the tie securing my ponytail. Fanning my hair over the shirt, he grinned. "I've loved you since the first time I saw you, and now, the more I learn about you, the more I love."

He continued his slow sweet torture as he moved in and out, building the tempo, without rushing. During this brief reprieve, it was as if we didn't have the fate of nearly a thousand people in our hands. It was just us, husband and wife, making love on a warm summer day. I lifted my hips, wanting to be closer, needing him deeper.

"God, Sara, you feel so damn good."

I smiled. "I do." It wasn't a question. I felt good—stretched, filled, and good. Pressure began to build as my back again arched and my toes curled. Jacob knew exactly what I wanted, exactly what I needed. He didn't back away, but pushed me higher until the trees and the beams of sunlight disappeared, and my body convulsed around his. Whimpers replaced the rustling of the leaves as I clung to his shoulders while wave after wave of pleasure momentarily washed reality away. I opened my eyes in time to see the expression that I loved, strain morphing to bliss and a contented smile.

When our breaths began to even, Jacob collapsed, his chest flattening my breasts, and he brushed my hair away from my face. I was home in the arms of a man whom, if life hadn't been so cruel, I'd never have met. Despite it all, I'd found the place I wanted to be. In that moment I knew we'd make it. I did love Jacob.

CHAPTER 22
Sara

It was more than a little disconcerting to sleep in a room that we knew had cameras, but we didn't have any choice. Father Gabriel had messaged both Brother Micah and Jacob in the evening to inform them that we wouldn't leave for the Northern Light until the next afternoon. Apparently it was because he had plans. Last night the music and voices could be heard as the *celebration* ensued up at the mansion. I really didn't care what Father Gabriel did in his free time. I was just happy to know he wouldn't be doing it much longer. Today he had three Assembly and Commission meetings to attend before we could leave.

Thinking about the flight back to the Northern Light made me uncomfortable. I would need to ride in the cabin of the plane with him and didn't know whether he'd expect me to talk. My plan was to busy myself with reading his word and pray that he ignored me.

A little after three, Jacob looked up from his phone as the color drained from his cheeks. "Sara, finish getting ready. A car is coming to pick us up in fifteen minutes."

"A car . . ." I began to question, but his narrowing gaze reminded me of the cameras. "Yes, Jacob."

The timing was right. The last Commission meeting would have recently ended.

To finish getting ready, I just needed to gather our things and touch up my hair. I was thankful Jacob had told me to prepare for the possibility of spending the night. If he hadn't, I wouldn't have had clean clothes. Not only had yesterday been long, beginning at the Northern Light, but also our walk in the woods had covered my shirt and skirt in twigs and dirt. From the way my cheeks blushed at the memory, I wasn't complaining.

I was standing in front of the mirror when Jacob entered the bathroom. I knew the routine and waited for him to roll the towel blocking sound from escaping at the bottom of the door. He spoke first, his volume low.

"I don't like any of this. My gut tells me we need to run. I just don't know how."

"Where are we going in the car?"

He shook his head. "I'm not sure. I just spoke to Micah. He didn't receive the same invitation."

I took Jacob's hands. "It's probably that test. I mean, other than when we first arrived, I haven't seen Dylan. Why bring me all this way, if that's the test, to let me leave without seeing him?"

The muscles in Jacob's neck tensed as he inhaled and exhaled. "I'm going to have a fucking heart attack before this is over."

Smiling sweetly, I said, "I told you yesterday—I can do this. I can do it because of you." I shook my head. "It's more than me not wanting to mess this all up for you or me wanting to help bring this travesty down. I meant what I said. I really do love you. I won't be lying when or if I have to speak to Dylan. The only part I'll be lying about is not remembering him, but I'm a woman of The Light. I shouldn't be talking to him anyway, not without your permission."

"I thought of that. Father Gabriel supersedes your husband."

How had I forgotten that?

I did my best to sound confident. "Don't worry. I can do this."

Jacob stood behind me and moved us in front of the mirror. For a split second, I had visions of seeing us for the first time in the bathroom of the pole barn. Now our faces were familiar.

With his arms around my waist and his chin on top of my head, he said, "Your bruise is getting lighter."

Nodding, I grinned.

"You're still beautiful."

I lowered my eyes as my cheeks flushed.

"Sara, look up. I want you to know, I'm getting us out—away from The Light and away from the dark."

Spinning in his arms, I brushed my lips over his. "Where does that leave?"

"The real world."

"I trust you with my life. I have and I'll continue to do it. I also want Father Gabriel stopped. If I didn't before, after yesterday, I want him locked away forever. So, as much as I'd love to run, you've put too much time and energy into this. We'll make it a few more days." I had a thought and scrunched my forehead. "Do you think that's the Kool-Aid plan—drugs?"

He nodded. "I do. Some kind of drug, more than likely ingestible. I don't think even Father Gabriel could expect a thousand people to inject themselves."

His lips met mine.

"I never planned on falling in love," he confessed. "But I did. Do you know what I want, someday?"

I shook my head.

"To call you Stella McAlister."

My cheeks rose. "Was that a proposal?"

"No." His eyes sparkled. "You're already my wife."

The knock at the outer door shattered the warmth of his embrace as his arms stiffened. My heartbeat quickened as he whispered, "Only a few more days."

I inhaled his cool aroma of shower gel and replied, "Yes, Jacob."

Once again Brother Elijah was the one who came to get us. I'd forgotten to tell Jacob that I'd remembered Brother Elijah from before. I was certain he was the man who'd knocked on my car window when I'd been at the other buildings in the other neighborhood in Highland Heights. He had also been the parking lot attendant—my last memory.

This time I sat alone in the backseat, as Jacob sat in the front. Our ride didn't last long, and I wondered why Father Gabriel had sent a car at all, because once the SUV left the gate, it was barely a minute before it entered another gate, the one for the main house. My stomach twisted as the gate I'd tried to see past nearly a year ago opened, revealing a tree-lined cobblestone driveway.

Bloomfield Hills was an older, prestigious neighborhood, and many of the mansions had been built by the auto-industry moguls of the past. As we approached the stately home, its exterior a combination of red brick and limestone, I got the sense of American nobility.

Once Brother Elijah parked, I waited until Jacob opened my door. As soon as he did, I read the panic in his eyes. He'd told me more than once that he'd never been invited to the house, and here we were, about to enter. I'd seen the back of the house and the limestone balcony from the outbuilding, but up close it was even more stunning, showcased by the landscaping and the fountain in the center of the driveway.

As we walked up the steps, the door opened. At first I wondered whether it was on a sensor, but then I saw the woman who had opened it. She stood silently beside the door, and though she was never acknowledged, the blue scarf around her neck caught my attention. Other than that small bit of color, her plainness made her invisible. She never looked up, but in a few seconds I took in her fair complexion and the way her dark hair was secured in a low bun. The way she stood statuesque wearing a knee-length white shapeless dress and soft flat slippers facilitated the illusion that she didn't really exist.

As I entered the mansion, my senses on high alert, as if I were pre-paring for a story, I took in everything from the high two-story foyer with the domed ceiling and large chandelier to the mirrored set of curved staircases. With each step our shoes echoed against the opulent marble tile as Brother Elijah led us down a hallway. We came to a stop outside a set of French doors, their windows filled with thick ornate beveled glass, making it impossible to see inside.

As we stood, I tried to swallow, but couldn't. My mouth was sud-denly dry, a contrast to my palm in Jacob's grasp, which slid against his, clammy with perspiration. Brother Elijah's knock shattered the rever-berating silence as the recurring rap of his knuckles ricocheted off the intricate woodwork and marble floors.

Without lifting my eyes, I knew who'd opened the door. The faded jeans and boots were my first clues; the way Jacob's hand flinched, tightening his grip, was another.

"So nice of you to join us," Dylan said condescendingly as he opened the door.

Together we stepped over the threshold onto incredibly soft carpet. It was deep red, the color of blood. I tried to push that thought away. Brother Elijah entered last and shut the door. When I glanced in his direction he was standing with his arms crossed over his large chest, blocking our only means of escape.

What the hell? Did he think we'd try to run away?

I turned away from the door in time to see Dylan sit in a chair beside Father Gabriel. They were both on the other side of Father Gabriel's desk. From the way Dylan leaned back with his ankle resting on the opposite knee, I knew Jacob was right. Dylan and Father Gabriel were somehow connected. I'd never seen anyone appear as casual around the leader of The Light.

I waited to be told where to go before I looked up; however, we weren't directed to do anything. Instead we were left standing while Father Gabriel remained silent. When I gazed upward and my eyes met the piercing blue of my memory, my head tilted questioningly to the side, and then I shook my head, so fast it would be *almost* imperceptible, and lowered my gaze.

"Brother Jacob and Sister Sara," Father Gabriel began, "is there anything you'd like to say?"

"No, Father," Jacob replied.

"Sister?"

My breaths became shallow, and the room spun. "No, Father."

Dylan stood and stepped toward us. Just as quickly Jacob pulled my hand, moving me behind him as he stepped in front of me, blocking Dylan's path. Though Jacob didn't speak, from the way his body tensed and the closeness of their shoes, I envisioned the two men standing chest to chest. I was sure Jacob was taller than Dylan, but after what had happened yesterday, I feared that wouldn't stop Dylan from being the aggressor. As the silence grew, I closed my eyes and bit my lip.

"Gentlemen," Father Gabriel said, breaking the quiet. "That is not why I asked Brother Jacob and *his wife* here this morning."

At the phrase *his wife*, Jacob's grip loosened.

"Dylan, you'll have plenty of time to speak with Sister Sara. First we have business."

"Father, I'd prefer for Sara—"

"Brother Jacob," Father Gabriel interrupted, "I told you yesterday that I had questions. Dylan"—his tone became impatient—"sit down or leave."

I swallowed.

Why am I here? Why am I involved in this?

When Dylan sat, Jacob stepped to the side and pulled me forward. Once again we were standing side by side. Raising my eyes, I kept them locked on Father Gabriel.

"Brother Jacob," Father Gabriel continued, "since your entry into The Light, I've been impressed with you and your ability to learn quickly. You've known that, though, haven't you?"

"I've done my best to please you, Father."

"I spoke to Brother Michael."

Who is Brother Michael?

"He said he was pleased with the delivery," Jacob replied.

"Yes, he did. He told me the same. He also said that you refused the offer to stay the night at the Western Light."

"Yes, I had flight plans to fly into Lone Hawk."

"Did you fly into Lone Hawk?"

"Yes, I did. I borrowed the airport manager's truck and drove to Whitefish, and although I'd alerted them that I was coming, their inventory of supplies was shamefully low."

"Therefore, after completing one of the biggest shipments you've ever been entrusted with delivering, you took it upon yourself to change your prescribed flight plans, the same flight plans you weren't willing to alter for a Commissioner to stay at the Western Light."

I didn't understand what was happening or what they were saying. Maybe I should've asked more about his delivery and the envelope. Then again, my not knowing was the way it should be.

Jacob shifted, standing taller. "Yes, as an Assemblyman, I took it upon myself to decide that securing supplies for the nearly five hundred people at the Northern Light was most vital."

"And yet you called Brother Daniel."

"Yes, he's my overseer. I call him often."

"And Brother Benjamin?"

Shit!

"Father, if you're asking if I spoke with Brother Benjamin, I did, and Brother Luke, and Brother Abraham, and others on the Assembly. I wasn't aware that was a problem. If it is, I can certainly discontinue."

"It's no longer an issue."

What the hell does that mean?

My hand flinched, but Jacob secured his grip.

"Brother," Father Gabriel continued, "tell me where the envelope is that Brother Reuben gave to you."

"I'm most certain it's at the Northern Light. I apologize. I was distracted once I returned to the Northern Light."

"Distracted?" Dylan asked.

When Jacob didn't respond to Dylan, Father Gabriel told him to explain. Now Jacob was going to have to relay our cover story, in front of Dylan.

Jacob turned to me and let out a deep breath. "As you can see, Sara's been corrected."

"Yes," Father Gabriel replied.

"It happened Thursday night. Brother Benjamin called me on Friday after I'd left the Western Light to inform me that Sara had not been to work. When I arrived back to the Northern Light, as a husband, I needed to concentrate on my wife and why she'd missed work."

"Sister . . ."

My heartbeat raced. It wasn't Father Gabriel speaking to me. It was Dylan. When I didn't respond, he repeated himself.

Finally Father Gabriel said, "Since your husband obviously isn't going to give you permission to reply, I do. Answer my nephew."

Nephew, there it was.

I lifted my gaze to Dylan. "Yes, Brother."

"No . . . I'm not . . . never mind. Why didn't you go to work on Friday?"

"I was embarrassed that I had a visible reminder. I didn't want people to think poorly of my husband." I looked up at Jacob. "He's a good man."

"This is bullshit," Dylan mumbled under his breath. Louder he said, "So what happened once he came back?" His jaw clenched. "Did he *correct* you again?"

"Yes."

Dylan's hand slapped Father Gabriel's desk.

"Dylan, it's the way of The Light. You knew that," Father Gabriel replied. Then he asked me, "What did Brother Jacob do?"

"Because I was ashamed and didn't want to face people, my husband took me to the coffee shop, and later, after the Commission meeting, he took me to Brother Raphael's. I apologized to him for being selfish. I should've gone to work; instead I ran in the north acres and stayed there."

Father Gabriel stood. "I've heard enough. Brother Jacob, the envelope you received was not meant for you. I need it, and I need it now. I believe you need fewer distractions. Obviously you've been privy to an extraordinary amount of private information, even being here, in this house. I've been content, even pleased with your confidentiality in the past. The change of plans to Fairbanks bothers me. I assure you, if I had evidence of wrongdoing, we wouldn't be having this conversation. You've been trusted with a great deal. I want to believe that The Light is your first priority, and that you're as dedicated to The Light as The Light has been to you. I've decided that we will be going back to the Northern Light as soon as possible."

Thank God!

I exhaled.

"To facilitate your ability to not only remain focused and find the envelope Brother Reuben wrongfully gave to you but to also continue the duties you've been given, Sister Sara will remain here at the Eastern . . ."

No!

Jacob caught me as my knees buckled.

"Please, no," I begged, new tears blurring my vision and ability to witness the horror on Jacob's face.

"Sister!" Father Gabriel said. "Questioning me was one thing, arguing with my decision is quite another."

"B-but"—I said a silent prayer that this wouldn't make it worse— "I'm pregnant."

Jacob's eyes closed as both Father Gabriel and Dylan asked, "What?"

I collapsed in Jacob's arms.

CHAPTER 23
Jacob

What the fuck is happening?

I scooped Sara's limp body into my arms, her cheek against my chest. With everything in me I wanted to run out of this house, into the street, and beyond, yet I knew with Father Gabriel and Richards demanding answers, we'd never make it. Sara and I would be dead before we escaped this room.

"What the fuck? She's pregnant?" Richards asked, his volume louder than necessary.

"Dylan! Brother Jacob, Brother Elijah will take her," Father Gabriel offered, nodding toward Sara.

I readjusted Sara in my arms. "She's fine. I have her."

"For God's sake," Father Gabriel said, "at least put her on the sofa."

I turned to the wall behind me and saw a sofa I hadn't noticed when we arrived. Nodding, I gently laid her on the soft leather and smoothed her hair away from her face. For only a millisecond her eyes opened and I knew the truth—she was awake. I feigned a smile at her, wanting her to know how proud I was of her, and what a great job I thought she'd done. Damn, I'd wanted to pick her up and swing her in my arms when she'd called Richards *Brother*, but now . . . now . . . it didn't fucking matter. Now it was all falling apart around us.

"Brother Jacob." Father Gabriel demanded my attention.

I turned and straightened my stance, my leg against the sofa, not willing to leave Sara.

"Did you authorize your wife to stop taking her medicine? As an Assemblyman, you should know this is too early. She's only been on it for less than a year."

I exhaled. "No, I didn't. She's been counseling a female follower who works at the day care. After visiting the day care a couple of times, she began talking about children."

Richards shook his head in disbelief.

I went on, "I told her we'd decided to wait." I shifted my stance and exhaled. "I didn't know she'd stopped taking her birth control until Thursday night, after prayer meeting."

Father Gabriel's dark eyes opened in understanding as his brow disappeared behind his un-slicked-back hair. "I see."

Richards glared in my direction, sending more daggers with each second. If his uncle weren't right next to him, I suspected he'd try to give his right hook another workout. "You fucking beat her because she's pregnant?"

"No," I replied matter-of-factly. "I didn't *beat* her. I *corrected* her, and not because she's pregnant, but because in The Light, it's not her place to make such decisions. It's mine. She was willful. Her thoughts are my thoughts. She was disobedient not to share her plans for a child and make an unauthorized decision . . ." The entire time I spoke, regurgitating Father Gabriel's rules, Father Gabriel pressed his lips together and nodded, while the vein in Richards's neck pulsated and his nostrils flared.

Richards stood and walked around his chair to the window. The large pane looked out over the backyards, pool, and tennis courts, and beyond, to the outbuildings and landing strip.

"Dylan," Father Gabriel said, "do you have anything to say?"

He quickly turned. "Oh, yes, I have a shit-ton of things to say."

"Father," I began, trying to stop Richards's speech. With the pounding of my heart, the heart attack I'd mentioned to Sara earlier this morning seemed as if it was about to happen. "I'm not questioning your decision. I agree that I momentarily put my wife and her behavior above my duties. I assure you, I bought supplies in Fairbanks. Brother Noah can verify the purchases. Brother Micah can verify the supplies from the manifest, as the plane was unloaded. However, if I may, I beseech you to reconsider Sara's fate. You gave me a wife and instructed me to bring her into The Light. As you can see, I did that. Even without her medication, Sara is a woman of The Light—part of the chosen. If you find fault in my behavior, correct *me*. Sara hasn't been well. The morning sickness has been severe. Please let me take her back to the Northern Light, to our home, to Dr. Newton."

Richards's hands came together, the clap echoing as another one filled the air, their recurrence coming faster and faster. "Bravo, Brother, for an abuser you almost sound sincere."

"Shut the hell up!" My nerves were fried. "You want her back. Why? You don't care about her. If you did, she'd still be with you. If you did, she wouldn't be with me!"

"You don't know what the hell you're talking about!"

Father Gabriel's hand went in the air. "Enough. I've had enough of this pissing contest. Sara is staying here."

I clenched my teeth at the pain as he ripped my heart from my chest. After closing my eyes, I opened them in time to see Father Gabriel nod. I turned as Brother Uriel lifted a syringe from the bookcase.

"No! Wait! What the hell is that?" I asked as I moved between him and Sara.

"Step back, Brother," Brother Elijah warned.

"Father? What is that?"

"It's a syringe of the high-dose memory suppressor," Father Gabriel said, as if he were discussing a glass of water.

"Why?" Panic infiltrated my words as I remembered Sara's reasoning for not resuming her medications. "She hasn't gotten her memory back!" I took a deep breath, still keeping Elijah at bay. "Father, she knows your word. If you allow this, she'll have to relearn it all. She studied hard, well enough that she counsels other females. She's been doing *your* work. Why take that all away from her?"

"Don't you see?" Father Gabriel asked. "With no memory of the Northern Light or what she's seen here, she can be reassigned. I can't allow her to go back and tell others of what she's seen."

Reassigned?

"She won't! I haven't. You know I haven't. Sara may be strong-willed, but she's obedient. She won't disappoint you or me. And what will that drug do to our baby?"

"Brother, you said she stopped the medication of her own volition. You said you didn't authorize a child. Besides, she can't be reassigned if she's pregnant."

"I said I didn't authorize it, not that I didn't want it. Father"—my voice held more emotion than I wanted—"don't punish Sara and our child for my indiscretions. I'll do whatever you want. Please let my wife go back with us to the Northern Light."

Father Gabriel waved Elijah away and looked at Richards.

"No medicine, not yet," Richards said, looking directly at his uncle. "Obviously she doesn't have her memory. Fuck! She called me *Brother*." He turned back toward the window. "I don't understand how the hell it all works. Will I ever get Stella back?"

"You gave her away," I repeated for the millionth time.

He spun toward me and through clenched jaws sneered, "I saved her fucking life!"

"Enough!" Father Gabriel commanded. "I will *not* tolerate any more of this debate." He waved his hand toward Elijah. "Take her."

"Father—" I said, once again blocking Elijah's way.

"Brother Jacob, if you do not step aside at this moment, I'll be in need of a new pilot, and my nephew's efforts will have been for naught. I'm tired of this. A female is *not* worth this much trouble."

Yes, Sara is.

"You gave her to me. May I say good-bye?" I couldn't stop the tears now descending my cheeks.

He nodded. "Be quick about it. You may carry her to where she'll stay. Dylan will show you the way."

Richards's shoulders drooped, but he didn't argue or turn back around.

My body trembled as I turned and looked down at Sara. Her cheeks were coated in tears, though she'd managed to keep her emotions unheard. Hell, I didn't know whether she had or not. If she'd made noise, we'd made more. However, even Elijah seemed unaware that Sara had been listening. Once I had her in my arms, I turned back to Father Gabriel. "I promise I'll do all you ask. I've devoted myself to The Light and you. Father, I'm asking you to please keep her alive and safe. Please, after I've given you the envelope and earned back your trust, let me have her back. I'll be the perfect follower, Assemblyman, and pilot. I'll do anything you ask."

Father Gabriel stood, put his hands on the desk, and leaned forward. "Brother, because of your past performance and not based on anything you've said today, I'll reconsider my decision *after* I see results. In the meantime she'll stay alive."

I exhaled.

"However," he continued, "this female has caused me more problems than any who've been granted the same privilege. *If* the time comes to grant you your plea, be warned, you may not like what you find."

What the fuck?

"*Me,*" I tried one more time. "Me, correct me. None of this is her fault."

I couldn't see Richards's face, as he was still peering out the window. Though his voice was low, I heard every word. "It's *all* her fault. If she'd only listened."

I wasn't supposed to understand, yet I did, and the clarity his words provided sent a chill down my spine.

"Dylan," Father Gabriel demanded, "show Brother Jacob to Sara's new room. Hurry, I have a plane to catch and I need a pilot."

I turned away, unable to look at Father Gabriel a second longer. I'd crash the damn plane if I thought it would save her.

As Elijah opened the door, I looked directly into his dark eyes. Instead of meeting mine, his gaze dropped to the floor. We were Assemblymen. It was a fucking brotherhood, and yet here he was, holding the damn knife as Father Gabriel twisted. Richards remained quiet as I followed him down the hallway past an archway that led to a large kitchen. I didn't pay any attention, but noticed women in the kitchen, all wearing the same white dress as the woman I'd seen by the door. Finally we came to another door.

When Richards opened it, he hit a light switch and said, "Watch your step."

Really? Like he gives a shit.

My entire body chilled as I stepped out of the opulence and into a cold, dreary world. As if she could sense my apprehension, Sara's body shivered in my grasp, and her sad blue eyes peered up toward mine. I didn't want Richards to see, but in our brief gaze I tried to convey as much as I could. I tried to tell her I loved her, I'd move heaven and hell to get back to her, and I didn't want to do this.

Step by step, down into the underbelly of the mansion we went. The length of the staircase told me that this was more than the lower level—it was a subbasement. Even the temperature dropped as we continued down. When we neared the bottom, the wall to my right ended, and I stood in disgust at where we were, at what I saw. Unpainted concrete blocks created thick walls, while instead of crystal lighting fixtures, as I'd seen upstairs, naked lightbulbs hung from the ceiling. The room was nothing more than an unfinished cement box—even the floor was smooth, cold cement.

The permeating odor of disinfectant stung my lungs and reminded me of the clinic at the Northern Light. When I looked up to the ceiling there were exposed wooden beams with thick insulation stapled in between.

I didn't want to think about its purpose. Was it to keep the cold from the floor above or sound?

The only furniture in the room was four worn couches, appearing as if they belonged in a fraternity house or a garage sale, not a multi-million-dollar mansion. Four doors interrupted the concrete block. The first one was open, and I stopped, glancing inside. The room reminded me of barracks I'd inhabited, but more cramped. In a space I doubted was bigger than ten feet by ten feet were three sets of bunk beds with thin mattresses. As in an army barracks, each bed was made, the sheets perfectly folded and tucked in place, and like the larger room with the couches, this one was without color. Gray walls, gray metal bed frames, and gray blankets. Only the pillows were different. Still void of color, they were white.

"Over here," Richards said, reminding my feet to move.

Each step physically hurt; the pain inside me was excruciating. I couldn't leave her here. I'd promised her I'd stay with her. The sound of an opening door caused me to look up, away from Sara's face, which was burrowed into me, as it had been when I first lifted her after her accident.

Suddenly the smell made sense. The door Richards opened revealed a room that looked like our clinic, or more accurately one room of our clinic. This room had two hospital beds. I swallowed, knowing that the newly acquired wives were kept in a clinic in the building across from the church.

Why was there one here, in Father Gabriel's house?

My feet forgot to step as I saw the occupant of one of the beds. Her face was black and blue, as Sara's had been when I found her at the clinic. Her eyes were covered in bandages, and around her neck was a thick, leatherlike collar. Though I was sickened by the woman's injuries—or more accurately the girl's—it was her identity that shocked me. Attached to an IV was Sister Salome from yesterday's service.

When I turned to the other bed, I saw the IV pole with the clear bag of solution. I recognized it from Sara's accident.

"You said no medicine," I said, more as a question. I didn't want to trust this asshole, but I was out of options.

Richards nodded. "I meant it." He shrugged. "I just can't promise for how long."

He pulled back the sheet and blanket of the unoccupied bed. At least it all appeared clean. When I laid her upon the mattress, the déjà vu almost knocked me off my feet. It was as if I were back nine months in the past. I wished with everything in me that I were. If this were nine months ago, I would call my mission complete before Sara ever stopped taking her medicine. I would take her away, make her safe, and call for reinforcements.

Sniffling like a child with a cold, I gently smoothed her beautiful blonde hair away from her face, and turned to Richards. "Please?" I was too devastated to fight.

After he nodded and stepped from the room, I collapsed upon Sara's chest. "I'm so sorry. I'm so sorry." My words were indistinguishable as they ran together and overlapped one another. "I love you, Sara. I won't let this be the end. Stay strong. I know you can do this. Believe in yourself. Give this to me. I'll take it. I'll make sure you're safe any way I can. Never forget me or how much I love you."

The eyes that stared up from her bruised face shredded me. If I stared at them much longer there wouldn't be anything left. I reached for her hand and whispered, "Like before. Remember? Do you trust me?"

She squeezed my hand once, and despite the hell we were in, I smiled.

"I will get you out. I promise."

She squeezed again.

"I love you and our baby."

She squeezed again.

"Only a few days," I said, softer than everything else.

As she squeezed my hand she tugged me closer.

With my ear near her lips, she whispered, her words barely audible, "Bring him down. Don't think about me. I'll figure a way. You worry about your mission. I know after everything we've been through, we won't fail."

I started to shake my head. It wasn't her place to be the strong one.

She tugged me closer.

"We won't. Because one day I'm going to take you up on that promise of a new name."

I took a deep breath and closed my eyes. As much as I wanted to be the one to save her, I knew I had to have faith in her. I had no idea what was in store for her, but I believed that while Sara knew how to survive The Light, Stella would be the one to figure out how to escape.

Covering her with the blanket, I kissed her forehead.

"Jacob," Richards called from the other room. "You'd better hurry. My uncle's already pretty pissed."

I swallowed my emotion and whispered, "It will happen"—I lowered my voice more—"Mrs. McAlister."

And then I did the hardest thing I'd ever done in my life. I walked away.

CHAPTER 24
Dylan

I pulled the door closed, but not before taking one more look at Stella. She had to be unconscious. She hadn't moved since she'd collapsed in Gabriel's office. Maybe if she could stay out cold for a little longer I'd be able to get back to her. Once I was sure Gabriel was in the air then I'd be in charge.

The tumblers echoed against the cement block walls as I locked the door.

"Tell me you're the only one who has a key to that door."

My teeth clenched at the sound of Jacob's voice.

I wished I were the only one with a key. I really did. If he hadn't fucked up and gone to Fairbanks, she'd still be at the Northern Light. It wasn't as if I wanted her there, but it was a hell of a lot better than what Gabriel had planned.

I found my cockiest tone. "Are you now saying you'd be OK with that?"

His hands balled into fists, but at least he was keeping them at his sides. "No. I'm not OK with any of this. You're pissed because she had a blackened eye. Have you looked around this place? Did you see the woman in the other bed?"

I put my hand up to make him stop. "I'm serious. My uncle will be more upset than he is, if he has to wait for you."

"That's it? You're going to leave her here. What do you think will happen to her?"

I knew damn well what would happen. Did he think I was a fucking moron? But this place did have one advantage. I took a step toward him as my answer came out staccato. "I. Think. She'll. Be. Away. From. You."

Hatred glowed in his eyes. I'd seen it before, but not in a follower. Most of these Light psychos had the intellectual fortitude to be frightened or at least respectful of me. That wasn't the vibe this guy was giving. His expression wasn't like that of a normal follower. It reminded me of the look I'd seen on more than one asshole's face as I was about to arrest him. They were the ones breaking the law, but they blamed me for locking them up. It was the same thing. This guy had been the one to screw up, to cause my uncle to question his loyalty. He'd been the one who blackened Stella's eye, yet from the way his nostrils flared, he was blaming me because she was here.

Before I registered his movement, he was on me. His words spewing with spittle through clenched teeth. "You asshole! You think what you just did is better?"

He was the asshole. One word from Gabriel and me would turn him into polar bear food.

Before I could tell him, his forearm came against my throat, pinning me to the wall and momentarily halting my breathing.

"I could kill you right now," he threatened. "No one would hear or find your body until your uncle's forty-three thousand feet in the air, flying across this goddamn country at nearly seven hundred miles an hour."

I pushed toward him and backed away, giving myself much-needed air. "Asshole!" I seethed. I was a fucking cop. I dealt with lunatics like this before breakfast. I didn't care how fucking big or strong he was, I knew what I was doing.

My hands came up, and as they did, so did my leg. My boot planted to his torso. As soon as my leg straightened, he was the one gasping for air, his body tumbling backward against one of the filthy old couches before he regained his balance.

If I told my uncle now, Stella wouldn't have a chance. "You're really losing it," I said. "If I fucking tell Gabriel any of this, you're the one who's dead."

"I don't give a damn about *myself*. You think I give a shit about me when my wife and child are locked in there? If I can't help Sara, I don't—"

Wife and child? As if any of this shit was real.

I ran my hand through my hair and slowed my words. "That's *not* her name."

"I know that. I was told the name she used in the dark, but now she's in The Light—where you put her."

"She'd be dead if I hadn't, and you were wrong earlier. It *is* all her fault. I tried to stop her. Hell, Mindy hadn't gotten as deep into it, and they took her. I did everything I could to stop both The Light and Stella. She's stubborn as hell, and too damn good at what she did. By the time she was too deep, Gabriel wanted her dead. I convinced him to take her as far away as possible, and do the memory thing. I didn't know how it all worked. Fuck, I can't be seen around the temple or any of the buildings in Highland Heights. I'm mostly only here. I don't want to know what happens *here*, much less over there."

Jacob stilled before tilting his head to the side. "Wait, who's Mindy, and are you saying Sara's a cop? Or she *was*?"

This guy really was clueless, and the last thing I needed to do was be the one who filled him in. I shook my head. "No, and fuck, I shouldn't be saying any of this, but I did try to save her. Now, Gabriel's pissed at you. I overheard the conversation. You did something that's made him suspicious. That never ends well. I know enough about how this works to know that if you don't get your shit together, your days are numbered, and if you're banished, so is she."

I went on, "I had to think of something, so I asked Gabriel for confirmation that she was alive. For some reason he agreed. There were never any plans for her to go back to Alaska. Reassignment was, is, her only hope." I shrugged toward the locked door. "I even tried to have her given back to me, but he was adamant that wasn't an option. They're too concerned that allowing her back to her real life would result in the return of her memories."

I refused to think about my uncle's plans—the brides. I had a plan too. It was to get Stella assigned to the Western Light. It was better than here. I respected my uncle and all he'd built, but he was a sick twisted bastard when it came to women.

The shrill ring of Jacob's phone filled the basement, echoing off the walls. From the look on his face, the way the color drained from his cheeks, I had a pretty good idea of who was calling. *Father Gabriel* didn't like to wait.

I shook my head. This guy was doing everything he could to be polar bear food. Pressing my lips together, I leaned against the wall and watched as he pulled the phone from the pocket of his jeans.

He took a deep breath, and his chest inflated and deflated before he answered. "Brother Jacob . . . I'm on my way . . . Yes, I understand . . . I'll go through the yards."

I gave the guy credit. He held it together on the call.

His eyes met mine. "They've already driven to the landing strip. I'll get your uncle everything he needs. I'll find that damn envelope, and *get my shit together*." He emphasized my words. "Please, watch out for her."

I nodded. "It's safer here right now, with him at the Northern Light."

That was the truth. Part of me actually felt sorry for this guy. No matter what he did, he wasn't coming back. Once he found the information that Gabriel needed, he was as good as dead. I'd even heard they had a new pilot set up to take his place.

Gabriel didn't put up with shit from anyone. Half of this fuckup had started at the Western Light. The envelope Reuben was supposed to give to this idiot had been simply a test. Somehow either Michael or Reuben had given him the wrong one—the one with the pass-phrase needed to access overseas accounts. Michael might be one of the original three, but I'd bet he'd received an earful from my uncle on that move.

Personally I would have laid Michael out too. Then again, if he hadn't given Jacob that envelope, even by mistake, Jacob probably wouldn't have made it back to the Eastern Light, and then neither would Stella. If he had made it here with the envelope, tomorrow on the police scanner I'd be hearing about some tall white dude with no fingerprints dead in an abandoned building in Highland Heights.

They really needed to spread out the bodies better. I'd told them more than once.

"If you ever cared about her—"

I lowered my voice. "Haven't you listened to a goddamn word I've said? I cared. I still do."

"Then watch out for her, and try to hold off on that medicine."

I nodded, though the medicine was exactly what she'd get. It was the only way to reassign her to the Western Light.

I glanced at my watch. Right now he needed to get out of here, so Gabriel would be gone. That would give me at least a few days to figure out my plan. I tilted my head toward the steps. "Let me show you the best way to the backyards."

I hesitated on the second step while Jacob stared at the door to the room where we'd left Stella. When I cleared my throat, he squared his shoulders and turned toward me. I didn't turn back around. I didn't need to. The heavy sound of his boots stayed close behind as I walked back up the stairs and closed the door to the basement. We walked silently through hallways and rooms, down another set of stairs, and finally out to the back lawns.

There were things I could say, things to hurt him. Part of me wanted to. By all rights I should do more than that. I imagined pulling my gun from the holster and planting a bullet in his forehead. After what he'd done to Stella, not just the eye, but changing her, turning her into one of the zombie wives, he deserved it.

I didn't need to be the one to dirty my hands. As soon as the envelope was found, his fate was sealed. The way I saw it, he'd never see Stella or even Bloomfield Hills again. Jacob was yesterday's news.

As he passed me he didn't turn in my direction. That was all right. As I watched him start running through the grass toward the landing strip, an appropriate movie quote came to mind.

Under my breath I muttered, "Dead man walking. No"—I smirked—"running."

CHAPTER 25
Jacob

Sara's words haunted me, while at the same time they reinforced my resolve.

"Bring him down." Her determination and faith in me repeated over and over as I ran down the hill and through the yard.

It took everything I had to walk away. I wasn't sure I could have done that without knowing that Stella was awake inside her. Sara's conditioning could have left her vulnerable, and I'd have been responsible for that. But Stella, she was the backbone behind Sara, and I had to have faith that she'd make it.

If it weren't that the Cessna Citation required two pilots, I'm certain Father Gabriel would have had Micah leave without me. As I passed the pool and tennis courts, I recalled the other reason that he wanted me to return to the Northern Light. It was that damn envelope.

I forced my mind to do what Sara had said and think about the future—the mission. Why would Brother Reuben give me something so important that Father Gabriel was asking for it? Had he? Or was this some mind trick—some dumb test—some move to get me back to the Northern Light where my banishment would be more easily hidden?

I tried to remember what I'd done with it. At the time I'd concentrated more on the way Reuben removed it from his jacket, purposely exposing his firearm. I'd never suspected that it contained something important.

Richards's words came back, blaming Stella for all of this, and indignation rose up. He was wrong. The Light was to blame, and so was Father Gabriel. It wasn't her. Being good at her job was why she'd decided to come back to The Light. She wanted them to go down as much as I did. I said a prayer that the stubbornness he'd mentioned would keep her alive.

Though she'd sworn to save herself, I couldn't stop the weight of responsibility that bogged down my steps as I neared the outbuildings. Regardless of what Richards said, Stella Montgomery was in this compound, in that basement, for one reason. Because of me. If she hadn't agreed to help my mission, she'd be safe in witness protection. Barring some miracle that would allow her to escape, the only way to save her, once I left for the Northern Light, was to authorize the raids.

In the chaos a small smile graced my lips. Damn, he was right about her stubbornness, and I loved it. I wanted it.

Sara and I ran farther than the distance from the mansion to the landing strip all the time, but today was different. Today I was running for my life, for her life, and consequently, by the time I reached the outbuildings, my breathing was heavy and labored. As I opened the door of the building Sara and I'd shared, the scent of floral shampoo caused my chest to clench.

Instead of my giving in to the overwhelming urge to crumble, the aroma gave me strength. I needed to be strong too. I couldn't let leaving her here at the Eastern Light ruin me. If I did, all that I'd accomplished over the past three years would be for nothing. For her future as well as my operation, I needed to face Father Gabriel and convince him that I was a changed man. I wasn't the man who had stood in front of him and pleaded for his wife. I'd learned my lesson, and was now the best damn follower he'd ever had. It was the only way—our only chance.

As I'd said—*the best performances of our fucking lives!*

Taking a deep breath, I remembered that today was Monday, only three days since Sara had left the Northern Light. A glance at my watch told me it was just after four in the afternoon here in Michigan. With the time difference and the time it took to fly to the Northern Light, we'd land about half an hour after we left Bloomfield Hills. Taking a deep breath of the floral-scented room, I turned, straightened my shoulders, and walked back out into the Michigan sunshine.

My goal was that both Sara and I would make it until Wednesday. Just two more days.

Micah and I were scheduled to fly to Fairbanks on Wednesday for supplies. There was a special distributor that provided the ingredients for the pharmaceuticals. We made the exchange only once a month. I'd been included on those runs since I first came to the Northern Light. Since it was only raw materials, this exchange didn't require the higher clearance I'd needed to deliver the actual pharmaceuticals. However, due to the sensitivity, it had always been done with two pilots. It was one of the reasons Father Gabriel had insisted I return to work after Sara awoke. When we made it to Fairbanks, I'd buy a burner phone and authorize the raids. It wouldn't happen immediately, but it would happen.

Sara and I both had to make it a couple of days.

As I walked toward the Cessna, my eyes met Micah's. He didn't need to speak. I saw the combination of question and devastation in his expression. Ten minutes ago that look would've crushed me, but not now. Pressing my lips into a straight line, I nodded. "I'm sorry I made you wait," I said, looking around for Father Gabriel.

Micah grabbed my arm and whispered, "Jacob, I-I'm . . ." He didn't finish. There were no words.

I stood taller. "I'm getting her back. Let's go, so I can come back. Where is he?"

"In the plane, with Brother Elijah."

My eyes opened wide. "Is Elijah going to the Northern Light too?"

Micah shrugged. "I don't know what's happening, with anything, and I hope you're right."

I nodded. His expression told me that he didn't believe my declaration that I would get Sara back. If I were only Jacob Adams, I wouldn't believe me either; however, I wasn't Jacob Adams. I was Agent Jacoby McAlister, and I was fucking doing this.

Step by step I climbed the stairs, ready to get this show started. Standing at the top of the stairs, with the glare of the sunshine behind me, I was waiting for my eyes to adjust when Father Gabriel spoke.

"We're not off to a good start."

It wasn't enough information. Micah wouldn't know what he meant, but Elijah, sitting across from Father Gabriel, did, and so did I. I saw Elijah's dark eyes staring in my direction. No longer did they convey the pity I'd seen at the mansion. Father Gabriel was referring to the promise I'd made standing in front of his desk, the promise to be the best pilot and follower he'd ever had. And instead of doing that, I'd made him wait—something I'd never done before.

Of course I'd never been forced to leave my wife locked in a dungeon either.

Exhaling, I held my hands behind my back and spread my stance. "I apologize, Father. As you've assured, I no longer have distractions. My devotion is fully with you and The Light."

He nodded to me and turned to Elijah. "It seems things are under control. I'll contact you once we're at the Northern Light. For every minute my call's delayed, you know what to do."

I clenched my teeth, but refrained from speaking.

Elijah looked at his watch. "Father, what time did you plan on making that call?"

A smirk came to Father Gabriel's lips. "I'd planned on leaving here no later than three-thirty. With that schedule I'd be calling by eight."

Fucking asshole!

"Then we'll stick with the original plan. It'll be my pleasure," Elijah replied.

Yeah, so much for the brotherhood of the Assembly.

The next time I saw Elijah, I hoped it would be in a holding cell. Kool-Aid was too damn good for him. Our eyes connected as he stood, and this time he didn't look away. Once he made his way down the steps, Micah came aboard, lifted the stairs, and locked the cabin door.

The sound reminded me of the lock Richards had secured and momentarily opened a floodgate of thoughts. As I worked to corral them, Micah spoke.

"Father, is there anything you need before we take off?"

"No," Father Gabriel said, looking at me. "However, I don't want the curtain closed to the cockpit."

What the hell did he think I'd do? He'd just threatened my wife in my presence. My main goal was to fly this $30 million tin can as fast as it could go. He'd be back to the Northern Light in time to make that damn call. As Micah and I entered the cockpit, I went for the pilot's seat, but Micah blocked me. We'd always agreed to switch off responsibilities with each flight. We'd been doing that for years, and he'd piloted us to the Eastern Light, which meant it was now my turn. However, instead of arguing, I nodded, thankful, as Micah spoke wordlessly. His eyes told me that he was upset too, but he'd be able to concentrate, better than I. My mind would be somewhere else.

"As fast as possible," I whispered.

He nodded.

Once we were airborne and had given our coordinates and plans to the Detroit airport, I settled back. With the open sky and setting sun ahead of us, continually out of reach, I let my mind go somewhere else. It was as Micah had predicted, but it was different. I wasn't allowing my thoughts to linger in the mansion in Bloomfield Hills. I let them go there only long enough to say a prayer that Sara would make it two more days. Then I switched gears and allowed my mind to focus on the future, one different from the one the man sitting in the cabin of this plane predicted, a future I planned on delivering—sooner rather than later.

With each mile I formulated my plan. Wednesday's shipment couldn't be canceled or changed. It had to happen. Too many alarms would sound if everything didn't go as scheduled. The Light was a too-well-oiled machine. I didn't mean the religious organization. I meant the large moneymaking enterprise.

That was when I remembered Thomas. I wondered when he was next scheduled to fly to the Northern Light and if anyone had figured out that he was missing. If someone had, would that lead to unwanted attention on the Northern Light? The flight plans I'd been happy he'd made last Friday now had me worried. If Father Gabriel had been notified of his disappearance, I hadn't been informed, and I doubted Thomas was scheduled to return on the weekend. It would be today or later this week.

I didn't know whether Father Gabriel's concern over the stupid envelope was real or not, but either way it needed to be found.

I worked to mentally retrace my steps. The obvious conclusion was that I'd put it in the pocket of my coat; however, Montana wasn't Alaska. I didn't remember whether I'd worn a jacket at the Western Light. If I had, that was probably where it was. If I hadn't and I'd had it in my hand when I boarded the plane, maybe I'd left it in the cockpit. Or I could have taken it with me into the airport in Lone Hawk. Hell, I couldn't remember. Maybe I'd taken it in the truck I borrowed or left it in the motel room . . .

Perspiration dotted my brow. The possibilities were multiplying, and each one added to my apprehension.

As soon as we arrived, I planned to check the cockpit of the smaller plane, after I made damn sure Father Gabriel got to his apartment or the temple, or wherever he wanted to be to make that damn phone call to Elijah.

Delivering that envelope was the first step toward buying me the time I needed—just a couple of days.

CHAPTER 26
Sara

Though my eyes ached to open, I stayed still, contemplating my next move as questions bombarded my mind, momentarily quelling the fear I should have been feeling at my new circumstance.

Was I being watched? How would I escape? How, in this day and age, could this be happening? How did one man have so much power?

The answer to the final question was simple. We, Father Gabriel's followers, had given it to him. With each follower—chosen or otherwise—we'd given him our minds and our bodies. We'd willingly done his bidding, physical or psychological, without considering the consequences or the human toll.

Each day without my medicine made the world clearer. I could look upon The Light with a new perspective. The daily psychological warfare was fierce and perfectly executed. If it were only a religious cult, it would be well planned, but now, considering the numbers I'd seen at the lab combined with the small bit of information Jacob had shared during our late-night talk about the pharmaceutical enterprise, the operation as a whole was flawless.

Each and every person in The Light fortified Father Gabriel's strength. He couldn't do what he did alone, but with nearly a thousand people, he moved mountains and ruined lives. He did it in the name of

God, but he was the only one profiting. Each of us was made to believe that without him we'd be no one. The reality was the opposite.

Without us, he'd be nothing.

I recalled the young couple at the temple yesterday. In front of more than a hundred followers, Father Gabriel had ordered their deaths. Then today he'd ordered mine. Not literal death, but the death of Sara Adams. He'd said the loss of my memories of the last nine months was necessary for reassignment.

Were women so worthless in his mind that he could manipulate their lives as if they were toys he could take from one man and give to another?

As my memories of life in the dark and in The Light continued to blend, I recalled a prayer Jacob had said on one of my first days as Sara. At the time I hadn't understood the full impact. I hadn't been able to comprehend. Now I did. Jacob had said the prayer as I was about to eat for the first time. He'd said, "Let this food be a reminder that privileges given can be taken away." That's what Father Gabriel had done today. The life Jacob and I'd built, no matter how perverse our circumstances, had been a privilege, and in a simple declaration Father Gabriel had taken it away.

Perhaps I was suffering from dissociative identity disorder. As I lay motionless, I had the unreal ability to see everything from two different perspectives—Sara's and Stella's. I recognized how well The Light had conditioned me. If it hadn't, I would have fought the descent into this cold dungeon. Most normal people would. However, from this dual perspective I could assess that as Sara I was no longer normal. I'd been conditioned to accept that the men knew best and to never question.

Though there was a sense of peace in that mentality. I would fight heaven and hell to stop them from doing it to me again. I wasn't in the circumpolar North. I was in an upscale community in Michigan. All I had to do was get out of this compound and get to the FBI. Though that seemed a difficult goal, considering the obstacles I'd already survived, it wasn't impossible.

As both mind-sets settled into my psyche, I took Sara's peace and put my trust in the man who'd kept me safe for the last nine months. I also took Stella's fear and let it come to life. Fear had a purpose. It kept people safe. It was that little voice that said not to go down the dark alleyway, or the rapid pulse that occurred when things weren't as they appeared. Fear happened for a reason, and I needed to embrace it.

To survive this, I needed both, the peace and the panic. I needed out of this basement.

Muffled voices continued to waft from the other side of my locked door. Though some were louder than others, I couldn't make out the words; however, I recognized both voices. I also heard the emotion in both. I had difficulty comprehending that Jacob and Dylan were even talking to each other, but recognized that the absurdity was more than coincidence.

I tried to recall all I'd heard in Father Gabriel's office. I didn't have enough understanding for any of it to make sense. We had been prepared for the test. When I'd called Dylan *Brother*, it hadn't been a Herculean effort. Though I'd known him in what seemed like another life, he hadn't been introduced to me. Until Father Gabriel gave his permission, I hadn't been told I could even speak to him. Therefore, once I was granted permission, the title came without thought. After all, as Sara, I knew that all men deserved a title.

Definitely dissociative identity disorder.

I'd hoped that after announcing my pregnancy I'd be allowed to stay with my husband. Since that'd been my goal, I'd failed. However, the announcement may have helped me avoid the drug Brother Elijah had planned to inject. Though Jacob was the one who initially stopped Brother Elijah, we both knew Jacob's power was limited. He and Brother Elijah were both Assemblymen. Father Gabriel's decrees were the final word. Then again, it wasn't any of them who'd stopped the injection. It was Dylan.

How did Dylan have that much power? Had he always, even when we'd been dating? How could I have dated someone involved in The Light and not known?

I remembered my boss, Bernard Cooper, his concern about Dylan, and how he'd had Foster, my coinvestigator, look into his private life. I'd been the one to tell him to stop. I also realized that I'd discovered all the information I had about The Light while Dylan was right there. He'd gone with me to the morgue. He'd seen my pictures of the white building in Highland Heights. I'd given him a key to my apartment. Suddenly I wondered if my research had ever been found. I wondered if Bernard or Foster had gone through all I'd uncovered.

Of course they hadn't.

My inner turmoil turned to anger as I thought that like my memory, more than likely, my research had been cleared away. Then again, Dylan had been the one to stop the medicine—the medicine that would allow my reassignment. What Brother Elijah had been about to inject wasn't like the pills that Jacob had wanted me to restart. Father Gabriel had called it the *high-dose* memory suppressor.

I didn't want to think about it. Instead I held tightly to a sliver of hope that maybe together Jacob and Dylan could buy me some time, time I needed to save myself. I continued to believe until the voices stopped.

A muffled sob erupted from my chest and my breath stuttered. The voices were gone. They'd left me and soon Jacob would fly back to Alaska. I was truly alone.

The new silence came like a thick cloud settling in the chilled basement. In some ways it reminded me of my psyche after my accident. Time lost meaning as only my breaths moved me, and then slowly I became aware of the world beyond my closed eyes. I fought the cloud and pushed it away. The fine hairs on my arms stood to attention as Stella's fear was realized. I wasn't alone.

Slowly I opened my eyes and turned my head. On one side of my bed, radiating coolness, was a gray wall. In the dim light I made out the rectangles and knew it was made of cement blocks. The far wall was also made of cement blocks. There was the one door, the one Jacob had walked through, and the one I'd heard lock. A dim light came from a lightbulb hanging from the ceiling. Unlike the grand ceilings upstairs, this ceiling was nothing more than insulation and boards.

As I turned to my right my breathing hitched. There was another bed in the room and someone was in it—a woman. Opening my eyes wide, I quickly sat and backed away, scooting myself to the top of the bed. Backed against the cold cement wall, I pulled my knees against my chest, while my heart beat erratically and I stared at the silhouette of a body. Memories of bodies on Tracy's table in the morgue prickled my skin with goose bumps as I tried to determine whether the woman was alive.

I released a breath as recognition propelled me from the remnants of my fog. Despite the bruises, contusions, and bandages around her eyes, I recognized the girl in the bed. Moving as quietly as I could, I eased myself to the cold hard floor. With my gaze narrowed to the other woman, I gasped as I nearly toppled an IV pole holding a bag of clear liquid near my bed.

Shit! Have they medicated me?

Quickly I scanned my arms. For only a moment, I feared that somehow I'd lost time, but my arms were clear of IV marks. Step by step I moved closer. Standing at her bedside, I saw the thick leather collar around her neck. Only a few inches wide, it wasn't a brace, and seeing it, I was once again reminded of the bodies in the morgue. The one I recalled seeing with Dylan had had a thick bruise around its neck. Taking a deep breath, I reached for the woman's hand. In the dim light, the tips of her fingers had the same ghostly hue as mine, and even in the coolness, her hand had warmth.

Thank God!

She was alive.

She might have been alive, but the swelling and black-and-blue contusions of her face peering out from the bandages over her eyes, as well as the ones on her exposed arms, told me she'd lived through hell.

Attached to her other arm was the IV, with two bags hanging from the pole. One was the same as the one near my bed. I hoped the other was pain medicine. I eased her blankets down and found a cast on her right leg. I knew where I'd seen her before. She was the girl from the service.

"Sister Sara, leave her alone."

I turned at the voice. I'd been too interested in the unconscious woman to hear the opening of my cell. In the doorway was the figure of a woman. By her attire, I wondered whether she was the same one who'd opened the door when we first entered the mansion.

"Come with me," she said.

Nervously I tugged the silver cross on my necklace and ran it up and down the chain. This was my means of escape. It couldn't happen from within this cell. I needed to comply, no matter where she led. As I followed, I squinted—not that the outer room had natural light, but it was brighter than the room where I'd been held. I quickly scanned the new room. It was depressingly like the one I'd just left, unpainted cement block and cement floor, with only old couches as furniture.

"In here," the woman called from another room.

As I followed her voice, my steps slowed at the threshold of the room where she'd led me. It was a bathroom.

"You have three minutes, strip and shower."

"Excuse me?" I asked, my knees once again feeling too weak to hold me.

Up close I saw that she wasn't the same woman who'd opened the front door. This one had dark-blonde hair in a bun at the back of her head and was wearing the same shapeless white dress and soft shoes, but her scarf was a darker shade of blue. Her lips pursed and her eyes narrowed. Stepping closer, she lifted my silver cross and pulled. I gasped as the fine chain snapped.

"Strip and shower. That means your jewelry. You're no longer chosen nor are you married. I personally don't care if you succeed or fail. However, I'll give you a bit of advice—follow directions the first time."

When I didn't reply she went on, "We all know the chosen think they're so much better than the rest of us."

Defensive at her tone and words, I stood taller.

She closed the distance between us until we were nose to nose. "Do you have a problem with following directions from *followers*?"

"No, I don't know what you think about the chosen, but I assure you we follow directions. We are also used to sisters being helpful, not cruel. Give me back my necklace." I wasn't sure where my strength came from, but I'd spent nine months subservient to men. I didn't plan on adding women to that equation.

She smirked. "Well, like I said, your success or failure is no skin off my back." She laughed. "It will be off yours. And I *am* being helpful. Strip, shower, you'll not need the necklace. Here we wear something else, something that defines us as Father Gabriel's personal followers, *the brides of The Light*. So do as you're told and shut up. You may live long enough to understand the honor of being here."

Brides of The Light?

I couldn't process. All I knew was that I needed to play this damn game long enough to get out. What I didn't know was what that would entail.

"Please," I tried, hoping for compassion. "I don't know what's happening. Give me back my necklace. I'll keep it and my ring hidden."

She stepped past me. "You now have two minutes."

Biting my lip, I began to shut the door when she stopped me.

"You're on constant surveillance. I'm not getting punished because of you. Hurry."

I turned toward the shower and began to take off my clothes. Once I was down to my underwear, I turned on the water. The trickling stream was freezing cold. I tried to adjust the warmth, but my clock was ticking and the temperature wasn't changing. When I looked back over my shoulder, my new sister shrugged.

"You don't have time to wait for it to warm. Besides, down here, it doesn't."

"Why do I need to shower?"

"You have a lot to learn. Did your husband allow you to question?"

"No, but you're a female. I can question females."

She pointed at her scarf. "Only if you've earned a darker color. Today you'll receive your white scarf. You may only question females with the same color or lighter. To everyone else you don't exist. Now get in."

Removing my underwear, I stepped under the ice-cold shower. My teeth chattered and my skin prickled as I wet my hair and body. The entire time I avoided turning toward the woman who watched my every move.

"Time's up," she announced, turning off the water. "Follow me."

Soaked and without a towel, I shivered as I wrapped my arms around myself in an attempt to shield my body. Next she opened a door to a new room. My eyes opened wide as I took in another concrete cell. This one was empty of furniture. On the cement floor was a white dress similar to the one she wore, a pair of underwear, and shoes.

"Sister?" I tried asking. "Could I go back into the bathroom? I didn't get a chance to use the toilet."

She rolled her eyes. "Hurry."

Thankfully no one else was around as I walked nude back to the bathroom, leaving a wet trail. On the floor, where I'd seen it earlier, was the silver cross that had come loose from my necklace. She'd put the chain in her pocket. As I sat on the toilet, I covered the cross with my bare foot. Seconds later she was watching me again. I kept it hidden as I washed my hands.

When she stepped away, telling me to hurry and dress, I reached for the cross. With no other alternative, I ran it under the water and placed it on my tongue. Swallowing, I vowed they weren't taking everything from me. Once back in the other room, I dressed, the material of the white shift clinging to my wet skin. Just as I was beginning to feel better about being covered, I held my breath at the sound of heavy footsteps crossing the outer room. They were getting closer.

Instinctively my chin dropped and my head bowed. With no bra, the cold temperature, and the light weight of my dress, I was keenly aware of my hardened nipples. Turning my shoulders forward, I tried to hide my breasts, which rubbed against the shift.

"Sister Mariam, will Father Gabriel be pleased?"

Mariam must be the name of the woman who'd been directing me. Through veiled eyes I watched the large man I'd never seen before talk with her, while at the same time scanning me up and down. When his gaze lingered on my breasts it added to my unease.

"No, Brother."

What were they talking about?

"That's too bad. We can't disappoint Father Gabriel."

"No, Brother. She'll learn this is an honor."

The man brushed Mariam's cheek. Though the action could have seemed affectionate, in reality it twisted my stomach.

"Leave us."

"Yes, Brother Mark."

Still barefoot, I backed away as Brother Mark stepped closer. When my back hit the far wall I gasped, causing him to laugh.

"Sister, Father Gabriel is particularly interested in your lessons and your correction. He's put a strict zero-tolerance policy on you. Assuming you're allowed to continue your lessons, we'll get well acquainted."

I flinched as he brushed my cheek.

"Please."

"Sister, I'll tell you when it's time to beg. Now it's time for your first lesson."

The bile from my stomach surged upward as Brother Mark reached for the buckle of his belt.

CHAPTER 27
Jacob

With the winds in our favor and more acceleration than we usually needed, we landed with time to spare for Father Gabriel and Elijah's timetable. As we unbuckled our seat belts Micah nodded in my direction. Taking a deep breath, I reined in my nerves and walked to the cabin of the plane. It was time to make the same speech I'd made numerous times. "Father Gabriel, would you like either Brother Micah or me to drive you to the community or would you like one of us to call for another member of the chosen?"

Leaning back against the soft leather, he casually looked up at me. "It does seem we've made excellent time."

"Yes, the winds helped to keep you on schedule."

Father Gabriel stood. "I need that envelope now, yesterday even. I'll contact Brother Raphael, you two do what you need to do for the plane, and you find me what I need. I expect to hear from you this evening. I don't think you want to disappoint me."

"No, I don't. The call to Brother Elij—"

He lifted his hand, stopping my words.

"Is no longer your concern. Remember, we've eliminated your distractions. Finding the envelope is your only concern."

Eliminated? I swallowed my retort as cool Alaskan summer air filled the plane and we turned toward Micah and the open door. "Father, I will get the cart," Micah offered as he lowered the steps.

Ever since we'd seen polar bears on and near the landing strip, Father Gabriel had decided he needed a ride to and from the hangar. While that normally didn't bother me, right now I secretly thought how fortuitous a bear mauling would be.

"Go, Jacob," Father Gabriel said, "you have things to do."

I nodded, following Micah from the cabin and down the stairs. A quick scan of the trees and open space revealed nothing out of the ordinary. As we walked toward the hangar, Micah was a few steps ahead of me.

"I'll get the cart. You get the tug," he called.

That was fine by me. I'd much rather secure the Cessna than transport Father Gabriel. Quite frankly, if it had been up to me, I'd have tied fresh meat around his neck and left him for the bears.

Getting the tractor and the tug, I thought about the parts of this mission I'd miss. The flying and even ground crew duties were at the top of my list. I purposely didn't put Sara on that list, because after this was over, I wasn't losing her.

I had the Cessna pushed back and inside the hangar by the time Micah made it back inside. I'd just started the post-flight checklist when he said, "Go. Do whatever he keeps telling you to do."

I nodded, but the idea of setting foot back in our apartment without Sara had me trembling with both anger and fear. Though I kept trying to think of other things, I couldn't stop the thoughts of what she was enduring at the mansion in Bloomfield Hills. No matter what it was, as long as she was alive, we'd survive.

"Did someone come get him?" I asked.

"Yes, Brother Raphael. I'm probably paranoid, but I get the feeling there's something up. As soon as I'm done with this checklist, I'm heading back to the community. I want to get to Joanna . . ." His expression saddened. "I'm sorry, Brother."

"Don't be sorry. Take care of her and little Isaiah." I tried to not think about the man who'd become my friend and his small family. The human side of The Light was the reason we were back here, why we'd risked everything to give the FBI a few more days.

"I'll do my best. You know I've been praying for Sara."

"Thank you." It was all I could say. My first job was to focus and try to remember what I'd done with the envelope. Walking toward the small plane, I imagined the cockpit and where I could have stashed it. If I hadn't been looking at the floor, I wouldn't have seen them, but I was and I did. On the concrete floor, every few steps were small drops of something.

Anger swelled inside me, causing my pulse to race as the thudding of my heart filled my own ears. Was it blood? Was it Sara's? Had Thomas done this?

I scuffed one drop with the toe of my boot, and the dot smeared. It couldn't be from Sara. If it were, it would have happened last Friday. It wouldn't still be moist enough to spread. Why was there fresh blood in our hangar?

Just as I was about to open the door and enter the small plane, my phone rang. Father Gabriel's tone echoed throughout the large space. Micah's eyes flew to me, filled with both question and trepidation.

I answered before the third ring. "Father, I just started to—"

"Come into the community immediately. We're convening an emergency Assembly."

Shit! What does that mean?

"Father, the envelope?"

"At the moment, you're still an Assemblyman. You need to be here."

The line went dead.

I took a deep breath and contemplated my options. Without a phone to call the FBI, I had none. "I'm headed into the community," I said to Micah. "Forget that checklist. Go to Joanna."

⁓

Parking my truck as near our apartment as possible, I went directly to the temple. The sense of impending doom lurked around every corner. As I neared the Assembly room, I saw Luke and grabbed his arm. "What's happening?"

He shook his head. "I'm not sure, but it's not good. Not good at all."

When we entered, a sea of eyes turned in my direction, and for the first time I could remember, Brother Timothy's expression wasn't contemptuous; instead I'd describe it as smug.

"Now that we're all here, have a seat, Brothers," Brother Raphael said, standing to the right of Father Gabriel.

I peered around the table at the sixteen men. With Father Gabriel present, there should be seventeen. "Where's Brother Benjamin?" I asked.

"Apparently, much has happened while we were away," Father Gabriel said.

Yes, a lot *had* happened. My wife had been left at the Eastern Light.

"Brother Timothy," Father Gabriel began, "please tell the entire Assembly what you just relayed to me."

Timothy stood. "It's possible that not all of you are aware of the lengths we go to, to supervise our campus. We monitor the use of cell phones and the activity of the cell tower very closely. The Light can never be too careful or too trusting." He looked directly at me.

Shit! The cell tower. My pulse quickened.

"Other than an occasional hunter or pipeline worker, our cell tower is monopolized by us, the chosen, the only ones who have cell phones in this community."

Suddenly Father Gabriel's comments about whom I'd called came back to mind.

Fuck!

"You can imagine our confusion when last Friday an unknown number called from our tower. Incoming calls do happen with wrong numbers. This call originated from our campus."

From the sober expressions of the Commission, I gathered they'd already met and discussed this; however, most in the Assembly appeared shocked.

Brother Timothy went on, "That unknown number made five outgoing calls and received one call."

"Brother, does this have anything to do with Brother Benjamin?"

The table murmured at Brother Peter's question.

"Brothers," Father Gabriel commanded. "Let Brother Timothy continue."

"This could be attributed again to a hunter or pipeline worker except that the five outgoing calls all went to a familiar number, one that received the calls from a tower near the Western Light."

Perspiration dotted my upper lip.

Where were Benjamin and Raquel? How long had Father Gabriel known this? Maybe I'd been right and the envelope had been only a pretense to lure me back to the Northern Light.

"That doesn't make sense," Luke interjected. "Who'd even know to call anyone at another campus?"

"That's a good question," Brother Timothy replied. "It was something we would've questioned if it were not for the one familiar number the unknown number called initially—five times."

I took a deep breath. "Father, Brothers, did the unfamiliar number spend enough time on the call to speak to the familiar number?"

"No," Brother Timothy replied. "The only call that was answered resulting in a discussion was the one *received* by the unfamiliar number."

"Father, Brothers," Luke implored, "could the five calls to a familiar number have been made erroneously, a wrong number?"

Father Gabriel nodded. "That could be possible, unlikely, but possible." He stood and nodded to Brother Timothy. "This meeting is to inform you, members of the chosen, that the guilty parties have been punished. While Brother Benjamin will be missed, The Light will not tolerate deception of any kind on any level. We've unfortunately lost members of the Assembly in the past. It's never an easy decision, but I support the stance taken by Brother Raphael and the Commission in my absence."

My heart clenched as I peered toward Luke. His eyes now glistened with unshed tears as the muscles in his jaw clenched.

"While I've decided to not publicly call out the coconspirator in this travesty, rest assured, he too is undergoing correction."

The room stilled as everyone but me nodded. I couldn't move.

How had I not thought that they'd monitor the tower? Was Sara currently paying the price for my mistake?

"Nominations for the open position on the Assembly," Father Gabriel continued, "will be heard at tomorrow's meeting. Brother Luke, you have a wide knowledge of the followers here at the Northern Light. Bring a list of possible candidates. We may be in need of more than one nomination, depending on the near future."

My lungs forgot how to breathe at his last statement. I couldn't move, much less speak, as everyone but me responded.

"Yes, Father."

"Brother Noah, please pray for our Assembly, and we'll adjourn this meeting."

Fuck!

I needed to get to Fairbanks. Two more days.

Lost in my own thoughts during the prayer, I didn't realize it was over until Father Gabriel said my name.

"Brother Jacob, were you listening?"

All of the other Assemblymen were standing and moving toward the door.

"I'm sorry, Father. I admit I wasn't."

"I thought we'd eliminated your distractions."

Why does he keep using that word?

"Father, you said you'd keep her alive."

Brother Abraham nodded and closed the door, leaving me alone with Father Gabriel and the Commission.

"And she is. Your job is too valuable right now for you to meet the same fate as Brother Benjamin. Sister Sara's current position is your warning."

I looked to Brother Daniel, but his jaw was set and his eyes were on Father Gabriel.

"Father, I won't fail you. I promised that."

He narrowed his dark gaze. "You already did. Tell us what was said during your discussion and why it couldn't be done on your real phones. Explain to us why you needed deception."

The obvious answer: because that our real phones were monitored wasn't acceptable. I fought to make sense of the lies we'd told while I simultaneously wondered what Benjamin and Raquel had said. With my elbows on the table, I held my head. Three years of hard work and this was going to end over a damn phone call.

"Brother, speak now or I will make a call to the Eastern Light."

The room blurred as I summoned my Light persona and ignored his blatant threat. "Father, I'm sure Brother Benjamin explained."

"No, he didn't. As a matter of fact, you can cut to the chase. We know it was Sister Raquel whom you spoke with, not Brother Benjamin."

Brother Timothy replied, "We have the technology to triangulate the location of the phone. The call came from the Assemblymen's apartment building. That was the best we could isolate it. Everyone was accounted for, except Raquel and Sara. When Raquel was questioned, she finally admitted to having the phone, and swore Benjamin didn't know anything about it. She said she called about Sara and used the phone to not get Sara in trouble."

"Brother Raphael, remember Sara's confession?" I asked.

"Yes."

I ran my hands through my hair. "Ever since the time Sara was corrected by Brother Timothy and Sister Lilith, I've been worried about her when I'm gone." Timothy sat back and crossed his arms over his chest. "I asked Sister Raquel to alert me if anything unusual happened while I was away. This is my fault. I should be banished, not Benjamin or Raquel and not Sara."

"Brother Jacob, decisions made by this Commission can't be unmade. Go on."

"Sister Raquel was worried when Sara didn't go to work, especially when she couldn't find her. That was why she called me using the phone I'd given her."

"I'm going to ask this one more time," Father Gabriel said. "Why did you go to Fairbanks?"

"Because Raquel was afraid that Thomas took Sara. She said she'd seen him in the community."

"You lied, to me and to Brother Daniel."

"Yes, I did."

"Why?"

"Because I found Thomas and eliminated him as a problem."

Father Gabriel leaned back as the rest of the council shifted in their chairs. "You killed him?" he asked.

"He was a threat to The Light. I didn't want anyone to know what I'd done. After I did it, I worried that it could somehow come back on The Light."

"Why did you kill him?"

"He'd been in the community. Xavier never comes into the community. Thomas threatened to expose things he'd seen as well as our location."

"His body?"

I shook my head. "I brought him back here. That was my true distraction, not Sara. I brought him back here, and left him for the wildlife."

Father Gabriel nodded. "I believe that in light of this new information, we'll need to reconsider our safety measures. You're correct that he should never have been given access to the community. How did he learn the codes?"

"I don't know the answer to that," I answered honestly.

"Each Assemblyman and Commissioner has his own code for the gates. We could go back through and assess the surveillance . . . ," Brother Timothy offered.

"The video's on a loop. It erases every third day," Brother Daniel replied, finally meeting my eyes. "Besides, there's also the code used by followers who work at locations outside the walls."

"Change everyone's codes," Father Gabriel said as he turned to me. "Thank you, Brother Jacob. It seems as though we may have rushed to assume the worst. Pilots are in precarious positions. I'll take this new information into consideration regarding our situation at the Eastern Light."

"Thank you. I was only thinking of The Light."

"What you did was acceptable; however, it was outside of your scope of decision making. The proper way to have handled it would have been to tell Brother Daniel the truth, and then follow the guidance of the Commission."

"I apologize. I was afraid that he had Sara," I admitted.

"Well, as we've stated, that's no longer an issue. Now produce that envelope, and I'll reconsider your current correction."

"Yes, Father."

I stood and nodded toward Brother Daniel.

"Brother Jacob," Father Gabriel said, "call me as soon as you have it."

Benjamin and Raquel's fate hit me as I closed the meeting room door. The weight of my knowledge staggered my steps as I contemplated their consequence for helping me.

CHAPTER 28
Sara

Vomiting on Brother Mark's shoes wasn't intentional, but that didn't stop me from receiving additional correction. Never had Jacob whipped me like what I'd just experienced. Though Brother Mark hadn't told me to count, I had. I couldn't ask, but eventually I suspected he wasn't going for a particular number. His belt continued to strike my cold skin until it opened and blood ran from his lash.

"So dark," he said, assessing my blood, as he roughly spun me around to face him. He said my correction was to remind me to listen to directions the first time. From the bulge in his jeans, I believed it was also about his pleasure. The sickening thought came accompanied by a shiver of fear. In my current position, I was powerless to stop any other type of pleasure he might choose to require of me.

Before he'd started my correction, he'd made me remove my dress. I'd wanted to remind him that only husbands were supposed to be able to do this, but I knew it wouldn't help. Crying and wearing only my panties, I covered my heaving breasts with my arms and studied his vomit-splashed shoes. While I was afraid to ask whether I could get dressed, the longer he stood there staring at me, the more afraid I was to remain exposed.

Finally he simply turned and walked away, leaving me alone with blood dripping from my back and tears coating my face. The cool temperature of the basement added to my trembling. Biting my lower lip, I stood still, watching the door, unsure what I was expected to do. My dress lay near my feet, while my shoes were still where I'd found them. And near the back wall was the puddle of my vomit.

Though I knew my back was bleeding, I wanted to be covered. When I reached for my dress, I noticed the naked ring finger on my left hand. My thumb reached for the missing wedding band as my trembling, as well as tears, increased. I would survive this, not only for me but also for him, for Jacob, for his mission.

With my hair still damp, I pulled the dress over my head. The material irritated my fresh wounds, while the cold water and blood glued the fabric to my skin. I slid my feet into the soft formless slippers.

The next time the door opened, it was Sister Mariam. She didn't speak; instead she scrunched her nose, shook her head, and disappeared. When she returned she had a bucket of antiseptic-scented water. Placing it on the floor, she handed me a scrub brush.

"Clean your mess," she commanded, and walked away.

I tried to do as she said, but too soon the water was filled with pieces of my long-ago-eaten lunch. All I was doing was spreading it around. When the door opened again, I lowered my head, knowing Sister Mariam would reprimand me. It wasn't her. Another woman wearing a white dress, this one with a white scarf, entered. It was the color of the one I'd been told to expect. Remembering Sister Mariam's words, I knew this was one of the women I could question, but with my back sore from my latest reminders, I didn't want to risk it. She didn't speak either. Silently she took the bucket I'd been using and replaced it with one containing fresh antiseptic water.

The scent of the cleaner combined with the pain of my back had me on the verge of vomiting again, but I continued swallowing, scared of what would happen if I didn't do as Mariam had said. Tears mixed with the water as I scrubbed the concrete floor for the second time. Each time I moved my arm, the material of the dress tugged and rubbed my back, intensifying the sting of Brother Mark's reminders.

I would have done a better job on the floor with better tools. The scrub brush she'd given me was as dilapidated as the old couches in the main room. The bristles were short and worn. Though I didn't notice it at first, the tip of one of the fingers on my right hand was raw and bleeding from scraping across the floor. As I was almost finished, footsteps and voices came from the main room. I wasn't sure how many people were out there, but I knew it was more than Sister Mariam. As I waited for the door to open, I wondered whether it would be better in here with the wet strong-smelling floor or out there with them.

"Sister Sara," Sister Mariam said, as she unlocked the door. "Come out. It's time you understand the honor you've been given."

Honor?

As I stood, my muscles and wounds cried out. My legs ached from washing the floor on my hands and knees. And the white dress I'd been told to wear was damp and dirty from being on the floor. Without bandages over my back, surely I'd bled onto the white material.

Five women, all wearing similar shifts, stood in the main room forming a semicircle. Four of them wore blue scarves in varying shades. The one who'd brought me the fresh bucket of water was the only one wearing a white scarf. I recognized the one with the lightest shade of blue as the woman who had opened the front door.

I never had time for a sorority in college. I was too focused on my grades. But as I stepped in front of them, I had the strange sensation of some sick college movie. What I feared was that I was about to be the unsuspecting participant in the deranged hazing scene.

"Kneel, Sister Sara," Mariam demanded.

Willing to do almost anything to avoid Brother Mark's return, I did as she said. The weight on my tender knees caused me to grimace.

Apparently Sister Mariam was the designated speaker, because everyone else remained silent, watching my every move.

"Father Gabriel has chosen you to be one of his personal followers, a bride of The Light. You used to call yourself chosen, but you weren't. We, the brides of The Light, are the true chosen, the only ones privileged to care for his needs."

My thoughts moved from my physical discomfort to her words as I struggled to understand their meaning.

"It's a calling," she went on. "Now you've been called to share that privilege."

With my stomach twisting, I lowered my chin, trying to hide my disgust—the privilege of caring for Father Gabriel's needs? I didn't want this honor or privilege. I didn't even want to know that any of this existed.

Mariam continued, "We care for the house and for him. Sara, look up."

When I did, my eyes widened. In her hand was a leather collar like the one Salome wore, in the hospital bed in the other room.

My hand went to my throat. "No, please."

"Sister Leah, take off your scarf."

The woman with the white scarf untied the soft material and revealed the collar beneath. Seeing the purple bruising around the edges, I was reminded of the body I'd seen in the morgue. At the time I'd thought that whatever had left the bruise around the victim's neck had been in place for a period of time. When I turned back to Mariam, she'd removed her scarf to show the same collar, and then they all did.

"Sister Leah was our most recent sister given the honor to perform the duties of brides, or she was until you. She's a fast learner." Mariam turned toward Leah. "Take off your dress."

A tear slid down Leah's cheek, but she didn't hesitate to carry out the command. As she lifted the white material, I covered my mouth to keep from speaking. Dropping her dress to the ground, she slowly turned around. On both her back and front were various shades of lash marks, some newer than others. Bruises prevailed, but silvery-white scars as well as crusted scabs indicated the places her skin had been sliced. The markings extended beneath her panties and onto her thighs. When she made the full turn, I winced, seeing the lashes on her stomach and breasts. Thinking how badly my back hurt, I couldn't imagine a belt striking my tender breasts.

"Leah," Sister Mariam continued, "had the honor of spending the most time with Father Gabriel the last time he was home."

"Did *he* do that to you?" I asked.

Lightning-fast, Mariam stepped forward and slapped my cheek. "You don't ask questions. You listen. Apparently you're not as fast of a learner as Leah. Our leader is more than a man. He's The Light, and The Light needs fulfillment to be its brightest. We, the brides, are fortunate to be chosen for that duty. Everyone within The Light has their job to do.

"Being as close as we are with Father Gabriel, giving ourselves in all ways to The Light, we must willingly allow all darkness to be removed from us. Father Gabriel's pleased when he sees the stripes we gladly bear to exorcise the darkness from our bodies. After all, he wouldn't be able to enter us if we harbored darkness."

My stomach rolled.

"This"—she held up the collar—"also pleases Father Gabriel. As we wear it, it's a constant reminder that our lives are in his hands, and we have no choice but to trust him in all ways. He knows what's best for us."

My body trembled at the realization of what she was saying. These women served as Father Gabriel's brides, his wives, his *harem*. I had no doubt that when he tired of one, she ended up on the table in the morgue. The collar served as a reminder that these women belonged to Father Gabriel. If they didn't do as they were told and willingly accept their calling, if they didn't meet his needs, they would meet the ultimate punishment, banishment into the dark.

"There have always been *seven* brides, since the beginning of The Light. The collar you're about to wear was worn by brides who failed to fulfill The Light. We all wear the collars of brides who've failed. It's another reminder to do our best to please Father Gabriel, to do our best to keep The Light bright."

Do these women actually believe this is an honor?

"Sister Sara, do you accept this honor?" Mariam asked.

"I want to go back to my husband."

My cheek stung as she slapped me again. "You're really not very smart. I don't know why Father Gabriel would want you to be part of us." Grabbing hold of my hair, she lifted my face upward. "Let's try this again. Do. You. Accept. This. Honor?"

Though I kept my lips together, my scalp screamed as she moved my head up and down.

"That looked like a yes to me." She turned to the others and asked, "Do you think it looked like a yes?"

The other women agreed.

"Lift your hair or it'll be taking space you may want for breathing or eating."

With trembling hands I gathered my still-damp hair and lifted it while Mariam secured the leather collar that had been worn by other women, women who were now dead. I worked to be sure I could swallow as the heavy collar applied pressure to my throat.

"It must be tight enough," she explained, "so that Father Gabriel can see the darkness leaching from your skin. Until our skin no longer bruises, there's darkness within us that must be removed.

"Beginning tomorrow, you will be given responsibilities within the household. Can you cook?"

"No, she can't."

All six of us gasped at the deep voice, as our eyes immediately dropped to the floor. That wasn't all. Suddenly the other five brides fell to their knees. I didn't need to see the man with the deep voice to know who'd spoken. In one sentence I recognized Dylan.

My eyes darted to Leah, who was still wearing only her panties. She'd never been told to dress. Even with her face down, I saw her cheeks glisten as new tears descended and her body trembled. However, instead of covering herself, she had her hands at her sides, like everyone else.

"Stand," he commanded.

We all simultaneously did as Dylan said.

"Sister, put your dress back on."

Through veiled lids I peered in Dylan's direction. Unlike Brother Mark, who'd scanned me up and down when I was in front of him in only my panties, Dylan had his back to us. I quickly moved my eyes back to the floor as he turned back toward us.

"Sister Sara, come with me."

I swallowed and, while keeping my eyes down, I walked toward him. With each step my heart beat faster than it had before. My palms moistened, and I fought the sense that the world would tilt.

Silently he motioned for me to go up the stairs first. Nodding, I stepped past him. As I did, he touched the small of my back.

Wincing, I flinched. Though I bit my lip before I said anything, undoubtedly he was able to see the blood that had seeped through my dress.

"Fuck," he murmured, removing his hand.

CHAPTER 29
Sara

Step by step, as I ascended the stairs in front of Dylan, I contemplated what I'd say, what I'd do. Standing before him with Jacob at my side had been difficult enough. Doing this alone would be nearly impossible. I tried to think rationally; however, the more absurd the situation became, the more determined the Stella part of me was to come forward.

The echo of Dylan's hard-soled shoes alerted me that he was only a few steps behind me. I had no idea what the back of the dress looked like, but he was getting a good view. For some reason that made part of me happy. I was here because of him and he'd had the audacity to be upset with Jacob over a blackened eye that Jacob hadn't even caused. Besides, the way the women downstairs reacted to him, they knew him. They feared him—I'd sensed it and wondered whether I should too.

I rationalized that it wasn't so much that I should fear Dylan, but *any* man in this depraved house. This place was worse than the Northern Light, by far. My stomach twisted at the thought of the duties of the brides. Sister Leah was so young, as was Sister Salome. Not only would I call Father Gabriel crazy, but also he was practically a pedophile.

Each new bit of information about Father Gabriel made me more disgusted.

With each step I clung to the promise of the FBI. Surely enough time had passed. All that needed to happen was for Jacob to get a phone or for me to get free. Though I wondered what was going on at the Northern Light, I tried not to worry about Jacob. I reminded myself that he was an agent and had been doing this for a long time. I had to believe he'd survive—that we both would.

Passing through the door at the top of the stairs gave me the sensation of coming out of a black-and-white photo. Once again the world had color. The marble floor below my soft shoes glistened with golden flecks, while the walls glowed with a rich beige hue and shiny white ornate trim. Even the door was different, gray on the side of the basement, but pristine and white on the side in the house. I stepped to the side and waited, eyes down, for Dylan to emerge from behind me.

Except for the echo of Dylan's footsteps, the mansion was silent as we made our way down the long hallway. Every few feet we passed white pillars supporting arches, and between the arches crystal light fixtures sparkled, sending prisms of color reflecting rainbows that danced upon the floor. When he stopped, I recognized the French doors with the beveled glass and bit my lip, praying that Father Gabriel wasn't in here.

Opening one of the doors, Dylan gestured for me to enter.

Through the window the sky had darkened since the last time I'd been in the office. I wasn't sure of the time, and while I was certain I'd missed a meal, Brother Mark's whipping and Mariam's speech had taken away my appetite. The pool in the distance caught my eye. In the middle of the darkness, its illuminated beauty reminded me of a tropical resort. Underwater lights changed its color, while around it the landscaping sparkled with tiny white lights. The mini-paradise appeared to be surrounded by nothingness. The tennis courts, outbuildings, and landing strip that I knew were there were all cloaked in darkness.

When my eyes settled on Father Gabriel's desk, my heart fluttered. In an ordinary plastic container—the type to store leftover food—was Fred, swimming in circles, unsure of his new bowl. Lowering my chin,

I sucked my lip between my teeth and worked to contain my smile. A simple blue betta fish should mean nothing to Sara.

Oh my God! This is hard!

I hated Dylan and, at the same time, remembered thinking I could love him. Even with all that had happened, he'd kept Fred. Refusing to look up, I stayed rooted to the soft red carpet as Dylan walked to the front edge of the desk. Crossing his arms, he casually leaned back and studied me. It was his detective look, the one where he assessed, analyzed, and silently stared. Finally his broad shoulders sagged as he sighed and ran his hands through his dark-blond hair.

"I brought you in here," he began, "because it's one of the few places in the house that isn't under constant surveillance. There're no cameras or microphones . . ."

My pulse raced.

". . . Stel—Sara, will you please talk to me?"

Not lifting my eyes, I hid behind The Light's expectations of a female. I couldn't look directly into his piercing blue eyes. "Yes, Brother, Father Gabriel gave me permission to speak to you."

"My name is Dylan, not Brother."

I shook my head. "All men deserve a title."

"No, they don't. Fuck. Most don't deserve anything." He uncrossed his arms and they fell to his sides. "I know that I sure as hell don't."

I closed my eyes, and a tear escaped my lids. "I'm sorry. I don't understand."

"Will you fucking look at me?"

He reached for my chin, but I backed away. Too many thoughts were swirling about.

"Jesus, I'm not going to hurt you."

Maybe not physically, but he had hurt me, and now hearing the emotion in his voice was hurting me more. I wrapped my arms around myself, as my cold hands gripped my own elbows and hugged. The dirty white dress pulled against my new reminders as I gave in to the emotion. Tears burned my cheeks as my shoulders shuddered, and I gasped for air.

"I'm sorry," I mumbled, thinking that I would never have reacted this way before, but now I was. My off-the-chart emotions were real. "Why do you want to be away from cameras?" I hiccupped a cry. "I shouldn't ask. Questioning is my greatest weakness."

Dylan reached for my arms, and I froze, paralyzed by the thought of anyone but Jacob touching me—first Brother Mark and now Dylan. It was wrong.

If he sensed my discomfort, he didn't say anything. Instead he sighed and led me to the sofa, the soft leather one where Jacob had laid me earlier.

Dylan's tone overflowed with compassion. "Why don't you just sit for a minute? I wasn't trying to upset you. I'm not going to do anything away from cameras. I wanted to talk to you."

I shook my head. "Please, may I stand?"

"Oh, shit. I wasn't thinking. Yeah, sure, stand." Releasing my arms, he paced a trek around the office, stopping again at the desk. Picking up the plastic container, he said, "I brought you something. I know you don't understand why, but, well, I was hoping maybe you would." He put Fred back down and shook his head. "It's dumb. I shouldn't have done it. If I hadn't taken the time to go get it . . . if I hadn't, maybe I could've stopped whomever . . . goddamn it! I can't do this again."

Handing me a tissue, he collapsed in the same chair where he'd sat earlier. "Are you really pregnant?"

"I think I am. I haven't taken a test."

Dylan nodded. "Yeah, you're kind of emotional."

Really? I wonder why.

"I'm scared," I confessed truthfully. "And I miss my husband." It pained me to say that to Dylan, but, like my first statement, it wasn't a lie.

"I don't get it. How can you miss a guy who does that to you?"

I swallowed. "I'm not certain I'm allowed to speak so freely to you."

Though my Sara answers were saving me, the Stella side of me made the mistake of looking up. For only a moment, our eyes met. In his stunning blue orbs surrounded by lush lashes, I saw what I'd been hearing: remorse swirling with regret. It was the storm from my dream, clouds covering the clear sky. The ache in my chest grew.

"What?" he asked, as I broke our momentary connection and bit my lip.

"Nothing," I replied softly.

"Nothing?"

"I was in an accident almost a year ago. I drove my husband's truck and crashed. During the time of my recovery, I kept seeing—not really seeing, imagining—blue eyes." I shook my head, unsure which part of me was speaking. "I'm sorry. It's not appropriate, but, Brother, your eyes remind me of my dreams. I really don't think I should say more."

"Dylan, not Brother, and I give you permission," he offered.

I smiled and lowered my chin. *Damn, if only it were that easy.* "Bro . . . Dylan, only my husband or Father Gabriel has that authority. But I will say my husband has never done what Brother Mark just did to me. He's never harmed me."

"Mark?" he questioned, and then went on, "You don't think what he did to your eye was harming you?"

I forgot about my eye.

"It was the first time he'd done that, and it was my fault. I shouldn't have made the decision to start a family without his permission."

"What if he'd decided to start a family, and you weren't ready?"

"I'd trust his decision."

"What if he told you not to go somewhere, like Highland Heights? Would you go?"

I shook my head. "No. Obeying isn't optional." It was one of the first things I remembered Jacob telling me.

Dylan stood and walked toward me. "Turn around."

Though his proximity caused my trembling to resume, my conditioning wouldn't allow me to refuse a man's command. Slowly I did as he said, but when he touched my hair, I sucked in my breath.

"Don't worry. I'm not going to do anything," he explained, "except take this damn collar off you."

I nodded as he gathered my now-dry hair to one shoulder and fumbled with the buckle. Once it was off, I sighed and massaged my tender neck. "Thank you."

"Why are you shaking?"

"I'm scared. I don't know what's going to happen to me or to Jacob. And I'm . . ."

"Yes, you're pregnant," he said, with palpable defeat evident in his voice.

"No, well, yes, but that's not what I was going to say. I know I can't question, but I'm hungry. I was downstairs. No one brought me anything to eat."

For the first time, I saw Dylan's smile, the one I remembered. "Of course you are, it's after ten o'clock, and this is something that I can do something about. Let me get you some food."

My skin prickled with alarm. "I don't know."

"What?"

"You're being nice, but so far, you're the only one. What if someone sees me, and I'm not allowed to eat? Withholding nutrients is an acceptable decree."

Dylan's eyes closed as his jaw clenched. "I hate hearing you spout doctrine."

Bowing my head, I whispered, "We all study Father Gabriel's word."

He touched my chin, and this time I didn't flinch. "I don't need to hear it. And don't," he said, lifting my face to his, "be sorry. I'm sorry." He reached in his pocket and pulled out his phone. "I'll go get you something from the kitchen. No one will say anything to me. You can stay in here. Lock the door and don't let anyone but me back inside. Here"—he swiped the screen of his phone—"I have two phones. One's for MOA . . . never mind . . . anyway, I just put the number of my other phone in this one. If anyone tries to get in here before I get back, call me." He put the phone in my hand. "Can you do that?"

"I don't know."

The warmth of his grasp encased mine as he closed my fingers around the phone. "You can. I give you permission."

I shook my head. "That's not how it works."

"Here it does."

The sound of my own heartbeat echoed in my ears as I stared down at the phone in my hand. By the time I turned, Dylan was opening the door, and before he walked away, he turned the small latch on the inside doorknob. With only a nod and a half smile, he closed the door, locking me in and him out.

This was my chance, my chance to escape this hell.

Careful not to drop his phone with my shaking hands, I stepped cautiously to the door and jiggled the handle. It was locked. Really lifting my eyes for the first time, I scanned the office and searched for cameras. I couldn't be sure whether Dylan had been truthful when he'd said this room wasn't under surveillance, nor was I adept at recognizing secret cameras. My only experience was with the ones Jacob had pointed out in the outbuilding's living quarters. From what I could assess in the nice office, there weren't any.

That would make sense. Father Gabriel probably did a lot of business from inside this room that he didn't want recorded.

Hurry! Call someone! How much time do I have?

My list of candidates came fast and furious—my parents, my sister, Bernard, Foster, or Tracy. If only I could call the FBI. Calling the police was out of the question. Dylan was police—not Bloomfield Hills, but he was a detective. I zeroed in on Bernard. My old boss could help me.

He was the only one with the connections to help. As I searched my memory, I had the strangest sensation of knowledge so close, yet out of reach. And then I remembered.

I remember Bernard's cell number!

I swiped the phone and backspaced through Dylan's number. The trembling in my hands increased, not out of fear, but out of excitement and relief. This was really almost over. *Holy shit!* This would be the biggest news story of Bernard Cooper's career, of my career. I'd be just like Jacob, going undercover and infiltrating The Light.

My heart clenched. *Just like Jacob . . .*

Jacob . . . all his work. The FBI. Kool-Aid. My friends.

Oh my God! If I do this, I may save myself, but at what cost?

CHAPTER 30
Jacob

The door to our empty apartment weighed hundreds—no, thousands—of pounds. The simple act of opening it was almost more than I could bear. Since I was back in the community, checking our apartment first for the envelope made the most sense.

Once inside, I stood, slowly turning and taking everything in. It was all her. Yes, the other sisters had decorated so Sara would think we'd lived here, but over the last nine months, she'd added her own touch. I stared at the throw pillows she'd been so excited to find at the store. Knowing she couldn't do it without my permission, she hadn't purchased them on her own. But I remembered the night, at dinner, when her eyes sparkled as she told me about them. *A splash of color* was what she'd called them. Though I was tired, and it was one of our few nontemple nights, we hurried to the store before it closed. If it were possible, I'd never tell her no.

The deafening silence tore at my insides. Not only was our apartment silent, but so was the one next door, Benjamin and Raquel's. I palmed my temples and squeezed. This was so hard. Maybe I wasn't cut out for this. School, training, academy . . . fuck! None of it was like real life. With every fiber of my being, I wanted Father Gabriel to go down.

Hell, after what he'd just pulled, as well as three years' worth of offenses, I wanted him to suffer, but he wouldn't be the only one.

The Light offered its followers enlightenment—knowledge of God's purpose without the darkness of everyday life. The entire organization was a well-oiled machine. Each voluntary follower sold their earthly possessions and abandoned the dark, willingly entering a world of slave labor. While the chosen had the elite jobs, the average follower worked in more physically demanding jobs like those in the production plants. Whether producing the pharmaceuticals at the Northern Light, the Preserve the Light preserves at the Western Light, or the illegal drugs, mostly meth and crack, at the Eastern Light, or working at the packaging and distribution sites, followers eagerly devoted ten or more hours a day to be enlightened.

Father Gabriel's teachings preached the promise of clarification by devoting one's life to others, being part of the body, and fulfilling Father Gabriel's missions. In the process the followers were relieved of the burden of pressures and decisions that plagued their lives in the dark. Hours worked in their assigned jobs earned followers credit in the commissary as well as the clothing and furnishing stores. The more hours worked above the required sixty-five a week, the more credits they earned. As long as followers worked their prescribed jobs, every need had the potential to be met. The Light provided anything they needed. If it wasn't available or within their reach, then it wasn't necessary.

One of the most frequently mentioned reasons for entering The Light that I'd heard since I began counseling followers was that The Light offered the ability to walk away from the stress and struggles they faced in the dark. In The Light they were free to devote their lives and be enlightened. Working as part of the body gave them purpose.

Before Sara I saw The Light for the sham it was. After Sara I admit that I fell into the rhythm. That may have been part of the reason the Commission had insisted I take a wife. When Sara and I were in Fairbanks and she'd confessed to not hating the life she was now able to look back on and see as depraved, I hadn't told her that I understood exactly what she meant, but I did. The months following her initial indoctrination could be labeled pleasant. Without meaning to I'd fallen under The Light's spell.

As I brushed the burned tips of my fingers over the cover of our bed, memories of our short time together ran like a highlight reel through my head. I remembered the way her lower lip disappeared when she was nervous or excited and the way she looked first thing in the morning. My skin chilled as I thought about her warmth as I'd wrapped my arms around her and spooned her soft yet firm body. Those terms seemed contradictory, but they weren't. Her skin was as soft as velvet and so was her body, in all the right places. At the same time, running and genetics had blessed her with firm muscles and a flat stomach.

I sank to the bed, my knees suddenly weak.

Will her stomach change? Is she really carrying my child, our child?

I looked at the clock on the bedside stand. It was after six in the evening here, which meant it was after ten at the Eastern Light. I'd left Sara over six hours ago. Six hours, and I was losing it.

How am I supposed to make it until Wednesday?

I refused to believe she'd meet the same fate as Benjamin and Raquel. I refused. If she didn't survive until Micah and I made it to Fairbanks on Wednesday, when I would contact the FBI, there would be only one person to blame, and it would be me.

I could try to point the finger at Richards or even Father Gabriel, and my accusations wouldn't be unfounded; however, three nights ago she and I had been in a cheap motel in Fairbanks. As the continued silence echoed throughout the apartment, I knew I wasn't her savior or anyone else's. Despite all my grand proclamations, I had a good chance of experiencing the same fate as Benjamin. If I did, at least I had Sara to thank that the FBI now had a case against The Light. I hadn't given them everything in our short debriefing, but they'd gotten enough.

Even if I were banished, I'd die knowing Father Gabriel would soon be going down.

Fuck! I needed to snap out of this.

I walked to our closet. As I opened the door, the fresh scent of fabric softener knocked me backward. Before Sara, my laundry had been done by female followers whose job it was to do the unmarried men's laundry. Though they were efficient, it wasn't the same. Then I'd find my clothes packaged outside on the stoop of my apartment. Now I never saw laundry done, or rarely, but the clean clothes appeared, hanging perfectly straight, ready for me whenever I wanted them.

I fought the onslaught of emotions brought on by something as stupid as fabric softener as I searched for my jacket. It was my lightweight one, the only one I could've possibly worn at the Western Light. It was hanging exactly where Sara would've hung it, on my side of the closet. I anxiously ripped it from the hanger and fumbled through the pockets, coming up empty except for a wadded-up tissue and a piece of gum.

No envelope.

Dropping the jacket on the bed, my hands went to my hair. I once again held my head and pushed, forcing myself to think. I could envision Brother Reuben handing the white envelope to me as Brother Michael and I laughed about the production. I recalled my phone vibrating again as we laughed.

I rushed to the clothes hamper and searched for the jeans I'd been wearing. My phone had been in my front pocket.

Did I stuff the envelope in there after I got my phone out?

There was nothing in the pockets of my jeans.

I knew I hadn't taken my phone out of my pocket until I was in the air. I hadn't wanted Brother Michael, or anyone at the Western Light, to misinterpret my talking on my phone. The damn envelope had to be in the plane. I considered calling Micah to check, but then I remembered that he'd left the hangar right after I had.

That meant that at this moment he was where he should be, at home in his cramped apartment with Joanna and Isaiah. Clenching my jaws tightly together, I prayed that nothing would alert Father Gabriel and the Commission before the FBI arrived. The loss of Benjamin and Raquel hurt too much. I'd need more than deprogramming if anything happened to the followers I oversaw and those I considered friends.

Quickly I searched the top drawer of our dresser—nothing. One last look and I grabbed the jacket and walked out of Sara's and my private world. I needed to go back to the hangar and search the plane.

It was still bright outside as I drove toward the gates. This time of year, on the edge of the circumpolar North, the skies were never fully dark. Twilight extended from one day to the next. For some reason the northern lights came to mind. They were something I'd add to my list of things I'd miss about this mission. During the winter months they were spectacular.

DENIED.

What the fuck?

I entered my code again into the inner gate—the same message flashed across the screen—*DENIED*. I pounded my palm against the steering wheel and took out my phone. Brother Timothy oversaw security. He was undoubtedly the one who'd figured out the cell tower.

I had to get back out to the hangar if Father Gabriel wanted that envelope.

I dialed Brother Daniel.

"Hello, Jacob."

"Brother Daniel, my code won't work at the gate. Have they all been changed?"

"Yes," he replied drily.

"Father Gabriel asked me to find something for him. I didn't have time when we first landed due to the emergency meeting. I need to get back to the hangar."

"I'm on the Commission, but this is beyond me. You can understand your actions regarding Fairbanks and, well, the call. I'm sorry, I am. Only Father Gabriel can authorize your new code."

Fuck!

"I understand. Thank you, Brother Daniel. I regret not being straightforward about Thomas."

Brother Daniel sighed. "In the end you did what was best for The Light. That's what matters."

"Sara?" I couldn't say her name aloud without its overflowing with emotion.

"Jacob." Brother Daniel paused. "It's beyond me."

Swallowing, I nodded. "Thank you, Brother Daniel. Whom should I call?" I wasn't thinking straight. Following his orders seemed like the best course of action.

"I'll call Father Gabriel. Stay at the gate. No one else will be leaving the community today. I'll call you back."

"Thank you. I'll be waiting," I said, ending the call. A few more pounds on my steering wheel and I ran the palms of my hands over my growing beard. Nothing helped to calm my nerves. I couldn't sit in the truck. I had to move. Keeping my phone in hand, I got out of the truck and paced, back and forth, back and forth. The hard cracked ground beneath my boots reminded me that it hadn't rained in weeks. The climate at the Northern Light was a far cry from the humidity in Michigan.

My palm struck the side of the truck, once, twice, three times, each strike sending shock waves up my arm, pain from each impact. It wasn't enough. The pressure was mounting, and I was about to explode.

The sound of tires against the gravel made me turn, back toward the community.

Brother Daniel had said no one else would be leaving the community. Only the chosen had their own vehicles. There were also panel trucks used by followers to transport supplies and product to and from the hangar. This was a car, and the closer it got the more my chest clenched. I recognized it—Brother Timothy's.

Widening my stance, I stood, waiting beside my truck, as both doors opened. Brother Timothy came from the driver's side and Brother Abraham from the passenger's door. My chest inflated as I stood taller. There was no love lost between me and either one of these men.

Not knowing what they wanted or intended, I sized them both up. Brother Timothy had to be in his early sixties, and though he could be intimidating in voice and with the power he wielded on the Commission, physically he wasn't. Abraham, on the other hand, was in his early thirties, a little younger than I and maybe an inch or two taller. I was bigger, wider, and undoubtedly stronger. Doing my share of ground crew duties as well as running had kept me fit.

I took a step toward them as they approached.

"Brother Jacob," Brother Timothy said.

"To what do I owe this pleasure? After all, we just saw each other at the Assembly meeting. Did you miss me?"

Not amused by my greeting, Brother Timothy formed a straight line with his lips. "Brother," he continued. "Due to the recent events, as we said in the meeting, all codes have been changed."

"I understand not wanting Thomas or other unauthorized individuals entering the community. However, I'm hardly an unauthorized individual. The last I heard, I'm still an Assemblyman."

Brother Timothy shrugged and tilted his head toward Abraham. "Brother Abraham, also on the Assembly, is here to escort you to the hangar and back. We want to be sure there are no unforeseen changes in your flight plans."

My chest inflated and my fingers balled to fists as I suppressed the first response that came to mind. Instead I swallowed my retort and replied, "I don't anticipate any, unless I am forced to once again protect The Light."

"Father Gabriel wants the letter you need to find. Brother Abraham is merely joining you to help. Once you retrieve what you've lost, then the future is up to Father Gabriel."

I knew he was baiting me about Sara, but I couldn't let him know how close to losing it I was. I stepped closer. "Father Gabriel will see that I'm devoted."

As the two men exchanged glances, it took every ounce of self-control I possessed not to knock the smirks off their damn faces. "Of course he will, Brother," Brother Timothy said, still using his overly placating tone. "I spoke with Brother Mark from the Eastern Light. Your devotion has been noted."

I audibly exhaled.

"Now," Brother Timothy continued, "Father Gabriel wants the message in the envelope from Brother Reuben. Go out to the hangar and find it. Brother Abraham has a new code. He'll help you." He turned toward Abraham. "Won't you?"

"It'll be my pleasure." Abraham turned my way. "I'm always willing to do what the Commission and Father Gabriel ask of me."

This wasn't good.

"Fine, get in the truck," I said, turning around. "I have an envelope to find."

"Give him your keys, Jacob."

What the hell?

My expression, as I spun, must have spoken for me, because Brother Timothy continued, "The security codes are entered from the driver's side."

"They're in the ignition," I replied through clenched teeth as I walked past both men to reach the passenger's side. Slamming the door, I waited. In the side mirror, I watched as they conversed about something. Finally Abraham walked to the driver's door. Before getting in, he smiled through the window.

I hated that man, well, both of them, with a passion. Every time I looked at Abraham I remembered what he'd done to Sara, and how he'd planned to do more. Out of the corner of my eye I watched as he consulted his phone before entering his new pass-code. By the third gate he had it memorized.

What a genius!

The truck jiggled over the rough terrain of the road as we traveled toward the hangar in relative silence. Only road noise and the occasional screech of a hawk flying low could be heard until we neared the pole barn.

Turning toward me, Abraham asked, "Thomas? You said you dumped his body out here?"

CHAPTER 31
Sara

I stared at the phone's screen, representative of a number pad but devoid of numbers Dylan had programmed. And then it changed. The keypad vanished and the time—10:36 p.m.—appeared. Biting my lip, I sighed.

A few more days!

That was what Jacob had said. I was numb. The hunger that had rumbled earlier in my stomach was gone, and so was the excitement. In the middle of Father Gabriel's office, I was without direction. With the solution in my hand, literally at my fingertips, I couldn't proceed.

Calling Bernard would risk the entire FBI mission. It risked everything and everyone.

Bernard may have had contacts, but would he be able to get to the right people? Involving my old boss risked too many lives—the lives of all my friends at the Northern Light, the lives of terrible people I didn't honestly give a damn about at the Eastern Light, including those in this mansion, and even the lives of people I'd never met at the Western Light. Involving Bernard could put his life at risk, yet as I stood motionless, staring at a now-dark screen, the only life that I honestly cared about was that of the man I'd called my husband. If I called Bernard, I would jeopardize not only Jacob's mission but also his life.

I couldn't do it.

With my freedom a phone call away, I couldn't dial the numbers. It was clear that I loved Jacob more than I craved the biggest story of my career, and somehow even more than I feared this terrible house.

A lump formed in my throat as I imagined explaining to my dark-haired, dark-eyed son or daughter that it was I, the child's mother, who'd made the call that had cost my child his or her father.

Turning slowly, I laid the phone on the desk near Fred and walked toward the large window.

As time passed and the scene through the window went unchanged, I concentrated on what I could do. I made a mental note of each person, each name I'd encountered at the Eastern Light. I'd recall their names and faces as I testified to whoever would listen. This might be Jacob's case, but I was a witness and I wanted a part in bringing down The Light.

It wasn't until the doorknob rattled that my attention came back to the present. Through the beveled glass, all I could make out was that the figure was a man. With trembling hands I reached for Dylan's phone. Swiping the screen, I realized my mistake as my stomach dropped. The numbers he'd programmed into it were gone. I'd erased them when I contemplated calling Bernard. The door once again rattled, this time with a knock, and my eyes darted around the office as I searched for a place to hide. For a moment I considered locking myself in the attached bathroom.

"Sister Sara, it's me," Dylan called in a stage whisper. "I'm alone. Please open the door."

Relief momentarily flooded me as I grabbed the desk for support and stared at his figure. Slowly I stepped toward the door, listening for any sound to indicate that he'd lied and wasn't alone, but there was nothing except another faint knock and request for me to open the door.

"Brother Dylan, is it really you?" I asked, pretending not to recognize his voice.

"Shit, yes, it's me."

My cheeks rose as a small smile crept across my lips. I'd never before noticed how much he cussed. Living in The Light, where vulgarities were frowned upon, made each one he uttered sound foreign. I marveled at how, in the Northern Light, even my thoughts had been without vulgarities—well, until my memories returned. Using vulgarities was the transgression Jacob had chosen as being in need of correction in Fairbanks.

Turning the small latch within the doorknob, I opened one of the doors. Keeping my eyes down, I watched as Dylan's boots crossed the threshold onto the red carpet, then quickly shut the door, mindful to again turn the latch. The tray he'd been carrying clattered as he placed it on Father Gabriel's desk near Fred and his phone.

"I made you a sandwich and brought you some water," he offered, as if a sandwich could make up for what I'd been through. "I almost got you a beer, but then I remembered the pregnant thing. I didn't know if you should have tea. So, well, I settled for water. I hope that's all right."

Beer. I hadn't even thought of beer in months. Suddenly memories of the two of us came to mind. I recalled evenings on his back deck with beers while he grilled, but just as quickly I remembered that he was the one who'd handed me over to his uncle. Taking a deep breath was all I needed to solidify my more recent memories, those of hours ago in the basement of this horrible place at the mercy of Brother Mark. When I inhaled, the white dress tugged and pulled against the new lashes, pushing any pleasant thoughts away and doing what they were intended to do: remind me.

"Thank you," I said quietly. "It's very kind of you."

He motioned toward the food. "Do you want a chair, or would you rather—?"

"Standing is fine," I replied, hoping that my pain inflicted guilt.

When I didn't move closer, he asked, "Are you going to eat?"

"I'm waiting, for you."

"Me? I ate earlier." The confusion in his voice was audible.

"Brother Dylan, I'm waiting for you to bless the food so I may eat."

"Shit, yeah, well, I did that already. So go ahead and eat."

When he reached for the phone I'd left on the desk, my heart skipped a beat. I was grateful I hadn't made a call.

"You erased the number I put in here? What if someone had come?"

"I'm sorry. I didn't know what to do. I was holding it. I think I touched something, and it went dark." I smiled at my own creativity as I took a long drink of water. My amusement quickly faded as I noticed my empty ring finger and my thoughts went to Jacob.

"It's all right. I'm back."

"Why?" I asked, taking a bite of the turkey sandwich. As my teeth sank into the soft bread I realized how hungry I'd become and almost hummed at the taste of mayonnaise. I hadn't eaten that since before The Light, and the unique gooiness was like heaven on my tongue.

"What?" Dylan asked.

I put the sandwich down and lowered my chin. "I'm sorry. I know better than to question a man. It is my biggest struggle. I just don't understand why you're being nice to me. No one else is."

"I had a talk with Mariam. Things will be different."

I nodded, again reaching for my sandwich. When I did, my breathing hitched as Dylan covered my hand with his. "I know it doesn't make sense to you, but if it did, I'd tell you that I didn't have a choice."

Bullshit! We all have choices.

I bit my lip, doing my best to keep my Sara persona intact. The part of me that was Stella was no longer reliving pleasant memories. She was ready to take Dylan out for the hell he'd put her through.

"My uncle won't be back here for at least a few days. I'm trying to come up with something."

"Brother," I said, conscious that the title made him uncomfortable, "I don't want to stay here. I want to go back to my husband." A real tear crept down my cheek. "I don't want to be a bride of The Light. I know by not accepting this honor that Sister Mariam spoke of, I deserve to be punished, but I don't want the honor."

With each word I spoke about brides of The Light and honor, Dylan's hand upon mine tensed.

"Here," he said, scooting the phone closer to me. "Take this again. I put my number back in it. Don't touch anything unless you need me. I have a few more people I need to talk to before I can leave you alone. Just stay quiet and finish your dinner."

"Yes, Brother."

He huffed and pointed toward a door I'd explored earlier. "There's a bathroom, if you need it. Remember, don't let anyone in but me."

"Yes, Broth . . . Dylan."

And just like that, he left me alone for the second time. I wasn't sure whom he was going to speak to or whether it would help. No matter how convenient it would be, I wasn't willing to put my faith in him. It was already taken by Jacob's promise.

After I finished the sandwich and water, I looked out the window at the colorful pool. No matter what I did, my mind drifted to the Northern Light. I worried about Jacob and the envelope Father Gabriel had mentioned. I worried about Benjamin and Raquel. Father Gabriel had said something about speaking with them. He'd said it was no longer an issue. I didn't want to even consider what that meant.

I eyed the computer at Father Gabriel's desk. Could there be something, anything, there that I could access? Could it help Jacob's case?

Carefully I sat in Father Gabriel's large chair, but as my fingers hovered over the keyboard, I feared that trying to access information would set off an alarm. Instead I opened drawers and peered inside for anything.

Certainly, once the raids occurred, the FBI would thoroughly search the entire mansion. Maybe it would be better if I didn't disturb anything.

Sometime around midnight, my tired muscles cried for rest. It might have been only after eight at the Northern Light, but unfortunately I'd awakened at the Eastern Light, and was still here. Not only were my muscles tired of standing and walking, but also exhaustion tugged at my eyelids. Over the last hour I'd formed a fleeting sense of security locked away in Father Gabriel's office. I didn't know where I would be told to sleep, but since I was here and so was the sofa, I decided to see whether I could sit. Though the leather was incredibly soft, sitting was too painful to allow me to rest; however, after maneuvering around, I found that if I lay on my side, I could get comfortable.

With Dylan's phone tightly in my grasp and his number still available, I sighed and my tight muscles eased a bit. I closed my eyes. Lost in the familiar leather scent, in no time at all I drifted to sleep.

In my dream I was no longer a hostage in Father Gabriel's mansion, and the talk of *brides of The Light* was forgotten. I wasn't holding Dylan's phone; instead my palm was warmly and safely encased in Jacob's. In a gentle breeze, we were walking through the north acres at the Northern Light.

The warm kiss of the sun touched my hair and our arms brushed each other's as we walked. When I looked up, I squinted. The bright sky behind him created a glow, but it was Jacob's gaze that brought a rush of blood to my cheeks. I quickly looked down. I didn't need to ask why he was looking at me or what he saw. It wasn't because I wasn't allowed to question. It was because I knew. I knew the swirl of emotions behind his soft brown eyes. I knew his consuming thoughts that words could never fully describe. I knew where we'd gone and what we'd done when merely his expression had the ability to accelerate my heart and twist my insides.

Leaning closer to my husband, I melted against his strong arm, closed my eyes, and drank in his intoxicating scent of leather and musk. While tall grass rustled all around us, Jacob pulled us to a stop, removed his jacket, and laid it upon the cool ground. In the middle of the circumpolar North he'd provided us with the perfect place to sit. When I did, he laid his head in my lap, and I ran my fingers through his dark, wavy hair. His deep voice and soft laugh were but drugs to my already-inebriated system, electrifying my senses as they reverberated from him to me.

As we spoke, the gentle breeze tousled my blonde hair, fluttering pieces around my face. Jacob's large hand gently tucked a renegade strand behind my ear. Eager for more of his touch, I inclined my cheek toward his palm. His warmth combined with the rough tips of his fingers lingered, cupping my cheek as he wordlessly encouraged me forward until our lips were but a whisper apart.

Their contact overloaded my body—soft yet firm, demanding yet giving. My chest heaved as a moan escaped. With the increase in my pulse, my nerves came to life, and impulses sparked synapses that only he could ignite.

Noise.

Commotion.

Startled.

The office door opened, rattling the beveled glass with excessive force. Lost in my dream, I couldn't make out the words or accusations hurtling from his lips, though my skin prickled with goose bumps at the tone and volume. Blinking away the haze of sleep, I momentarily focused on Brother Elijah, our eyes meeting, mine scared and confused while his burned with hatred and vengeance. Lowering my eyes, I searched for Dylan's phone, but before I could find it, my scalp cried out in pain.

Grabbing a fistful of my hair, Brother Elijah threw me from the sofa to the floor. Dazed and sore, I tried to make out the words as his threatening voice boomed through the office, echoing in my ears.

". . . playing us for a fool. No one leaves The Light! Your zero-tolerance policy has expired."

"I don't understand," I managed as he pulled me to my feet. However, as I stood I saw his fist, not even an open hand as Thomas had hit me with, and I turned, shielding my face. Unfortunately, my cheek hadn't been his intended target.

I coughed and spit as my lungs tried to inflate. The second blow to my stomach sent me back to the floor.

"No!" I screamed, covering my face and pulling my knees to my stomach.

This couldn't be happening.

Who would do this, knowing I could be pregnant?

As Brother Elijah's large foot reared back to kick where he'd punched, I closed my eyes and prayed for a miracle.

Sound.

Loud.

Deafening.

The room exploded. A flash through my closed lids sent shock waves that accelerated my already too-fast heartbeat. The vociferous bang echoed endlessly against the walls, submerging and drowning out everything else. The kick never came, as I floated in the waves of the explosion, and my heart ached at the loss I feared I'd already suffered.

A few days, that was what Jacob had said.

I didn't want to open my eyes. I wanted to go back to the north acres. Maybe if I gave in to the waves . . .

"Sara," the deep voice coaxed, as a warm hand smoothed my hair away from my face. "Sara, we have to get out of here."

I shook my head. No! This wasn't Jacob. It was Dylan. I needed Jacob.

"Sara," he said more emphatically, pulling on my hand. "Can you stand? Oh my God! I heard him. Get up. I need to get you out of here."

My eyes, filled with questions, opened.

Before I could process the idea that Dylan was taking me away, I gasped. Inches from where I lay, right in front of me, were the dark eyes that had looked at me with intense hatred. No longer did they send fear through my body. They were open and lifeless while around them Brother Elijah's black skin sagged and spit dripped from his partially open mouth.

Painfully I jumped to my feet.

"Oh! He's . . . he's . . ."

"He's dead," Dylan confirmed, tucking his gun back into a holster I remembered he occasionally wore beneath a sports jacket. "And we need to get out of here."

"B-but." I couldn't articulate as my stomach cramped, doubling me over and bending my knees.

"No, Sara. No fainting. We need to leave now."

I nodded, petrified to leave but terrified to stay.

Dylan seized my hand and pulled me toward the door. Just as my slippers hit the marble and I left behind the carpet that was now literally red with blood, I stopped. When Dylan's panicked blue eyes met mine, I said, "Fred! We can't forget Fred."

Immediately, I knew my mistake.

"Brother Dylan," I said, trying to recover, "wasn't that what you called the fish?"

For a millisecond his panicked expression changed and his eyes narrowed. And then, instead of speaking, he rushed past me, into the office, and grabbed Fred's container. Securing it in one hand and my hand in his other, he led me through unfamiliar hallways, pulling me until we emerged into the backyard.

"We need to get down to the outbuildings. There's a car down there. There's no way we can leave from the front of the house."

I gasped at the darkness. With the only indication of light coming from the pool, the expanse before the outbuildings seemed insurmountable. I stood unmoving, my midsection cramping and the reminders on my back still sore.

"I don't know," I said, "I'm not sure if I can make it."

He gripped my shoulders and spoke slowly. "Listen, Stella, I know you fucking remember. I also know I need to get you out of this house. We don't have any choice. I'm sorry that I'm not as big as your damn *husband*, and I can't carry you all the way, but if we don't move now, there won't be a later."

I didn't understand what Dylan was saying, but the urgency in his voice was loud and clear. Even though I'd blown my charade with Fred's name, it seemed like with whatever was happening at this mansion, leaving with Dylan was my best option. I nodded, bit my lip, and ran through the pain. I concentrated on my footing, careful of the wet, slippery grass, made that way from sprinklers. By the time we reached the outbuildings I was clammy with perspiration and my slippers were soaked.

I waited as Dylan disappeared into the building where Micah had stayed. The still night hung heavy with a feeling I couldn't identify as I searched the sky for stars that were more visible during the dark season at the Northern Light. Looking up to the heavens, I knew the feeling I was having. It was an impending sense of doom, and it was getting closer with each passing minute. The opening of a garage door caused me to turn and face the far end of the building.

"Get down here!" Dylan yelled.

Standing still after running had intensified the cramps, yet I pushed past the pain and made my way to the SUV that he'd pulled out of the small garage. It was older than the one Brother Elijah drove and reminded me of one of the vehicles I'd seen nearly a year ago in Highland Heights.

Dylan opened the back door. "Get down on the floor. If the cameras at the gate are still working, they won't be able to see you."

Loud, angry voices cut through the thick, humid air, coming from Father Gabriel's mansion. Momentarily I turned back, peering through the darkness toward the mansion.

"Get in, now!"

Dylan didn't need to tell me again.

CHAPTER 32
Jacob

"You were told what I'd said to the Commission?" I asked Abraham. My fried brain couldn't remember who'd been present when I'd told my story, but I thought it was only the Commission.

Abraham smugly turned in my direction. "I've been told lots of things—things about here, Fairbanks, phone calls, and the Eastern Light."

I turned away, watching rows of small trees clear to large areas of open land to be swallowed up again by trees. As the landscape passed by the windows, I tried to assess what he was saying. "Congratulations," I finally replied. "You're apparently *in the know*."

"You'd better hope whatever it is Father Gabriel wants you to find is out here."

Abraham stopped the truck and pushed the button for the garage door. After he pulled inside the pole barn and as the door was going down, I turned in his direction. "Wait a minute."

Abraham's eyes widened as his brow furrowed.

"He has it, doesn't he?" I asked. "Father Gabriel already has it. Someone went through our apartment while I was at the Eastern Light and found it, or came out here. What the hell am I doing out here if he already has it?"

Abraham shook his head. "That's not what I was told. I was told that I'm supposed to be here until you find something that Brother Noah needs . . . something Brother Michael from the Western Light never intended for Brother Reuben to give to you. I heard you screwed up and if you don't find this thing, you're not the only one who'll suffer."

Veiled threats against Sara were becoming less veiled.

I opened the truck's door and started walking in the direction of the hangar. Pointing behind me, I called over my shoulder, "There's the living quarters. I don't need a damn babysitter." Without turning, I knew Abraham hadn't listened and was following in my direction. As I opened the door to the middle part of the pole barn, the area before the hangar, his footsteps got closer.

"I was told to *not* to let you out of my sight. *I* follow Father Gabriel's orders."

Asshole.

The hallway veered to the left and ran through the center of the building, allowing space for the offices on the right and workshops on the left. If I wanted to be nice, I could have flipped the switch and turned on the lights, but I wasn't being nice. Besides, the hangar had windows, and the beams from the perpetual sunshine created a literal light at the end of the tunnel.

"Fine, whatever," I offered sarcastically. "Knock yourself out."

Only our boots echoed against the concrete floor as we made our way down the hall. When I reached for the handle of the door at the end of the hallway, the one leading to the hangar, my steps stopped. I spun backward, my movement precipitated by a loud *thud* followed by another odd noise that had come from behind me. I watched, in shock, as Abraham fell to the floor, his knees buckling before he fell backward. A sickening squish—like the sound of a dropped watermelon—filled the hallway as his skull made contact with the concrete. Within seconds a dark pool of liquid began to form around his head.

When I dragged my gaze away from Abraham, my eyes met Benjamin's. In his shaking hand was a large wrench, now dripping with the blood of our Assembly brother. I rushed toward Benjamin and, before he could say a word, wrapped my arms around his shoulders.

"You're alive! I'm so sorry." My emotions were jacked. Guilt flooded through me, guilt at what had happened to him and to Raquel because of me. "I'm sorry about you and Raquel. I never thought about the cell towers."

Benjamin's shoulders hunched forward as his head moved from side to side. Very quietly, he whispered, "Microphones? Out here?"

"Didn't used to be," I answered softly, flipping the switch to acknowledge his concern. The bright light brought crimson to the dark pool around Abraham's head. I looked away, focusing on the ceiling and seams in the tiles. I scanned the floorboards and door frames. "No, there're none in here. There are some out in the hangar, but we usually only turn them on during loading and unloading of merchandise and supplies." I shrugged. "That doesn't mean they're not on now. I don't know what the hell's happening."

"Sara?" he asked.

Pressing my lips together, I slowly shook my head. "She's still at the Eastern Light. Father Gabriel's holding her there until I get him some envelope I was given at the Western Light." I ran my hands through my hair. "I just can't remember what I did with it. It was when Sara . . ." I let my words trail away. We both knew what'd happened. We were both living with the consequences.

I took a step back as the loud clank of the wrench hitting the floor reverberated through the air, and scanned Benjamin up and down. Normally, he was well dressed, always neat and clean. Not now. Today his pants were torn and the knees were covered with dirt and grass stains. His shirt hung loose and was equally filthy. On his shirt were smears of blood, and, judging by the color, it was dry and hadn't come from Abraham.

"What happened? I thought they said . . ." I didn't want to say the word *banished*.

It was as if someone had deflated Benjamin, as if he were a balloon losing air. His entire body shrank and lines covered his face as he cleared his throat to speak. "Him," he said. "Him!" He spoke louder, kicking Abraham's side. The man didn't move. With the way his skull was opened, with some sort of gray matter visible, I was pretty sure he never would.

"*He* what?"

Benjamin took a step back, avoiding the growing pool of blood. "While I was at the lab, *he* went to our apartment, to the place we lived, our home! He *questioned* Raquel."

My already knotted stomach convulsed. "Questioned?"

In Benjamin's dark eyes, which usually held compassion and understanding, I saw an unfamiliar glare of hatred.

"Questioned," he repeated through locked jaws. "I had no idea it was happening. It wasn't until I was called to the temple to the Assembly room that I knew anything about it. Something to do with isolating the location of the phone and only two possibilities."

I nodded. "The Commission told me, Raquel or Sara."

"I told them I'd talked to you, on our regular phones. I had no idea where it was leading, but with all four of them sitting there he"— Benjamin nodded his head toward Abraham—"brought her to me." Tears descended his cheeks, clearing paths through the dirt, grime, and blood. "She was crying, and bruised, and upset, and apologizing. I wanted to kill Abraham. I wanted to kill them all."

I looked down and lifted my brow. "Looks like you accomplished part of your goal."

Benjamin shook his head. "I know it upset him."

I doubted it had upset Abraham at all.

Benjamin went on, "He was my overseer, *our* overseer. I worked with him every day, but Brother Raphael said he didn't have a choice."

"But you're not . . ."

"Dead," he said, finishing my sentence. "Not yet, but I will be. Brother Raphael told us to run, to go into the dark and see how long we'd last."

The flicker of hope that was born when I saw Benjamin grew to a flame, fearful of being snuffed out. "Raquel?"

He nodded toward the hangar. "She's in there, but Abraham beat her pretty bad. I've never been so scared. Even if we had a place to go, she can't walk. I carried her here."

"Wait," I said, lifting my finger to my lips. Opening the door to one of the offices, I went to the computer and prayed they hadn't changed the password. A sigh left my lips as the screen came to life. A few clicks of the mouse and pass-phrases later and I was into the hangar's security feed. With Benjamin over my shoulder, I nodded. "The cameras are off. The last recording was the day I came back from Fairbanks."

"Does it have Sara? Had they seen her?"

I shook my head. "No, I knew it'd be running and got her out of the plane before I tugged it into the hangar."

"I'm getting back out to Raquel."

"Take her to the living quarters. This computer oversees all the security. Nothing's being recorded in there either."

As we stepped back into the hallway, I kicked Abraham's side. "We need to get him outside."

"I'm moving Raquel first."

Nodding, I reached for Abraham's jacket and took out his phone. Holding it in my hands, I suddenly wondered whether I could use it to call the FBI. But first I needed the envelope, praying it would buy me time.

"I need to check the plane in the hangar for something Father Gabriel wants," I explained as we started to walk away from Abraham's body. "How did you know he'd be here?"

"I didn't."

I turned toward Benjamin with my eyes wide. "So the wrench was for me?"

The very corners of my friend's mouth moved upward. "I heard the garage door and was on my way to see if it was you when I heard your voice and his. The wrench was just handy, and someone should have done that a long time ago."

I patted his shoulder. "No argument from me, Brother. Take me to Raquel."

As we walked toward the far end of the hangar, I saw the drops of blood I'd seen earlier on the floor and tried to scuff one. This time it didn't budge.

"You were here when we first got back from the Eastern Light, weren't you?"

Benjamin nodded. "We'd just gotten here. The door on the far end by the landing strip was unlocked. I'd just gotten her inside. That's how I knew about Sara. I overheard you and Micah talking when you arrived from the Eastern Light."

"I'm getting her back."

He didn't respond. No one believed me, except me.

Benjamin led me to the far corner of the hangar, behind a row of skids and shelves filled with boxes of supplies. I stopped walking as the bile rose from my stomach. Raquel's normally pretty face was red, with areas of darker blue. One cheek and eye were swollen so badly that it didn't appear as though her eye would open. She was lying unmoving on her side.

As I stared at my friend, I felt no remorse about Abraham. I was glad he was dead and hoped he rotted in hell. How he could continue to do this to women was beyond me. The man was a psychopath who'd found an acceptable outlet for his desires. I hadn't thought of his wife until this moment, but I doubted that Deborah would mourn her husband's loss.

"Raquel," Benjamin said softly, kneeling by his wife's side. "Brother Jacob's here. He said for a little while we can move you to the living quarters. It'll be better than having you lie on this hard floor."

She nodded and her face contorted as Benjamin helped her sit.

"B-Brother Jacob . . . I'm sorry . . ." Her voice was weak.

I knelt beside her. "No, Raquel. You have nothing to be sorry about. It's my fault. All of this."

"But Sara . . ."

"Raquel, don't worry about her. I'm going to get her back. I just need to find something first."

We all jumped as the phone in my pocket buzzed. Benjamin's eyes met mine. "Yours?" he asked.

Pressing my lips together, I shook my head. After a deep breath, I swiped the screen of Abraham's phone and read his new text.

Father Gabriel: HAS HE FOUND IT?

I looked up to Benjamin. "Well, that blows my theory that Abraham brought me out here for something else."

"You'd better answer him."

I hit "Reply" and held the phone so we could both read.

Abraham: NOT YET. STILL LOOKING.

Father Gabriel: DON'T LET HIM OUT OF YOUR SIGHT AND GET ME THAT ENVELOPE.

Benjamin's and my eyes locked. "What about you?" he asked. "Is he supposed to take you back to the community?"

Fuck!

My heart raced as I hit the buttons.

Abraham: JACOB?

We waited.

Father Gabriel: AS WE DISCUSSED.

I blew out a puff of air as Benjamin shook his head. Well, that wasn't informative. I slid his phone back into the pocket of my jacket.

Raquel winced as Benjamin lifted her from the ground. As he did, her blouse rode up, revealing a large purple bruise. I opened my eyes wider. Her side wasn't only black and blue as Sara's had been, the skin was distended. I'd seen it before, not at The Light, but in Iraq. I swallowed.

"Is that hard to the touch?"

Benjamin nodded.

"Brother, I think she has internal bleeding."

His eyes glazed over as his chin fell to his chest.

If she didn't get medical treatment soon, she wasn't going to make it. I wasn't a medic, but I transported enough injured soldiers in that C-12A and heard enough discussions. Images I'd hoped would remain buried came to the forefront of my mind.

I closed my eyes and whispered, "I'm so sorry." I was. My heart was breaking as my friend held his dying wife.

Raquel turned toward me, her one blue eye staring directly at me. "It was me. My doing," she said. "I agreed to help Sara. Don't ever be sorry." She looked up to Benjamin, whose cheeks now contained multiple tear paths through the grime, descending to his chin. "What happened to me," she went on, "would've happened a lot sooner in my old life. I know that. I was destined to die this way." She smiled. "I'm just thankful that before I did, I got to know love. I know there's a lot of things wrong with The Light, but I don't regret a day I spent as your wife."

I was suddenly an intruder in their private conversation, a voyeur watching as Raquel's eyes closed and she leaned her good cheek against her husband's chest.

My temples throbbed as I contemplated Abraham's phone. This had to end.

"Oh," Benjamin said, stopping and turning around. "My wife didn't do as you told her." He peered down at the crumpled woman in his arms. "However, as it's at my discretion, I've chosen not to correct her."

What the hell is he talking about?

Benjamin walked back to me and stopped. "In the inside pocket of my jacket. Can you reach it?"

I carefully pulled at his jacket, trying not to disturb Raquel.

"There's the phone. She didn't destroy it as you'd told her to do. She turned it off and hid it."

My heart raced. This was it. I needed to call. I couldn't wait for two more days.

I spoke with new purpose. "Benjamin, I was never told the plan, if there is one. What would happen if Father Gabriel believed his dreams were threatened? Is there a plan, a Kool-Aid plan?" I added the last part to emphasize my meaning.

"There isn't one for here. No one can find us up here, and there's no place to run."

I inhaled. "OK, what about at the Eastern Light?"

He shrugged. "Mandatory service. The followers know too much. If The Light is threatened, it would be time for communion."

Please, God, I prayed, *don't let Sara take communion.*

I flipped open the cheap burner phone and brought it to life. Undoubtedly the call would show up on the cell tower. I just didn't know how long it would take for it to be discovered. After all, Abraham, who worked under Timothy, wasn't exactly on the job right now. I dialed the number I'd memorized.

Special Agent Adler answered after the first ring. "McAlister, where are you?"

"Northern Light, sir." I held Benjamin's stare, and briefly wondered what he was thinking.

"We're forty minutes out, on all campuses."

My mind spun. "What? I didn't authorize . . ."

"That boy the marshals took?"

"Thomas," I said. "What about him?"

"Someone fucked up. Over an hour ago he was allowed to make a phone call."

The world dropped out from under me and I fell to my knees. "Bloomfield Hills, sir. Eastern Light, they have Sara . . . Stella there. Go now, don't wait. Please go get her. Please."

"She's not with you?"

My vision blurred. "No, you have to get her. Do it now! There's no Kool-Aid here, but there is there."

"Agent, if you have any way to get out, do it. They don't know everything, but I listened to the recording of Thomas Hutchinson speaking with someone named Xavier. Hutchinson told him about Sara and the marshals. We were able to trace Xavier's next call to the cell tower up there at the Northern Light." My thoughts overlapped while Agent Adler was still speaking, ". . . don't know who he spoke to, but someone knows why you were really in Fairbanks."

"Shit!" Now Abraham's question about Thomas's body made sense. From the time I'd been speaking to the Commission to the time I made it to the gate, they all knew I never killed him or dumped his body.

"Agent, get out of The Light now. That's an order."

"Sara?"

"We'll move."

CHAPTER 33
Jacob

"Benjamin, don't take Raquel to the living quarters. Come with me."

His quizzical expression asked more than his words. Still Benjamin tried, his voice unsure: "What's happening? Who did you just call?"

"We need to move." I pulled out Abraham's phone. "Let's pray this buys us some time."

Benjamin didn't speak as I began to text.

Abraham: HE JUST FOUND IT IN THE PLANE.
I'LL BRING IT TO YOU, AFTER I TAKE CARE
OF THINGS.

"What if we were wrong and there wasn't a plan to do anything to you?"

I gritted my teeth. "If there wasn't, after what they just learned, there is now. I'm sure of it."

"Are you sure enough to bet our lives?"

I nodded and then inclined my head toward Raquel. "Benjamin, what you do is up to you. Take your chances with the dark up here, or come with me. I'm tugging the smaller plane out to the strip. It's fueled and I'm getting out of here. Come with me and I'll explain everything.

First we can get Raquel in the plane, and then you can help me get the plane out."

Confusion came and went in Benjamin's eyes. "I don't know. We . . . I thought . . . weren't we friends? I don't know what's happening."

I grabbed his arm. "Listen to me. Do. You. Want. To. Save. Her?" Before he could answer, I continued, "Because I sure as hell plan on saving Sara. I'm leaving now. Come with me or don't. It's up to you."

His chest inflated and deflated. "Let's go."

Normal procedure was to return the tractor and tug to the hangar before taking off. I wasn't worried about following normal procedure. Benjamin sat in the cargo section of the plane, strapped into one of the jump seats beside Raquel. She was now unconscious. It wasn't the first time I'd transported an unconscious woman, but it was the first time I'd felt good about it. This was her only chance. Besides, Raquel's state of unawareness was probably better. At least now she wasn't in pain.

Just before takeoff, I looked back and he was holding her hand.

Benjamin and I had talked the entire time we strapped her in as well as while we got the plane ready. Our freedom of speech was no longer restricted. The black box that recorded all our words was within the plane. It didn't broadcast. The physical box had to be removed to be analyzed. We'd be away from The Light before anyone learned what we'd said, and then it wouldn't be The Light that learned it. It would be the FBI.

As we spoke I told Benjamin everything. I told him the truth of who I was and what I was. I told him about Stella, that Sara had gotten her memory back, and that she had agreed to play along until the FBI could organize enough force to raid all three campuses simultaneously.

Just as we were about to take off, Abraham's phone buzzed. I looked back at Benjamin, our eyes met, and I tossed him the phone. It was my gesture of faith. He was letting me take Raquel and him out of The Light. With Abraham's phone he could alert Father Gabriel, the Commission, and the Assembly to everything.

Catching it, he swiped the screen. As I flipped switches on the panel before me, he spoke through our headphones: "Father Gabriel told Abraham to wait at the hangar. He said Xavier's on his way and should be here in less than ten minutes. He wants Abraham to drive him into the community."

"It's going to be a crowded airspace and landing strip," I said.

If Agent Adler's timeline was accurate, the FBI was twenty to twenty-three minutes out. I'd texted my handler the new code to the gates to enter the community, the one I'd gotten from Abraham's phone.

"What should I text back?" Benjamin asked.

"That's up to you."

The roar of the engine grew louder as we rolled forward. I didn't concentrate on Benjamin's movements. I couldn't be sure how long it took him to text back or what he texted. It wasn't until we'd reached about twelve hundred feet that I had visual confirmation of Xavier's descent. If we'd been in the dark season, I might not have seen his white plane with the blue letters and numbers, but it was the light season and I did.

For only a second, I thought I saw the nose of Xavier's plane move upward, changing course toward me, but it was too late. In order to crash into me or send me off course, he'd need to be proficient in maneuvers most often seen at air shows. I was above and passed him. At that realization I closed my eyes and let out a long breath.

The Northern Light was behind me. With Xavier there, Father Gabriel would have two pilots; he could get away. Hell, he could get away in Xavier's plane and leave Micah behind. I couldn't worry about it. The drive to the hangar was over twenty minutes from the community. By my calculations the FBI would land before Xavier's plane could be refueled and back in the air. My cheeks rose as I realized that with the emergency meeting and everything that had happened, we hadn't refueled the Cessna Citation X. Assuming Father Gabriel would want to leave The Light and go into seclusion somewhere unknown via the luxury of the Cessna Citation X, the FBI had more than enough time to arrive first.

Now my only concern was Sara. I prayed that the FBI had already conducted the raid on the Eastern Light, and that agents had found her. With the increased altitude my phone was useless. I wouldn't learn anything until we landed.

I rolled my neck, trying to relieve the tension that wouldn't lessen. As I did, my eyes veiled and I looked down. Beside my seat, wedged next to the controls, was something white. Fumbling for the corner, I squeezed my fingers into the tight space and pulled.

Whatever Father Gabriel had been so desperate to find was in my hand. I read the front of the plain white envelope: *Father*. Instead of opening it, I folded it in half and slid it into the inside pocket of my jacket.

Father Gabriel's teachings came back to me with new understanding. I suspected that after three years, it would be a long time before all the doctrine I'd learned didn't come to mind. However, the one I was thinking about wasn't necessarily perverse. It was one of the ones I'd recited to Sara and made her recite to me. It was about a wife giving everything to her husband, releasing it and being free. I'd seen the relief in her beautiful face more times than I could count—times when she was upset or sad, times when she was scared or guilty. Even when she knew that sharing her concerns or confessing her transgressions would result in correction, the process of giving it over to me had given her peace. Whatever was bothering her was no longer her concern, but had become mine.

That same overwhelming rush of relief that I'd seen on her face filled me as I pocketed Brother Reuben's envelope. I was no longer responsible for deciding whether its contents were important. I was no longer alone in this fight. As soon as we landed in Anchorage, I'd pass the envelope and all my information on to my team at the bureau. What they did with it was at their discretion and no longer my concern.

I planned to leave Benjamin and Raquel in Anchorage. I'd gladly debrief for the entire flight to Detroit, but getting to Sara was now my main concern. The FBI could handle The Light. I now fully understood the gift that lesson had been to Sara. For a moment, as I flew above the white rolling clouds, my neck lost its tension.

"How long until we get to Anchorage?" Benjamin's voice reminded me where we were. In my mind I was already beyond Anchorage and on my way to Sara.

"It's about an hour and a half. Agent Adler will have teams waiting for us. They'll have an ambulance ready for Raquel. How's she doing?"

"I'm scared. She's cold, but I feel a pulse."

"I'm praying for her, and doing my best."

"Are you?" Benjamin asked.

"Am I what?"

"I'm just confused. What was real?"

"I don't know," I answered honestly. "I know I had a mission. I know there were parts of The Light I recognized as wrong. I also know there were parts that I understood and made sense. I know what I feel for Sara, or Stella, isn't fake. We spent a lot of time talking after I confessed who I was and knowing who she was. I don't know if she's pregnant or not, but either way, just because this is over, I don't want to give her up."

"Pregnant? Really?" he asked.

Shit!

He and Raquel had been trying for a few years to get pregnant.

"We don't know. She's been sick and, as you know, she quit taking her birth control, but we don't know if she's pregnant. There's been a lot happening. She might just be ill and throwing up because of nerves."

"Yeah, I remember when Raquel got her memory back. It was a rough time, but at the same time, it was good. It felt liberating to finally be honest with her."

I sighed. "It did, but we haven't had much of a chance to discuss it." I looked at my watch; it was only ten after nine. "She left Friday morning. Monday isn't even done. Our whole damn lives have changed in less than four days."

"Tell me about it."

I looked back. He was still holding Raquel's hand with his head back against the seat, and his eyes were closed.

"Tell me about Raquel. What did she mean when she said she was destined to die that way?"

"I don't like to think about it, but"—his voice hitched—"I suppose it's easier than seeing how she is now."

"Hey, you don't need to say—"

He interrupted me. "No, talking keeps my mind off the future." He paused. "Before she was brought to The Light she was a prostitute in Highland Heights, a runaway. Her parents died and she ended up in the foster care system. When she was seventeen she hitched a ride with a trucker. It was her first time, and she said he wasn't terrible. Afterward he gave her cash, and she'd found her new profession. She doesn't exactly remember how she ended up in Highland Heights, but if you were to ask her, she'd tell you it was divine intervention. She'd also tell you that despite the indoctrination, she was thankful she did.

"I can't imagine her living that life. Even the thought of it breaks my heart. When Brother Raphael released us, I knew we'd die out there, in the dark. I just wasn't willing to let her die alone. That's why I took her to the hangar. I honestly thought someone would find us and just kill us. It would've been easier than starvation, exposure, or animal attack. I knew about banishments, but I'd always suspected that we would . . . I really didn't even consider."

"I'm sorry . . ."

"Don't be. You heard Raquel. She wanted to help Sara. I should have figured. I mean, I guess banishment is a very viable option when you accept a seat on the Assembly. It's not like seats become vacant because the previous Assemblyman resigns. The thing was, I was proud to be part of the chosen, and after the life Raquel had suffered when she was younger, I was proud that through me she could be part of the chosen too."

The airwaves fell silent as I thought about his honesty. No doubt the stress and turmoil, as well as holding his dying wife's hand, had fueled his words.

"Who else?" I asked.

"What?"

"I know about some of the followers, but I wasn't privy to any of the chosen who were banished. Who else on the Assembly or Commission has been banished?"

"Well," he said, "I've never known of anyone on the Commission. The first Assemblyman I know of, after I was on the Assembly, was Brother Joel and his wife, Sister Chloe. You can imagine how difficult that was."

I shook my head. "Was I there? When did that happen? I don't recognize their names."

"Oh, you're right. It was right before you came, and you probably don't recognize their names because no one is supposed to talk about it. Probably your coming was one of the reasons it was able to happen."

"I don't understand. Who were they?"

"Brother Joel was a pilot. It's a job with a lot of scrutiny, as you know. The thing was, no one ever suspected Joel of anything. After all, he'd been raised in The Light, not actually in The Light itself. Before The Light even existed, he followed Father Gabriel as he preached around the country. Timothy and Lilith were some of his first devoted followers. They took Joel everywhere with them. He'd known Father Gabriel most of his life."

"Wait a minute," I said. "Joel was Timothy and Lilith's son? He was the pilot who was banished just before my arrival?"

No wonder they hate me.

"Yes, and Chloe was the daughter of Brother Raphael and Sister Rebecca."

"Holy shit! What happened?"

"The Commission was given evidence that Joel was in contact with people outside The Light. I never heard the particulars. It went over the Assembly straight to the Commission—"

"Which contained two of their fathers," I added in amazement.

"Yes."

"And Timothy and Raphael went along with it?"

"They believe that Father Gabriel's word is divine."

This news definitely shed new light. Timothy and Lilith disliked me because I'd replaced their banished son. If I hadn't been available, Joel might have been forgiven or found innocent.

"We're making our approach in Anchorage," I said. "I need to talk to the tower. Soon we'll learn more."

"Thank Father Gabriel," Benjamin said under his breath.

I looked back. His eyes were closed and he was clutching Raquel's hand. I doubted he even realized what he'd just said.

CHAPTER 34
Sara/Stella

From my vantage point on the floor in the back of the SUV, I couldn't tell where we were going. When the SUV finally stopped, I tried to see where we were. It was the rumble of the garage door that let me know we were inside a new building.

When the back door opened, I looked up at the blue eyes of my dreams. He offered me his hand; however, in those piercing eyes, I didn't see the Dylan I'd known. It seemed as though his learning my deception had changed something. What I witnessed was a growing harshness I didn't recognize.

Was this the hard-ass Dr. Tracy Howell had warned me about?

"Dylan," I began, meeting his gaze. "What happened? Where are we?"

As he helped me from the SUV, his head tilted and his lips formed an unnatural grin. "I thought you weren't supposed to question. Maybe I should correct you. That's what happens according to the doctrine you've been spouting all night, isn't it?"

"That's not you," I pleaded. "Tell me the truth, and I'll tell you the truth."

Grasping my upper arm, he forcefully ushered me up some steps and through a door into a very nice house. Judging from the amount of time we'd been in the SUV, we were still in Bloomfield Hills. With each light switch that he pushed, the beautiful interior came to life.

Once we were in the designer kitchen, he led me to the table and motioned for me to sit in one of the chairs. For a brief moment, I considered refusing, but the Sara side of me obeyed. The lashes on my backside were no longer as big a concern as the man who had now taken me somewhere that I wondered whether Jacob would be able to find.

In a matter of minutes, Dylan's demeanor had morphed into something neither part of me recognized, but he seemed to be the kind of person the Sara part had more experience dealing with, someone who expected obedience.

Pacing near my chair, Dylan appeared to collect his thoughts and rein in his words.

"Truth," he began. "You want the fucking truth? Well, so do I."

My ability to keep my chin down was waning by the second, as were my eyes' ability to maintain the conditioned submissive pose. This wasn't a man of The Light. This man had at one time been my boyfriend. And never in our relationship had I allowed him to speak to me with that tone.

Slapping my hands on the granite tabletop, I glared. "OK, truth. Let's start with the fact you fucking gave me to The Light. Do you have any idea what kind of hell I've lived through?"

He reached for my chin. Clenching his jaws, he spoke slowly and deliberately. "No. Stella. Do. Not. Talk. To. Me. Like. That . . . I. Saved. Your. Goddamn. Ass . . . Show. Me. Some. Fucking. Respect . . . For. Once. In. Your. Damn. Life . . . If. You. Can. Give. It. To. *Him* . . . Then. I. Fucking. Deserve. It. More."

I searched behind the manic blue for the man whom, at one time, I'd thought I loved. "Explain it to me, Dylan. Tell me what's happening, what happened. I thought we . . . I thought we were going someplace. I didn't lie earlier. After my accident, which wasn't real, but some drummed-up scenario that The Light put me through. A scenario that harmed me—like broken leg, concussion, injured me—I *did* dream of you, of your eyes. When I was finally able to see, Jacob's brown eyes upset me. I couldn't remember you, because of the medicine they gave to me, but I wanted to remember. Please tell me why you did it."

"How can I trust you?" he asked, taking a breath and sitting in the chair to my left.

Trust me? *Is he serious?*

"You lied about remembering," he went on. "You acted like you didn't know me."

"I was afraid, and I didn't lie about that. I'm still afraid." I met his gaze. For the first time with any man other than Jacob, I felt empowered, back on an even keel. I wanted information. I just needed to figure out the best way to get it. "If I ever meant anything to you, tell me what's happening. What was Brother Elijah saying? Why was he so mad?"

Dylan shook his head. "It's you. It's fucking been you. You have that effect on people."

I waited as he ran his hand through his hair and leaned back with a look of utter exhaustion.

Reaching out, I covered his hand lying on the table. "I don't understand."

"I fought to keep you alive and now, this is what happens. Gabriel must be . . . shit . . . I can't imagine." He removed his hand from mine and pinched the bridge of his nose. Suddenly his eyes widened. "Where's my phone?"

I looked from side to side. "I-I don't know. I reached for it, but Elijah threw me to the ground. I think I left it on the sofa."

"Fuck! I won't know what Gabriel is thinking, unless he calls this one. I need to get my phone out of his office."

"What? Why? And what is Gabriel Clark or Garrison Clarkson to you? How are you connected to all of this? I mean, you didn't seem like"—I looked down and took a deep breath—"with me, you were never like them."

Emotions flooded his expression, creating a spinning kaleidoscope. Happiness and sadness battled, and at the same time, I saw loss and duty as well as pride and shame.

"You may think you know The Light," he said with an eerie calmness. "But you don't. You only know what you've been allowed to see, and," he added exasperatedly, "what you learned in your fucking research."

I knew more than he thought because of Jacob, but I wasn't going to correct him.

"Then tell me," I said, adjusting in my seat as the cramps continued to ache. "Help me understand."

"It's bigger, so much bigger than you know. I'm not part of this fucked-up religious sect. I don't beat or use women. The man you knew, that's who I really am. And believe it or not, Stella, I tried to save you. If you would've had a damn ounce of the obedience you appeared to have with that asshole, you could be living your own life right now."

My back straightened, rebelling at Dylan's description of Jacob, but I decided that learning more about The Light was more important. "What do you mean, it's bigger? And what did *I* do that caused Brother Elijah to be so upset?"

"You left. Nobody leaves and talks about it! Did you think you'd get away with it?"

Shit!

"I left the Northern Light and came here, because Father Gabriel ordered it. I didn't, no, I *don't*, want to be here. I'd rather be there."

His gaze narrowed. "Truth? Really? Stop the fucking lies! You left the Northern Light four days ago with some douche bag named Thomas. I don't fucking know if he took you willingly or unwillingly, but I know he said that you begged him to help you get away. He said you claimed you'd been kidnapped."

It wasn't only the cramping from before that caused my discomfort, but also nausea, bubbling, no, gushing and churning the sandwich in my stomach. If Dylan knew this, then so did Father Gabriel, so did the Commission at the Northern Light.

Where is Jacob? What have they done to him?

Perspiration dotted my brow and lip as the blood drained from my face. "Dylan, I-I . . ." I looked down, unsure what to say.

He reached for my chin. "What's the matter?" he asked in a tone I didn't recognize. "Cat got your tongue? I don't think I've ever seen Stella Montgomery speechless. Is that who I'm talking to now, or is this *Sister Sara*?"

"How? How do you know that?"

His palm slapped the table. "I told you, The Light is bigger than you think. What The Light doesn't know is how the US Marshals became involved. Why would they be there when you landed and how did Jacob find you?" His expression softened and his tone morphed to that of the man with whom, at one time, I'd considered sharing a life. "That's what I need you to tell me." He reached for my hand. "Come on, sweetheart, I'll show you mine, you show me yours. We used to be good at that."

I pulled my hand away. "Stop it, your bipolarness is scaring me."

"Really?" His chair scooted across the expensive flooring as he stood and began pacing. "*I* scare you? I never gave you a damn black eye."

"Neither has Jacob!" I retaliated. "This came from Thomas. The man you're willing to believe. He's the one who did this, and I didn't want to go with him. He not only took me against my will but threatened to rape me once we got to Fairbanks. I don't know why the marshals were there when we landed, but I'm sure as hell happy they were. They left me alone in an interrogation room for hours. They fed me, but kept promising I'd see another marshal and get to make a call.

"Guess who I wanted to call? Guess who I thought would be my knight in shining armor. You! I was going to call you! But the female marshal never came. Instead the first marshal walked in and told me *my husband* was there to get me. It was Jacob. I don't know how it all went down, but I was fucking terrified."

"Of?"

"Of everything! I was scared to go back with Jacob and scared not to. These last nine months have screwed with my mind. I didn't know who to believe or what. I mean, I was with the US Marshals for Christ's sake, and I thought my nightmare was over, but it wasn't." A tear slid down my cheek. "It still isn't, and I'm with the person who I thought would save me."

"You lied to me!"

I couldn't reply; instead I crossed my arms over my chest and pressed my lips together. For the first time, I looked at the room around me and saw the tall, dark cabinets, high ceiling, and designer lighting.

Where are we?

"So," Dylan said, "you and dear old hubby concocted this lie about you missing work . . ."

I nodded. "Yes, he was afraid of what could happen to me if The Light knew I was off one of their campuses. I was afraid to tell him I'd gotten my memory back. So I told him Thomas took me."

"How did he know where you where?"

I shook my head. "I really don't know. Don't you get it? I'm not allowed to question."

Dylan smirked. "Stella Montgomery couldn't question. How did you function?"

I slapped the stone table. The sting in my palm took a bite out of my response. "Not well, not at first. It wasn't easy. It was my biggest difficulty."

"I can see that."

"Dylan, you said The Light is bigger than the three campuses. What do you mean?"

"How do you know there are three?"

"My husband, I mean Jacob, is a pilot. He'd tell me when he'd fly to the Eastern Light or Western Light. He never told me where they were, but he'd use those names. I also knew we were at the Northern Light."

We both stopped talking as the earth shook. Wineglasses hanging upside down from racks clinked against one another as the table trembled under my grasp. My eyes opened wide as we waited for it to stop.

Did we have an earthquake?

Dylan hurried to a wall of windows and then rushed to another room. The next thing I heard was a long tirade of curse words. Scooting my chair, I quietly made my way toward his voice. The house wasn't nearly as large as Father Gabriel's. From the front window of the living room, I could see other homes. From their size I presumed we were still in Bloomfield Hills. It wasn't the neighbors' homes Dylan was watching, but a glow in the distance. Above the glow, suspended in the night air, was a plume of smoke.

He reached for his other phone and dialed a number. Though I could barely make out what he was saying and my conditioning told me not to intrude, the Stella part of me wanted to listen to every word. Quietly I inched closer. I heard the name *Joel* and more curse words. He asked something about *all of them*, but he was speaking too low for me to make out anything more.

Once he put the phone back in his pocket, I asked, "What happened?"

Dylan spun toward me. "You, and I don't know what fucking else. I won't. I don't have my damn phone!"

"I don't understand," I said to his back and broad shoulders as he turned again toward the window. On the wall I saw a clock, a quarter past one.

Pulling his other phone back out, Dylan swiped some numbers and turned toward me with disgust. "Damn circuits are overloaded."

"Dylan, what happened?"

As I asked, the air filled with the shrill wails of sirens; though muf-fled by the walls and windows, they seemed to be coming from all directions. For a moment I prayed they'd be coming to us, and I might be saved, but that didn't happen. Just as fast as they'd come, the sirens faded away, growing fainter with distance. I stepped toward the large window and watched as the dark Michigan sky filled with red and blue lights speeding toward the glow.

"I guess I won't get my phone back or my car," Dylan stated matter-of-factly.

"W-what?" I asked in disbelief. "That's Father Gabriel's—"

I couldn't finish before Dylan turned back to me. "Go back to the kitchen. You wanted answers? Well, Stella Montgomery, you're going to get them. Go sit the fuck down and listen."

More sirens roared, only to fade into the general chaos occurring in the distance. Unsure what I had to do with any of this and why Dylan blamed me, I did as he said and went to the kitchen. He followed close behind.

After pulling a beer from the refrigerator, he turned a chair back-ward, sat, and stared. Once I sat, he took a long swig of his beer and began, "As I was saying, The Light is bigger than you think. The three campuses your *husband*"—each time he said *husband* he made a point of exaggerating the word—"told you about, that's only a portion. The Light is everywhere. It's not just about the followers on the main cam-puses. The Light needs followers in the field, in *the Shadows*, willing to do what it takes to bring light to the dark. Those followers are in law enforcement, like me. They're in the medical field. They're in every profession throughout the United States and Canada. The Light reaches beyond those borders, because only The Light can stop the dark."

My heartbeat raced. I'd never seen Dylan like this. His blue eyes glowed with conviction, yet he wasn't looking at me, but seeing things I couldn't. In that moment I had no doubt he was part of it. "Why? Why you? How long?"

He shook his head and took another long drink from the brown bottle. Grinning, he said, "I bet good old hubby had a field day with your questioning. Did he get off beating your ass? I remember you having a mighty fine ass."

I gritted my teeth. "Is Father Gabriel really your uncle?"

He nodded. "My mother's half brother."

"And when your parents died?"

"They were part of it. They died doing work in the Shadows for The Light."

"So he took you in?"

"I lived with my grandparents, like I told you. But Gabriel and I had always been close. He never had any children." Dylan shrugged and lifted a brow. "None that he let be born. He always wanted me to work with him, but I refused to be involved in the shit like you've been doing. I prefer the Shadows."

"So those brides, have you ever . . . ?" I wasn't sure I wanted him to answer.

"Hell no! They are, or were, his. They just know I'm a man with high ranking. That gives me unlimited power. I told you, I've never been into that shit. But, up until now, I never stopped it."

"Until now?"

"Elijah. Shooting him. I'd given orders to keep you untouched." Dylan lifted his shoulders and cocked his head dismissively to the side. "He disobeyed. When it comes to the Eastern Light, being Gabriel's nephew, I hold my share of power. You said it yourself, earlier tonight, disobeying isn't an option."

"Those women . . . you said . . . *were* . . ." I swallowed the churning bile. "Are they dead?"

"Didn't you see the fire? Did you feel the explosion?" he asked. "No one in that house survived."

"Why?"

"Damn, Stella, have you lost your ability to comprehend? I told you. This all started because of you and the fact that Thomas Hutchinson was in the dark, making threats. There's always been a contingency plan. Witnesses are too dangerous."

Oh, God!

Because of me?

"Kool-Aid?" I whispered.

"Only at the Eastern Light. Uncle was confident the other campuses are too well hidden."

Thank God!

No Kool-Aid at the Northern Light.

"What did you mean that Thomas was making threats?"

"He was part of the outside Light, a follower in the Shadows. But when he called his connection, he told him that he wanted out of prison, where the marshals had taken him. He knows The Light is capable of getting him out."

"Will it?"

"The Light can do anything. Will it? No, and it's his fault."

"The threats?"

He smirked. "Maybe you are listening. Yes, he didn't just ask to be released. He said that if it didn't happen soon, he'd start talking to anyone who'd listen." An amused grin graced Dylan's lips and his eyes narrowed. "The Light is everywhere. I'm sure that if it hasn't already happened, very soon, the asshole who threatened to rape you will no longer exist. Who knows, if it's another inmate, Hutchinson may get to know your fear of rape before he leaves this world. If I have anything to say about it, and now that I know what he did to you, I'll suggest it."

Part of me cringed at the idea that Dylan had that much power. The other part of me liked the idea of Thomas suffering for what he'd done to me. The evidence was mounting supporting my diagnosis of dissociative identify disorder.

"But you're a policeman, a detective. You help people."

"I do. I just helped you, for a second time."

I looked down at my hands and lifted my fingers for him to see. When I did he closed his eyes and took another drink. I waited for him to finish before I said, "You knew. When we were at the morgue and the woman, the one who we were afraid was Mindy, you knew she was part of The Light?"

He nodded. "What do you want me to say, that I'm sorry? Because I'm not. It's the way it is. You work the game in your favor or you lose. I'm not a loser, neither is Gabriel."

I took a deep breath, my cramping nearly gone. "Mindy?"

"Last I heard, she made it to a campus. I'm not sure which one, and I honestly didn't want to know."

"But she wasn't investigating The Light. Why did they take her?"

"She was investigating a business from outside The Light, Motorists of America, MOA. It's a shell corporation. She stumbled across too many things, like you."

I recognized that name. It was the company Foster had told me about—the one I had been too impatient to listen to him discuss. Oh, shit, it was the one that Foster had found when he was investigating Dylan. Dylan's name was on a utility bill for a house in Bloomfield Hills that was owned by MOA.

Could that be where we were? Was this the house Foster had found by researching Dylan's name?

Dylan ran his hands along the dark-blond scruff lining his defined jaw. "I fucking warned you. I told you to leave it alone, but you were too stubborn."

I closed my eyes. "Did Bernard or Foster ever see my research?"

"Come on, you're smarter than that."

A tear trickled from my eye. "So they never knew what I'd learned?"

"No."

"My parents?"

"Your mom still calls me."

My chest clenched as I laid my head on my arms. "How could you do this and talk to her like you didn't know?"

"I didn't see any other options. Do you?"

"Yes," I whispered. "Yes." My words gained strength as I lifted my head. "I see *many* other options. Tell the truth. Tell law enforcement. Do something. Stop this travesty. What The Light is doing is human trafficking and drugs. Oh, God . . ." My volume decreased. "Do you know what happens? Last Sunday, here at the Eastern Light, I witnessed a man and woman—"

Dylan raised his hand. "I don't want to know."

"What? That doesn't make sense. You're supporting this, condoning this, and you don't want to know?"

"We are all part of a greater good, part of the body. I have my responsibilities. I don't need to know about the others and what they do unless it interferes with what I do."

It was time for my eyes to narrow. "I don't know what your responsibilities entail, but let me tell you, I watched a man be murdered. The woman, she survived to end up in the basement . . ." My stomach knotted again. "Now she's dead."

"If you're talking about the woman in the bed, in the room where you were left, she was unconscious. The explosion was probably easier on her than the others."

"How can you be so callous? How can you talk about life like it doesn't matter?" Suddenly a thought occurred to me. "How? Wait a minute. Why are you being this open with me? Why are you telling me all of this?" My hands began trembling. "Are you going to kill me?"

Dylan stood and his footsteps moved about the kitchen. "Glass of water, Stella?"

What?

"No." The hairs on the back of my neck rose to attention and my skin prickled with goose bumps. "Tell me." My volume rose and I stood to face him. "Dylan, tell me." I stared into his piercing blue eyes and tried again. "For old times, for what I've been through, please tell me what is going to happen to me." My volume rose. "If you're going to kill me, be man enough to own it."

He reached out and caressed my cheek. I sucked my lip between my teeth and forced myself to remain still as his words rolled forth and his warm beer-scented breath skirted my cheeks. Though his tone was soft like an apology, his words were sharp in their meaning. "Stella, I know you may hate me, but you should know, at one time, I thought I could love you. The you I loved was strong and sure. I've been around subservient women all my life. My mother was one. I loved her but hated the way she acted around my father and the other men." He looked deep into my eyes, his finger tracing my cheek and lips. "I loved your fight, sharp tongue, and stubbornness. I loved all of that, but it wasn't worth the cost. The price was too high—not only to you, but to me and The Light."

His tone softened as his touch dipped to my collarbone and his gaze lingered at the neckline of the dress. "Besides, they took those parts of you away. That asshole you call your husband did that."

I wanted to tell him it hadn't been Jacob, it had been his uncle. It was Father Gabriel who was responsible, but I kept my lips closed and let him continue.

Dylan took a deep breath. Bringing his eyes back to mine, he tucked a piece of my hair behind my ear. "Even so, for all the reasons I said, I wanted you to know the whole truth. I wanted you to understand that I tried. I really did."

I took a step back. "Please . . . you're scaring me."

"Don't you understand? Don't you see it now? The Light can't be stopped."

I nodded, again pulling my lip between my teeth.

"That explosion changes everything," he explained. "I'm trying to make you understand. No matter what happens to me or to you, The Light is here and there and everywhere. There's no escaping it. My uncle was right. Allowing you to go back to Stella's world would be impossible."

I shook my head. "No, it's not! I won't tell. I promise. I'll pretend, like I was doing earlier. I can do that."

He took a deep breath. "Believe me when I tell you this hasn't been an easy decision."

"What hasn't been easy?"

He leaned closer, once again cupping my cheek. "Do you remember how good we were together? Do you remember how easy it was?"

I nodded, tears raining down my cheeks.

He cooed, "It was easier with you than anyone. I wanted . . ." He touched his lips to mine, the cold contact feeling more like a good-bye than a hello. "But," he went on, "we don't always get what we want. I've known it all my life. The Light is bigger than me, than you, than both of us.

"I told you everything, because things changed tonight—because of you. I wanted to be honest, for old times' sake . . ."

I saw the syringe from the corner of my eye. It was like the one Elijah had tried to use on me earlier.

". . . even though I know that when you wake up, you won't remember a word of it."

"No!"

The sharp pain in my neck transported me back to the parking lot in Detroit, just before my world went black.

CHAPTER 35
Jacoby

I landed the small plane in Anchorage a little ahead of schedule; however, as we rolled to a stop along the runway, my mind wasn't thinking about the time or even about the blur of commotion on the tarmac. My mind was in Bloomfield Hills. The raids should all have been started if not carried out, and I wanted details. I needed to know Sara was safe.

"Thank you." Benjamin's voice came through the earphones, reminding me that I wasn't the only one worried about a wife. "Jacob, I mean Jacoby, Raquel's pulse is weak, but she still has one. Thanks to you. I know if you hadn't . . . she wouldn't . . ." His voice trailed away.

I turned and, with a strained smile, nodded in his direction. "They're waiting on us. They'll have her in surgery soon."

Though it was after ten at night, the airport where I'd been told to land was alive with activity. Just as Special Agent Adler had promised, there was an ambulance, and as I unbuckled my seat belt, it was moving slowly toward the plane. I opened the hatch door and lowered the steps before going back to help Benjamin.

As I reached for Raquel's seat belt, Benjamin grabbed my hand. "I don't know if she'll make it, but I know she wouldn't have made it up there. I owe you. Anything. You've got it. You can count on me."

"Right now, concentrate on Raquel. Until we know how the raids went and what's ahead for us, listen to the FBI. They'll keep her safe. They know what we're dealing with better than we do. I'll do my best to convince them to let you stay with her, but . . ." I shrugged. "Honestly, you were on the Assembly. There's a case against you. You knew things. You worked in the lab, but really your future is up to you."

Benjamin took a deep breath. "*It's up to me*, like we told followers. Nothing was up to them, and I have the feeling that nothing's really up to me now either."

"It is. I'll talk to my handler. I'll do all I can to persuade them to allow you to stay with Raquel until she's no longer critical. If you want more time than that—"

Benjamin looked away, his red-rimmed eyes downcast. "I want forever. Is that too much to ask?"

"No. I want the same thing. You just need to talk to the agents— be one hundred percent honest with them, be willing to turn state's evidence and testify. That's what you can do to get back to Raquel." I patted his shoulder. "I'm behind you. I hope you know that you've got my support."

We turned as paramedics made their way into the fuselage.

"What about Abraham?" Benjamin asked in a hushed tone.

I shook my head. "You should get a damn medal. You also saved my life. I'll tell them what happened."

"What about her?" he asked, looking at Raquel as the paramedics lifted their gurney. "Legally, I mean. Is there a case against her too?"

"It's not up to me. It's all up to the FBI, but I'll tell them what I know, which is, as far as the Assembly wives are concerned, from my knowledge they were all blissfully unaware. They were never informed of the workings of the Assembly or Commission. I'll be truthful in everything."

"Sir, is this your wife?" the young female paramedic asked, looking to Benjamin.

Benjamin looked at the paramedic and again at me.

"We," I said to Benjamin, "were married under The Light. I plan on using that legality to find Sara. Until it's disproved, your answer is yes."

Benjamin nodded and turned toward the young woman. "Yes, she is."

The woman's eyes widened as she scanned Raquel's injuries and looked back to Benjamin, seeing his bloodstained shirt.

"Miss," I said, attempting to derail her obvious train of thought. "I'm Agent McAlister of the FBI. This woman was attacked and beaten by someone who has been dealt with, not by her husband. I'll testify to that."

"Yes, Agent. Sir," she said to Benjamin, "please come with us. They're waiting for us at the medical center."

"Miss"—I read her name tag—"Kellogg, this woman's husband and another agent need to stay by her side."

"Agent, they can follow—"

"No, they will be *with* you."

"Yes, sir," she said, tightening the restraint and securing Raquel on the gurney. Without another word she and the other paramedic wheeled Raquel down the stairs toward the ambulance.

I handed Benjamin the burner phone. "I'll get one from the bureau and call you. I plan on heading east immediately."

He nodded and tucked the phone in his pocket. "You know, the last time I accepted this phone . . ."

I shook my head. "I know. I'm sorry."

"No, Raquel was right. She wanted to help. Just find Sara."

I took a deep breath as Benjamin stepped through the doorway and followed his wife.

As I descended the steps, the weight of three years lifted from my shoulders. I'd done my part. The Light was behind me. Looking out at the sea of faces, I searched for ones I recognized. When my eyes met one man's, that of an agent probably fifteen to twenty years my senior, a weary smile graced my lips. I'd spoken to him, but I hadn't seen him in over three years.

When he nodded in my direction, my grin broadened toward Special Agent William Adler. While he'd grown a few more gray hairs and even gained a few pounds, I recognized my handler immediately. When I reached the bottom of the stairs, he met me and patted my shoulder.

"Agent McAlister, you're a sight for sore eyes." He scanned me up and down. "It doesn't appear that you're too much the worse for wear. Maybe you'd like to do another three years in The Light?"

"No, sir. Let's flip that switch and move on."

Adler's welcoming expression faded. "Come with me, Jacoby. We need to talk."

The four words *we need to talk* splintered my already frayed nerves, leaving them in shreds. Before I could speak and ask him what we needed to talk about, he ushered me away to a waiting vehicle. I tried to protest, letting him know I didn't want to go to the field office. I couldn't go to the field office. I needed to get on a plane to Detroit. Instead of listening or even acknowledging my protests, he and two other agents flanked me and herded me into the large black SUV.

Once we were safely away from listening ears, Special Agent Alder turned toward me. "Listen, Jacoby, you're not authorized to leave, not yet."

"What do you mean? I told you on the phone that Sara's at the Eastern Light. I told you that you needed to get to her . . ." My shoulders drooped and words failed to form as the weight I thought I'd shed fell heavily back upon me.

"Listen to me," Adler said. "Can you do that?"

I nodded. I could listen, but first I needed to quiet the mayhem alienating the words and phrases coming from his mouth. Though his lips were moving, I wasn't seeing him. All I saw and heard was her. I was back in that damn bathroom in the outbuilding at the mansion with Sara in my arms. Her sweet trusting voice filling my ears while her beautiful blue eyes dominated my vision. With her hand reassuringly upon my chest, she said, "I trust you with my life. I have and I'll continue to do it."

Her confidence was steadfast, and I'd left her, walked away and abandoned her.

"Agent, did you hear a word I just said?"

The vehicle had pulled away from the small airport, taking me farther away from Sara, not closer, not where I'd promised to stay. I looked beyond my visions and searched for the ambulance. It must have already left. If I strained I could hear its sirens wailing in the distance.

"I'm sorry," I replied. "What? You completed the raid at the Eastern Light?"

Agent Adler nodded. "When's the last time you slept?"

"That's not relevant."

"I'm sensing you're in shock or going into shock. That's understandable. You deserve to rest. Without you this would never have been as successful—"

"Special Agent, you were telling me about the Eastern Light— about Sara."

He nodded. "After I spoke to you, we moved on the Eastern Light first. That raid began earlier than the rest. Once you told us there was no mass suicide or homicide plan at the other campuses the timeline seemed safe. Being that we struck after one in the morning, we believe that helped decrease the number of casualties. We found everything you promised on the campus and hidden in what appeared to be abandoned buildings, including four women who were in a room resembling a clinic."

My heart clenched.

"Sara?" I asked.

"We don't believe so. Due to their injuries, it's difficult to be sure. Once we get to the field office we have pictures you can check for visual confirmation. There were only eighteen casualties on the campus in Highland Heights. They appeared to be the crew of followers working within the production plant. Identification is underway, but given the lack of fingerprints, we have our work cut out for us."

"The rest?"

"Taken into custody."

I nodded. "Sara wasn't on the campus."

"No one came forth with that name, or Stella Montgomery, under questioning. Of course, few are talking, especially the women. According to the agents at the scene, they believe the women were too afraid to speak, even with female agents and interrogators. However, after my brief conversation with Miss Montgomery on your phone, I'd assume that she would talk and give her true identity."

I nodded. She would. "Bloomfield Hills, sir?"

"Agent, the raids were *planned* simultaneously. The timing was close."

Oh, fuck! I was going to be ill.

"Close? What does that mean?"

"The subdivision that housed Gabriel Clark's home in Bloomfield Hills is gated. The mansion on Kingsway Trace is also gated. By the time we gained access, there was a five-minute discrepancy."

Though the vehicle was moving, I couldn't feel it. I couldn't focus. The weight was crushing, suffocating. My body fought to complete involuntary tasks. Expanding my lungs and contracting my heart required thought. The life-sustaining processes were chaotic at best. I worked to speak. "What happened in five minutes?"

I waited, wondering whether I'd actually spoken.

He reached for my arm. "They must have known we were coming. The entire mansion blew. The way it exploded, it was a planned defensive measure. The home must have been sitting on a powder keg of explosives or maybe it was an intentional natural gas explosion. ATF is working on it. It's still burning. The investigators can't get close enough to even start looking for bodies."

"Bodies? What about survivors?"

"Jacoby, no one survived that blast."

"Maybe they got out first," I tried. "There are other exits, down by the airstrip?"

"Our agents had the property surrounded. We had aerial confirmation of the property and all the possible ways on and off. Every gate was blocked at least ten minutes before we tried to enter, even before the initiation of the raid on the campus. No one tried. Whoever was there is gone."

"Ten minutes? Then why weren't they up to the house five minutes earlier?"

"Agent." Adler's voice was calm, as if it would make what he was saying any easier to comprehend. "The bureau did the best they could. We only had eighteen casualties, forty-six overall. If we'd made it into the mansion five minutes earlier, we would have lost agents in the explosion."

"Forty-six? Does that include victims in the mansion?"

"No, but it includes all the campuses. Over one thousand people are in custody. Those outcomes are very good."

Incredulously I sought the right words, yet none came forth. "Outcomes, numbers? Shit! This isn't about numbers. I need to see the pictures of every woman you found, alive and dead, at the Eastern Light. And once they get in that mansion, I need to see that too." I turned my blurry vision out the window, before I turned back. "Special Agent, I request permission to go to Detroit. I need to see for myself."

"Agent, we understand that you became close—"

"She was assigned to me as a *wife*—nine months ago!" He didn't seem to understand. "She's pregnant with my child."

The interior of the SUV went silent. Not even road noise registered any longer.

"She's not dead," I said.

"Agent, we don't—"

"No. I know. I don't know if I ever believed in this shit before, but I would know. I would feel it if she were dead. She's not, and I'm going to find her."

He didn't respond as we continued to drive. Finally I managed to pull my thoughts from Sara and broaden my scope to the entire mission. "What about Gabriel Clark?"

"We have him. We have them all—him, the members of the Commission and Assembly. Well, unfortunately, we're missing one member of the Assembly at the Eastern Light. He could have been at the mansion. Also, one of our forty-six casualties is a member of the Assembly at the Northern Light. I don't know if you know anything about that. He was found in a hallway of the pole barn near the offices attached to the hangar."

"I know he was sent to accompany me to the hangar"—it was then I remembered the envelope—"to recover"—I reached into my jacket and pulled out the envelope and handed it to Special Agent Adler—"this. I have no idea what's inside, but whatever it is, my gut tells me that I owe my life to it. Father Gabriel was suspicious of me since Fairbanks, four days ago. I'd received this letter from a brother at the Western Light. I'd forgotten all about it, with everything that happened with Sara." Saying her name caused my heart to clench. "I have the feeling if he didn't need me to fly him back to the Northern Light or need whatever this contains, I wouldn't be sitting here right now."

My handler looked closely at the innocuous-looking envelope. "We'll take it in to the field house and have it analyzed." He turned toward me. "Jacoby, you have hours, days, and maybe even weeks of debriefing ahead. You have more knowledge of The Light than you're even aware. As you know, we have people who can help you recover that information. I'm deeply sorry about Stella Montgomery. Maybe in all that information floating around in your head you'll see how what you did, what she was willing to do, was beneficial to the success of this mission. Agent, because of you and her, we've opened a Pandora's box of illegal activities. You're right. We don't have a body count at the mansion, but there have been hundreds lost to this organization, even one more is one too many. Your sacrifice will not go unnoted—and neither will hers."

I did my best to hold it together, to be the agent I'd been trained to be, but I couldn't. "I promised her I'd keep her safe. I promised her a few more days. I even pleaded . . ." My teeth ground together. "Where is he?"

"Who?"

"Where is Gabriel Clark?"

"He's still at the Northern Light. We're arranging transport here to Anchorage."

"I need to see him as soon as he's here."

Special Agent Adler's head moved slowly back and forth. "You know we have protocol."

Anger and hatred seethed from my every pore.

"I want to look the motherfucker in the eye and tell him that I was the one who brought him down."

"Agent, one thing at a time."

CHAPTER 36
Dylan

"Good-bye, Stella Montgomery," I whispered as her body fell limp against mine.

Damn her! This was all her fault. She could fucking listen to *her husband*, but she wouldn't listen to me. I didn't want the submissive shell he'd created. But how hard would it have been for her to keep her damn nose out of The Light?

None of that mattered anymore. I wasn't sure what exactly had happened in the last hour. On the phone, Joel had said all the campuses had been raided. *I mean, what the fuck? How all?* My mind was a cyclone. This was never supposed to happen. The Eastern Light, sure. There was always that possibility. That was why I hated going over to that place. But *all* of them?

I tried to rein in my nerves as I laid Stella on the couch. Somehow she had something to do with this. US Marshals? I needed information and I needed it yesterday. Someone in the Shadows will know something. *If I only had my real damn phone! It was cleared to access the network on the dark web.*

The medicine I'd given Stella wasn't the memory suppressant, not yet. What I'd injected was only something to knock her out. The other shit was touchy, and I didn't know enough about it to risk administering it. If I gave her too much, too quickly, all of her memories could be lost—everything including things like eating and speaking. I'd heard stories from when they'd first started using it. On more than one occasion they'd been left with an infant in a woman's body. Then again, if not enough was given, there was that chance it wouldn't work.

She'd already had the medication in her system once. Did that mean she'd built immunity and she needed more, or that only a little would work?

I ran my hand through my hair and exhaled. I wanted to know what the fuck was happening. Where the hell were Joel and Chloe? I needed to prioritize. I also knew that if Gabriel were here, he'd never think a woman was worth this much trouble.

The way I planned it, once Joel and Chloe arrived, Joel could help me carry Stella to one of the bedrooms. Before they were banished, Chloe had worked with her father in the lab at the Northern Light. She understood all the science stuff and how the medication worked. She could administer the memory suppressant while Joel and I figured out what the hell was happening with The Light and the Shadows.

Once Chloe erased Stella's memories, Sara Adams would be gone forever. If she really did have feelings for that guy, this would be easier anyway. More than likely, Jacob was already gone—polar bear food. Gabriel had forbidden me from keeping Stella, but as I grabbed another beer from the refrigerator, I reasoned that if he was now in FBI custody it was no longer his decision. It was mine. And once Chloe was done, the woman with me wouldn't be Sara or Stella. We'd find her a new name.

I paced from the kitchen to the couch and back, fisting my hair.

Too fucking much!

All of this was on me. I tried again to call Joel, but the circuits were all still busy.

I flipped on the television. The first thing that came on was an interruption of normal programming. On the screen in front of me was aerial coverage of the Bloomfield mansion explosion. The caption read, "Gas leak suspected as the cause of an explosion in Bloomfield Hills. House is believed to be the part-time residence of accused cult leader Gabriel Clark." As I was about to change the station, a reporter appeared, broadcasting live from Whitefish, Montana. Behind her were buses filling with followers.

Clenching my teeth, I didn't listen to what she had to say. Instead, I shut the damn thing off.

Taking deep breaths, I reassured myself that I'd learned how to do this. Most of my life had been spent in preparation for my role in assuming power. I needed to take the lessons I'd learned from Gabriel and put them to use. First and foremost, no one would or could argue with my decisions. As long as Gabriel was out of commission, I was in charge. Second, as leader, I could authorize and/or witness activity, but I was always to stay at least one step removed.

Keeping his hands clean was what Gabriel had done. It was how he would survive whatever was about to happen. No matter how far and wide the Shadows were scattered, we all knew Gabriel Clark would survive. Like a phoenix he'd rise again.

When I finally got a hold of Joel, he was both shocked and elated to hear from me. He'd tried my other phone and I hadn't answered. He said the chatter among the Shadows was that I'd been in the mansion.

Maybe I was the phoenix, rising from the ashes of the explosion.

My plan was to lie low for a few days and let the dust settle. This house was a great place to do that. It didn't have any connections to me or to The Light. It was connected to MOA. After a couple of days of organizing our strategy, we'd be ready. And after a few days of pumping the drug into Stella, she'd be ready. When we woke her, she'd be whomever we wanted. I would convince her that she was part of the Shadows.

In our brief conversation Joel told me that Gabriel had passed the mantle. He'd told the Shadows I was in charge. I just hadn't known it, or seen it. I looked over at Stella.

"Because I don't have my fucking phone!" She couldn't hear me, but saying it out loud made me feel better.

While my temples throbbed with the task ahead and the responsibilities Gabriel had bestowed upon me, I still managed to grin, knowing I wouldn't be doing this alone. Shit, in The Light Stella had been chosen. In the Shadows she'd believe she was married to the leader—to me. It didn't get much fucking higher than that.

I wasn't interested in a harem or brides of the Shadows. There was one woman I wanted. And now that I was the leader, my every desire was obtainable. I wanted the old Stella, but I'd take an improved version. She really was smarter than shit. I liked her quick tongue and questions. In the new version, I'd encourage her strengths, as long as she knew that when it came to my word, it was indisputable. I smoothed her hair away from her face and tried to ignore the blackened eye. With her beside me, and the Shadow resources, we would be unstoppable.

My first official proclamation after Joel arrived with a new phone would be to assure Thomas Hutchinson's fate. My neck straightened as I brushed my thumb over her swollen eye. Before he died, that fucker would know the fear Stella had experienced when he threatened to rape her.

I paced by the large window, the glow of Gabriel's house still lightening the horizon. Shaking my head, I tried again to log my MOA phone onto the private network, but it didn't have authorization. Fuck! I'd missed so much by not having my real phone. At least now I didn't need to worry about anyone finding it and connecting it to me. With that explosion, they might not even be able to identify my car, and they definitely wouldn't find Elijah.

That stupid asshole.

Under my regime things would change. Then again, I wasn't as narcissistic as my uncle. I understood that not everything had to be my way. He believed he was invincible. I'd warned him to have contingency plans at all the campuses. He wouldn't listen. He was so damn sure that the isolation would be enough.

I didn't need to worry about that with the Shadows. Our growth over the last few years had knocked the number of followers on the campuses out of the damn water. We'd also known that what had happened tonight was always a possibility.

My phone buzzed. Finally. Maybe the damn circuits were catching up.

Joel: WE'RE HERE. LET US IN.

I glanced at Stella, still sleeping like a baby, before I walked through the house and opened the front door.

"Shit, D. This is worse than we imagined," Joel said, shaking his head as they entered. By their expressions they both looked as if they'd just suffered through an FBI raid, not heard about it.

"Get your head in this," I said as I patted Joel on the shoulder.

Chloe buried her tearstained face in my chest as she wrapped her arms around my waist. "Dylan, I never thought . . . do we know yet? They have Gabriel. Don't they?"

I shook my head and gently rubbed her back. The three of us had been friends for most of our lives. Their parents and mine had been some of the first followers. While their parents had gone to the campuses, mine had gone to work in the Shadows. Gabriel had known he needed reinforcements scattered about. "I don't know," I replied. "I don't have my real phone, only the MOA one, and it's not authorized for the network. Besides, the damn circuits have been swamped. If Gabriel did try to reach me, well, he couldn't."

"The last communication didn't sound good," Joel said.

Slowly Chloe released her hug, and I led them back to the kitchen.

"We can't reach anyone at the Northern Light," she stammered. "M-my mom. My dad . . ." She walked toward the back living room.

As Joel reached into the refrigerator and pulled out a beer, he asked, "Where's your phone? Why don't you have it?"

"Dylan!"

Joel and I turned toward Chloe's scream. Her lips were pressed together and her arms crossed over her chest as she stared at Stella's sleeping body.

"This! She? Are you crazy?" She didn't wait for my answer as her earlier sadness morphed to indignation. "This is *that* woman, the one you were dating, the one that was sent away. Isn't it?"

I pulled my shoulders back. "Yes."

"Gabriel told you—"

I took a step forward. "Gabriel isn't in charge anymore, at least not currently."

"But he said—"

"Chloe," Joel warned. "D's right."

"Either you're with me on all decisions or on none," I declared.

Fuck! I sounded just like my uncle, but at the moment I didn't care.

Chloe took a deep breath. "Fine. Is this why you wanted me to bring the drug?"

"Yes. She's spent the last nine months at the northern campus. When she first disappeared there was a lot of press and police activity. It's safer now. She's old news."

"D, man, I'm not questioning you, but are you sure?"

I nodded. "Yeah, I'm sure. When I first brought her here, I was thinking I could get her to the Western Light." I ran my hand through my hair. "She's a pain in the ass, but I'm not ready to let her be banished." I scrunched my nose. "I also wasn't going to leave her at the mansion."

Chloe's lips moved upward. "So instead you're decreeing that she's *banished* like us."

I scoffed. "I guess I am. I didn't think of it like that, but yes. Your exit from the Northern Light was a little more voluntary, but the end result is the same. She knows too much to be released, and while carrying out ultimate banishments doesn't bother me, like I said, not with her." I stood and watched as my childhood friends stared, first at Stella and then at each other. When they didn't respond, I said, "Help me carry her upstairs."

I got my arms under hers and lifted her shoulders while Joel lifted her feet. I continued talking as we walked. "I figured we could lay low for a couple of days. Gabriel's directions were for radio silence. We'll do what he said. It'll be easier on the Shadows if things progress the way they expect. Then, once we wake her up, we can move. She's smart. She'll adapt. Fuck, she adapted to the Northern Light. This time she'll have her real life back, well, kind of."

Chloe wrinkled her nose as she watched us lay her on the bed. "She's going to need to be cleaned up. Who the hell did that to her back? And why is she dressed like a bride?"

"Mark," I replied. "We had words. There was only so much I could do." I clenched my teeth together. "Fucking Gabriel told me I couldn't have her, and then I found out he planned on making her one of them—one of his brides."

"Jesus!" Chloe said, shaking her head, "I'm not questioning Father Gabriel, but I just don't get it."

Joel looked to his wife and narrowed his gaze. "Just because we're in the Shadows . . ."

Chloe continued to move her head slowly from side to side, her brown hair falling over her shoulders as she tended to Stella. The Shadows didn't follow all the doctrine of The Light. That was part of the reason Joel and Chloe had asked to move into the Shadows. The extent to which each Shadow followed varied, but Father Gabriel's teachings were still the cement, the binding that held the Shadows to The Light.

"You need to keep the messages going, for those who want it, who need it," Joel said, talking to me.

I nodded as I watched Chloe set up the medication. "I've been thinking about that. Man, you're my first Commissioner. I was wondering if you . . ." My words trailed away. The Light doctrines and preaching weren't my thing. I'd spent most of my life avoiding them. Joel knew the lessons backward and forward. He and Chloe had lived it before they were married, and after at the Northern Light.

"If I wanted to preach, I'd have stayed in Alaska."

I stood taller. "As my first Commissioner, I'm not asking you." Joel's lips thinned, but he didn't respond. "The way I see it," I went on, "you two know that side better than I do. I can oversee the operations and the money. You're right. There are Shadows who'll need to hear Gabriel's word. I figure you two can give them what they need until the dust settles. We have Shadows everywhere: police, judicial, fuck, even federal: FBI, CIA, Homeland Security. I could keep going.

"What happened tonight will be big news. I was just watching some coverage on TV. It'll be like Stella's disappearance was. Give it some time and then it'll die down. When that happens we'll do what we do. It just takes one—Raphael, Michael, Uriel, one of them. Once we get one of them out of custody, the Shadows will eat it up. It'll be like he was raised from the fucking dead, and then he can do the preaching."

Joel nodded. "Fine. We'll do it. But I don't know why we should stop there."

Chloe began putting bandages around Stella's head.

"What are you doing?"

"The loss of vision," Chloe answered, "is vital. I remember reading my father's research. If you want her to believe she's someone else, it takes time."

"Father Gabriel," Joel continued. "He needs to rise again. The Shadows have the power. If they think getting one of the originals out of prison is a miracle, getting Father Gabriel out will be better than walking on water."

I nodded and smiled as I watched Chloe cover Stella with a blanket.

When she turned my way, she said, "I'll need to get some more medical supplies if she's going to be unconscious for a few days."

"Thank you, Chloe. We all need to bide our time." I slapped Joel on the back. "But I agree, man. We can't let Gabriel rot behind bars any longer than necessary. In the meantime—"

"You're the boss, man," Joel said, finishing my sentence. *"Father Dylan?"* he asked with a smirk.

"I'd rather not."

"You know what you need to do," Joel said.

Chloe put her arm around my shoulders. "It'll be like when we were kids."

I hadn't used my The Light name since my parents died. At first Gabriel had tried to get me to go by it, but my stubbornness won. "Not *Father*, though. Gabriel's coming back. We just don't know when."

"*Brother* David," Chloe said.

Though my gut twisted with the title, I couldn't be the leader of the Shadows as just Dylan. I nodded.

Joel shook his head. "All right, *Brother David*, we need to stop playing nursemaid and get down to business. If you're sure we're safe here, this is a great place to get our plan in gear. The computer system in the lower level is stellar. I know how to use it and backdoor us into some sites. It won't be long until I've got us not only on the dark web but authorized to broadcast. I'd say by tomorrow morning, we will be able to get a message out, something short to the Shadows. Not enough to sever Father Gabriel's orders of radio silence, just enough to let everyone know that you didn't die in that explosion—that Brother David is alive and ready to keep this going, to move the Shadows to the next level."

"It's nearly four in the morning. Do you think that this could wait until morning?" Chloe asked.

They both looked at me.

"I'd say it already did. Let's keep going and see what we can learn. We can't call the campuses, but shit, let's start contacting individual Shadows."

"From what I've learned," Joel said, "This was an FBI operation. Somehow they coordinated it with all three campuses."

"Our fucking Shadows in the FBI have some explaining to do. How the hell did it get this far?"

"I don't know, but I'd suspect that just like we have people inside the FBI, they had people or a person inside The Light."

"How in the hell didn't we know that?" I asked.

"That's what we need to find out. What are you going to name her?" Joel asked as we walked down the stairs.

I'd already thought about this. I knew the name she deserved. Yes, she'd been a pain in the ass, but in a few days, she'd be awakening with a new life for the third time. "Stacy," I replied. "It means 'resurrection.'"

Chloe nodded as both of their phones buzzed.

"Hello," Joel answered. "Yes, all three of us are here." His eyes opened wide as he disconnected his phone and turned to me. "That was a Shadow on the inside of the FBI. We need to get out now! I'm sorry about Stacy, D. But the FBI is only minutes away. Shadows first, we need to flee."

CHAPTER 37
Jacoby

For the middle of the night, the Anchorage field office was a hive of activity. Each new agent who came up to me slapped me on the back, congratulating me on a good run. They were all proud of the end results: no fires on the campuses, no mass suicide. Special Agent Adler said that the president had even called the director, pleased that he didn't have a PR nightmare on his hands.

After a few more congratulatory pats and affectionate ribbing as a few of my old colleagues called me *Brother Jacoby*, I made my way back to the evidence room. Standing at the doorway, with my mouth agape, I took in the other side of my mission. I'd lived it, been in the trenches, but this, the boxes of evidence, as well as board after board of pictures, creating theories and trails, was the end result of years of research.

"Jacoby, come in," Special Agent Adler called from his temporary office. I wasn't sure how long the operations would be located in Anchorage. Usually Adler and all the unit's operations were housed in Virginia.

I followed him into the small private room and shut the door.

"I wanted to let you see these pictures in private."

"Thank you." No one other than Adler and the other two agents in the SUV knew about my relationship with Sara.

Opening the folder, I pulled each glossy photo out and studied the faces. Every one of the women had bandaged eyes. It was standard protocol; however, that wouldn't impair me from being able to tell whether one of them was Sara. I'd spent three weeks looking at her with her eyes bandaged. I'd still recognize her nose, cheeks, hair, and lips.

Even those features weren't easily distinguishable on some of these women. Their injuries were extensive, yet the bruises and fractured bones barely registered. I'd flown women in similar condition more times than I cared to admit. I'd helped to carry their unconscious bodies onto my plane and taken them across the country. The only thing that mattered to me as I stared at the pictures was identifying Sara. I hated the thought of her being in that bad a shape in less than twenty-four hours, but if it meant she was alive, I'd nurse her back to health. I'd done it once before.

Sighing, I shook my head and placed the folder back on Adler's desk. "None of them are Sara."

"Every other agent who's looked at those photos has commented on the extent of the injuries. You didn't say a word."

I met his gaze. "I've seen it, firsthand. There's nothing new to me in those photos."

Special Agent Adler whistled as he blew a gust of air between his teeth. "We need to get you some rest and start debriefing. There's so much I want to know."

"Not yet. I want to meet Father . . . Gabriel Clark when that plane lands." I ran my fingers over my face, and as I did, I recognized the familiar disconnect with the tips of my fingers. Lowering my hands, I turned them over, showing them to Special Agent Adler. "See my fingers?"

"Yes, we've been seeing a lot of that."

"No, don't you get it?"

"What?"

"I want an alert sent out to all the area hospitals, homeless shelters, airports, police, everywhere."

"Jacoby, I don't understand. We have all the followers corralled from the campuses."

"We don't have Sara. I refuse to believe she's dead. Have the FBI tell all the places I just mentioned that we're looking for women who have no fingerprints."

"As soon as they get the fire extinguished—"

"No, let's say she escaped. If she did, she could be wandering about. If she is, she could be picked up and that is the way to identify her."

"I'm not sure that's a good idea. There's more you need to know. Let me show you something that we're only beginning to understand."

I nodded, and waited for Adler to make his way around his desk and back out into the evidence room.

An hour later, as I drained my second cup of coffee, I continued to read and follow the magnitude of evidence compiled within this room. The caffeine was essential. I was currently going on twenty-four hours without sleep and the adrenaline from Benjamin's and my escape was quickly dissipating. Undoubtedly the emotional roller coaster of the last four days was taking its toll.

I'd lived in The Light for three years, and Special Agent Adler was right. My work had paid off. Because of me nearly a thousand people would now be free to live real lives, no longer manipulated by a narcissistic psychopath. However, as I followed the leads and information accumulated on the large boards, I was flabbergasted by what I hadn't known.

"So what the hell are *the Shadows*?" I asked, my brow furrowed in confusion.

"The Light outside of The Light," Agent Brady explained. He was a young man, part of the small obscure team at Quantico on the special task force that investigated The Light. His knowledge was as profound as mine. Instead of living it, he'd infiltrated The Light through cyber-space, through the dark web. Admittedly I felt a pang of jealousy when I learned that he'd discovered so much without putting himself or those he cared about at risk.

"It's an interesting phenomenon," Brady went on. "When you were first sent in, we had no idea that there were even three campuses. We'd identified the Western Light, but not the Northern. Your final corre-spondence nearly two years ago confirmed its existence."

I remembered making that call. I'd been living at the Northern Light for a time and felt the need to at least notify the FBI that the campus existed. I'd made that call from Bloomfield Hills on a burner. Thankfully, those cell towers weren't monitored like the ones at the Northern Light or even the Western; there was too much cell activity to identify unknown users.

"It wasn't until we started following the cyberactivity from the Northern Light that we were able to identify a connection out in the real world."

"The dark," I said mindlessly.

"Excuse me?" another young agent asked.

I looked up from the aerial photograph of the Bloomfield Hills mansion. "The real world, in The Light it's referred to as *the dark*, the area beyond The Light."

Adler had been right. It would take me weeks of debriefing to give up all the information I'd obtained, because some things, like the term *the dark*, seemed like common knowledge to me. The FBI had people to help scour my thoughts and memories. I was more concerned about the deprogramming. Obviously I was in need of that too.

"Yeah, we've heard that term. Well, the cybertrail led me to *the dark* . . ." Brady's voice trailed away as he hit keys on a keyboard and a large screen came to life.

I pinched my brow and stifled a yawn. "Yes, I understand the term the Shadows, but who or what are they?"

The screen became a map of North America. The three campuses were identified.

Brady went on, "The cyberactivity has been the strongest and the easiest to identify from your campus. It's the isolation. A lot of the activity was intercampus communication. At first that was difficult to intercept. The firewalls were commendable, hell, better than some used by our government. They were layered, even triple encrypted. We'd make it through one only to be stopped by another."

"You're saying The Light's security was good."

"I'm saying it was excellent. Only recently did we penetrate it enough to see the broadcasts of the meetings and sermons. By doing that we could pinpoint Gabriel's location. We could tell if he was at Bloomfield Hills, which is where the majority of the broadcasts originated, the Western Light, or the Northern Light. We thought that most of the activity was intercampus, until we discovered this." He hit a button and suddenly the United States and Canada lit up like a virtual Christmas tree. He zoomed out and lights lit all over the world.

"What is that?"

"Hits on the latest broadcast."

"How?" I asked. "If the communication was solely between campuses?"

"Agent, welcome to the Shadows. There's a highly encrypted website on the dark web that allows followers outside of the campuses to obtain access to the broadcasts. The last broadcast was short, sent fifteen minutes before the FBI touched down at the Northern Light, moments before the explosion in Bloomfield Heights."

I couldn't think about the explosion and concentrate. I had to be Agent Jacoby for a little while. "Do you have the broadcast? Did you see it?"

I gripped the table in front of me as Father Gabriel's face covered the large screen and his voice filled the room. How many times had I watched his broadcasts? He looked exactly as he did when he delivered a sermon, not a hair out of place.

"Children of The Light, a very unfortunate chain of events has occurred. You will hear things and see images. Remember, my children, the dark is everywhere. While The Light may be temporarily dimmed, we know it cannot be extinguished. You, my children of the Shadows, must stay vigilant and keep the vision alive. You've been given enlightenment to discern the truths. Those who wish us harm are our enemies. You are the soldiers in this war. Though I may be unavailable for a time, know that time is irrelevant to our cause and mission. My power will be held by the one who would inherit the legacy, until it is mine again. I entrust it thereupon, but never give up, never accept the lies told in the dark. Know that The Light will forever shine."

My knuckles blanched and the blood drained from my cheeks as the screen went black. "What the fuck does that mean?"

Special Agent Adler had entered the room during the broadcast. "Jacoby," he said, "there are a few bunks here. I suggest you get some sleep. We have a lot to discuss."

I spun toward him. "It's not gone? Three years, lives, Sara . . . all for nothing!"

"No," he replied calmly. "It wasn't all for nothing. The campuses were the main source of The Light's revenue. They were a hotbed of illegal activities hiding behind the separation of church and state. *You* brought that down. You did it! Over a thousand people freed. That wasn't for nothing."

"But"—I pointed toward the now-blank screen—"that earlier graphic, there are ten or fifty times as many Shadows." I used the new term. "Not everyone you're taking into custody was brought to The Light unwillingly. Their campus is gone, but with the right connections they'll be able to rejoin the force. What will stop them?"

Agent Adler shook his head. "The mission *was* successful. You do realize how unusual it is to be able to infiltrate three separate locations with the exercised precision and such a low number of casualties."

"Sara," I whispered.

"Going back last Friday made the difference in our success. We didn't have the manpower ready."

I nodded. "Have you issued the APB for Dylan Richards?"

"Not yet. The charred remains of his car were found on the grounds in Bloomfield Hills. Right now we're assuming he was in the mansion when it blew."

My knees gave way as I collapsed in a nearby chair. "No. No." My volume increased. "I don't care if it was five minutes or one, there was a plan to save Richards and I know it. Besides, did you hear what Gabriel said? He said something about his power going to someone who would *inherit*."

Brady nodded. "We've been searching, but we're coming up blank. He must mean it as a transfer of power. Gabriel Clark or Garrison Clarkson never had children."

"Not a child, Richards is Clark's nephew. He's alive; I know it. Even that asshole wouldn't allow his nephew to be blown up. I saw the two of them interact just the other day—fuck, I don't even know what day it is."

"Tuesday," Brady offered.

"Yesterday. There's no way Clark allowed that."

Agent Adler shook his head. "I don't see how—"

"Did you have constant aerial surveillance?" I asked.

Brady tapped his keyboard again; however, before he hit the key to play the time-lapsed video, he asked, "Are you sure you want to see this?"

My fight was gone. "I'm sure. Go back ten minutes before the blast."

He did. Ten minutes played in less than thirty seconds. The explosion made me gasp. Adler's hand came down on my shoulder as I wiped a tear from my tired eyes. There was nothing preceding it, just a catastrophic eruption. Obviously the means to produce such an explosion had been in place for an event such as this.

I agreed that on the video there was no activity on the grounds. If Richards had received a warning call, he hadn't heeded it.

"Is there any way he could have known earlier?" I asked out of desperation.

"It's doubtful. The timeline is tight."

While Adler answered, Brady brought up the video again and rewound to sixty minutes before the explosion. Moments after he put the time-lapsed footage in motion, I saw a blur of white in the darkness near the pool. The lights around the pool were the only illumination on the rear grounds.

"Wait," I said. "Go back and run it in real time."

Both men stilled as Brady did as I asked. Thankfully, the government had sophisticated cameras with immense zooming capabilities. Though it was grainy, there were definitely two figures who appeared to have run the length of the yard, the exact trek I'd run the day before.

"Was she wearing white?" Brady asked, interest as well as concern in his voice.

"No, not when I left, but, shit, I remember there were other women there in white. It could be one of them, or it could be that they made her change clothes." The possible reasons for the change of clothes turned my stomach. I wouldn't allow myself to let my thoughts linger there as I stared at the screen.

"It's difficult to see the other figure. I'd assume it's a man."

"Have they thoroughly checked the outbuildings?"

"Yes, and the wooded area. No one's there."

"There's a back gate. Can you access the video of that gate?"

Brady shook his head. "No, the main center for the surveillance was in the house. When it blew, we lost our connection."

"That neighborhood is within Bloomfield Hills and is gated," Adler said.

"Yes?" I asked, wondering where he was going with that.

"The neighborhood has cameras!" Brady said.

My exhaustion gave way to one last surge of adrenaline. "Can you . . . ?"

I didn't even need to finish my question before the screen came alive with nearly twenty feeds time-stamped at 00:00:00 Tuesday morning. The house wouldn't blow for over an hour, but in general the streets and intersections were quiet, except for a late-model black SUV. It stopped at one stop sign long enough for us to see the driver.

"Shit! It's him!" I said, the hairs on the back of my neck standing to attention as Dylan Richards's image came into view.

"I don't see anyone else in the vehicle," Adler said.

"But we saw the woman in white near the pools. If the bureau has thoroughly investigated the rear grounds and there's no one, or no body, down there, she has to be in the vehicle. I can't imagine him taking any of the other women from that house. It has to be Sara. I told you, she's not dead."

Brady isolated the SUV and followed it to another home within the neighborhood. Once he zeroed in on the home, a smaller screen emerged and we were shown the owner of the home: Motorists of America.

I turned with my brow furrowed. "What the hell is that?"

"It's a shell corporation. One that's been on our radar as part of the Shadows. It's worth millions, probably more."

"So even stopping the production at the Northern Light won't stop the money?"

"It will stop the influx of new money. There's already a good amount out there. We just need to prove that it was obtained illegally. Hell, it could make a small dent in the national debt."

"Send agents to that house now."

While Agent Adler dialed, Brady switched to a time-lapsed feed of the house. With the time stamp reading 03:04:50, another SUV pulled up to the house. A man and woman got out and went into the house. I looked at my watch. That had been about an hour ago. By the time Special Agent Adler had given the order to go to the house, Brady had the screen on the live feed.

Less than two minutes after the order was given, three people came out of the house and got into the new SUV. It was the new man and woman plus Richards.

"Shit! What the fuck just happened?"

Special Agent Adler's eyes narrowed. "Shit!"

"There must be agents at the mansion. Get someone there now! Catch him!" I was screaming orders at men, one of whom was my superior.

Brady followed the SUV through the streets of the neighborhood; however, once the SUV left the gates of the subdivision, we lost the feed.

"I gave them the license number. We need to sit tight," Brady said.

"Please." I turned to Agent Adler. "I need to be on a plane to Detroit."

Special Agent Adler nodded. "I'm going with you."

CHAPTER 38
Stella

Thick fog penetrated my thoughts, its tentacles clawing at my memories. It wasn't new, my mind knew its tricks. I'd played this game before. Steel shutters of internal defenses snapped shut and barricades went up. From somewhere deep I knew to stop the invasion. Its deception was difficult to fight. There was a tunnel and a light. The brightness enticed, pulled me closer, and my battered, exhausted body longed to surrender.

The promise of reprieve it offered was real. All I needed to do was lift the shutters and allow the fog to infiltrate. My reward would be rest and time to heal. The appeal grew as pain from my back and cramping from my midsection remained on my side of the barricades. If only I could open them a little, enough to allow the fog to enter, it would save me from the pain.

My desire grew . . . maybe I could allow just a little . . .

CHAPTER 39
Jacoby

Pictures from the home in Bloomfield Hills came via the agents' cell phones as Adler and I were driven back to the airport. I lost any semblance of professionalism as Sara's picture materialized.

She was there and she was alive, unconscious and alone in the house.

I didn't know why Richards had left her, but at that moment I didn't care. My cheeks dampened as tears of relief freely flowed. I wiped them away, watching as Agent Adler's iPad continued the slide show of images. As they materialized, I saw her bandaged eyes and my gut twisted. Thankfully, even though her eyes were once again bandaged, I didn't see injuries like those of the other women at the Eastern Light. What I did see, what made my heart skip a beat, was the bag of clear liquid hanging from the pole near her bed.

"Tell them to disconnect the medicine, immediately," I said, my body shaking with fear. That motherfucker had told me he'd try to keep her off the medicine. Now there it was.

"But Jacoby, you don't know what it is—"

"I do." My volume grew. "I don't know the name of it, but it's a memory suppressant. I've seen it attached to more women than I want to admit. Tell them to disconnect it immediately."

Agent Adler handed me the phone. "Here, you're not only an agent, you're her husband. You tell them."

"Agent?" I said, speaking to someone in Bloomfield Hills.

"Yes, sir, this is Agent Billings."

"Billings, disconnect the medicine immediately."

"Sir, by what authority . . ."

"I'm Agent Jacoby McAlister." My name had made the rounds. They all knew I was the one who'd been inside The Light.

"Sir, it's an honor—"

"Disconnect the medicine. As soon as the paramedics get there, have them start her on IV fluids. We need to dilute the medication in her system. Make certain that they *only* give her clear fluids. How is she?"

"She's unconscious and, well . . ."

"Tell me, Agent."

"Sir, her eyes are covered, but there appears to be bruising around one eye that has drifted down her cheek. I'd assume it's not new."

I shook my head. "It's not. She was struck on Friday. Is there anything else?"

"We haven't tried to move her, but there's blood on her dress." He gasped.

"What?"

"I haven't removed her dress."

"Don't!"

"Sir, her back is bloody. I'd wager to guess she's been whipped."

My teeth clenched together as rage surged through my veins. I was going to kill Richards when I saw him. The asshole got all up in arms over a blackened eye and he whipped her! "Get her to the hospital. I want an agent beside her every minute. Do not let anyone prescribe any medication. There's a possibility that she's pregnant."

"Yes, sir, but . . ."

"What is it?"

"I'm not a doctor, but she's bleeding, and not just from her back."

My chest became tight. "Get her to the hospital. Make sure she's safe. That's all that matters."

When the line was disconnected I handed the phone back to Adler and turned toward the window. The sun was rising in Anchorage, creating long shadows over the streets as we neared the airport.

As I fought the overwhelming sadness of the loss of something I hadn't realized I wanted, I tried to concentrate on the positive. Sara was alive. I cleared my throat. "What about Richards?" I asked.

"We lost them," Adler replied. "We found the SUV abandoned on Highway 1, but they're gone. We're staking out his house in Brush Park as well as the one in Bloomfield Hills. He hasn't reported in with the DPD either. We're still looking. His cell phone has been silent. We identified the other people through facial recognition. They go by Joel and Chloe Beechen."

"Joel and Chloe? I believe they're banished members of the Northern Light. I don't understand how they're still alive." I turned toward my handler. "If they were informed of our impending raid on that house, it means that someone from The Light or the Shadows somehow tipped them off. It means there's someone or multiple people within the FBI."

Special Agent Adler's lips pressed together. "Up until the raids, this task force was very small. I know it was secure. If it hadn't been . . . well, you would have been discovered. But with the raids, all the acquisitions, and then the explosion in Bloomfield Heights, the number of agents has increased dramatically. We'll begin an internal investigation, but first we need to be sure all of our witnesses are secure."

I ran my hand through my hair.

Shit, I need a shower.

As we pulled up to the airport, my eyes widened. Being ushered from an airplane to a waiting van was a line of men, all ones I recognized, all with their hands cuffed behind their backs. I reached for the door handle and Adler reached for my arm.

"Protocol. You don't want to ruin three years of work by saying the wrong thing. Let it go until you have Sara back."

My neck stiffened and my eyes narrowed. Getting out of the SUV, I moved so that I'd be in plain view of each Commissioner and Assemblyman, and especially in view of Father Gabriel.

I waited as each person passed, each member of the chosen.

Perhaps the Commission and Father Gabriel thought Abraham had killed me; maybe they hadn't given it much thought. When I saw the suit and the silk shirt, I knew.

I couldn't speak. Nevertheless I took another step forward.

My movement must have caught his attention. When our eyes met, the look Gabriel Clark gave me was classic and unforgettable. At first it was as if he couldn't believe what he was seeing. His dark eyes widened in question. It was as his gaze scanned my body and lingered on the badge hanging from a lanyard around my neck that I smiled. In his glare I witnessed unadulterated hatred. I knew the look, because if I hadn't known that Sara was safe, I would have been giving him the same expression. The next second an officer pulled Clark's elbow and he looked away.

My smile had been more of a Cheshire grin, and I didn't shine it just on Gabriel Clark. No, I maintained it with my cheeks high as Timothy passed by, his beady eyes narrowing in disbelief. It was only with Daniel and Luke that I found myself wanting to offer to help. I told myself I would, but first I wanted to get to Sara.

My sleep-deprived mind was a blur as I pushed my way through Henry Ford Hospital. As soon as we landed, I received an update. Stella Montgomery was in stable condition. After we left Anchorage she had undergone a minor medical procedure commonly referred to as a D & C.

I told myself to concentrate on the first sentence. She was safe and in stable condition. That didn't mean that I could ignore the rest of the update. I was an FBI agent. My job was dangerous. Hell, I'd almost been killed in the past twenty-four hours, and because of me, so had Stella. I'd never considered children, never wanted them. Until now.

There was a special security detail outside Stella's room. With the news of the Shadows, the FBI was taking every precaution. Although my face-off with Gabriel Clark had been gratifying, it was also stupid. Now I was a target. And if I was, so was Stella.

As I approached Stella's room, I struggled with what I'd find. Mostly I worried about how she'd take the news about the baby. That was, if she remembered—if they'd disconnected the memory suppressant before it had time to do its job. No one, except Brother Raphael, knew exactly how it worked or how much of the drug it would take to destroy her memory. She'd already had it in her system. Would even a small amount take her back to a blank canvas? The last messages had said she hadn't awakened, though the anesthesia from the procedure was wearing off.

"You're her husband?" the doctor asked, just outside her door.

"Yes," I said. Despite everything we'd been through, seeing her, even from a distance, made me smile. That was, until I noticed the bandages. "Why are her eyes still covered?"

"We thought maybe you could tell us. We didn't want to remove the bandages if there was a previous trauma."

I shook my weary head. "No, there's no trauma. The D & C?"

"Agent McAlister, from Stella's HCG levels, it's difficult to say if she was ever pregnant. However, due to the trauma she endured to her torso and the heaviness of her menstrual bleeding, the D & C was completed as a safety precaution."

"Trauma? What happened?"

"It appears as though blunt force was delivered directly to her uterus."

My fists balled. I'll kill him. So help me God. I was going to kill Richards.

The doctor placed a hand on my shoulder. "There's no permanent damage, if that's what you're concerned about. Your wife will be fine. Future children are possible."

I nodded. "How much longer until she wakes?"

"It could be anytime."

As we turned I saw Stella's hands move shakily to the bandages. "No! Not again! Please no!"

Her pleas were music to my ears. *She remembers!* I rushed to her side, pushing the nurse out of the way.

"Sara, I'm here. We're getting these off. You don't need them."

She blindly reached in my direction. "Jacob? Is that you? Are you here? Oh, God. Where am I?"

I fumbled with the bandages until they fell away. The small dark domes landed upon the covers, and from beneath them the most beautiful blue eyes blinked and focused on me.

"It's me. I'm here and you're safe."

Her shoulders shuddered as I wrapped her in my arms.

"I tried to help," she said. "I kept asking him questions, trying to get him to tell me information. But then he said I was going to forget everything, and then he stuck something in my neck." She pulled back. "Why? Why didn't it work?" Then her face dropped, her mouth slightly open. "Our baby? Did I . . . ?"

I shook my head and pulled her close. "You didn't do anything but survive. I'm so sorry I left you. I swear to God I'm going to kill him. I can't believe he did this to you."

Her face burrowed into the nape of my neck. "I'm so sorry."

"Stop it," I whispered as I rubbed small circles on her back. "You have nothing to be sorry about. The doctor said that they couldn't confirm you were pregnant. They said the hormone level was low. They also said they did a procedure for precaution, but if you ever decide to have children in the future, it's still an option."

Stella stilled in my arms. When she finally looked up to me she asked, "Me? If *I* ever decide?" She pulled her left hand away from the grip she'd had on me. "They took my wedding ring."

I lifted her hand to my lips and kissed her left fourth finger. "I'd be happy to put another one on that finger."

She sat taller and wiped the tears from her cheeks. "I'm done being Mrs. Adams."

"That's good." My cheeks rose as my first real grin surfaced. "I don't know anyone named Adams anyway." I brushed my thumb over her bruised eye. The color had lightened to a sickening green. "I was wondering how you feel about the name McAlister?"

The tips of her lips moved upward. "I think I like it. Sara"—her grin grew—"Stella McAlister." Burying her face in my chest, she looked up again, with her nose wrinkled. "Stella and Jacoby. That's going to take some time getting used to." She brushed my cheek. "You know, I don't care what your name is, as long as we're both safe. I love you."

"I love you too." I smoothed her blonde hair away from her face. "They told me I'd lost you. When I landed in Anchorage, they told me about the mansion."

She covered her face with her hands. "Jacob, there were women there. They called themselves *the brides of The Light*. They . . . belong . . ." Her hand fluttered around her neck, and I saw the faint bruise. "They said I would be . . ." Red blotches began to surface as her eyes filled with tears.

"Shhh . . . it's over." I pulled her close. "It's over for them too, I'd suspect. The authorities are waiting for the house to cool enough to check for remains."

She shook her head. "Dylan told me things, things I need to tell you."

"You never *need* to tell me anything. Your thoughts are yours. I'll take whatever you want to share."

Her lids fluttered with the ongoing battle Stella and Sara had been having since she'd left the Northern Light. And then her stare met mine. "I don't think that's what I meant. I meant, you're FBI. The FBI needs to know all the things he said. He told me that The Light is bigger than we know. He called it the Shadows."

I took a deep breath and exhaled. "You and I both need to spend time with agents who'll help us debrief and deprogram. I only hope that after our time in Virginia is complete, you still like the idea of Stella McAlister."

She reached for my hand and, as they'd done a thousand times, our fingers intertwined. "I can't make any promises, because I know from experience that life has a way of throwing curveballs, but if I were to guess, I will always like that name, and maybe one day when we're both ready, I'd like to verify the doctor's prognosis and create some little McAlisters."

"I can't tell you enough how sorry I am. I'll spend the rest of our lives trying to make up for leaving you. I shouldn't have done that."

"And what?" She brushed her lips against mine. "Father Gabriel would have killed you." Her light-blue eyes opened wide. "Wait! How did the raids go? What about all the others? What about our friends? Do they have Mindy? What about Brother Benjamin and Raquel?"

I laughed. For the first time in over a week, my chest rumbled, and I wrapped my wife in my arms, sending the vibrations from me to her. "I don't think I'll ever tire of your questions."

She shook her head. "That's good, because I can't seem to stop asking them."

"I've noticed." I took a deep breath. "The raids went well. Father Gabriel's in custody. I don't know anything about your friend Mindy. I saw Luke and the rest of the chosen men in Anchorage. The other followers were being transported from the Northern Light. I'm sure Mindy is among them, but there are over five hundred. It'll take a while to get them all to Anchorage and identified. As for Raquel and Benjamin, they'll be OK, but that's another story."

Her lip slipped between her teeth before she asked, "I remember Father Gabriel saying something?"

"Raquel was pretty badly injured, by Abraham, but we got her to Anchorage. I spoke with Benjamin on the way here from the airport. She's still critical, but the doctors are encouraged. They believe she made it to surgery in time. The FBI's allowing Benjamin to stay with her until she's better. All in all, there were few casualties—forty-six, not including the bodies yet to be discovered in the mansion."

"So we did it?" she asked. "Going back made a difference?"

"Yes, it made all the difference. There was a Kool-Aid plan for the Eastern Light. Lives were definitely saved there. Also, like you'd said, if Gabriel Clark had been in Bloomfield Hills, he probably would be gone with Richards."

Stella's eyes opened wide. "He's free? Dylan is still out there?"

"He's a fugitive now. Everyone is looking for him." I reached for her cheek. "I can't believe he hurt you after his show of pretending to be upset about your eye. I swear, when we find him, I'm going to—"

"Dylan? He didn't do it."

"He didn't?"

"He's the one who gave me the medicine, but he didn't hurt me. Brother Mark, who I got the feeling was on the Assembly at the Eastern Light, was the one who whipped me. It was Brother Elijah who hit me. Sister Mariam was the one who put the collar on me."

"What the hell? Whip? Hit? Collar? What?"

Stella reached out and covered my hand with hers. "We both have long stories. Let's find out about everyone first. I want to call my parents and let them know I'm all right. And Dina Rosemont and Bernard—"

I stilled her list with another kiss. "I know I haven't said it enough, but Stella Montgomery—"

"I definitely like McAlister better," she interrupted.

"Stella *M.*," I corrected myself. "You're an amazing woman." I ran my fingers through her hair. "So strong and brave. As we go through the next few months and try to undo what was done, I want to be the one there for you, the one to make your dreams come true."

She cupped my cheeks and her eyes glistened. "Waking up and having your brown eyes in front of me was my dream. You've already made it come true." She leaned forward and our lips united. "I'm all yours, Jacoby McAlister. I don't care what we need to go through to debrief or deprogram. What I feel for you isn't programmed, it's real, and I don't want you to ever question that."

I grinned. "So now I'm the one who can't question?"

"I believe that was a question," she said with a sparkle in her gorgeous eyes. "And as much as I want what you said, I want to be there for you too. It wasn't fair to give you all the burdens. I want to be a team."

"I think I'd like that."

As I stood I thought of something else. "Did Richards get a warning call telling him about the mansion?"

Her forehead furrowed. "No. I know he didn't, because I had one of his phones. The other one didn't ring until later."

"You had his phone? Did you try to call?"

She shook her head. "I thought about it, but I didn't want to jeopardize the FBI's mission and mostly I couldn't risk your life."

I was momentarily mute, imagining the hell she had been going through, and yet, with freedom in her grasp, her thoughts had been about me and the mission.

"You never cease to amaze me. But if he didn't get a call, why did he take you out of the mansion?"

Stella shrugged. "It was after Brother Elijah attacked me. Dylan shot him."

What the hell?

"And then he pulled me out of Father Gabriel's office and said we had to get away. In all the commotion I must have dropped his phone. If someone called him, he never got it."

There were too many things in her last statement for me to even articulate a question.

After a minute she added, "He did make a call, after the mansion blew. I tried to listen, but I couldn't hear him very well. I think he spoke to someone named Joel or Noel . . . something like that."

Joel? The one on facial recognition. I had to wonder if he was Brother Timothy and Sister Lilith's son. Were the Shadows made up of supposedly banished members of The Light? Ones Father Gabriel entrusted to hold important positions in the dark, supporting The Light's activities?

As I contemplated, I walked to the door and motioned for Special Agent Adler to come in. Turning toward Stella, I smiled. "Special Agent Adler, I'd like you to meet—"

"Agent McAlister's wife," Stella interrupted. "I'm Stella Montgomery McAlister."

Agent Adler was shaking her hand. "Ma'am, it's nice to meet you. You had us all very worried." He tilted his head toward me. "This one in particular. I don't think he's slept in nearly two days."

"I don't think he's showered either," she said with a grin.

"I just spoke with the doctor," Special Agent Adler said. "Now that they know your eyes are all right, you can be released. The FBI would like to put you both up with your own security detail for a few days. We can assure you each a secured hotel room with room service. Once you've rested, we'll send you to Virginia. You both have a long debriefing ahead."

"Agent," Stella said, "please tell the FBI thank you. If it's all right with Agent McAlister, I'd just as soon save our government the additional charge. I believe one room is sufficient."

"You heard my wife," I said with a grin.

"Then it's settled," Adler said. "Oh, and another thing, that friend you mentioned on the phone, Mindy Rosemont, we've confirmed her identity as one of the women still on the Northern Light. It will take some time to get everyone to Anchorage."

Stella looked from Special Agent Adler back to me. "I want to see her. I want to help her. I tried talking to her after my memory came back, but she didn't know me. Once her medication is gone, I want her to know we were looking for her."

Was she asking? For once I didn't have the answer. Instead I looked back to my handler.

"It'll take some time," Agent Adler said, "but I'm sure we can get that worked out. Also, we've contacted your parents. They're on their way to Detroit as we speak."

Stella's face suddenly paled.

"What is it?" I asked.

"I wanted to speak to my mom. It's Dylan"—her eyes filled with panic—"he mentioned that she's been calling him every week. If she knows I'm all right, she might try to call him. Then he'll know the medicine didn't work."

"I'll call your mother's cell phone right away," Adler said. "Don't worry. No one will know your location."

"The Shadows?" I asked, not wanting to know the answer.

"I'll personally screen the agents protecting the two of you."

I reached for Stella's hand and nodded. "We'll be all right."

She nodded. "Since I dropped Dylan's phone at the mansion and it likely blew up, I doubt my mother could reach him. Dylan said the Shadows are everywhere. Does that mean they're in the FBI?"

I took a deep breath. I'd promised her truth, but at this moment I didn't want to be truthful. I wanted to make her feel safe. Nevertheless, she deserved honesty. "We believe that it was a member of the Shadows who tipped off Richards. If that's the case, the call came from within the FBI."

Agent Adler shook his head. "That hasn't been confirmed. We're investigating. But like I said, we'll keep your location undisclosed."

"My parents?"

I squeezed Stella's hand. "Sorry, Agent. I can testify that she never stops asking questions."

Agent Adler grinned. "We're happy you're both safe. Let me get you a phone."

"Thank you," Stella said, her cheeks pink and her eyes down.

I reached for her chin. When our eyes met, I said, "I'm looking forward to a lifetime of them."

CHAPTER 40

Jacoby McAlister

Agent, Federal Bureau of Investigation

Two months post-raid:

CONFIDENTIAL FINAL REPORT: THE LIGHT
Following Agent Jacoby McAlister's final debriefing, his
forty-one-month-long infiltration of The Light officially
concluded. The results of his investigation include:
  The Light, a religious, tax-exempt organization, has
allegedly been discovered to be a front for illegal activi-
ties. The activities identified by A-Jacoby McAlister were
divided among three campuses. On the three campuses
a total of 1,070 followers were identified. These follow-
ers include men, women, and children. At the Northern
Light, located in northern Alaska, was a fully func-
tional pharmaceutical production plant, capable of cre-
ating various knock-off drugs. These medications were
transported to the Western Light, located in northern
Montana, where they were packaged and then trans-
ported to Canada under the cover of Preserve the Light

preserves. Once out of the United States, distribution and logistics occurred via unidentified members of the extension of The Light known as the Shadows.

The Eastern Light, located in Highland Heights, Michigan, served primarily as the point of entry for new followers, both voluntary and involuntary. Women abducted for The Light were brought through this campus and transported to the other campuses. Along with the acquisition of new followers, a small production plant was also located on the Eastern Light. This plant produced illegal substances that were then transported out of the United States via the cover of Preserve the Light preserves.

Alleged charges uncovered during this mission into The Light include: multiple counts of first-degree murder, felony murder, human trafficking, kidnapping, sexual assault, physical and psychological assault, drug manufacturing, drug possession, drug trafficking, and labor code violations.

Gabriel Clark, aka Father Gabriel and Garrison Clarkson, as well as the twelve members of his Commission, are being held without bond in various high-security facilities throughout the United States. Due to his association with the current threat of the organization referring to itself as the Shadows, Gabriel Clark is currently incarcerated at ADX Florence, near Florence, Colorado. This facility is a supermax prison for male inmates with extreme limitations on communication with outside sources.

Thirty-three members of The Light's Assembly were interrogated individually by the FBI. Through hours of questioning, the level of knowledge into the illegal activity of The Light was determined. The level of knowl-edge and roles in activities varied. Twenty-two members were determined to have extensive knowledge and were unwilling to testify on behalf of the state. Those members are currently incarcerated awaiting trial. The remain-ing eleven Assembly members are undergoing voluntary debriefing and deprogramming as state's witnesses. Due to the alleged danger posed by the Shadows, the eleven members will enter witness protection until time of trials.

Wives: Of the eleven Assemblymen to cooperate, ten of their wives under The Light have volunteered to accompany their husbands into witness protection. It has been determined that none of the Assemblymen's wives held a significant level of knowledge regarding the inner workings and operations. The wives of the uncooperative or deceased Assemblymen agreed to undergo deprogram-ming. Those whose true identities could be determined have been reunited with family outside The Light, if fam-ily could be found. Even after discontinuing the memory-suppressing medication, three Assembly wives have yet to know their true identities. The FBI is still working with the Kidnappings and Missing Persons department in this endeavor.

Nine of the twelve Commissioners' wives have been determined to have knowledge of illegal activity and to have participated in various illegal activities. These nine women have been charged with crimes, resulting in their incarceration. The other three Commission wives have undergone deprogramming and have voluntarily been reunited with their families outside of The Light.

The three physicians, one at each campus, are also incarcerated and awaiting trial for various felony charges.

The envelope Agent McAlister had been given from a Commissioner (Brother Michael) at the Western Light contained a sequence of numbers as well as a pass-phrase. After diligent work by the FBI cyber division, overseas accounts were discovered and accessed. Until the information in the envelope was decoded, the financial side of The Light had been the missing link in McAlister's investigation. The contents of the accounts uncovered a large portion of The Light's allegedly illegally obtained wealth.

Dylan Richards is still at large. Cybertracking has identified him as the heir apparent to the operation of the Shadows, now referred to in their communications as the leader, Brother David. It is currently believed that Richards is outside the United States.

After tedious searches, most of the followers on all three campuses have been identified. While it is impossible to account for all followers, one female follower from the Northern Light is currently misplaced. Mary, aka Mindy Rosemont, was identified while on the Northern Light campus. However, when the followers were later cataloged at the Anchorage FBI field office it was discovered that she was not among the female followers. This turn of events is currently under review by an internal subcommittee.

As the bureau's key witness, A-McAlister will enter the witness protection program until the time of Gabriel Clark's trial, as will his wife Stella McAlister.

EPILOGUE
David

"I want confirmation as soon as you have it," I said, my grip on the phone growing tighter by the second. From the way Agent Fisher was stumbling over his words, he knew from my tone that I wasn't playing around. "He needs to pay the ultimate price for his deceit."

My blood boiled.

Agent Jacoby McAlister, fucking Jacob Adams.

I'd had that motherfucker in my grasp. I should have killed him in the basement of the mansion. If I had, The Light would still be making the money we needed for operations. Hell, if I'd killed him then, Gabriel would still be free. I gritted my teeth. If I'd killed him, he wouldn't be at Quantico, married to Stella.

Damn her. Damn him.

At least I had a connection—a Shadow—at Quantico. Now if he'd stop stuttering and do his damn duty.

"Brother David, I-I have the necessary clearance. I'll learn where Agent and Mrs. McAlister are assigned."

Mrs. McAlister. The name made the hairs on my arm bristle.

"When you do, tell me. Don't, I repeat, do not, proceed on your own. I want the last thing that asshole remembers is that he fucked with the wrong organization. And I want him to know he didn't stop us or any of our plans. He may have slowed us down a little, but The Light is everywhere."

"Yes, Brother."

I didn't wait for the phone to disconnect before I hit the red button and sent it flying across the room. As it collided with the wall, Stacy jumped. She shook her head, and with a sassy grin looked in my direction.

"I'm going to guess that wasn't the news you wanted?"

I ran my hand along the scuff of my jaw before extending it in her direction. Without hesitation she stood from the couch where she'd been reading and came to me. I pulled her onto my lap and cupped her chin. "You don't need to worry. I've got you now. I don't want her."

Stacy smiled. "I'm not worried. But it is strange how this all worked out. Who would've thought me and you and the Shadows? I mean I'd never even heard of them and I remember when you were my best friend's boyfriend."

I wrapped my arms around her waist. If I didn't think about it too much, I could imagine she was Stella. They looked that similar. That was the reason she'd been brought to me. It was a peace offering from the idiot who'd let the FBI task force exist without his knowledge. He'd heard about Stella and for some reason thought Mindy was her.

Too bad for him it wasn't enough to stop his banishment.

"Your best friend?" I asked with a smirk.

She shook her head, her long, blonde hair moving slowly over her slender shoulders. "Not anymore. Now that I remember, I remember how she didn't help me, how she was part of the chosen—"

I touched her lips. "Baby, that's the past. Look at you now. Fuck the chosen. Most of them are in prison. You're the wife of the leader of the Shadows. And soon, very soon, she and that agent will pay."

"If you say so, David."

"I do. No one stops The Light."

ACKNOWLEDGMENTS

Thank you to everyone who has worked to make The Light series a reality. Thank you for believing in my crazy world with twists and turns on every page. To my agent, Danielle Egan-Miller, your support has been invaluable. To my PR representative, Danielle Sanchez from Inkslinger, thank you for having faith in this series long before the world ever had the chance to read about it. To my betas and early readers, thank you for loving these characters enough to encourage me. To the wonderful editors and cover artists at Thomas and Mercer, thank you for seeing the potential in our story and helping to make it the best it could be. Most importantly, thank you to my readers. It is because of you that I can live my dream.

ABOUT THE AUTHOR

Photo © 2015 Erin Hession Photography

Aleatha Romig is a *New York Times* and *USA Today* bestselling author whose work includes *Into the Light* as well as the twisty, darkly romantic series Consequences, which has graced more than half a million e-readers, Tales from the Dark Side, and Infidelity. Aleatha was born, raised, and educated in Indiana, where she reared three children of her own. She lives with her husband just south of Indianapolis.